WALKING SHADOW

A Stone/Darke Mystery

MICKEY LEWIS

MIDNIGHT
MACHINATIONS

PO Box 67, Bridgewater, MA 02324

DEDICATION

To Mum and Dad, wherever you are now—I finally wrote a crime novel for you! Pity you can't read it, though it's probably too extreme for your tastes. Love you both always.

To Bear and the Mole, with equal love.

PART ONE
INSERT CASSETTE AND PRESS PLAY

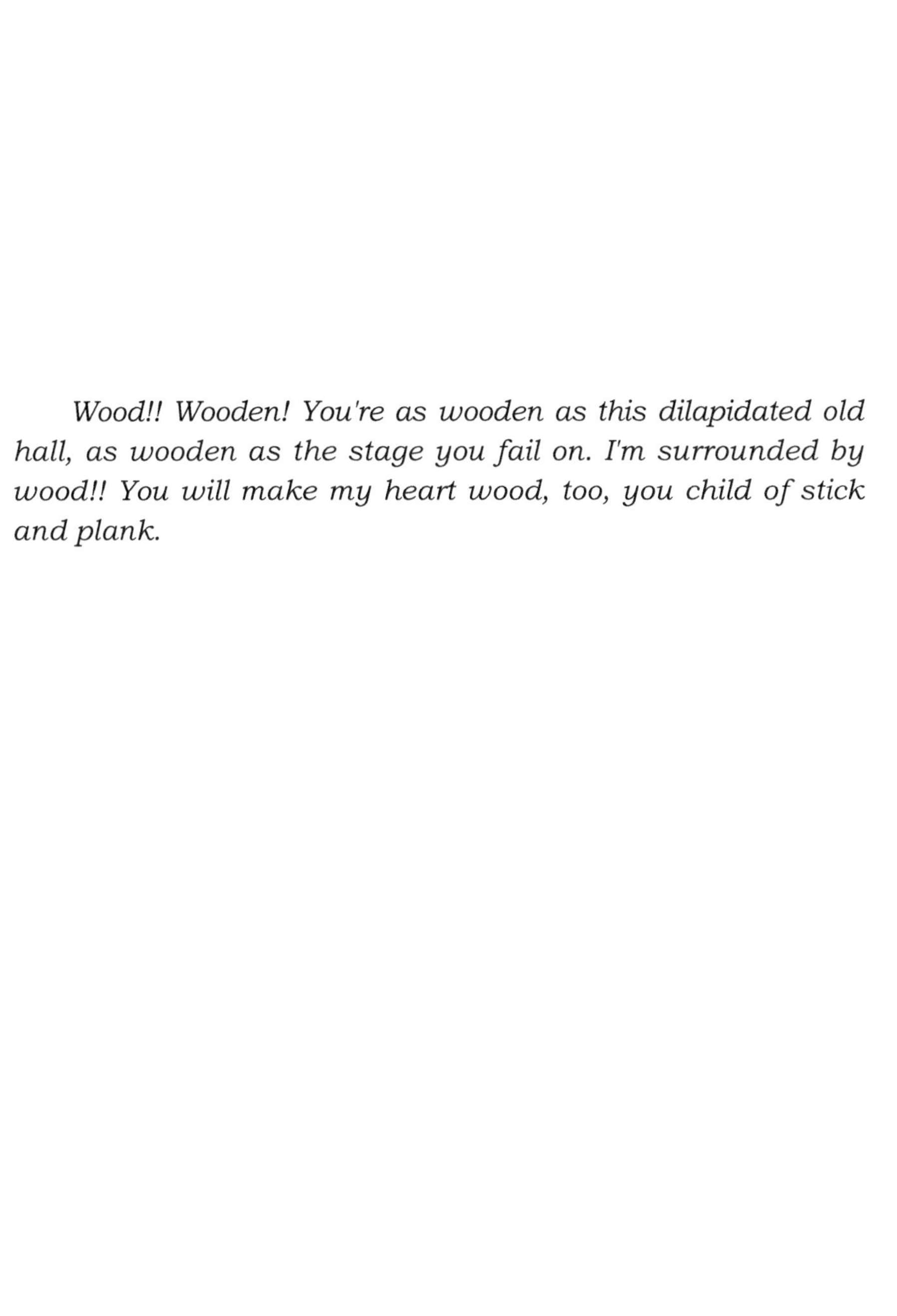

Wood!! Wooden! You're as wooden as this dilapidated old hall, as wooden as the stage you fail on. I'm surrounded by wood!! You will make my heart wood, too, you child of stick and plank.

CHAPTER ONE

Seven Romans in a Horsebox at 4:00 a.m.

Five Brits, one Irish, and one German.

It sounded like the beginning of a joke, but the German had traveled twelve hours just to take the lowly paid job, so it was more like the end of one.

They were cold, they were hungry, and they were dog-tired.

"Fuck this," one of them said. He was skinny, in his early forties, with wild eyes made even more prominent by the early hour, and it was his distinctive curved nose rather than his acting skills that had got him the role in the first place.

"Fuck what?" asked another Roman. Geoff was tall, as cockney as eels buried in pie and mash, and constantly ready to take the piss.

"This," the skinny Roman, Jem, elaborated. "Why the fuck do we do it?"

Nobody answered him. Through the Horsebox entrance they could see the actors' tent lit brightly with multiple storage heaters. They'd seen a young Assistant Director walk past with an urn of steaming hot chocolate ten minutes before and disappear with it into the tent.

At least the heavy rain had stopped. But they were already soaked from an earlier scene in which they'd been expected to stalk through the reeds on the bank of the River Severn, supposedly searching for a

Druid Princess. The rain had been remorseless. Jem had collided with the princess in the dark as she broke cover to run, and both of them had ended up on their backsides in the wet reeds. The young actress found it hilarious, but then she had a warm tent to drink hot chocolate in. All the Romans had been offered was water.

"I need a fag," Jimmy said. He was stocky, with a bush of dark hair, and was a notorious camera whore. He always liked to be at the front of every scene. He and Jem didn't speak as a rule, apart from Jem telling him to fuck off earlier when Jimmy suggested where he should position himself in the scene. Jimmy liked to think of himself as an A.D. as well. He had gotten quite aggressive in response, and the two had a stand-off, facing up to each other in wet armor and soaked capes. Not the first time they had clashed on set by any means.

"Think you're something special, don't you?" Jimmy had barked at him.

"Compared to you, yeah."

"You ain't in no fancy play now, mate. What was it called? *Epic of Gilgapish*?" He laughed at his own joke.

"Gilga*mesh*," Jem corrected him through clenched teeth. "But you couldn't be expected to know that; just stick to watching *Hollyoaks*, babes."

Jimmy bristled. "On this series, all you need to be able to do is not fucking walk into the main cast and knock 'em over, mate. Think you can do that? You're a fucking extra, not an actor." Jimmy was yelling now, hand on the hilt of his polyurethane sword in its sheath as though contemplating drawing it. As if what they were doing was real, as if they were genuine legionnaires actually invading Britain. But everything they did was "as if" in this fabricated world of Horseboxes, wet sandals, and plastic swords.

The A.D. interrupted hastily, and the cohort of Romans had all been sent back to their Horsebox while the next scene was set up.

Two hours later, Jimmy got up from the wooden bench he'd been squatting on and moved toward the open door of the Horsebox. The German got up to join him.

"Where d'ya think you're going?" Jimmy snapped, turning to face him.

"I don't need you to hold my fag, *or* my dick."

"No, take him with you," Geoff said quickly. They were all tired of the German's constant wittering[1]. They'd all heard the meticulously told story of his twelve-hour journey to get here the previous day far too many times during the course of the night shoot.

Jorg turned reproachful eyes on Geoff. "I think you don't like me."

"We fuckin' love ya. Just not at four a.m. Go and have a piss with Jimmy."

But Jimmy had already jumped down from the box. Jorg looked undecided for a moment, then followed.

"Fuckin' nutter," Geoff laughed when Jorg had gone. He adopted a ridiculous German accent. "It take me twelff hours to arrive, by ze boat, by ze coach, by ze foot. I am happy to be arrivink."

Jem's smile was very thin. He was bored by the joke and Geoff's xenophobic attitude. And he liked Jorg. The fact the German had traveled so far for a lowly supporting artist job showed commitment and tenacity. Besides, he had his own source of irritation to focus on. "I hope that twat Dixley falls in the river while he's pissing."

Geoff patted Jem's lorica, the leather Roman breastplate that was still damp from the rain. "Ya gotta let it go, mate. Really."

"He's a wanker. You know it. Always telling the other S.A.s what to do. Always putting himself in the best positions. Camera 'ho'."

"The A.D.s know what he's like. They'll kick him off before too long. Don't let it fuckin' eat yer head."

"I think they've got more important things to worry about than keeping an eye on a dick like him. Like making sure the NoMeansNo campaigners don't break onto the set and screw up the shots, for one."

Dougie, the Irish extra, who had been quiet for most of the night, suddenly piped up. "They're not gonna be bothering us at four a.m., man."

"They've been hanging about all day, though," the smallest member of the troop butted in. His face was fox-like with a basin of dark hair. Bazzer was working toward the stunt register and made sure the Horsebox legion was well aware of it. "Said they'd boycott the entire production."

---

[1] Babbling.

Jem shook his head. "And yet they all went home to their beds when the going got tough."

"They've already made their point, I guess, just by being here." Alec, the Horsebox's generic tubby Roman, added from the furthest reaches of their "green room." He was suffering the most from the lack of food.

"When we weren't filming anything," Geoff barked. "Fuckin' pointless. And then they run off home when it gets a bit cold and dark."

"They don't have Jorg's dedication to the cause, it seems," Jem said.

"I agree with what they're protesting about, though," Alec asserted.

"'Course ya fuckin' do." Geoff put his boot up on the bench opposite, in the spot vacated by Jorg and Jimmy Dixley. "You agree wiv everyfing the social justice warriors tell ya, Tubby. You think that makes you a decent person? It just makes you a fuckin' virtue-signaling sponge."

"Fuck you, Geoff."

"Strong." Geoff looked offended.

"Leave him alone, Geoff," Jem warned. But the cockney was warming to his tune now.

"An' if you'se so fuckin' inspired by the PC Brigade, what the fuck you doin' on this production anyway? You knew they was boycottin' it."

Alec said nothing.

"Or are ya gonna pretend you didn't know anyfing about the notorious rape scene? And the wanton display of boobs 'n' fanny? Not that we get to see much of that, more's the pity. We just get rain, mud, and fuckin' reed beds." He snorted back some phlegm. "But this series has had enough negative publicity; you couldn't have fuckin' missed it, so don't even pretend. The twenty-first century answer to fuckin' *Caligula*—ain't that what the tabloids are bleatin' about? Sayin' it's takin' standards back to the rough 'n' ready seventies, undoin' all the progress made over the last few years. You knew what you was gettin' yourself into, so don't fuckin' play the snowflake wiv me, mate." He kicked the bench.

Jem got up. He was tired, he was cold, and he was bored of the arguments, the bullshit.

"Where you off to?" Geoff watched him stump toward the entrance. "You wanna hold Dixley's dick, too?"

Jem didn't answer. He jumped down from the Horsebox. A very fine mist of rain was veiling the production unit base, ghosting the moon. The warm glow from the actors' tent drew him like a moth, but he knew better than to enter.

He knew his place.

Contented conversation came from within the large, brightly lit tent. He could smell food and hot chocolate. He'd heard an A.D. telling one of the principal cast earlier that there would be wild boar hot dogs for the actors later.

He wondered what the extras—the supporting artists, to give them their less-demeaning title—would get. Curled sandwiches, if they were lucky, that had already been picked over by the crew.

He headed for the mobile toilet, the "honey wagon." He was so sick of it all.

This was not what he'd signed up for in life.

Seven Romans in a Horsebox. Five Brits, a German, and an Irish.

It really did sound like a joke.

But at 4:00 a.m., nobody was laughing.

Jimmy was all too conscious that Jorg was following him.

He was heading for the reed bank that partially masked the River Severn, intending to have a smoke in solitude. He'd had enough of the attitude inside the Horsebox. Mostly, he'd had enough of Jem. Mr. "I'm an actor really, not an extra" was getting right up his nose. Too many like him in this industry, unfortunately, and they made Jimmy see red. They weren't fucking actors. They hadn't been to Drama School. They were chancers, trying to edge their way into acting the easy way. But it never worked like that—not in this country anyway. Proper actors looked down on extras. They were the grunts of the industry, living props, furniture that breathed and stole the crew's sandwiches as soon as they appeared from the caterers. But Jimmy was happy with his lot. He had no aspirations. He knew what he was and what the rest of the industry thought of him, and he didn't give a fuck. It helped pay his rent, and he got to appear in big films and TV shows alongside major stars. He didn't have to pretend he was something special. Not like that twat, Jem: the geezer thought he was a proper actor 'cause he was in some crappy semi-professional play about ten years ago. Big fuckin' deal. From what Jimmy had gathered, *The Epic of Gilgamesh* had been an absolute flop on its brief run in Bristol. They'd tried to take it to the Edinburgh Fringe and been laughed off the stage, and it certainly hadn't been a comedy. Twats. And the best bit: they'd apparently sacked Jem before they even went to Edinburgh, so he must've been crap, though he'd tried to brush it off as jealousy from one of the other actors who got the director to push him out. Nah, he was probably just shit. Just *shit*. An extra in a Horsebox: that was Jem's destiny, not the red carpet, for fuck's sake.

He didn't know why Jem got to him so much. Everyone else seemed to get on with the guy, to have a laugh with him. But Jimmy could barely stand being in the same room with him, let alone a cramped Horsebox.

He became aware that Jorg was continuing to follow him as he headed away from the brightly lit unit base with its collection of dining buses, production vehicles and tents, so he quickened his pace along a footpath that skirted the reed bed to lose him. The drizzle was lessening, and the smoke would warm him up. But he wanted to be alone now.

Jorg kept on after him. Jimmy stopped and turned to face the German.

"No offense, mate, but can you just fuck off and leave me in peace for a bit?"

The German paused beside one of the lighting cranes. He stood perfectly still, silhouetted by the flare of illumination above him. He didn't reply, just kept staring at Jimmy. He'd even put his helmet back on. *Fucking moron.*

"Fucken sie offski, yeah?" Jimmy turned and continued ambling along the path, leaving the silent figure behind. The cast and crew were all inside the tents, having a break and prepping the next scene. Soon they would be out in the reed bed again for the subsequent setup, but for now, Jimmy had the riverbank to himself. The full moon was sharply etched in the sky now that the rain was ebbing, and Jimmy could see the path clearly, and through the gaps in the tall bulrushes and reeds, he could see the vast expanse of the Severn estuary, too, spangled by starlight.

He picked a spot where a gap allowed a broader view across to the dark bulk of Wales and pulled a lighter and a pack of JPS from under his lorica. He placed a ciggie between his lips, spun the lighter wheel, and took his first puff.

Tilting his head back to exhale the smoke, he reveled in the tranquility. Thoughts of Jem slipped away, and a profound sense of calm began to settle on him.

The call of night birds drifted across the estuary. The gentle lap of the tide soothed his fatigue. He took another pull on the JPS.

A tall shadow fell across the reeds in front of him, distorted by the overhanging crane light. He turned, and Jorg was still coming.

For fuck's sake. "Thought I made it plain I wanted to be alone." He threw the stub of his ciggie into the reed bed. Jorg continued marching slowly and implacably toward him, face in shadow beneath the Roman helmet. "Gonna have a piss now; do you wanna see my cock or something?"

The Roman remained silent, clutching a plastic Sainsbury's bag in one hand, and for the first time, Jimmy began to suspect it might not be Jorg after all. It had been difficult to shut the German up in the Horsebox and on the set earlier. Now he wasn't saying a word, just stalking purposefully along the path toward Jimmy.

He stopped when he was ten yards away. Jimmy stared at him, trying to distinguish his features beneath the helmet, but the tall light behind continued to make a silhouette of the Roman.

"*Was ist los? Die Katze got sie tongue, mein freund?*" His tone was jovial, but he was beginning to feel a thread of unease now. It was the way the Roman legionnaire was just standing there, not moving, not speaking. Another thought struck him. Was it Jem? Coming for a rematch? For fuck's sake. But he could handle the jumped-up prick.

"That you, Mister Gilgapish? Come to defend your honor as a top-flight actor while dressed up as the cheap extra that you really are?"

The figure moved again, taking a few more steps nearer, and his free hand moved to the hilt of his sword. *What the actual fuck??*

The rasp of steel on steel was all too clear in the stillness. That certainly didn't sound like one of the fake polyurethane swords the rest of the supporting artists had been given. Only the actors and stuntmen had access to the real deal.

The sword was clear of its scabbard now, glinting in the light from above. The figure moved forward again.

"You think you're scaring me, Whateley?" Jimmy's own scabbard was empty; the armorer had even taken the fakes away from the S.A.s, so little were they trusted. So how did Jem manage to get hold of a real one?

The figure remained silent. It held out the plastic bag and dropped it at the side of the path. Took another step closer. Jimmy still couldn't discern the features properly, and his nerves were beginning to stretch.

The sword was held out in front of the shadowy Roman, like a challenge.

Of course, it might not be Jem. Was it one of the actors fucking around, trying to freak him? Maybe they'd heard Jem boasting about being an actor and got that twat and Jimmy mixed up and wanted to give Jem a scare.

It was beginning to work. There was something menacing about the silent, remorseless figure in the Roman helmet, lorica, cape, and sandals.

"Who the fuck are you?" The first trickle of fear seeped through Jimmy's body.

The figure continued to advance. Five yards away, darkness masking the face, light gleaming from the helmet, along the length of outstretched blade.

Then suddenly the Roman started to run, coming at Jimmy in a mad rush.

The blade was pulled back, and before Jimmy even understood what was happening, it was slamming forward again, tearing through his legionnaire focale scarf and into Jimmy's throat, exposed above the leather lorica.

A night bird crooned across the water.

Jimmy lay gurgling on the path. The shadow of the Roman knelt over him. The plastic bag had been retrieved and the figure was shaking something from it with its free hand as Jimmy's blood ran black under the arc light, dampening his lorica and tunic more than the rain had ever done, pooling on the grass of the path. A square plastic object dropped from the bag. The Roman let the empty bag drift to the path, picked up the object it had released, and held it toward Jimmy's face.

Jimmy's vision was swimming in and out of focus now. He stared at the box his killer was presenting him with as agony shook him to the core, concentrating on it as if understanding what it was would alleviate his pain. He'd seen boxes like it before, of course, years ago. Obsolete now, the only place you'd find them would be charity shops or car trunk sales… His thoughts swirled, as unfocused as his vision, struggling to make sense of this offering while his life bubbled away from his throat.

The Roman placed the VHS box on Jimmy's lorica, the body beneath jerking and twitching, and the blade in his other hand rose again, some of its gleam dimmed by blood.

The legionnaire brought the sword down with a brutal stab, plunging it deep into Jimmy's right eye socket, and Jimmy's career as an extra was well and truly wrapped.

Chapter Two

At 45, he really should have been consolidating all the successes in his life and enjoying his family.

The tired-looking man stared morosely out of the window of the Boeing 737 at Bristol International Airport as it loomed beneath the aircraft.

Trouble is, there weren't any.

Oh sure, he'd been promoted over the years, but he had reached the firm realization that he had got as high as he was ever going to get—and he'd be lucky to keep that fairly modest position, considering his reputation and lifestyle. As for family… Forget it. He'd left it too late, and he wasn't fundamentally suited to settling down.

He was a sad excuse for a bloke really… But hey, at least he could accept his faults—if only to himself. To everyone else, he appeared arrogant, overbearing, bullish, thoughtless, and always had to be right.

Was that all just an act, then, Derek? Because underneath that brash, unlovable exterior, you're really just a misunderstood sweetheart, right?

Right.

He smirked ruefully as the plane banked for its final descent.

He'd managed to encounter a scrap of affection over the last few days, even though it had been cynical and transient, just like everything in his life. But Krakow had been just what he needed to take his mind off the cul-de-sac his life and career had stalled in.

His smile widened as he thought of Aneta. And Maja, too. Hell, how could he forget Maja? How, indeed? But he'd managed to, pretty well. Couldn't remember anything about her, apart from an insubstantial image of her face and the luxurious hotel rooms he'd fled from at six the previous morning. He supposed he could lay the blame for his poor recollection squarely at the feet of her two male friends, though.

He remembered meeting Maja well enough. That was still firmly embedded in his mind. He'd been sitting in Prozac 2.0, a club just off Krakow's popular main square, and he'd been on Tinder—messaging Aneta and trying to arrange a date with the Polish girl—when he became aware that an attractive blonde had settled on the seat next to him and was waiting for him to notice her.

Derek hadn't paid her much attention at first, other than almost unconsciously checking her out as she moved over from the bar. Blonde, nice figure, attractive. Then he'd switched his focus back to his phone, and Aneta, who was waiting patiently for an answer to her questions. Was he married, did he have any children, what was his job? She sounded a little too demanding, and he was wondering if he should make excuses and leave her to find another fool. His decision was made for him when he realized the blonde was looking at him.

"Hello," she said when he turned toward her.

"All right?" he responded gruffly, managed a grimace of a smile. He wasn't good at introductions.

She held out a hand and told him she was Maja from Sweden. Derek hesitated. This never happened to him. Attractive women just didn't hit on him. Not in the U.K. anyway. So there had to be an angle. The club was throbbing and thudding with house music. Derek had to be the oldest person there, but as he'd been drinking all day in the Jewish quarter, he didn't really give a shit about what a fish-out-of-water he must appear. He was pretty sure drugs were being exchanged in the club, which was surely her angle.

Two tall men sauntered over from the bar, each carrying a bucket of ice with a bottle of expensive champagne nestled inside, and sat down in chairs facing Derek and the blonde. He felt his defenses rise automatically, and the young woman must have sensed his apprehension because she introduced them straightaway as her traveling companions.

"I know them from school. We always travel together. People always assume I'm with one of them, but I'm not." Her English was flawless, and her statement emphatic. A trace of desperation flicked across her features and disappeared. What was she after? His suspicious instincts kicked in, rebuffing the fog of alcohol in his brain.

He assessed her in his own special way. Mid to late twenties—far too young for him. Judging from the expensive champagne in the buckets and her chic clothes, hair, and attitude, she was rich, playing at being wild. The hidden trait of uncertainty puzzled him.

"You want to lick Maja's pussy?" asked one of the men, the tallest. His friend laughed heartily. Maja didn't react. She was obviously used to this male teasing. Was this the cause of the self-consciousness she tried to bury? Why would she still hang out with school friends if they continued to bully her? He pictured her then as a child in a Swedish playground, two bigger boys of her age laughing at her, picking on her, probably because they fancied her and didn't even know it, or want to know it.

He leveled his gaze for a second at the big bastard who had spoken while nobody said anything. Then he shrugged. "I'd rather lick hers than yours, if that's all the same to you." He raised his glass and took a swig. The tall man didn't know whether to be angry or amused at first, but then he howled extravagantly with good humor, his friend already cackling, Maja smiling.

She was twenty-eight, that much he did remember. When he told her he was 45, she looked a little disappointed, but when he asked if that bothered her, she shook her head. When he tried to kiss her, however, she told him she didn't kiss in public places. Feeling like he was on some unlikely rollercoaster in an unfamiliar amusement park, Derek gulped at the champagne the two men cheerfully offered him.

They were in a taxi an hour later, heading for the hotel Maja shared with her two friends. They'd insisted he join them to continue the party 'til the morning hours. The copious amounts of alcohol Derek had consumed were beginning to work on him by now. He was entirely confused by events, but in his befuddled state, he was quite happy to let them unfold in any way they liked. At one point, Maja leaned against him in the back seat. She smelled good. He put his arm around her shoulder. "I don't want a relationship," she told him earnestly. He'd been too drunk to even laugh.

Their hotel rooms were three times the size of his. Plush and elegant, exuding the affluence mirrored by the three Swedes themselves. He'd glimpsed a massive infinity pool outside. Inside, ceiling-to-floor glass windows, chrome, and high-class furnishings dominated. The two men wasted no time laying out lines of coke on a polished glass tabletop.

Derek frowned as Maja hoovered up two in quick succession. "Here," she said, holding out the 100 Zloty note she had tightly rolled. He waved it away, but she put a hand on his knee and asked again. This time he did as he was told, like a good boy.

Maja didn't wait for the effects to kick in. She was already scooping up a small pill that the tallest man—Oleg? Olaf?—had dropped in a saucer next to the lines of coke. She held one out for him. "Don't be a pussy," Oleg—or was it Olaf?—rebuked him. But it wasn't until Maja nuzzled him on the side of his neck and held out the pill a second time that he acquiesced. He was going to hell. But with Maja next to him, her hair a curtain of pale silk in the low lighting, it seemed a fine way to get there.

The tall bastard was dancing to more house music that his only slightly shorter friend was playing on his iPhone, and Derek's vision was receding down a dark tunnel.

"You want to lick Maja's pussy?" the big man asked again.

Derek could only nod this time.

The tunnel stretched.

He remembered kissing her. "Not so much of a hurry," Maja scolded him gently. He relaxed his kissing. "Better."

Then… Bright sunlight.

He was lying in a wide, super king-size bed. A puddle of blonde hair draped the pillow next to his.

Nothing made sense. He couldn't remember where he was or how he'd got there. The young woman next to him didn't move. He leaped out of bed and pulled his clothes on, his head a muddle of confusion and spaced-out detachment. One overwhelming drive forced him to put his shoes on and leave the room. He had to get home.

Or to his hotel, at least. He was in Poland, not Bristol. It was the instinct that always drove him after a heavy session. He hated waking up in other people's properties, and as he got older and his self-destructive, hedonistic urges lessened, that tended to happen a lot less frequently these days.

But right now his primal need was to get back to his own bed, away from crazy Swedes, from pills and coke and strange blondes.

He staggered out of the hotel, bright sunlight digging at his overloaded senses. He checked his pockets. His wallet and phone were where they should be—as were his kidneys. Or at least he assumed so, judging from the lack of pain in that general area. Cross off that urban legend, then. He located his hotel on Google Maps and thumbed up the directions. Forty-minute walk? It would do him good. But he had to get a move on.

He was due to catch the coach to Auschwitz in an hour and a half.

"Auschwitz?"

Aneta paused and gazed quizzically at him over her glass of red wine. Why did every woman he'd ever met look at him that way? As if they couldn't work him out and weren't sure they wanted to?

"I felt the closest to death I've ever experienced on that coach," Derek told her as they sat in the fading warmth of the September afternoon outside a bar on the main square. A white fairy carriage drawn by elaborately decorated horses clattered slowly past, carrying tourists on a tour of the

Old Town.

He remembered lying across both seats of the coach, face pressed against the glass, staring at the stark trees, his insides wrung out, his dwindling breath forced up a long, dry pipe. Across the aisle, a young couple swigged at bottles of water and watched the video of SS atrocities unreeling on the TV screen above the driver's head. Derek would have begged them for a sip of their water right then, but his throat was too parched to speak, his body too battered to move. Sweat oozed from every pore, his clothes sopping with it. He'd stopped staring at the screen; the footage had made him feel even sicker.

This was it. He'd finally done it. He wondered what his boss and colleagues would say back home when his dead body was repatriated. Death by ingestion of a lethal cocktail of alcohol and drugs. The shame.

By the time the coach had pulled up to the museum, Derek had barely been able to stand.

"So you went all the way to Auschwitz and lay on a coach the whole time?" Aneta scowled at him. She wasn't as pretty as her Tinder profile pic had promised, but she had amazing dark brown eyes and long, lustrous black hair. The cynical nature of her bombardment of questions and comments on the dating app had prepared Derek for her scathing attitude, but not for the playfulness that underlay it.

"No." He sipped at his beer. More alcohol. *Hadn't his body suffered enough?* But this was hair of the dog, and boy, did he need it. "I staggered out to the café and drank a whole two-liter bottle of water in one go. Then I bought another. By the time we'd finished at Auschwitz 1, I was beginning to feel better. Then they took us to Birkenau, and I—"

"Yes? You felt sorrow and despair for the fate of millions of human beings who died there?"

He shrugged. "I threw up against the barbed wire fence, next to a sentry post. I felt a bit better after that." He took another sip. He couldn't believe that had all occurred today—that all of this had happened in the last twenty-four hours: Maja, drugs, Auschwitz, and now Aneta. He was living on the edge. And now, after agreeing to meet Aneta as it was his last evening in Poland, he was really beginning to wish he didn't have to return to reality the next morning.

"So why *did* you go to Auschwitz?" She twisted her smooth features interrogatively, fixing him with those dark eyes.

"I—" He started to say something, then stopped.

"You don't even know, do you?"

He shrugged.

"Just something to do, I think?" Her English, like Maja's, was perfect. Her accent, though, was thoroughly Polish, and thoroughly enticing. He felt his tired body respond to her presence, to her unabashed stare (and, he hoped, interest), and it felt good to be alive again.

"Many of my countrymen died there, and you go as a tourist with a hangover. What an asshole."

He shrugged again. He couldn't argue with her. He thought of one of the other tourists who'd been refused entry at the gate of Auschwitz 1. The sleeveless Motorhead T-shirt had sent the guide into apoplexy. *What an arsehole,* Derek had thought as he looked at the young man with his long hair and cut-off denim shorts.

Aneta leaned forward to study him, her expression irascible. "But you're actually quite attractive for an asshole."

For the second time in twenty-four hours, Derek was puzzled. *Was he?* He'd never believed so, and compliments were certainly thin on the ground back in the U.K. Maybe he should come here more often...

"I've never been called that before."

"An asshole? I doubt that."

He laughed, warming to her more. She was petite, maybe five-two, and she clearly spent a lot of time in the gym. He wanted to stroke her dark hair but managed to refrain from doing so. He took another gulp of beer instead.

"So you don't remember fucking this Maja?"

Why had he told her? It was another of his faults. He always blurted out shit. Could never keep it in. Brutally, painfully honest, at times. It had cost him. Probably another reason why he'd never progressed beyond his current professional level. He shrugged again. "I have no idea."

"James, you are an English asshole."

Okay, he wasn't honest *all* the time. "Er. My name's not really James. I just used that for Tinder."

She scowled at him again. "So what is your real name, Englishman?"

"Derek."

"That is an asshole name." She laughed.

He bridled. Maybe he wasn't going to get to take her back to his hotel after all. He'd blown it at the last hurdle—his name.

"It's a cool name," he said defensively. "Del, for short. Like Del Boy."

She looked confused.

"Only Fools and Horses."

She shook her head. But her eyes were full of amusement at his exasperation.

"Wow, Poland really is a cultural vacuum."

She nearly choked on her wine. "Says the asshole Brit with his Brexit death wish."

"I appreciate culture," he protested. "Just before I met you, I walked all around the old quarter. Looked at the castle."

"I bet you were looking for sex workers. You can find them easily enough if you persevere."

He met her gaze. "I tried my best. I booked one from an escort site. Klaudia, she was called. She looked really classy on her profile. Blonde, big tits, legs that could straddle a rhino. When I turned up, she wouldn't let me in 'cause I was swigging from a can of beer." He smiled cheekily at her. "Arrived in a taxi full of English swagger, returned to my hotel on the bus with my tail between my legs and my beer still clutched in my sweaty hands."

She studied him for a moment, not smiling, her pale, unblemished face impassive.

"I don't know if you are joking or not, but I *do* know you are an asshole. An English Asshole."

"Something to be said for that," he said and lifted his glass in salute. "And it's *arse*hole… just so we're clear."

Two hours later, when he finally rolled on top of her in his hotel bedroom and let out an inelegant gasp of pleasure as he entered her, she pressed her lips against his ear and whispered, "So… do you *still* want to pull out of the E.U.?"

The Boeing landed with a heavy bump, jolting him back to the present. The plane taxied along the runway, and while he waited for it to stop, Derek pulled out his phone and switched it on.

A flurry of text messages burst onto his screen. He groaned.

His presence was urgently required at a TV production located on the banks of the River Severn just outside Bristol. Body found amongst the reeds, multiple stab wounds. It never ended.

So much for a breather, a chance to clear his head…

His three days away had left him even more weary and confused than ever, as the cocktail of drugs and alcohol he had wantonly consumed continued to work their way around his system. Images of Maja and Aneta faded into the bleary background.

Detective Inspector Derek Stone collected his rucksack from the overhead luggage rack and reluctantly made his way off the plane.

Chapter Three

Detective Sergeant Samantha Darke was waiting for him when he pulled into the production unit base car park, ten miles out of Bristol.

He got out of the eleven-year-old Merc he'd retrieved from the airport and straightened his shoulders. She was looking at him like he'd just climbed out of a sewage inspection pit, but then she always did. Her bright eyes skewered him with that old, familiar quizzical look. She shivered slightly in her dark suit, her dirty blonde hair ruffled by the breeze coming straight off the river behind her.

It was 9:30 a.m., and the mists were lifting along the Severn banks beyond the cluster of production trucks and trailers. He could see across the wide expanse of water to Wales. It wasn't an impressive sight today. The Prince of Wales Bridge loomed out of the gray morning a mile away to his left. Beyond the gigantic mile-and-a-half-long span, the industrial blot of Newport was just visible on the far shore.

"Good break?"

"You really don't wanna know," Stone replied. She would get no more out of him than that. He ignored the raised eyebrow and turned to the slender young man next to her.

"This is Alex Tamer," Darke said, smiling at the man, who looked pale and sick. "He's the A.D. who found the body."

"A.D.?"

"Assistant director, sir," the thin man said hurriedly, looking like he was going to hurl at any moment.

"So are we gonna stand here waiting for you to chuck up on my shoes, or are you gonna show me the body?"

Stone was already peering past the A.D. toward the reed banks, where a white C.S.I. tent had been erected, yellow police tape marking off a section of the footpath around it. A couple of uniforms stood stolidly by while a cluster of C.S.I. officers with cameras and dusting kits buzzed around the tent like ungainly white flies.

A plainclothes detective emerged from the thinning mists to greet them as they made their way along the path.

"A right strange one for you, boss." Simon Cooke was six-five and towered over everyone else at Avon and Somerset. During his fifteen years on the force, he'd mastered two expressions, cynical and snide. Today, he almost had a new one—puzzlement—but it was vestigial at best. He winked at Darke, who ignored the Detective Constable as usual.

"Do I…have to come with you?" the A.D. asked as they paused to converse with Cooke. "I… It's rather upsetting."

Cooke gave him a sneer. Stone turned to stare at him like he didn't understand the question. Darke touched the young man's shoulder, which was trembling despite the North Face jacket he was wearing. "We can talk back at the production trailer, if you'd prefer." She waited for Stone to argue, but he gave a brief nod. The A.D. looked so grateful that Stone was sure he was going to hug her before quickly slipping away.

"I love the smell of bullshit in the morning," Stone said, striding off along the path.

"Wrong movie, boss." Cooke easily kept pace with his superior officer. Darke followed behind.

"Meaning?"

"You'll see."

But Stone didn't wait for further elaboration as he reached the C.S.I. tent and a uniformed officer lifted a flap for him to enter.

A dead Roman lay inside, his right eye gouged out, several other wounds puncturing his throat. His period costume was patched with dried blood.

The pathologist, Dr. Hughgroves, a wiry, edgy man with facial tics, straightened up from his examination.

"What the fuck is this? *Carry on Cleo?*"

"More like *Caligula,* boss."

Cooke indicated a plastic VHS box positioned on top of the leather armor covering the corpse's torso. One of the C.S.I.s waited patiently for Stone to see it before bagging the item. Stone blinked at the garish cover.

It depicted a profile of Malcolm McDowell's mad Emperor "God" Caligula, designed on a large coin with blood trickling from his eye.

"This a joke?" The abuse Stone had subjected his body to over the last twenty-four hours was beginning to show. His voice was slurred, his vision shaky. He needed to sleep for a week. And the smell of coagulating blood was making him feel sick. As sick as an A.D. at a murder site…

"If it is, the punch line's not very funny." Darke tugged at the bridge of her nose, then handed him a pair of surgical gloves.

Stone took them, put them on before picking up the box. He studied the cover. *The most controversial motion picture in history…*

He opened the plastic jewel case. Inside, the tape looked battered and worn. A white sticker with the legend REWIND AFTER VIEWING had been stuck across the video label.

He handed it to the C.S.I. and turned to Darke. "I need a coffee."

"Been crackin' on in Krakow, boss?" D.C. Cooke smirked.

"Cookie, just give your bloody gob a day off for once." He could barely focus on the D.C.'s grinning face.

Dr. Hughgroves, never one to waste words, knew what was coming next and beat Stone to it. "I don't know the exact time of death, of course."

"I wouldn't expect anything else."

Hughgroves's right eye twitched at Stone's cynicism. "I'll know more—"

"After you've messed about with him back at the mortuary. I know the drill."

The doctor's twitch intensified, his pale, fish-belly complexion contrasting with the darkness of his empty eyes. He'd spent far too long out of the sun. "I'll get out of your way, Inspector."

"Wait."

The pathologist paused in the act of lifting the tent flap.

"Come on…"

Was that a smile on the doctor's bloodless lips? It was a ritual they'd played out many times before. Maybe this constituted fun for him. It was his turn to roll the dice on the pathology board game. "Between four and five a.m. You know I can't be more certain than that."

Stone waited. He wasn't in the mood for the pathologist's tricks today.

The doctor sighed. "Stab wounds to throat and right eye. First indications point to a sharp, smooth instrument approximately two inches wide and of indeterminate length. I'll be able to tell you more lat—"

"Knife?"

"Possibly." The pathologist's eyes gleamed momentarily before the right one gave way to a twitch. "Or a sword."

Stone turned to D.S. Darke as the doctor left, his headache worsening as he moved his body just a little too abruptly for comfort.

He sighed, screwed his eyes shut to relieve the pain. Opened them again, slowly, as if hoping he'd find himself somewhere—anywhere—else.

"So… Is anybody gonna tell me why we've got a butchered Roman lying by the banks of the River bloody Severn?"

"I hear you and Mister Dixley didn't get on?"

Jem Whateley blinked, but he met Stone's gaze without flinching. The act didn't fool Stone. That's what this prick was paid to do, after all. Although maybe that was giving this extra more credit than he deserved; running around in a Roman costume waving a plastic sword didn't involve much "acting."

Stone sat back in the swing chair in the production office trailer he'd usurped for his interviews and studied the man across the table from him.

There was something about him the D.I. disliked immediately. Was it the defensive, arrogant stare? The slightly haughty posture, as if this guy disliked the police in return? Could be a reason for that. Stone would have to look into his past. He stared him down, waiting for the thin, tired-looking man to drop his gaze. Which he eventually did, fatigue draining his reserves of attitude.

"I don't know where you heard that from." Whateley was good-looking in a weary, defeated manner, and Stone wondered how much of that ground-down air was due to the fact he'd been up all night. There was something deeper to it than that. Despite his show of antagonism to the policeman's questioning, Stone suspected this was a man on the cusp of middle age—What? 40? 41?—who had gotten used to being disappointed in life. His green eyes had a lost look, as though they'd almost given up being excited by life. *Loser.* That was it: this man had the classic loser look.

"Where *didn't* I hear it from? Everybody's been only too keen to tell me how you hated the guy. Is that why you followed him when he went for a piss? 'Cause you wanted to stick one on him[2]—or *in* him, as it were." He glanced over at Samantha Darke, who was sitting next to the window. She grimaced at his lack of diplomacy. Stone winked back at her, then returned his full attention to Whateley.

"It wasn't me," the supporting artist insisted, his eyes angry now.

"You sure about that, Shaggy?" Stone spread his hands. "'Cause I've got four or five Romans telling me you followed Dixley out of the Horsebox. You sayin' they're lying?"

Whateley sighed, rubbed his face with his long, thin hands: a poet's hands, or a pianist's. Stone wondered how someone with soft hands like that would cope in Her Majesty's special accommodation at Bristol. Or would it be Gloucester? Neither establishment rated five stars or had earned a Michelin. The guests tended to be a bit too rowdy, and the food too lumpy. He might have to remind Whateley what he could be facing. That might crack through his defiance.

"I went to the honey wagon. I didn't see Jimmy at all. The first I

---

2 Colloquial slang for hitting someone.

heard about it was when I heard Alex the A.D. screaming."

"Honey wagon?" D.S. Darke leaned forward curiously.

Whateley turned to her. "Mobile toilet. That's what they call it in the biz."

She nodded.

"And what do they call stabbing one of your fellow extras for real in the biz… Overacting?" Stone took a swig of his coffee. It was cold now, which didn't improve his mood. He could sympathize with the slender man in front of him in one area only: they both needed more sleep. His mind was a blank, felt in imminent danger of closing down. He should have let Darke do the interviews, really, but that had never been his way. He was a hands-on D.I. and would never settle for desk life. If he'd relented just this once, it would have been seen as a weakness by his enemies at the station. And he had plenty of them. Whereas maybe this guy only had the one.

"I didn't stab him. I told you, I went for a pee."

"Did anyone see you?"

"Jorg was already in there. He left as I entered."

"Jorg?" Stone looked down at the list of supporting artists and crew members the shell-shocked second assistant director had given him earlier.

"He's German."

"What difference does that make to his bloody statement? I take it he can still pronounce your name." Stone was rubbing his own face now in an unconscious mirror of Whateley.

"Speak to him. He'll tell you he saw me."

"He might tell me he saw you enter the hussy wagon or whatever the hell it's called. Doesn't mean he necessarily saw where you went next."

"I hung around the tent for a bit. Not long. Then went back to the Horsebox."

"Why were you hanging around?"

"I could smell the hot dogs. I was hungry."

"So why didn't you go in and get one?"

Whateley's laugh was bitter. "You've obviously never worked in the business, Detective."

"Just answer the question."

"Supporting artists don't mix with the actors. It's the law." His smile was sardonic and even more bitter than his voice. "Feudalism never died out in the T.V. and Film industry. We know our place."

"You seem resentful, Mister Whateley. Do you have a score to settle, maybe? Are you pissed off with your job? I hear from your Roman colleagues that Dixley was winding you up earlier and you nearly got into a fight. Did Dixley push you a bit too far and you snapped? Was that how it happened?"

"That's not how it happened. Yes, we were arguing earlier, but that was hours before he was found dead. We'd each said our bit and—"

"And what was your 'bit,' Mister Whateley? Would you like to tell me exactly why you were arguing?"

Whateley shrugged. He knew he was in a corner, but despite his exhaustion, he wasn't going to go under. He sighed again, then fixed Stone with his fiercest gaze. *Pretty good,* Stone had to admit. This guy knew how to fight back.

"He was taking the piss out of me being an actor. He was jealous. That's it."

Stone leaned forward, parried Whateley's gaze with his own. "But you're *not* an actor, are you? You're an extra."

Whateley stiffened but refused to lower his gaze. "We're called Supporting Artists these days, Inspector. And just because I'm an S.A. on this job doesn't make me any less an actor."

"Really? Been to Drama School then, have you?"

Whateley bristled, his anger threatening to boil over. "No. You don't have to go to Drama School to be an actor!"

"So what acting have you done then? I've certainly not seen you in *Game of Thrones.* Or even *Coronation Street.*"

Whateley sat back and looked up at the ceiling. Stone realized the man was laughing.

"You're good, Inspector."

"Am I?"

Whateley smiled wryly at the policeman facing him across the table.

"You're trying to get me angry, aren't you? To see how easily I flip."

"Wouldn't I like you when you're angry?"

Whateley barked out a tired laugh, turned to D.S. Darke. "Is he for real?"

Darke decided it was time to rein her boss in a little. "Was Jimmy Dixley taunting you about your aspirations to be an actor?"

"I *am* a bloody actor. I've played leading roles on stage. I've been acting since I was in school."

"And now you're running around with no lines dressed as a Roman in the background. Must hurt, that. But not as much as a sword in the bloody eye, eh?" He tipped Whateley a wink. "We have various crew members and fellow extras—oh do pardon my French—Supporting *Artistes*," Stone emphasized the term mockingly, "who all heard you threaten Mister Dixley. Then a few hours later, he turns up with a sword in his eye. I'm speaking metaphorically, Mister Whateley, because obviously the sword was no longer in his eye but had disappeared. Would you know where it went to?"

"In the bloody river for all, I know. I wasn't there at the time."

"How long have you known Mister Dixley?" Darke again. Stone was grateful for her intervention as he was beginning to flag. Bed was extremely inviting right now.

"I've worked with him on lots of productions. He's a veteran S.A. Unimaginative, unambitious. Just does whatever job comes along… You all right, Inspector?" Whateley suddenly leaned forward, sensing a weakness. "You look as knackered as me. Rough night at the Annual Policeman's Ball."

"I'm glad this is all so humorous for you, Mister Whateley. Now answer the bloody question."

"Your eyes are even more shot than mine. What *have* you been on? Tucking into the confiscated narcotics stash again?"

Stone nodded, playing along, tipped a glance at Darke. She winced again, not wanting to guess where this would end. She knew how unpredictable her boss could be.

"Keep going, son." Stone smiled.

Something in Stone's manic grin pulled Whateley back from the brink just in time. He lost the cocky gleam in his eye, and his words were slightly less combative. "Not nice being grilled when you're tired, is it?"

Stone leveled his no-prisoners gaze at the thin man. "You're a funny man, Mister Whateley. But I've met funnier. And so will you."

Whateley shrugged. "What the hell does that mean?"

"It means you'll be getting a nice, comfy bunk to sleep in soon enough. Plenty of amusing roommates we can double book you with."

Whateley actually laughed. "I was wondering when the threats would start. Look, as I said, I'm tired. *Very* tired. I haven't even had any breakfast. And that coffee was cold and awful. So let's skip to the end, shall we? Yes, I argued with Dixley. Yes, I thought he was an annoying, camera-hogging prick. But no, he didn't annoy me enough for me to want to kill him. You're talking to the wrong chap."

"So, who *should* I be talking to?"

"I don't know! Just not me. I even told the agency I didn't want to do this job because I knew Dixley was on it. They didn't listen. They persuaded me to do it because it was a night shoot and they couldn't get anybody else."

"And which agency would this be?"

"Brigstowe Casting. I'm hardly likely to make everyone aware that I didn't like the guy if I planned on killing him, am I?"

"Like I said before: he took the piss, and you snapped. You get angry pretty easily, don't you?"

"You're *making* it easy."

Stone grinned like a wolf. "You a vinyl junkie, Mister Whateley?"

Whateley looked confused. "Do I look like a hipster?"

"What about V.H.S. tapes? Got any lying around at your house?"

"Why? D'you want to come round and have a beer and watch a few flicks with me? Didn't think we were on such friendly terms. You've just accused me of murder, remember."

"Answer the question, please."

Jem Whateley shrugged. "Probably got one or two somewhere. From when I used to record films and shows as a kid. Why?"

Stone abruptly stood up. Whateley looked up at him. "Is that it?"

"Go home and get some sleep, Mister Whateley. We'll be seeing you again *very* soon."

When he'd gone, Stone turned to Darke. "Prick."

"He gave as good as he got." She chuckled, her freckled face dimpling.

Stone grunted. "I'm gonna take a stroll around. Speak to those wankers at the gate."

"You mean dedicated, morally outraged protestors, Inspector."

"That's what I said. How long have they been here?"

"Couple of hours. They're fighting for a good cause. Play nicely."

He turned to grimace at her as he opened the trailer door.

Outside, a weak September sun gleamed on the production vehicles and the now-dead arc lamps. Everything was on shut-down. The producer had arrived an hour after Stone had commenced his interviews, full of pretend concern over the fate of one of the extras but not wait-ing long before she got to the real cause of her grief: the length of time the production would have to be stopped while inquiries were undertaken.

The first person Stone had spoken to had been the young A.D. The D.I. could tell from his pale face and the smell on his breath that he'd been violently sick, probably several times. He'd told Stone about Dixley's argument with Whateley but couldn't provide much more. When Stone had questioned him about the murder weapon, the A.D. had insisted the extras were only ever supplied with fake swords.

Whateley's costume had been taken away to be thoroughly examined by forensics, but to Stone's naked eye, it had been clean, apart from the dried crusts of mud you would expect after a night shoot on the banks of the River Severn. It was the costume department that had provided more potentially interesting information: one of the spare Roman Legionnaire costumes that had been hung up in the wardrobe truck had disappeared. When Stone questioned the camp Head of Costume, the guy had been defensive in the extreme. No, he hadn't seen anyone take the costume because he wasn't stupid enough to spend all night in the wardrobe truck. He preferred the warm crew tent, and if Stone had cared to experience the temperature in the truck for himself—all the available heaters were in the tents—he was very welcome to do so. But he had been able to volunteer the info that the costume in question was one size fits all, which didn't help Stone at all.

The armorer had been up next. He gave a description of the exact sword that was missing. Again, he had been in the warm tent most of the night and had trusted that nobody would fiddle with his props, which were stashed in an easy-up not far from the Horsebox. Stone had questioned the wisdom of leaving dangerous weapons unattended, but the armorer had replied he had doubted people would be prowling around this remote stretch of river at 4:00 a.m. Stone sent him off with more than one flea in his ear, but at least he had a description of the possible weapon. Forensics would corroborate whether or not it matched the wounds. As for finding it, Whateley was probably right: he imagined the murder weapon was deep in the mud that covered the bed of the Severn by now. He had dismissed Darke's suggestion that they get divers to look for it, retorting insensitively (as she promptly told him) that if they couldn't find Richie Manic down there after all these years, they were hardly likely to find a relatively small sword. The prints would be washed away by now anyway.

Then, after he'd spoken to a few of the other extras, he'd sat back and waited for Whateley. He still had a couple S.A.s to speak to (the German and a cockney feller sprang to mind), but they could wait in the Horsebox. They were used to that, after all.

Stone glanced past the lighting crane toward the banks of the River Severn. Beyond the white C.S.I. tent and the thick bulrushes, the water sparkled and gleamed cheerfully. Even the stark architecture of the nearby bridge appeared softened in the glorious sunshine. His phone bleeped in his pocket. He pulled it out to find a text had arrived. He smiled sincerely for the first time that day. It was from Aneta. Would he like her to visit him in Bristol?

He put the phone away without replying. He would need to think about that. Could get complicated very quickly, and complications worried Detective Inspector Stone. He liked to keep things simple. Rock music, ballsy films, and seventies cop shows were the kind of simple things he particularly enjoyed. Where would this Polish chick fit in with those?

He didn't know if she would.

His smile disappeared as he spotted the producer and director emerging from the actor's tent to intercept him. As they approached, he could see their reserves of sympathy for the death of one of the extras had diminished even further.

The director let the producer do the talking, hanging back looking owlish and disgruntled, while the wasp buzzed in to do all the stinging. Stone swatted her way peremptorily.

"I'm sorry, Miss Connors. You'll have to speak to D.S. Darke. I'm in the middle of my inquiries."

The bullish woman puffed her chest out even more. Her sharp-edged glasses bore down on him over the bridge of her prodigious nose. "We're all very upset about the tragic circumstances, of course. But you have to give us some idea how long this is going to take, Sergeant. We have a very tight schedule to run."

"It's Detective Inspector. And I don't have to do anything except follow my duties. You'll find the Sergeant you're looking for in the production trailer." He walked away before she could bluster any further, though he heard plenty of indignant exclamations trailing after him as he strode along the dried mud of the track toward the production unit entrance gate. He almost grinned at that—*almost*—because he could see the group of protestors waiting for him on the other side of the closed gate and knew that nothing any of them could say to him would be remotely as amusing as winding up an over-ambitious, coldly calculating money watcher like Connors.

He saw the banners they were holding and girded his loins for the inevitable confrontation. He needed this like he needed a long-lasting, meaningful relationship and several kids. He'd rather face down a gunman high on coke than clash with the PC posse waiting for him. Their campaign against this particular production seemed suddenly misguided and insensitive in view of what had happened, yet they still didn't seem in a rush to go home. #Metoo? No thanks. Not after what he'd been through over the last day or two.

He nodded to the uniform posted by the gate and waved to the security man chatting with him, and as the bolt was drawn back, he found himself wishing, not for the first time in the handful of hours he'd been back in Britain, that he could just jump on the next plane back to Krakow.

CHAPTER FOUR

There were six of them, five women, one man. Four of the women looked to be in their forties, the other one younger. They all looked earnest and angry. Stone's balls shrank as he walked up to them.

Some of them were holding up placards with **#NoMeansNo** emblazoned on them. One shouted the slogan, **Stop Violence Against Women for Entertainment!** in lurid red paint. The man holding it had a full-on hipster beard, thick black glasses, and a Peaky Blinders haircut. He wore skinny jeans and a retro-red plaid jacket. Stone hated him on sight.

Stone pulled out his warrant card, waved it at their unimpressed faces, put it away. "You got what you wanted, so why are you still here?" He spoke to one of the women, probably the oldest, wearing multi-colored baggy clothes and a bobble hat. She lowered her placard as if agreeing, but her face was determined.

"They haven't stopped altogether, though, have they?"

The hipster held his placard up defiantly. "It's just a break in filming, isn't it? They have no intention of stopping."

"Are you aware of what's happened here?" Stone didn't look at the hipster. He didn't trust himself. Not today. He had promised Darke he would play nice, and he would. Or he'd give it a bloody good try anyway.

"We're aware something unpleasant has happened, yes, Inspector." This was from the younger woman, short, a dark bob, elfin features, and a smart leather jacket. She sounded well-educated, like they all did. Stone wouldn't have expected anything less. You didn't get housewives from the Knowle West Estates picketing films.

"We spotted the white C.S.I. tent and forensics team. We saw some of the actors being led into your office to be interviewed. We're not stupid, Officer. Someone's dead, aren't they? Is it one of the actors?" The hipster again. His face was young under the aggressive beard. Stone had promised Darke, so he refrained from turning to the man. He spoke to the younger woman with the bob instead.

"I can't tell you anything at the moment." He felt like he was making a statement to the press, which irritated him even more. Those bastards would be turning up soon. He was amazed they hadn't been tipped off already. Wouldn't be long, though. He hoped to be out of here and on his way back to Bristol before they swooped.

"But what I *can* tell you is that an incident has occurred that has resulted in the production being halted for the time being. So there really isn't any more need for you to stay. Like I said, you got what you wanted."

"And *they* got what they deserved."

Now Stone had no choice but to turn to the hipster. This wasn't going to end well.

"Martin…" one of the other women said, her tone scolding, like a school ma'am addressing a wayward child. "That's not very nice."

"And what do you mean by that, sir?"

The hipster looked to his fellow protestors for support, but they appeared embarrassed at his lack of sensitivity. He bristled. His face blazed with anger—whether genuine or disingenuous, Stone couldn't yet judge, but he strongly suspected the latter. This guy was trying way too hard to impress someone. Maybe the younger woman with dark hair?

"You wake up a wasp nest, you're going to get stung…"

"*Martin!*" The voice of the woman who had scolded the hipster was sharp with authority. *Yep, definitely a teacher or playgroup worker.* She lowered her placard even more. "Please don't listen to Martin. That's not how we feel at all, Inspector." She had a kind face with ginger dreads, a nose ring, and big Doc Martens. Stone put her in her mid-forties.

"We're sorry if something awful has happened. We're just here to protest the violent elements included in this production; we certainly don't have any ill feelings toward the cast or crew."

Stone was more interested in what Martin had to say. The hipster returned Stone's gaze, defiantly, scornfully. "Would you care to elaborate on what you just said, Martin?"

Martin opened his mouth to speak, angered even more by the policeman's informal use of his name, suspecting, quite rightly, that he was being goaded. The young woman with the bob put a hand on his shoulder, but Stone was unsure whether the gesture was a warning or in support. Martin pushed his specs up his nose before replying, his words a tad more measured this time, the redness gone from his face. "*Legion Britannica.* Not exactly a forward-thinking, representational addition to the T.V. schedules, is it?" His face twisted in scorn. "Haven't you read the papers, Inspector?"

Stone examined him intently. This was interesting. Maybe he'd let the hipster hang himself.

"Enlighten me."

"It's a scandalous production that revels in the exploitation of women for the sake of entertainment, officer." Martin's eyes were full of condescension. "There is a rape scene in it that is apparently going to be extremely degrading and does *not* promote the advancement of equal opportunities in any way, shape, or form. We need to stamp out this sort of degrading filth. Equal rights, equal representation for women. Rape is not entertainment."

Martin's face was shining with the sweat of his own conviction. Some of the other women were fidgeting uncomfortably at his zeal.

"The exploitation of women is something we're keen to eradicate from our T.V. screens." The older woman spoke up, shouldering the burden or dissipating the over-zealousness. "It's time for gender differences to be treated with equal respect. We're not just protesting against the casting couch any longer."

"It's time," repeated Martin fervently.

"And how do you know exactly what's in the series? It hasn't been completed yet?" Stone kept his eyes on the older woman for an answer, irritated beyond measure by the hipster.

"We received a leaked script," she replied. "We have our 'spies' in the industry."

"Do you, now? And have your spies given you any information on what's happened today?"

"No, of course not. We were turning up today as usual to picket the production and realized something awful had happened."

"Which, as I said, is bound to happen eventually if you peddle filth." Martin again. "Someone got overstimulated." He pushed his glasses up again. "Someone got *aroused*."

"Like you are now?"

The hipster's smirk vanished. He whitened, then the redness returned. "I don't like what you're suggesting, Inspector."

School teacher came to the rescue. "What Martin is implying—a little too over-earnestly—is that what we feared might happen if too many people were exposed to violent material such as this has unfortunately actually happened."

"I see." Stone was glad of the breeze carrying across the unit base from the river. The hectic last few days and abuse of drugs and alcohol in Poland had left him drained and nauseous. Exhaustion was closing him down, and he still had to initiate a murder inquiry back at the Criminal Investigation Department. He'd sent Cooke there to get the ball rolling, but he knew it was nearly time for him to follow him to stop the towering D.C. from upsetting too many people.

"The internet's alive with it. And the tabloid rags. *Caligula* for the twenty-first century is what they're calling it. And if that isn't a backward step for representation, then I don't know what is."

"*Caligula…*" Stone focused his blurry vision on the hipster again. "Interesting you should mention that, Mister…?"

"You don't need my surname. And it's not interesting, is it? Have you seen the original? One big, bloated bore. And that's disregarding all the vile disrespect of the female form."

"And the male form, if I remember correctly." Castrations galore.

But the hipster was right: it all got tedious in the extreme after a while. And as he recalled, the film was very long. "Helen Mirren was very good in it, though…"

But Martin didn't want to hear that. "It's porn dressed up as a historical epic. And we all know what porn leads to."

"Do we? Maybe you'd like to give me some more information about your campaign *and* your interest in *Caligula*. I'll get the constable here to take down your details."

Martin didn't look happy at all about that. Now it was Stone's turn to smirk.

He beckoned to the officer on the other side of the gate and then stepped briskly back through it, hurrying toward the production office. One more coffee with Darke, a couple more extras and crew members to interview, and then it was back up the A38 to Bristol.

He knew The Chief would be wanting a full brief as well. And he really couldn't face that right now.

"Did you do it?"

Jem sighed and forced a chuckle down the phone in reply to Christine's accusation. He knew she was joking. Or at least, he hoped she was. He never knew with Christine.

"Yeah, I hacked Jimmy Dixley to death 'cause he called me an extra. You sound just like Inspector Clueless."

Now it was her turn to laugh. And God, her chuckle was sexy. It was irreverent, sneaky, and provocative, and it got him more aroused than he knew what to do with. But then, that was always his reaction to Christine. Did she really fully understand what she did to him? She drove him wild with lust.

"You *are* an extra, you twat." *Even when she called him names.*

"Don't *you* fucking start."

"Bet you did…"

"Did what? Oh, fuck off, Christine." He sighed again, wishing he was with her instead of stuck in his lonely flat by the cemetery, looking out through the French conservatory doors at tombs and gravestones fighting against the onslaught of creeper, grass, and ivy.

"They've been forced to stop filming. I've lost a few days' work because of this bastard killer," he moaned.

"I'm so sorry some guy getting murdered has inconvenienced you so much."

"I didn't mean it like that." *Or had he?* He felt ashamed. "I'm sorry Dixley's dead. Of course, I am. I wouldn't wish that on—"

"Your worst enemy?"

"You *do* fucking think I did it."

She chuckled again. "No; you're too pathetic to actually kill someone."

"Gee, thanks. Remind me to pay your bill, counselor."

"You're *such* a twat."

"We've already been there. Have you got anything else to say, or are we done for today?"

"I'm running out of insults, so yes, time for bed."

"It's only midday. Want me to join you?"

"Prick. You never give up trying, do you? And you know I have M.E.[3] I need to rest a lot. Don't be so insensitive."

"Prick, too. Quite a repertory of abuse. And no, I don't give up easily. One day *you'll* give *in*."

"Will I? And don't forget you're still booked on *The Awful Dead* next week. You'll have the joy of my wonderful company, too. Lucky boy. Byesy bye, you murderous wanker."

"*And* a wanker? Not sure which is more offensive, being accused of self-pleasuring or being called a murderer."

"I *know* you're a wanker. I'm just not one hundred percent about the murderer bit yet. See you later, dahling."

"Love ya, you bitch."

He slid the Smartphone into his pocket and headed to his bedroom. He closed the curtains against the bright sunlight in the cemetery out-

---

[3] Myalgic encephalomyelitis/chronic fatigue syndrome (ME/CFS)

side and peeled his clothes off. He needed to catch up on twenty-four hours without sleep. Night shoots really messed with your body. *Not as much as they messed with Dixley's.*

He tried not to think about that. But as he climbed wearily into bed, his bones aching with the previous night's exertions, he knew he wouldn't be able to think about anything else.

CHAPTER FIVE

Cooke had actually done a reasonable job.

The incident board was up and even had a few photographs pinned to it. Jimmy Dixley was obviously central to the collage, and Cooke had written "multiple stab wounds, bank of River Severn" in purple Sharpie underneath the shot of the extra, taken in happier times, dressed in a Hawaiian shirt at a sunny theme park. Now he was smiling out at the Avon and Somerset Murder Squad.

Jem Whateley's pic was below the victim's, acquired from the *Legion Britannica* costume department, in full Roman Legionnaire regalia, and he didn't look half as cheery as Dixley. Cooke had written "Suspect" underneath the photo, accompanied with: "argued violently with victim." Next to Jem, Jorg Klaus's pic, also taken from the production. The annotation "followed victim out" had been written in Cooke's scrawl, which was surprisingly childish coming from such a large and bullish man. Cooke had scribbled various other notes the Inside Sergeant had passed on to him that he deemed important, along with various photos of the murder site, the production unit, and other ephemeral bits of info.

Stone nodded to the large D.C. in recognition of his efforts and took his place at the front of the room next to the board, perching almost nonchalantly on the edge of a desk. It was an act that would have made Jem Whateley proud, as Stone felt anything but nonchalant. Fatigue was crippling him. Darke pulled up a chair next to him.

Stone looked out across the large office filled with untidy desks cluttered with files and printouts, all the workaday paraphernalia of a live incident room. He'd already spoken to the Chief Superintendent, who had received his report as dolefully as Stone had expected. But then Doleful was D.C.S. Church's middle name. Stone had imagined the man's half-empty glass expression had been with him all the way through childhood, ruining any birthday photos his parents might have wanted. If he was aware they called him Cheery Church in the department, he never let on, and Stone doubted he would have cracked a smile at the nickname.

Stone cleared his throat, glared out at his murder squad of some fifteen detectives, all of them looking at him with that abated excitement that always accompanied the beginning of a major murder incident. And this one was hardly run of the mill.

He began by outlining the facts as he knew them, which were quite straightforward. It didn't take him long, for which he was glad. He hated talking in front of a crowd; it made him come across all gruff and bullish. But then, when he pointed this out to D.S. Darke in one rare moment of self-sharing, she replied sardonically that he *always* came across as gruff and bullish and was probably born growling and snapping at the mid-wife. After that, he hadn't shared anything else with her for a long time, especially not his beloved salt-and-vinegar crisps.

He got up off the desk and moved over to the incident board, pointed a finger at Jem Whateley. "This is our favorite. I like him, and I don't like him for it."

"That clears it all up, then," quipped D.C. Cooke. "Can we all go home now?"

Stone quashed the inevitable ripple of laughter. "You seem even more keen than usual to stand on a traffic island waving at cars today, Cookie." A bigger ripple of mirth. "Now shut your beak and listen." He tapped Jem's picture. "As our Squad Comedian has already informed us with his Primary School crayon," another burst of chuckles, which he quietened with a gesture, "Jimmy Dixley was reported by several witnesses to have engaged in a lover's tiff of sorts a couple of hours before taking his last stroll along the riverbank. Seems Dixley and Whateley had history, which is why I like our Jemmy for it. They hated each other. Put it down to professional envy, or one having a longer sword than the other, but they had a set to, which almost resulted in fisticuffs. Then our mate Jem leaves the Horsebox where the extras were waiting," he grinned wolfishly at the snorts that greeted this, "shortly after Jimmy goes for a Jimmy[4]. That's all fact. We know this. What we don't know is exactly what happened afterward. To complicate matters, we have our Deutsche friend here," he indicated Jorg's photo on the board, "going out for a James Von Riddle,[5] too. He claims he went to the honey wagon, or shit house on wheels to you and me, and saw Jem entering as he was coming out, which corroborates Whateley's story that he just went for a wee-wee and nothing else." Darke was rolling her eyes at his terminology, but he ignored her and strolled forward to confront the squad.

"So, the question is: did Jem then follow Dixley along the riverbank, or did he, in fact, loiter outside the actor's tent as he claims?"

"Anyone see him outside the tent, boss?" This was Ming, a Chinese D.C. who was more English in his mannerisms and speech than any-one else in the room. His little goatee had obviously earned him the nick-name Fu Manchu, but far from being offended by the cultural stereo-type certain officers might occasionally lapse into when using the name, he positively reveled in it. A big Marvel fan was Ming, but he obviously enjoyed a bit of Sax Rohmer, too.

"No, Ming, which doesn't help our friend, obviously."

"So why *don't* you like him for it?" D.S. Susan Fairchild was the In-side Sergeant, responsible for dealing with all the info streaming into the incident room consisting of witness statements, Crime Stoppers' info, contributions from members of the public. It was a remorseless and unforgiving task, and she handled it with very occasional humor. Right now, she was scrutinizing Stone as thoroughly as one of her wit-ness statement reports.

"Good question, Sue. I'll tell you why." He rubbed his hands to-

---

[4] Piss, urinate
[5] Piss, urinate

gether and considered his words, which didn't take long. As Darke had often told him, he was a doer, not a thinker. He believed she'd meant it kindly, but he had never been sure.

He turned to point at the photo of Jem in his Legionnaire lorica.

"His costume was too clean. Not a drop of blood on it. Obviously, forensics will give me a proper answer on that soon enough, but all that was visible to the naked eye was mud. If he washed off the blood, surely the mud would have gone, too. Obviously, he could have washed it and then muddied himself, but it would have taken a long time to scrub blood off, and it wouldn't have been easy to do that in a cramped honey wagon where any member of the crew could walk in on him at any moment. This is a problem for us. But it certainly doesn't count him out, and as I said, forensics will give me a better picture in time. On *all* costumes worn by both extras and actors. We're not as keen on hierarchy as the bloody film industry, I don't bloody care if I upset a big star by C.S.I.-ing his Roman knickers. Not that there are any on this cheapskate production."

"What about the missing costume, guv? Where does that fit in?" Cooke leaned back, his large frame dwarfing his chair.

"Well, there's the rub, Cookie. Does the fact that a spare costume was taken without permission from the wardrobe truck rule out the extras already wearing one in the Horsebox, or the honey wagon, or wherever the hell they were at the time of the murder? Not necessarily." He tucked his hands in his suit trouser pockets and pursed his lips. "The killer could have changed out of his own costume, or even put the nicked one over the top of the one he was already wearing, to protect it from blood stains. That might still put our friend Jem in the frame even if his costume comes up squeaky. And, of course, it's pure supposition that the killer was wearing a Roman costume at all. We're basing it on the fact one was reported missing, which seems an odd coincidence if it *wasn't* used in the murder. Now why the killer would want to put one on in the first place—if they weren't costumed-up already—is another question. Was it just to protect the killer's own clothes from blood, or was there another motive?"

He paced up and down, watching his squad expectantly. "Any offers?"

"C.C.T.V. cameras at the unit base?" D.C. Charlie Evans, his impossibly young face belying his age while his protruding ears, narrow eyes, and tuft of hair earned him the nick-name Stan Laurel in the Department. Stone liked nicknames. He positively *encouraged* them. He reveled in his own as well, of course, although after all these years, he couldn't remember if he had come up with it himself or not. But he would only let the squad use it when the D.C.I. or the Chief Superintendent wasn't around: Jack. As in Jack Regan. Darke refused to use it, obviously. She was always there to prick his balloon.

"None on the site, which is ironic considering the nature of the work they're doing. We need to get down there and check the nearby villages and roads for C.C.T.V. speed cameras, and A.N.P.R. cameras. I want every vehicle that passed or went into that base checked and a list of everyone who entered throughout the filming schedule. We're also looking for someone who might have trespassed on the site. I've spoken to the security team, but they've got nothing. Obviously, there are ways to sneak into the base without them seeing, but I want to know of vehicles or pedestrians in the immediate area who had no good reason for being there." He paused for breath, wished for a fleeting moment that he still smoked. He closed his eyes just for a blessed moment, which was dangerous. His bed was calling.

He waded on manfully. "Get me the Jimmy Dixley story. I want to know everything about him. Speak to his friends, family, neighbors, work colleagues—if he did anything other than waft around in fancy dress, that is. Mobile phone calls in and out on the day of his death. Disputes, girlfriends, boyfriends. Anyone he might have upset. Jealous exes. All the usual gubbins[6]. Likewise on our pal Whateley. I want his shoe size and the name of his barber. Everyone chats with their barber. He'll have told him something useful at some point." He was in his stride now. He could fight off the fatigue if he concentrated really hard. But now he was in his element. This was second nature to him. He could have reeled this stuff off in between snores. "I want the base searched meticulously for

---

[6] British slang. A foolish or futile person, a simpleton.

this bloody missing costume. Tents, Horsebox, reed beds, footpaths, bushes along the roadside, everywhere. We'll probably need to get the river police out to drag the Severn at some point. Who knows… They might even find the murder weapon, too…" He glanced over at Susan Fairchild. "Have another look over all the witness statements, Sue. I want to find something that doesn't add up."

Finally, he rounded on D.C. Cooke. "You a film buff, Cookie?"

The big detective frowned, his long legs stretched out lazily. "Depends on what type, boss."

"Roman porn. I've got your dream job for tonight. Watch *Caligula*. And I don't want you tugging on your gladius." Loud guffaws this time. "I want every relevant piece of info that fits this case. I want to know exactly why that V.H.S. tape was plonked on top of our Roman plonker."

"D.I. Jack Regan means 'unfortunate victim'," Darke added reprovingly.

"Sorry, Carter. Forgive my lack of… what's that 'S' word I always forget?" He winked at his sergeant, which only exacerbated his headache, causing the wink to turn into a wince.

"You all right, Boss?" asked Cooke snidely. "Looks like you need to shut both eyes, not just the one."

Stone gave him a look that made him draw his legs in. "Smart arses are welcome to try out the tall hats for size." He looked away from the giant D.C., addressed the whole team. "Let's achieve the impossible and put a smile on Cheery's face by cracking this before Christmas. D.S. Darke will allocate tasks to each of you. Let's rock and roll…"

And without another word, he turned his back on them and made his way toward his office.

CHAPTER SIX

Christine looked amazing.

She always did, of course. But today the wardrobe department had chosen clothes that really accentuated her figure—tight blue jeans, a clinging sweater, and a small leather jacket that hugged her waist. Her long, dirty blonde hair fell over the shining leather. Makeup had done their job, too. The sharp cheekbones of her elfin face had been high-lighted with a hint of peach. Her eyes were blue bolts sizzling from under arched, delicately plucked eyebrows, thin lips touched up with seductive scarlet.

She greeted him with a hug, which he would have had last longer. She smiled, revealing one ever-so-slightly crooked tooth on the right side, something she was continually self-conscious about, along with the shape of her slightly curved Roman nose. He told her she had absolutely noth-ing to worry about; he adored both features. They made her Christine, and not just some typical airbrushed blonde beauty. Of course, she could never understand that line of thinking. So he called her Snaggle, and Beaky if he was in a particularly teasing mood. He didn't think his insensitivity bothered her. She had plenty of unpleasant names for him, too.

It was another night shoot, although this one wouldn't go on 'til 4:00 a.m., thankfully. Wrap time was estimated to be midnight. Jem had been booked as a demon on the mid-budget horror production. He expected to be called to the makeup trailer any minute for his prosthetics and scary wig. He was already wearing the costume, which consisted of rotting farmer clothes—dungarees, a large, white shirt, and boots.

Christine sat beside him in the dining bus, which was the Green Room for Supporting Artists on most productions. The bus was full of extras in various costumes, but only three of them were to be made into demons. The rest were villagers, campers, farm hands—and that most dreaded of SA roles, "passersby." Not that there would be many passersby in the middle of the woods, but every production had to have them somewhere. Jem prided himself on having risen above that lowly position these days. Let the newbies and older S.A.s who didn't work as much fill those thankless roles.

Christine was going to be a villager, one of the crowd that would be terrorized later that evening when the demons materialized in this cabin-in-the-woods rip-off of the infamous Sam Raimi prototype.

"Why do you always get the good parts?" Christine grumped at him, sipping from her Styrofoam cup of green tea.

Jem swelled with pride. "Because I've been doing this a lot longer than you, and the bookers trust me. Keep at it for another year or so and stop saying no to most of the agency calls, and you'll get there, too."

She tittered. "You're such a dickhead. You still spend most of your time on near minimum wage, being looked down on by everyone else on set, either freezing to death 'cause you're made to stand in a muddy field with no coat in winter, or done up to the nines in a tux in the peak of summer. How long did you say you've been doing this for? Five years? Saddo."

"So why do *you* do it, then, Beaky."

She looked momentarily embarrassed at the nickname, in case anyone else on the bus had heard it. Her cheeks reddened slightly. "Because I obviously can't bear to be out of your charming company for too long, arsehole."

"Knew that was the reason. And because you can't bear to be out of the company of a camera for long as well, of course."

She pulled a face at him. "So what *do* you have to do tonight—apart from looking like a retard?"

"A retard with a walk-on, at least."

"Big fucking wow. You'll get an extra twenty quid or so to look like an absolute wanker."

"Jealous, Chrissy, dear? It'll be an extra fifty at least, plus a couple of lines of dialogue."

"You shagging someone at Brigstowe? You're obviously their favorite, you skinny, little twat. Can't think why. Anyway, I'm surprised the Po Po have allowed you on another film set, after what you did to that other guy."

"Christine, you're remarkably dumb for someone so sexy. Sometimes I wonder what it is I see in you. One day I'll wake up and smell the Chrissy. And it won't be a nice whiff."

She chuckled good-naturedly at that. Her eyes were momentarily wary, almost self-conscious. He knew that under the veneer of abusive snide and sarcasm, she was damaged. He had never quite ascertained why, apart from partly revealed hints of her past over drinks late at night in the Bristol bars. A previous boyfriend whom she had cared a great deal for, an absent father. An insubstantial outline. He had the straight edges of the Christine Jigsaw, but essential middle pieces were missing. She was vulnerable as well as sassy. And that was why he cared so much for her, not that he could admit to her the depth of his feelings. He knew she would run. Even now, with his jokey veiled allusions to fancying her, she looked like a flighty doe ready to take to her hooves.

"They can't arrest me for something I didn't do," he continued after a while.

"How many times have they been to see you now? I bet the neighbors think they've moved in."

"They're clutching. But there aren't even straws for them to find. I'm squeaky clean. Didn't do it. And you know it, too, or you wouldn't be sitting with me now."

"Maybe I just like the bad boys."

"Just as well, 'cause tonight I'm the baddest. Gonna make you poop in your sexy red knickers."

"How do *you* know I've got red knickers on?"

"You're a blonde. Of *course* you're wearing red knickers." He grinned wolfishly. "Besides, I saw a glimpse of them over the top of your jeans when you bent down to pick up your bag outside."

"*Such* a perv. If I were the police, I'd *definitely* run you in."

He turned serious for a moment. "It's been over a week now. I can tell from the questions that wannabe seventies detective asks that they haven't got anywhere on the case. If he's their best bet, they really are in trouble."

"Who do you think did it, then?"

He shook his head. "I only ever saw Dixley on film sets. Don't know anything about his private life. There could be loads of people who had it in for him. You know what an irritating bastard he was."

"Don't talk ill of the dead. He might have been an annoying twat, but he's a deceased annoying twat."

"Thanks for the sensitive interlude in Chrissy's normally thoughtless, vain, and self-absorbed broadcasts."

She tilted her head sarcastically. "I'm still surprised you're allowed back on a film set."

The A.D., Paul, jumped on the dining bus and began making his way toward them.

"Sorry, Jem. I need to change you out of that costume."

"What d'you mean?"

"We've got to switch you to crowd, I'm afraid. Director's decision. He wants someone with more stunt experience to play the demon."

"What? But I've played loads of monsters on *Doctor Who*—"

"I know, mate. Sorry. Nothing I can do. He's chosen someone else."

"What about my walk-on?"

Paul looked embarrassed and harassed all at the same time. "We haven't got much time, Jem. Got to rush you, I'm afraid. They need to get the other guy in costume. You're still needed as part of the crowd, though."

"I don't *do* crowds." Jem stood up angrily.

Christine sniggered. "Diva. What was that you were saying about being a retard with a walk-on? Now you're just a retard."

"Thanks, Snaggle. Fuck you." He pushed past her.

"You wish."

He followed Paul out of the dining bus, furious.

Twenty minutes later, he was on the phone with Brigstowe Casting.

Penny was full of her usual enthusiasm, but Jem wasn't in the mood for it. "Could I speak to Marcus?" She put him on hold. Jem was standing at the far end of the unit base, which was situated on the outskirts of Lords Wood, five miles east of Bristol. The dark trees pressed around the perimeter fence erected by the locations team. Not far away, a security man was smoking a cigarette in his bright yellow florrie[7]. It was five o'clock now. It would be dark in another hour or so, and they would have to start making their way into the woods to the shooting location. Marcus kept him waiting. When he finally came on, he was bright and cheery as ever.

"Hi, Jem. How are things on *The Awful Dead*? Not too awful, I hope?"

Jem ignored the humor. Not in the mood for it.

"They've dropped me from the demon role."

"Really? Why?" Marcus sounded dismayed, too. Either he was a good faker, or he genuinely did care about the S.A.s on his books. Every time Jem had met the agency team, he had been impressed by their bubbly, warm personalities. He had sometimes wondered if it was just superficial luvviness, but the geezer sounded like he actually cared.

"They said they needed someone with more stunt experience, so they went with Guy Johns. I was already in the costume and everything. And I've got S.P.A.C.T.[8] experience, too."

"I know," said Marcus soothingly. "You've got sword-fight training. You worked on *Merlin* and *Atlantis* for us."

---

[7] Fluorescent safety vest.

[8] Special Action

"And *The Legend of King Arthur.*"

"That wasn't with us, though."

"Besides the point, isn't it?" He might be sympathetic, but the guy was a bit of an idiot, too, it seemed.

"You've done such brilliant jobs for us, Jem. All those wonderful *Doctor Who* monsters."

"Exactly! Couldn't you ring them and tell them?"

There was a pause. "I'll try my best, Jem. Give me five or ten."

Jem thanked him and disconnected. He strolled around the base distractedly, waiting for the phone to ring. Passing the makeup truck, he saw the door open and a character appear at the top of the steps. A demon. *His* demon. The makeup was elaborate and scary, white face with heavy, black kohl eyes, red prosthetic blisters protruding everywhere. The filthy bramble of hair snaked around the eyes, which were concealed by white, pupil-less contacts. The demon began to descend the three steps from the trailer, treading carefully in the filthy farmer clothes.

"All right, Jem?" The demon waved a filthy claw at him. Guy Johns.

Jem shook his head. "Took my job, Guy."

"Sorry, mate. Awks."

Jem walked away. His phone vibrated in his pocket, set to silent in preparation for the night shoot. He answered it immediately.

"I'm *so* sorry, Jem. I spoke to Sheila, the second A.D., and she apologizes profusely. It's out of our hands. The director was insistent on having Guy for it."

"Why didn't they choose him in the first place, then? They're just messing me around."

"I know. I was pretty cross with Sheila, even though it's not her fault. Apparently, Guy's worked on another of the director's movies, and he remembered him when he saw him arrive. I'm as angry with them as you are. Of course, this Guy Johns character isn't even one of our S.A.s. He's come through another agency. But please don't be too upset. We'll get you something really good soon to make up for it. I know this is a setback for you, but don't let it demoralize you. You're our—you're one of our best S.A.s."

Jem sighed. "I know you tried, Marcus. You always go the extra mile. All of Brigstowe does. So thanks."

"Look, you're still booked for the night though. Even if it is as just part of the crowd."

"Sorry, Marcus. I don't do crowds."

He hung up, strode back to the dining bus. Christine was chatting animatedly with a guy in a demon costume. He waved his claw at Jem for the second time in five minutes. Christine didn't even look around.

CHAPTER SEVEN

Stone and Darke were at the bottom of two bottles of red, relaxing in the D.I.'s simple but pleasant two-up two-down in Fishponds.

It wasn't a frequent thing for them to share drinks at the end of a long day, but it wasn't altogether uncommon either. Stone was sprawled on one end of the sofa, his jacket flung onto a footstool, his shoes off, pale blue shirt a little crumpled, tie at half-mast. Sam Darke sat at the other end, facing him, one leg curled under the other, trim and smart in her own fawn suit. Though their posture indicated companionship, and even affinity with each other, there was never any sense of anything further between them. Of course, Stone had tried flirting when she first arrived at Avon and Somerset as a beautiful young D.C., but she'd soon set him straight. She'd made it clear she wasn't for the likes of Stone, with his dinosaur outlook, aversion to orthodox police methods and protocols, and childish predilection for 70s punk music. She was way too stylish and sophisticated for the likes of him. And besides, her girlfriend wouldn't have liked it.

Sonia had worried at first about her relationship with the "Christmas Cracker Diamond in the shit," as she referred to Samantha's superior officer. Sam knew she still did, deeming it unhealthy and impolitic. Sonia would never accept Stone as a man. He was everything she hated; the least P.C. policeman she had ever had the misfortune to meet, stuck firmly in the decade when men were men and women lay on their backs and did the washing up. He was a walking, swearing anachronism. Sam had tired of telling her there was a lot more to her boss than that, but whenever she tried to defend him to her girlfriend, she seemed completely at a loss to point out exactly what that "lot more" might actually consist of. But she loved Stone, warts and all—and there were plenty of those—but the idea of fucking him was obscene.

He was an attractive man in some ways. Not rugged, not handsome, exactly. Rough-hewn was probably how she would describe him. His mid-brown hair was spiky with gel but receding, his temples kissed by gray, the first lines sprouting under his eyes, a slouch starting up under his chin. But his eyes were firm and a magnetic blue. She could understand why certain women found him rather sexy—in a secondhand way. A Charity Shop Sean Connery? There was a used and faded tough glamour about him. Not that she would ever tell him that, of course. But despite his battered lack of charm that was somehow in itself charming, he never seemed to have much luck with women. So when his phone bleeped for the third time in a row, interrupting their conversation, and she happened to lean forward to read the caller I.D., her curiosity was naturally aroused by whom Aneta could possibly be.

Stone ignored the text, switching his phone off. But there was a glimmer of a smile on his lips.

"Aneta…sounds Polish."

Stone looked uncomfortable.

"She's not some sex worker you hooked up with over in Krakow, is she?"

"For fuck's sake, Darke! *I'm* supposed to be the politically incorrect one, remember? Just because she's Eastern European doesn't mean she has to be a prostitute."

"I wasn't being politically incorrect; I was speaking from insider knowledge of your seedy personality."

"Well, don't. She works for recruitment over there."

"And did she recruit you?"

"Pass us that bottle and shut it."

He poured himself another glass of mid-price Hardy's. They both enjoyed their wine, but neither was proficient in appreciating berries or provenance. As long as it cost between £5 and £10, they were happy. He had often teased her about her lack of sophistication when it came to drinking. It was one of the only things where she didn't mind slumming it— along with hanging out with him, of course.

"So?"

"So what. Change the fucking subject."

"Okay. Still fancy Jem Whateley for the *Caligula* Crime?"

"We really gonna talk shop? Enjoy your night off, Sergeant. And you sound like a tabloid."

"I bet Cooke enjoyed watching the film, though. Probably way too much."

"Don't think about it. You'll go blind."

"I'm surprised *Cookie* didn't. Didn't provide us with much help, though, did it? A killer who styles himself after a notorious film. There's got to be a whole load of clues in *Caligula* to help us as to motive, and all Cookie can comment on is the amount of vagina on display and Helen Mirren's breasts. Definitely think you put the wrong man on the job."

"So *you* watch it."

"Is that an order? Because it sounds more like a punishment."

"I'll watch it myself, then."

"Make sure you turn the sound down. Think of your neighbors."

"I'll try not to get too excited about all those seventies downstairs haircuts—or lack of 'em." Darke winced. "But you're right, there has to be a concrete reason why the killer left that video for us to find, and I don't think it was purely down to the similarity in subject matter… though, of course, that's the obvious correlation. But is it as simple as that, or is the perp trying to tell us something else? A week on, and we're still asking that question."

She frowned. "An ironic statement? On the T.V. and Film industry in general? A comment on the barbarity of our entertainment, comparing it to gladiatorial Rome? So what would that make the killer? A deranged film critic? A psychopathic social commentator? A failed director whose worthy efforts have been ignored in favor of blood 'n' boobs epics?"

"A disgruntled NoMeansNo campaigner?"

"I knew you would get back to them eventually. You've got nothing on them."

"Got nothing on Whateley either. Nothing that would stick. But in answer to your question. Yes. I still fancy him for it. But I'm a tart; I fancy a lot of other fellas for it, too."

"Predictably sexist. Just fellas?"

"Well, now you mention it, that dodgy NoMeansNo bird with the dreads would probably enjoy sticking it to the man."

"Don't we all."

"That's why I like you, Darke. You get me."

"I think I'm the only one in the force who does, Detective Inspector."

He suddenly lurched off the sofa, placed his glass on the small table piled with copies of *Vivre le Rock,* and squatted down next to a DVD shelf beneath his 55" Samsung.

"What are you up to now? We're not going to watch a film, are we? You know your taste hasn't a hope in hell of matching with mine. That's me and you all over: Chalk and Cheesy."

He'd found what he was looking for and opened a DVD case, turned to her, clutching the shiny disc.

"You call me Jack and you don't even know why. Just copying the lads at the station. So you're takin' the piss without understanding the reason. Jack Regan. Mean anything to you?"

She sipped her wine thoughtfully, looked up at the ceiling. "Dodgy porn star? Iffy punk rock singer? Used car salesman?"

He shook his head in disbelief. "I knew it. Not a clue. For an excellent detective, you've got a lazy mind. Didn't you ever think of Googling him? 'Course not. You just passed him off as some macho bullshit."

"I don't think I've ever called you Jack."

"Okay. It's mainly Cookie, I'll grant you. But you have said it a few times."

She shrugged. "Where's this leading? I hope it's not a drunken Derek

Stone diatribe about misunderstood Ford Capri drivers? Please don't tell me he's a boxer. You *know* I find that sport tedious and dumb."

He snorted, placed the disc in the player, pressed Play.

A Thames T.V. logo appeared, then a raunchy, primitive theme tune accompanied by stark illustrated images of a tough-looking man and his ruggedly handsome partner. Darke sat through the montage, waiting for the punch line.

"See, I told you there would be macho bullshit involved. Is he supposed to be a detective? He's just punched a villain wearing a sock on his head in the guts, and we haven't even finished the opening credits."

"Shut it, you slag."

"Is Jack the rugged one or the brute?"

He sighed, long and hard.

"Oh, Dennis Waterman. Isn't he the one Matt Lucas and David Walliams take the piss out of in *Little Britain?*"

"You're being deliberately stupid. And you know full well who John Thaw is."

"Obtuse is the word you're fumbling for, dear. And Morse is much more to my taste."

Stone flumped back on the sofa and paused the disc with a flick of the remote. "You telling me you've never seen *The Sweeney?*"

"Daytime T.V., love. We're out chasing villains at that time, remember, not watching actors playing them on the telly box."

"For a smart D.S., you can be incredibly dumb. It used to be prime time, back when I was a kid. I can only remember flashes of it as I was so young. Me Dad let me stay up and watch with him sometimes. He never missed an episode." Stone took a gulp of wine. "There was never a show that ever came near it. Thaw and Waterman. Not even gonna be so corny as to use the 'L' word. But they were. Proper geezers. The dynamic between those two. Nothing like it. The little improv they'd drop in so casually… Waterman looking for somewhere to chuck his takeaway coffee cup or fiddling with a faulty kettle. Thaw's scowls. Proper. They were fuckin' magnificent."

"You're drunk. It's just a seventies cop show with too much violence and disrespect to women."

"Bollocks."

"Too much of that as well. It's very dated. How many times have they said 'bird' in the opening five minutes? Make a great drinking game, if nothing else."

He ignored her. "You wanna know the real reason why I became a cop?"

"No, please. Don't say it."

"You might have joined the force because, I don't know, maybe because you wanted to arrest men. A power thing. Teach them how a 'bird' can get the upper hand. Don't even fucking try to deny it. But for me, it was that show. *Bang.* Changed my fuckin' life. And it wasn't just their performances; it was the realism of it all. For the first time on telly, you had cops who fucked up. Episodes ended inconclusively. There wasn't always a positive outcome."

"You can't live your life through a T.V. show."

"No, of course not. But if it inspires you to head in a direction away from what you were steamin' toward naturally—the slammer and a life of crime, like most of the rest of my no-good family, then I would say— and not lightly either—that it fuckin' saved my life."

He hit the Play button, and Jack Regan was slamming his fist into the villain's guts again.

And now it was Darke's turn to sigh.

CHAPTER EIGHT

Christine eventually noticed Jem's absence after an hour or two. She'd been too busy chatting with his replacement to notice.

When Guy Johns was called away to rehearse his scene, Christine stepped off the dining bus and made her way to the tea station.

It was dark now and had turned a little chilly. She was glad for her leather jacket, and the tea would be very welcome, too. She stirred her drink and flipped the tea bag into the waste bin, then pulled out her phone. She pressed Jem's call icon and waited. Nothing. "Wanker," she said aloud.

"What's that?"

Christine looked up to see one of the other supporting artists choosing a flavored tea bag from the box. She recognized her by sight but couldn't remember the name. Long, blonde hair like herself, but probably a good twenty years older. A fair few wrinkles. She remembered the lady telling her once she got whistled at by a lot of men, but when she turned around and they realized how old she was, they turned away sharpish. Bit harsh, Christine had thought. She had strong, attractive features and lovely twinkling eyes. Christine had warmed to her immediately.

"Oh, not you, obviously," Christine chuckled. "Just this twat who's supposed to be filming with us. He's done a runner. Sulking because he got demoted to crowd."

"Sounds like a bit of a prick."

"Oh, he is, believe me." They shared a smile and a titter. Christine found herself warming to her even more.

"So, who is the wanker in question?" The older blonde filled her cup from the hot water urn. Crew members and other S.A.s jostled around the tea station. Christine examined the older woman as she straightened up. Maybe early fifties, still got a good figure. Lovely hair, obviously dyed.

"Jem Whateley. Know him?"

"Oh, he *is* a wanker." The woman cackled good-naturedly. "No, actually, he's all right. Done many a job with him. He's a good laugh."

"Except when he's sulking." Christine sipped her tea. "He's the one who talked me into doing this job. I'm a relative newbie."

"It can be fun. And, of course, other times, it's a nightmare. You'll quickly find you're either too hot or too cold in this job, never just right."

Christine shivered dramatically. "Bit chilly, but not *too* bad at the moment, though, thankfully."

"You wait 'til eleven o'clock tonight. You'll be saying something different then. So… You and Jem…?" She gave Christine a little wink.

"God, no!" She paused. "Actually, that sounds a bit harsh."

"Yeah. He's not *that* bad. Quite good with his tongue, actually."

"What??" She frowned at the woman, shocked. "You and Jem?"

"Oh, it was very brief. We're just friends now. We had fun and left it there. But I still like him."

"Oh."

The older woman smiled knowingly. "For someone who seemed so adamant you don't fancy him a second ago, you seem awfully put out that he might have been with someone else recently."

"Recently. How… Oh, it doesn't matter." She grinned to show she wasn't bothered, *really*. She pictured him: thin face, messy brown hair that never looked styled. Lost eyes. Something appealing, though; she could see that. She could see why this cougar would have pounced on him. And he certainly knew how to make Christine laugh. They were on the same wavelength when it came to a sardonic outlook on the world, but as for anything else…

"He's cute," she found herself saying to the older blonde. "But I just don't know… There's a sadness…" She paused. This was the first time she'd articulated any of this to another person. "I can't put my finger on it. And he's a bit of a numpty, too. Daft and lost all at the same time, kind of like a little boy who never grew up. And I don't know whether that's attractive or tiresome."

The other laughed. "I think you two have a few things to work out."

"I think perhaps you're right. He's still, and always will be, a wanker, though."

They laughed together, and then the older blonde, whose name was Jane, suggested they both go and sit on the bus to keep warm.

They sat and chatted a bit further. Dinner was called, but they remained seated, watching through the window as the queue of crew and cast formed next to the catering truck. They knew better than to join the queue themselves yet. That had been one of the first things Jem had taught her on her first day. Know your place. And it certainly wasn't at the head of the queue. It was always at the back.

Jem had recounted to her how one day he had revolted against this feudal edict. He'd already been queuing in the cold for ten minutes when a second unit had broken for lunch, and a stream of crew members had headed toward them. Instead of joining the rear, they had formed an arrow formation next to where Jem was standing. A big, bearded grip had loudly told the rest of his colleagues to get in here, as he "didn't mind pushing in front of S.A.s." Jem had told him what he'd thought of that idea. "Crew first, buddy," the bearded man had insisted, looking for a fight. Jem would have given him one if an A.D. hadn't hurriedly intervened. Jem had simmered, but he knew his place. One day, he'd told Christine, his place would be at the head of the queue. One day.

Christine had teased him mercilessly about it. She knew exactly what buttons to push. Why hadn't he decked the bearded man? Too scared? Did he tug his forelock instead? *Yessir, mistah, nossir. Ise gonna go to the back like a good boy.* Jem had bristled and refused to speak to her for a while.

Why was she still thinking about him?

She missed him. He made her feel good about herself, even though he called her Snaggle and Beaky. He *got* her. She felt secure with him, and in her life, that had been a very rare thing.

"What are you going to choose? Lasagne or Prawn Curry?" Jane was peering out at the menu board with its sharpie-scrawled choice of meals.

She wished he hadn't stormed off, sulking like a spoiled brat. She wished he was here.

The scene was relatively simple. All he had to do was jump on the actor and tear a prosthetic wound open on his throat. Piece of piss.

The rehearsal had gone smoothly. He'd timed his action just right. The actor (Pete Somebody—Guy thought he'd seen him on *Eastenders* a few years back) had reacted scared enough as Guy stalked him. It wasn't Shake-speare. Any idiot in a mask could do it. But now they had to break for half an hour before filming the scene precisely *because* of a mask. Two demons, Guy being one of them, were marked out as lead creatures, or "Hero Demons," in the director's words, a generic and rather silly term that just meant they were more prominent in the scene. But the third de-mon was more background and so didn't need extensive prosthetics and makeup. A cheap demon mask had been produced for that per-former to wear, probably borrowed from another production or two, but nobody would really notice because the mask's wearer would be at the back of the shot. The problem was, the mask had gone missing.

After searching both makeup and wardrobe trunks, the second A.D. had given the instruction to do a quick makeup job on the third demon, which they were now in the middle of. Guy had seized his chance to take a pee while they did so. He wouldn't get much of a chance later, that was for sure.

He mooched over to the honey wagon and, opening the door, winced at the smell emanating from inside. Both cubicles were engaged, while the solitary urinal had a notice fixed on it saying OUT OF ORDER. He con-sidered slipping into the ladies' next door but rapidly thought better of it.

He didn't want to be marked down as a peeper, not with those #No-MeansNo clowns protesting outside the location site's perimeter. Could they see him from here? He peered past the brightly lit production vehicles toward the gap in the woods that marked the gate at the entrance. He could dimly see some shadows and an occasional bob of a flashlight. Silly sods. What were they protesting about? This wasn't Hollywood. Kevin Spacey was nowhere to be seen, and Harvey Weinstein obviously had nothing to do with this low-budget horror film—or any film anymore. So what did they want? He'd heard they'd been picketing various productions in the South West, and he could understand why they'd had a pop at *Legion Britannica*—the rape scene he'd seen leaked in the press had sounded nasty. There wasn't anything as bad in *The Awful Dead*. At least, he didn't think so. He hadn't read the entire script, obviously. He was just a lowly extra/creature performer. It was nasty and violent, and he expected the lead actress would bare her breasts. So what? That happened in horror films. As far as he knew, the producer hadn't demanded she toss him off to get the part. He would have read about it in *The Sun*.

He glanced over at the ladies' half of the honey wagon. Should he risk nipping quickly inside? As he contemplated it, one of the female grips trotted quickly toward the door, swung it open, and popped inside. That would be a no, then.

He began ambling across the clearing toward the track leading into the woods, nodding at a security man in his hi vis as he did so.

The prosthetics on his face felt tight, and an infuriating itch was beginning to bug him on his nose, which he couldn't scratch without ruining the makeup job so painstakingly applied a couple of hours earlier. But his need to piss was more urgent.

He strolled down the path and around a corner until the trees blocked the film unit from sight. He picked the nearest beech, ducking past hanging creepers, and fumbled around with his dungarees, lowering them to enable him to pee. He thought of Christine as he did so, which wasn't a sensible thing to do while he had his dick in his hand. He wished she'd take it in *her* hand. He hoped that replacing that loser Whateley as one of the demons would elevate Guy in her mind. She'd seemed interested in him, judging from their conversation earlier. He'd love to… He pictured her slender body, those amazing electric blue eyes, the fall of dirty blonde hair and imagined her following him out to the woods. *Damn it.* He'd never get to relieve his bladder if he kept thinking these happy thoughts. Think of something boring and ugly. Jem Whateley? Yeah, that was better. Man, what a prick. The way he'd stormed off set after being demoted to crowd. Fucking diva. That's exactly what Christine had said as well. *Don't think about Christine again or we'll be here all night.* And here he was, talking to his dick now.

A rustle of bushes behind him. He turned, still trying to pee, his head craning back over his right shoulder. It was dark in the woods. He could barely make out the path behind him. The twinkling of lights from the unit didn't do anything to alleviate the gloom this deep in the woods.

A shadow.

The unmistakable silhouette of a figure standing next to a tree just across the path.

"Christine?" *You dumb fuck. As if she'd really follow you into the woods.*

Then who was it? One of the other S.A.s? Another crew member forced to do the same as him? Of course, that's all it was. And yet the figure hadn't moved. There was no sound of urine sprinkling into the ferns around the tree. It was as if the shadow were watching Guy. *Or watching his dick.* Of course: a dirty peepin' bastard.

"See anything you like?" He waved it tentatively, then realized that wasn't the safest thing to do if the intruder *was* a pervert. "Can't a Guy even take a piss without somebody taking interest?" He hoped the perv would appreciate the play on his name. Probably not. His wit was always wasted.

The shadow remained motionless. Guy had lost all desire to pee now. Something about the figure's immobility and silence was unnerving him. He put his dick away and struggled to pull up his dungarees. He would have to take his chance back at the honey wagon.

The figure moved forward slowly. When it was halfway across the path, the glow from the unit picked out the dirty farm laborer-styled clothes, the makeup on the hands, the claws…the mask. *The* mask. The one that had gone missing.

It looked even more frightening in the dark woods. The eyes were black rips, the face shroud-white, pitted with latex scabs and scars, most of the detail lost in the night. The figure didn't make a sound.

"What you doing, Steve? You can't scare me, you twat." Steve didn't answer, just kept coming, stalking across the path, through the nettles and ferns, brushing aside the hanging creepers to where Guy was still fighting to button up his dungarees.

"Steve?"

No. It wasn't Steve, the background demon who had lost his mask. He knew it wasn't Steve. Steve didn't have the cojones to play a stunt like this. The joke was stretching too far. The punch line would come when he jumped at Guy, hands out like a Halloween monster.

He was carrying a Sainsbury's bag in one claw. He tipped the bag up in front of Guy, and a shiny, plastic object fell into the ferns. A box of some kind. Now Guy's attention was focused on the object in "Steve's" other hand.

Nothing to be frightened of—just a pencil. "Steve" held it up, and Guy could see the lead point was very sharp.

"Boo! Ya got me. Now fuck off and go scare someone who doesn't think you're lame."

"Steve" jumped at Guy, and the punch line came at last. But instead of throwing out his hands and shouting "Boo!," the figure suddenly dropped into a crouch and drove the point of the pencil through the sock on Guy's left ankle, just below the trouser bottom of his dungarees. Such was the force of the blow that the pencil dug through the thin material of Guy's sock and deep into the skin just above his ankle bone.

Guy screeched and fell back into the nettles. The figure stabbed the pencil into the same wound again, savagely hacking and twisting it into the vulnerable area, even though the point was shattered. Guy's shrieks were cut off as his assailant shoved a handful of nettles into his mouth with his other gloved hand, then dropped the pencil, moved behind him and curled an arm around Guy's throat. Guy was dragged backward, deeper into the woods, away from the dwindling lights of the film unit.

Guy choked, the arm constricting his throat. The lights dwindled even more. Then he was released, dropped into the ferns and nettles as his attacker reached for something dangling overhead. A creeper. The figure that was almost certainly not "Steve" withdrew something out of his own dungaree pocket. A glinting blade with which he commenced hacking at the creeper overhead while Guy struggled to get to his feet, his winded condition, wounded ankle, and general terror preventing him from doing so.

The figure swung on him again, a piece of severed creeper clutched in its right fist while the other held the knife. The mask stooped toward him, and cheap as it was, and no matter how clumsily made, Guy had never seen anything more terrifying.

And then the figure in the second-hand demon mask rammed the end of the creeper into Guy's mouth, and Johns finally got the deep throat he'd been craving.

CHAPTER NINE

The call came as Stone was finishing his sixth glass of wine.

"What the fuck do you want, Wells? I'm enjoying my evening off with much more attractive company than you could ever offer me, and I've got a nasty feeling you're about to crash the party."

"Sorry, sir. The Chief asked me to call you. We've got another one."

"Another what?" He put his glass down and scowled at Darke. She rolled her eyes, put her glass down, too.

"Another body, boss. And another video placed next to it."

Stone said nothing for a second, digesting this, waiting for the wine swirl to clear and allow him time to think. Excitement at the thought of engaging with the case again in a major new development merging with sizzled befuddlement and fatigue. But he was used to working on less than 100%. More than used to it; lately, it was becoming the norm.

"All right, come and pick me up. I'll grab a quick coffee. Hurry up before I fall asleep."

He could sense Wells's grin on the other end. The D.C. obviously believed Stone was entertaining a female guest, and not of the Detective Sergeant variety.

Terry Wells was a reliable, if occasionally unconventional, Detective Constable of second-generation Jamaican roots. Like Stone, he came from a tough, working-class background (in his case, the predominantly black district of St. Pauls in Bristol) that didn't tolerate the police. Like Stone, he'd grown up flirting with crime but had never quite fallen for it. And also like Stone, his subsequent career choice after a troubled youth resulted in family resentment and, in some cases, ostracism. They had both taken one of the two paths open to them, and in both cases, it was the hardest. As a result, they had a deep respect for each other, even if Stone had perverse ways of showing it and Wells of earning it. Stone enjoyed riling his subordinate officer, playing on racial stereotypes for his own amusement, while Wells did his best to live up to them. So while Stone constantly teased the D.C. with comments about him "smokin' da ganja and bangin' his ho's," Wells would merely grin artfully, and only *occasionally* enter the office with the smell of weed in his wake. It was a statement. He was taking the piss out of Stone, the Chief, the entire C.I.D. And while Stone had admitted to him that the D.C.I. didn't give a shit about such things—if he even noticed it—the Chief Superintendent was a different matter. He'd told Wells that if he came near the Super smelling like that, he wouldn't be working for the Murder squad for long. Wells heeded his advice—most of the time.

"You can't go," Darke reprimanded him after he'd hung up. "You're drunk."

"Sober as a fuckin' white wig. You forget, I've got a stronger constitution than the average geezer." He shrugged into his jacket, then headed for the kitchen to make them both a cup of coffee. Darke followed him.

"You mean more full of *shit* than the average geezer. The Chief can send somebody else. D.S. Fallen, for instance."

"Fallen is a phallus, and we both know it. The only thing he's good at investigating is snot up his nose. I'm the S.I.O. It's my case."

She stared him down, but she knew she wasn't going to win this one. They both sipped their coffees, waiting for Wells to arrive.

"At least have a shower," she suggested, which he knew was her way of asking if she could have one.

"No time," he replied. "And besides, you look beautiful as you are." He winked at her, and she threw a dishcloth at him, then retired to the bathroom to attempt to look respectable.

"You don't need to come," he called after her. She gave him the middle finger. Of course, she did. She was as invested in this case as he was. It was unthinkable that either of them would let someone else poke about at the murder scene without them.

Ten minutes later, they were climbing into Wells's BMW, Darke in the back and Stone in the passenger seat.

The first thing Stone objected to was the music.

"What the fuck is this bollocks?" he moaned as soon as he'd shut the door and Wells gunned the engine.

"Grime." Wells didn't look at him. Stone turned to stare at his subordinate officer. He didn't need to comment, his expression saying it all.

Wells refused to react, threading the beemer down the suburban street and onto the main road. He was in his late thirties, wiry and wary, sharp-eyed, ready to challenge and be challenged. Like his boss, he had a good knack for cutting through bullshit and unearthing hidden truths. But unlike Stone, he kept his opinions to himself most of the time. In that respect, he was far more shrewd. He would make the perfect D.I. one day.

Stone scowled at the grimy mix of rap and drum and bass. "Is this the sort of music an honest, law-abiding cop should be listening to?"

"No, sir. That's why it's okay for *me* to listen to it."

Stone reached into his inside jacket pocket and retrieved the CD he constantly kept there. It was his good-luck CD; he played it on the way to every murder scene. "Turn it off and play this instead."

"Can't do that, sir."

"Why the fuck not?"

"This motor doesn't have a CD drive, sir. Only plays MP3s."

"Wells, d'you think Mama Stone raised a clown? What the fuck is that slit on the dash, then?"

Wells grinned. "Caught me out, sir."

Darke chuckled in the back.

"Wells. I'll put this to you politely. Either you lose the Grimy shit and play this CD, or I assign you to Vice in St. Pauls."

"Permission to be disrespectful to a senior officer, sir?"

"Not given."

"Fuck you, sir."

"I said not given."

Wells played the CD. It was *Machine Gun Etiquette* by The Damned, a band that was one of Stone's earliest loves. His older brother had gotten him into punk at a young age, and it had stayed with him, driving his passions, his tastes, and his politics. He could lay a lot of the blame for his abrasive attitude and unforgiving refusal to be subordinate to anyone at punk's door. It had grabbed him at an early, impressionable age and shaped him. The rest of his prickly character was purely down to himself.

"Ladies and gentlemen, how do," a polite old voice announced on the first track before a tumultuous landslide of bass smashed the door in for the opening number, *Love Song*.

Wells scrabbled for the volume button.

"Now you know what I have to put up with," Darke smirked from the back as Stone duly turned it back up again.

The ritual was nearly over. Stone settled himself back in his seat for the drive. Only when he was good and ready, he turned to Wells, who knew full well not to divulge anything before his boss asked for it. Stone was sure the D.C. thought his boss was autistic. "Definitely on the spectrum" was a phrase often bandied about back at the station in reference to Stone. If Stone had heard such rumors, he certainly wasn't in a rush to squash them. But then he'd never been in a hurry to give a toss what anybody thought about him. If they wanted to think these things, then let them. It gave him added mystery, and it might even protect him from condemnation from above, considering his "unconventional" way of dealing with things.

"Come on, then. Haven't got all night, have we? Or would you rather I play the whole album a few times before you dish."

Wells told him all he knew, raising his voice over the din from the speakers. The call had come in from the producer of a low-budget horror movie being filmed just outside Bristol. One of their creature performers had gone missing. Wells repeated this job title with some relish.

"What the fuck is a creature performer?" interrupted Stone.

"What it says on the tin, sir. An extra who performs in a creature suit."

"What sort of creature?"

"Demon, sir."

Stone digested this. The alcoholic fog dissipated as the detective part of his brain—his most noble aspect—began to fight for dominance. His rumpled suit was a different matter, however, and the smell of his breath wouldn't fool anybody. Did Stone care?

"They'd waited an hour, then sent a runner to look for him. This guy, Paul White, eventually found their man in the woods nearby."

"And?"

"They didn't want to describe it to the uniforms, sir. Apparently, they said, 'We would need to see for ourselves,' whatever that means."

"Probably means it was too horrible for their middle-class palates, Wells. That it?"

"Video found next to the body. Old V.H.S. Like the one on the dead Roman."

"What was it?" Stone turned the volume down, and Wells's answer was loud in the sudden silence.

"*The Evil Dead,* sir."

Chapter Ten

"What the actual *fuck*?!"

Stone hadn't expected this when he entered the white C.S.I. tent, the flap lifted for him by a forensics officer.

"Quite a sight, isn't it?" A tic pulled at Dr. Hughgroves's right cheek. He looked subtly amused.

The body was lying face down across a tree stump, dungarees and pants around the man's ankles. A long piece of tree creeper had been inserted up the corpse's anus.

Stone felt the wine in his guts congeal. He'd contemptuously dismissed the green faces of the uniforms on duty outside, but now he was pretty sure his facial hue was emulating theirs.

"Oh dear Lord," said Darke behind him.

"For fuck's sake." Stone forced himself to approach the corpse, circled it gingerly. The dead man's face was caked with horrific movie makeup. Another creeper was rammed into its open mouth. Blood crusted the length of protruding root, pooled beneath it. Stone hunkered down on his haunches, deliberately keeping away from the bare backside and what had been slammed inside it.

There was more blood smeared on the left ankle, partially hidden under the shucked-down trousers and underwear. The underwear was decorated with Iron Man and the Marvel brand. A pencil was inserted into a nasty-looking wound just above the ankle.

Stone sniffed, controlled his rolling guts. He was developing a blinder of a headache. His eyes alighted on the large plastic VHS box nestled beside one outflung arm. He straightened up, pulled some C.S.I. gloves from his jacket pocket, waited for a C.S.I. to take one final photograph of the positioning, then picked it up.

"'The ultimate experience in grueling terror,'" he quoted from the back cover. He turned it over, frowning at the garish art on the front of the box. A green-faced demonic-looking hag was raising her ragged claws over two reels of film tape, a skull with a screaming mouth, and the primitive font of the title. "'The most ferociously original Horror Film of the year.' Stephen King seems to like it, anyway." He opened the clamshell case, peered at the tape nestled snugly inside. Besides the peeling PLEASE REWIND sticker, a bloody thumbprint was evident on the Palace Video label.

"Get that print checked," he told the chief forensics officer, Harry Grimes. "Bound to be a false trail, but have a look anyway."

"Obviously," came the sarcastic response.

"All right, Doris, let's not be so precious about it." He turned to Darke. "The print's a new addition. Either our killer is incredibly clumsy, or he's playing with us."

"Looks too blatant," Darke said.

"Doctor?" Stone passed the cassette box to Grimes, who promptly bagged it, then looked up at Hughgroves.

The pathologist shrugged. "Within the last two to three hours. The wounds haven't congealed entirely. May I take him now?" The photographer's camera flashed again at the pencil in the wound; then the C.S.I. stood aside while another officer removed it and placed it almost reverentially in an evidence bag.

"Patience. You can play with him all you like when I'm done." Hughgroves's tic seemed to have worsened. He didn't like Stone.

"Cause of death?"

Hughgroves sniffed. "Maybe it's the root that's been slammed down his throat, cutting off his air supply," the pathologist said. "Or had you failed to observe that?"

"And here I was wondering if it could have been the one that's shoved right up his ass that was making him so quiet. It hasn't stopped someone else I know, though, has it?"

Hughgroves's upper lip curled in distaste.

"Our perp's having a bit of a chuckle. Imaginative fucker. Why the creepers in both orifices, I wonder. And why the pencil in the ankle?"

"Perhaps the answer's in the film, Boss." Darke gave him a very thin smile. Her bluebell eyes looked bloodshot. It was easily 1:00 a.m. by now. They both needed sleep.

"You gonna watch it, or do I get to be the lucky one? Not trusting it to Cookie this time."

He prowled the interior of the tent, searching the rough ground around the body. Besides the smears and puddles of drying blood, there was nothing obvious he could use to point him toward what had happened. He gave the corpse one last look. "Playing an elaborate game."

"Sir?"

"The perp. The deaths are mirroring the content of these films. The Roman stabbed to death with a sword; this guy in demon makeup, a bit like the hag on the cover of *The Evil Dead*. The bastard's enjoying this." He signaled to Hughgroves, who left the evidence tent to look for some C.S.I. officers to transport the corpse.

"Psychopath, or someone with an ax to grind?"

"Against the film industry? Very possibly. Let's talk to someone who might know." He left the tent, followed by Darke and Grimes.

Stone paced around outside the tent, examining the trampled ferns and nettles, the occasional broken branch. He stopped when he got to a piece of dangling creeper. The root had been freshly severed.

"Already spotted it. It's been photographed," Grimes snapped.

"I should bloody hope so, too." His gaze wandered to one of the queasy-looking uniformed coppers guarding the tent. "You all right, son? You don't look well to me."

"Fine, sir."

"'Fine, sir,'" Stone mimicked the junior cop. "You don't have to bullshit me, son. I was born rolling in it. You look like you need a nice cup of hot chocolate and a bedtime story."

He tramped off down the path toward the film unit, illuminated by tall arc lamps. Darke shrugged at the uniform. "Don't worry, officer. He's always like that."

"What, full of shit?"

"Full of shit, *ma'am*," she chided him and followed the D.I. toward the production base.

"*The Awful Dead?* Not very imaginative, is it?" Stone was sitting in the production trailer, facing a harried-looking producer across a cluttered desk.

"I— It's an homage," the producer, Donald Wise, insisted. He had a florid face, a colorful tie that didn't match his purple suit, and very well-manicured nails.

"Is it now?" Stone looked up at the row of mug shots lining the walls of the trailer. "Looks like you've got your own wall of shame here. What are they in for?"

"I'm sorry?" Wise looked nonplussed. He looked at Darke for help, but the D.S. simply stared at him with a level, penetrating gaze. Finally, the penny dropped. "No, no. Those are photographs of our principal cast, not... not *criminals*." He looked aghast.

Stone's face was as inscrutable as Darke's. They were a double act, and they could keep it up all night long, until the victim of their routine finally broke. It wouldn't take Wise that long, though.

"Our demon chap isn't up there."

"No. No, he's... He was... Oh dear, this is so dreadfully upsetting. As I said, those are headshots of our principal cast."

"And our victim—Mister Guy Johns? He was just an extra, was he?"

"Y-yes. I'm afraid so."

"Afraid so? Why's that? Does it make a difference to you whether he was an extra or an actor?"

"N-no, I… Look, Inspector, this has all been a huge shock to us."

"But you're in the shock business, aren't you, Mister Wise? You should be hardened to this sort of brutality?"

Wise looked angry for the first time. "Are you being deliberately obtuse?"

"Beg your pardon? Obtuse?"

"It means—"

"I know what it means. How well did you know the deceased?"

Wise sighed, visibly relaxed a little. He was back on more obvious police interrogatory ground now. "Not at all."

"You must know something about him?"

"He was a supporting artist, not one of the cast. I've told you that. I'm the film's producer."

"And the two don't mix. I get it. But you must have people with their ears to the ground. Heard any rumors about dissent on set? Anyone with an obvious dislike of the deceased, perhaps one of your assistant directors moaning about clashes on set, things like that."

"I'm far too busy for that sort of thing, Inspector. You'll need to speak to the A.D.s."

"Oh, I will. Thanks for your time, Mister Wise." He waited in his seat. Wise waited, too, expecting the detective to rise to his feet. "I'm curious about something, though, and perhaps you could enlighten me."

Wise peered at him impatiently.

"Was it *supposed* to be a man?"

"I'm afraid I don't follow."

"In the script for your film. Was a man supposed to be killed in that scene? And did it involve tree roots?"

Wise wasn't sure what to say for a few seconds, but eventually, he shook his head and sighed. "A woman. Like in the original—it was our little pastiche. But it was scripted to be one of the female actors killed by the root, not a man."

Stone nodded, continued to remain where he was.

Wise glanced at his watch. "Now, if you've finished," he said pompously, "I really do have so much to attend to."

"Sorry to be a cliché, Mister Wise, but there's just one more thing."

Wise waited, not sure he would like what was to follow.

"I'm going to have to close your production down, keep all your cast and crew here for an unspecified time, and requisition your trailer as a temporary Murder room." He broke out with a cheesy grin. Darke pretended to find something very absorbing on the wall next to her.

"You can't go upsetting everyone like that," Darke said as Stone made himself comfortable in the producer's swivel chair and sipped a cup of coffee. "You know he'll only go complaining to the Chief."

"Let him. Give the Chief something to do for once, adding it to the list on his wall. That pompous fucker deserved it. 'He was an extra, and I'm a producer.' You still bleed like an extra, you still eat and shit like one, and you still have to give up your fucking nice, warm production office when I tell you."

"You enjoyed it too much."

"Damn right. So who's top of our list?"

"An A.D. who was in charge of Guy Johns, Paul White. Oh, and the uniforms have lined up the NoMeansNo campaigners, as well. Pretty sure they're the same ones from the other week at the Roman production."

"Haven't they got lives?"

"Seems their principles are their lives, sir."

"That a criticism, Detective Sergeant? I'm all for equality for women. But one of 'em in particular really gets my goat. What are they doing here this time of night anyway? They hoofed it back to bed when it got cold and dark on the Roman shoot. Bring them in one at a time after White. Save the twat with the attitude for last. I want him to sweat."

Paul White repeated what he'd already told the first uniforms to arrive, who had passed it on to D.C. Wells at Avon and Somerset C.I.D. He was a young, callow man in his mid-twenties, with a curly mop of hair on top, shaved at the sides. He looked as pale as his name. His hands shook slightly as he fiddled with a paper clip on the desk in front of him.

"He was a popular S.A. by all accounts. Sorry, that's supporting artist."

"I'm beginning to pick up the lingo. Popular? So, who do you think might have had it in for him so much they wanted to ram a creeper up his chocolate alley?"

White looked aghast. Stone wasn't sure whether by the reminder of the brutal detail or by Stone's insensitive vocabulary. Stone applied more pressure in his own special way.

"Did you like him? Did he try your patience on set at all?"

"What— What d'you mean? He was fine. A good performer. I think. I mean, he was under a lot of makeup. I—I liked him fine."

"What about everybody else?"

"I don't know. I—"

Stone examined the list of names of people who were working on the production. At the top were the cast, then the crew, and then a long list of SA names. Stone perused them for a moment in silence while Paul fidgeted with the paper clip.

Darke sat to one side, sipping her own coffee. Paul looked at her for support. He looked scared. She gave him a small smile. "Did you see anybody clash with him on set, perhaps?" she said.

"No. I don't think so."

"Anyone who might bear him a grudge?"

"Jem Whateley, maybe?" Stone looked up suddenly as he asked the question, his sharp green eyes riveted on White's.

"Who?"

"Jem Whateley. He's down on your list, I see. Supporting Artist. Seems to be cropping up like a bad penny whenever something nasty happens."

White nodded miserably. "Oh yeah, Jem. Yeah, yeah. I remember him now."

"Was he a friend of Guy Johns?"

Paul shrugged. "I don't know."

"Is there anything you *do* know?"

"D.I. Stone means is there anyone who could tell us more about Mister Whateley's activities on set and any possible relationship with Mister Johns?"

White thought for a moment. Stone could see him desperate to push someone else forward into the light so he could retreat from this nightmare.

"Christine Thomas. They seemed pretty close."

Stone scanned the list, matched the name. The S.A.s were all huddled miserably on the dining bus, waiting to be questioned. It would be a long time before any of them got to go home to bed.

Stone looked at Darke. "So let's speak to our pal Jem, then. See what excuses he's got for us this time."

"He—he went home," Paul said, then cleared his throat.

"He what? I gave specific instructions nobody was to leave the site."

"He left before—before the incident."

"Did he? How very interesting." Stone leaned back in his swivel chair. "Tell Wells to pull him in." Darke nodded, pulled her phone out, relayed the instructions to the D.C.

"Now, why would he leave?"

Paul's eyes brightened with the dawning implication of the line of discussion. "He was—disillusioned."

"Disillusioned? Why would that be?"

"He was hired to be one of the creature performers. One of the demons. It was a better job than your average crowd SA. More money."

"And?"

"And the director changed his mind, went for Guy Johns instead. Jem left the set in a foul mood."

"Really?" He exchanged a look with Darke. "I can't wait to speak to him about it."

When Paul had gone, Stone stood up and examined the row of headshots on the wall. He didn't recognize any of them. He looked at his watch, turned back to Darke. "While we're waiting for our friend Jem, let's see one of my other best mates: Martin, the NoMeansNoer. I've changed my mind, let's put Mister Hipster at the front of the queue. A good fight might wake me up a bit."

Darke winced. It was now 2:30 a.m. It didn't look like any of them would be sleeping any time soon.

Martin Thorogood slouched in the chair opposite Stone and played with his beard. Stone tried to hide his dislike and failed. He got up from his chair and paced the trailer.

"Why were you all still here? Last time you were in bed when it got too dark and cold. What makes this occasion different? It's like you were expecting something to happen."

Thorogood eyed him with equal dislike. "Of course, we expected something unpleasant to happen. That's why we were boycotting this production. Something unpleasant always happens on debased film sets like this, and it's normally to women."

"Not this time, though, eh?"

Thorogood said nothing. Again, he looked rather disappointed. Almost as if the victim being a man had derailed his purpose.

"Maybe you would have liked it to be a woman?"

"What does that mean?"

"Because then it would give you even better motivation to protest against it and other productions just like it."

"That's a disgusting thing to say."

"Isn't it? But wouldn't that help your just cause? It would make spectacular publicity for you and your friends. Gather the speed of your rolling promotional stone."

"I don't know what you're talking about, but I find your line of questioning obscene."

Judging from Darke's face, she was of the same opinion. She was shaking her head again, never a good sign.

"Did you leave your group at all over the last few hours?"

"You can ask the others."

"I'm asking you."

"No."

"Will they corroborate that?"

Thorogood hesitated. A weakness in his bristling armor?

"Of course, they will."

"You don't like horror films, do you?"

"I don't like any films where the object of repulsive violence and degradation is women."

"How did you know what was in the script? Another leak? Or do you have friends on the inside?"

"It's a cheap rip-off of another film where a woman is raped by trees. It didn't take a genius to work out this would follow a similar trail."

Stone stopped pacing. Returned to his chair, sat down to scrutinize Thorogood.

"You seem to know a lot about *The Evil Dead*. Watched it a few times, have you?"

"Don't be ridiculous. I would never stoop to watch such contempt-ible filth."

"Really? So how do you know what happens in it?"

"Because I'm obviously the deranged killer you're looking for."

"Not funny. Answer the question."

Thorogood shook his head. "This is beginning to bore me. I haven't seen the film, but its infamy is well-documented. The notorious rape by trees was one of the reasons it was slapped with the Video Nasty label in the early eighties."

Stone picked up his coffee, drained the last few dregs, his face giving nothing away. "Video Nasty… Tell me more."

"You can find out for yourself. I'm no expert."

"So what are you, Martin?" Stone leaned forward, elbows on the table, eyes boring into Thorogood's.

"I'm someone with principles. You should try it."

Stone allowed a very small smile to crack his hard face. "You're be-ginning to interest me, Martin. I mean, what drives a man to spend his days picketing horror films with a bunch of middle-aged women? Oh, and one young, attractive one."

"Are we finished here?" Thorogood's face was twisted with disgust.

"I don't think we are. Not by a long shot. I'd like to know all about Video Nasties, Martin. And I'd like to discuss in a lot more detail exactly why you hate horror films so much."

By the time he'd finished with Thorogood, Stone was beginning to hit a wall. It seemed like he never got to sleep anymore. He was getting too old to keep on going all through the night like he used to. He considered putting off interviewing the other #NoMeansNo campaigners until the next day but dismissed the idea. And he still had to talk to Jem Whateley, and he was very much looking forward to that. If he could stay awake long enough. He ordered another cup of strong coffee and waited for the next interviewee.

Tina Bell was the elfin-faced, youngest woman of the group. Her short bob of dark hair framed an interesting, inquisitive face. She held Stone's gaze unflinchingly, only looking at Darke occasionally throughout the conversation.

Stone tapped the pad of notepaper on the desk in front of him with a pen. On it were the words VIDEO NASTY scrawled in his spidery handwriting. After noticing it when she first sat down, Tina didn't look at the words again.

"How long have you known Martin?"

She shrugged. "Three years, maybe."

"How did you meet?"

"You don't think this has anything to do with Martin, Inspector?"

"You tell me. How well do you know him?"

"Not that well. But certainly enough to know he's not capable of anything like this."

"He seems pretty dedicated to your cause. One could even say overly so."

"Could one?" She was mocking him now. He sipped his coffee.

Came back for round two.

"Why do you think he joined your cause? He's not exactly the demographic, is he?"

"Isn't he? Passionate, principled, woke. I would say he's exactly the sort of person who would support our cause."

Stone was still wincing at the "w" word, Darke noticed, and she couldn't stop a little grin from escaping.

"Do you think there might be another reason why he joined your group?"

She blinked at him, disingenuously.

"Maybe he likes the company a little too much."

"Oh, really, Detective. I think you're confusing him with a sleazy, simplistic, misogynistic example of your gender."

Darke's eyes widened, but Stone simply smiled back at Tina.

"Maybe he'd do anything to impress you."

"Me? Now, why would he want to do that? Oh wait," she added sardonically. "Because he obviously fancies me."

"Does he?"

She stood up. "Anything else vital to the case that you'd like to ask me? Otherwise, I'd quite like to go home to bed."

Stone stood up, too, but stopped her on the way to the door. "Did Mister Thorogood leave your group at any particular time?"

She paused, hand on the doorknob, frowned. "I can't remember, Detective. Perhaps you should ask him yourself."

"I'm asking you."

She shrugged. "We all have to answer the call of nature at some point. Our dedication to standing by a fence all night is quite demanding."

"Think, Miz Bell. Do you recall him being absent for a particularly long time?"

She sighed. "Martin Thorogood is a welcome and committed member of our group. If you want to imply something untoward about him, then you're speaking to the wrong person."

Stone turned to Darke after she'd gone. "Is everybody I speak to tonight going to give me attitude?"

"You reap what you sow, Boss."

"What the fuck does *that* mean?"

"Try a more subtle approach… Oh, I'm sorry, thought I was speaking to somebody else."

"I could get tired of your cynicism, Darke. Who's next? Whateley here yet? That's all I need. More attitude."

"Wells said another ten minutes."

"Send in whatsername, then. Thomas. Christine Thomas. Let's see what shit she can give me before breakfast."

"Sir?"

"Yes, Darke?"

"I find civilized, sophisticated questioning can reap far better dividends than blunt chiseling in this more cultured age. Softly, softly…?"

"You know I prefer *The Sweeney*."

He sighed at her blank look. "I'm wasted here. And you imply it's *me* with no culture. Never mind. You think you're Miz Twenty-twenty-three; you have the next go. Gives me the chance of a breather before Mister Most Likely gets dragged in by Wells. I can have a little chat with the security guys while I'm out there. Knock yourself out, hot stuff." He winked at her and left the trailer.

D.S. Samantha Darke breathed a sigh of relief, sat down in the producer's chair so recently vacated by her boss, and reached for her coffee, which was now cold.

There was a brief knock at the door. Wells entered. accompanied by a tall blonde woman in her mid-thirties. She looked nervous, tired, and jittery.

Sam Darke looked up at Christine Thomas, cleared her throat, and signaled for the woman to sit opposite. Wells sat to one side, his expression closed.

As she opened her mouth to begin the interview, Darke wondered how long Stone would leave her in peace.

She hoped he got lost and ended up in the honey wagon. It was by far the best place for him, really. He was so full of shit that he needed a toilet roll moe than a warrant card.

"Hello, Christine. I'm D.S. Samantha Darke, Avon and Somerset police."

Christine nodded, wide-eyed. She was model-slender, insecure about her looks in the way of all naturally pretty women, with a touch of shyness that widened her eyes almost to the point of paranoia. She gave a nervous laugh. "Am I in trouble? I've heard what's happened, but there's not much I can tell you." She gave another nervous laugh that was more of a gasp.

Sam Darke smiled reassuringly and went to work.

Chapter Eleven

"I understand that you and Jem Whateley are close…"

Christine's eyes widened even more. "Is he… I mean, did he—?" Her voice was well-modulated, accent-free. She was either public school educated or hung out with people who were.

"Did he what, Miss Thomas?"

She looked away, confused, frightened.

"You can tell me."

She faced Darke again, her kaleidoscopic blue eyes bewitching fractals. Darke could see why Whateley would want to be "close" with her.

"I don't know anything."

"Ah, you can do better than that." She waited.

Christine's eyes roved the small production office trailer, alighted on the row of head shots, skittered away again. She was like a frightened pony. This was going to be easy.

"What do you want me to say? I don't know what you want me to say."

"I don't *want* you to say anything. Just tell me what you know. Let's start with you and Jem."

"But…" She studied her scarlet-painted fingernails. "There *is* no me and Jem."

"Just friends, is it?"

"He's my *best* friend." She shot a suddenly very earnest look at Darke, as if defying her to contradict the statement.

Darke nodded. "So you must know him pretty well?"

Christine studied her nails again. "Do any of us really know each other?"

Deep. Let's get this back on course. "What time did Mister Whateley leave the production set?"

She shrugged, still not looking up. "I've no idea. I didn't even realize he *had* gone."

"He didn't say goodbye to you? I thought he was your best friend."

"He was sulking. He'd just been downgraded from a monster to crowd. He…" She thought carefully about her next words.

"Yes?"

"He wasn't happy, okay?" She shot Darke a defiant look. "Why would he be? He loved doing special action and hated just being background."

"You're quite protective of him, aren't you?"

She shrugged again.

"That's good. Loyalty is an undervalued quality, especially in the film industry, I should imagine, where you're all trying to get ahead at the expense of everyone else."

"I don't know what you mean?"

Don't you? You look like the spoiled type who is always trying to get one step ahead. Using your looks and your hard, fit body.

"He makes me laugh. He's good company. He's not pushy or anything."

"But he felt slighted by his 'downgrading,' you called it? Was he particularly angry with Guy Johns, the man who replaced him?"

"He's not like that."

"What *is* he like, Christine?"

"I told you. He's my friend. He makes me laugh. He's not a maniac, if that's what you're getting at."

Darke had formed quite a picture of their relationship already. He probably had a crush on her, she liked him because he "made her laugh." It was a far-from-uncommon "relationship." The poor sap probably thought he was getting somewhere with her; she just wanted chuckles out of him and nothing more. Probably tormented him by talking about fit men she fancied all the time. Had she talked about Guy Johns in front of him, too?

"Was he jealous of Mister Johns in other ways?"

The kaleidoscope eyes bored briefly into hers, then skitted away. "Why should he be?"

"Were you and he 'close,' too?"

"Guy? I hardly knew him."

"Did you give Jem any reason to be jealous of Mister Johns?"

Christine was back to studying her nails. "Can I go now?"

"We're almost done." Darke scanned the list of names on the desk. "Anyone else on here know Jem Whateley?"

Another shrug. She lifted her head, scanned the wall over Darke's shoulder. "You could ask Jane."

"Jane…" Darke looked down the list of names again. "Jane Tighe?"

"Could be her surname. I don't know."

"Why should I speak to her?"

A pause. Then the blonde turned her full mesmerizing gaze on Darke again. "They used to go out, apparently. Or fuck, at any rate." A sneer, the eyes holding Darke's challengingly. The skittish pony had a rebellious streak, it seemed.

Darke smiled slowly. *Oh, you poor, silly girl… You really don't know who you're fucking with. I eat daft little bitches like you for breakfast.*

"Didn't that bother you?"

"Why should it?"

"Oh, yes. You're 'just friends,' aren't you? But if you're the best of friends, surely he told you all about his relationship with Jane."

She looked miffed now. Shrugged again. "Why should he? I don't tell him about every man I sleep with."

Oh, we both know that's a lie, don't we, Christine? I bet you tell him every single detail. You enjoy seeing his suffering, don't you? Watching the poor fucker wriggle around your little finger, desperate to have you himself, but with no chance in hell of that ever happening.

Darke placed a tick against Jane Tighe's name. They would speak to her shortly. But first, she had to break the pony in.

"So what time was it when you finally noticed Mister Whateley had vanished?"

Shrug. Back to the fingernails. "When all the fuss kicked off, I suppose. About two or three hours after I last spoke to him. I don't know if he left straight after I saw him or not, though. You'd have to ask the A.D. who signed him out."

But Paul White hadn't signed him out. Jem had stormed off without telling anyone, it seemed.

"Were you sympathetic to him?"

"I don't know what you mean."

Of course you don't. "He'd just told you he'd lost a great-sounding job. Demon character. Highly prominent in the scene being shot, I should imagine." *Don't fucking shrug.* She did, nails even more fascinating than usual.

"So, were you sympathetic to him? Did you try to make him feel better about it?"

"I'm not his counselor, am I?"

"Does he need one?"

"What?" Her eyes looked bored now, and obviously sleep deprived. Her skin still had the consistency of fresh milk, though, annoyingly. *Beautiful girl, aren't you?*

"A counselor."

"That was a figure of speech."

"So that would be a no, then."

"I don't know what you mean." Repeated like a bored mantra. The excitement of a murder happening at the same film set she was on was beginning to ebb.

"You weren't sympathetic at all, were you?" Darke leaned in for the kill. She had no time for women like this. Using their looks to play men to get what they wanted. Dangling them. Spoiled, probably came from a rich background. Got everything you wanted because you're hot. Isn't that right, honey?

"I bet you gave him a hard time about it, didn't you? I bet you *really* took the piss out of him, eh? There he is all puffed up and proud one minute 'cause he thinks he's going to impress you by playing a key character, and then bang! He's just an extra again. Wind taken right out of his sails. And I bet you *loved* it."

Christine didn't look bored anymore. No, sir. She didn't look happy either. Her milky skin took on an oven glow; her eyes became smaller, hawk-like, venomous.

"You don't know what you're talking about. He's my—"

"Of course, I forgot. He's your 'best friend,' isn't he? But isn't it true what they say? We *hate* it when our friends do well and we don't. We love to see them fall flat in the shit again, don't we? Or rather, *you* do, don't you, Christine?"

Christine's eyes flitted away again. Total surrender. Her bottom lip trembled. *Don't cry, little pony.*

"I want to go now."

"Feel free." Darke stood up. She'd gathered all she needed from this cruel, beautiful bitch. "Off you trot."

"You've really got a problem," Christine hissed as she made for the door.

"And if you want to tell us anything else, please don't hesitate to come see me."

"Come see you? In your dreams, lady." She shot Darke a final, knowing glance that she hoped was gloatingly triumphant but just looked bitter and sulky.

Darke sat down again. *Well, THAT went well. And she'd had a go at Stone for being a blunt chisel…*

She called Wells to bring in Jane Tighe. Hopefully, she would be the last for tonight. Tonight? She looked at the first gray flush beyond the window blind. What time was it? Her phone told her it was 6:15, but that made no sense to her. Like on the acid trip she had foolishly taken as a student, time had completely ceased to have any meaning.

The door opened, and Stone was back in the room.

"How did that go?" he asked as he sat in the chair against the wall.

"Brilliantly," she said.

Stone smirked. "I saw the look on her face when she came out. You're learning, Darkie."

She ignored him. "I asked to speak to another S.A. who might have some info on Jem Whateley. Jane Tighe. I thought that might be Wellsy bringing her in."

"Sorry to disappoint you. Whateley's with Wells now. Why don't you speak to Jane somewhere else while I grill Jizzy Jem."

Darke hesitated. "Can't Whateley wait five more minutes? I think Tighe's take on him might prove useful. Apparently, they used to date or something, according to Miss Thomas."

Stone pulled a face. He looked shattered now. Darke expected he wasn't the only one.

"Five minutes. Then we get on to the headliner."

Shortly afterward, D.C. Wells ushered in Jane Tighe. She looked even more tired than Stone as she took the seat opposite Darke. Darke put her at forty-eight, possibly fifty. Her face was lined, pouches prominent around her faded blue eyes. Her long blonde hair was lustrous, though.

Darke didn't waste any time. "I believe you and Mister Whateley have history."

Jane looked surprised and confused. "Jem? What's he got to do with all this?"

"You tell me, Jane. What time did you last see him yesterday evening?"

Dawning light in those pale, tired eyes. "You don't think—?"

"Just answer the question, please."

She looked aghast. "But Jem wouldn't..." Her face suddenly hardened. "Is that what Christine told you?" Her voice had hardened, too. "That he might be responsible for... for—"

"What do *you* say, Miz Tighe?"

"Whatever *she* told you is a load of bollocks. Jem wouldn't ever do anything like that."

"You sound very sure. How well do you know him?"

"Well enough. He's a sweetheart. Or at least he was, until he started hanging around with that—" Her face twisted.

Interesting, thought Darke. *Let's see what other buttons we can press.*

"Are you referring to Miss Thomas? Don't you get on well with her, Jane?"

"I hardly know her. Only met her tonight. She seemed pleasant enough to me; we chatted amiably enough, but I know women like that. All charm and fingernails, and a bitch underneath. I could see she's got Jem wrapped around her pinkie. She was really tearing into him about him losing that job."

"And what time would this have been?"

She rubbed her face, stretching the tired skin. "I don't know. Must have been eight or nine. I can't remember."

"And he left immediately after?"

"I don't know that either. I'm sorry. I haven't been much help, have I? But if you think it was Jem, then you're barking up the wrong tree. Like I said, he's a sweetheart. He might have been pissed off about losing the job, but there's no way he would have done this."

"How long have you known him?"

She tilted her head back. "Maybe three, four years. We met through doing this job. I often bump into him on set."

Darke made a note on the pad in front of her. "Do you tend to bump into the same people on these jobs, then?"

Jane nodded, smiled slightly. "The same sad faces keep cropping up, yep. A lot of us do it for a living. We don't make much, but just about enough to survive on. Most of the time. The A.D.s get to know us and keep picking the same people they know are reliable and won't mess them around."

"Reliable in what way?"

Jane looked a little confused. "Is this relevant? I know you want a background picture, but I don't see how this has anything to do with poor Guy."

Darke glanced at Stone, who raised an eyebrow. Darke turned back to Jane. "Did you work on the Roman production the other week, Jane?"

"The *Britannica* thing? No, why? Do you think these two murders are related, then?"

"You say the same faces keep cropping up on different productions. I assume Jem Whateley would be one of those?"

"I guess so."

"Well, he was certainly on the *Britannica* production, wasn't he? What about Guy Johns?"

"I don't know. You'd have to ask the agency."

Darke looked down at the list. At the top, the production secretary had typed: Supporting Artists provided by Brigstowe Casting. Darke ticked the name.

"And was Guy a regular on these productions, like you and Jem."

She shook her head. "I might have seen him once or twice. Certainly not that often. Quite a newbie, I think."

"And yet he got a very privileged job on this production, didn't he?"

"It happens. We call it beginner's luck. An A.D. or director takes a shine to someone on set, plucks them from the masses."

"Takes a shine?"

"I don't mean like *that*. I mean, they think they look good for a particular part."

"Must have been tough on Jem Whateley. That this particular director *didn't* take a shine to him."

"It's not personal. I've told him that many times."

"And does he listen?"

She hesitated. "He gets upset. Takes every rejection as an insult. I shouldn't be saying this…"

"You say what you need to."

"He gets wound up easily, complains to the agency. I'm amazed they keep booking him, really. And I shouldn't have said that either. He's a good bloke, honestly. He just wants to do well and takes it to heart when he keeps getting knocked back."

"Does this happen often?"

She sighed. She suddenly looked drained. "He's a supporting artist who wants to be an actor. That's never going to end well, is it?"

"You tell me."

"It doesn't apply to me. I'm happy to do what I do. I don't have pretensions to be anything else."

"And Jem does?"

"Yes, a bit. I mean, no. Well. He just wants to…"

Darke nodded encouragingly. Stone was rubbing his face, his eyes bloodshot. They would have to wind this up.

"He just wants to act. He's been trying all his life."

Darke scribbled this down, too.

"And how much does he want to act? How far would he go to make that happen?"

Jane shook her head. "Not that far, Sergeant. As I said, you're barking up the wrong tree."

"You like him, don't you?"

The question took Jane by surprise. And Stone, too; he stopped rubbing his face and gave Darke an enquiring look.

"What's that supposed to mean?"

"You had a relationship. For some reason, it didn't work out. But I can tell you wish it had. Did he finish with you, Jane? Perhaps when Christine Thomas entered the scene?"

Jane opened her mouth, then closed it. "I'm not jealous of her, if that's what you're getting at. And it was never a relationship between us. We slept together once or twice, that's all. Friends with benefits. That sort of thing."

"But you wished it could have been more?"

"I don't know where this is heading, and I'm really very tired."

Darke smiled. "Of course. You've been very helpful. We might need to be in touch again, though."

Jane nodded.

"So that's softly, softly, is it?" Stone said after she'd left. "You obviously used a whole different approach on Miss Thomas."

"I liked Jane. I went easy on her."

Stone laughed. "Come on, let's wrap this up."

"Jem Whateley and then sleep, Detective Inspector?"

"Let's give him nightmares before bedtime, shall we?"

"It's six-thirty-five in the morning."

Stone grinned. "He'll never sleep again after I've finished with him."

He reached for his phone, told D.C. Wells to bring Whateley to them.

"I suppose I could have interviewed him at home," Stone said, swapping seats with Darke. "But I might as well get as much use out of this office as I can. Bring Whateley back to the fold. Let him feel there's no escape."

"And you're the wolf in the fold?"

Stone grinned, showing his incisors theatrically. "I feed on bullshit before breakfast, remember? Send the little lamb in."

Chapter Twelve

Summer, 2013

For a play called *The Epic of Gilgamesh*, it was pretty cheap and shoddy.

Did Julian Swanheart (or whatever the pretentious twat was calling himself) appreciate the irony? Of course not. He believed he was directing a grandiose piece of theater that would stride the ages, a comment not just on centuries past but on our jaded, modern times.

But then Julian was full of shit.

Jem had known that from their first meeting. Julian Cranleigh, to give him his real name, was a product of the Bristol University Drama degree course. He was posher than Hugh Grant at a regatta, minus the charisma. A swoop of hair fell over a pale, earnest forehead while small, humorless eyes blinked out at a cruel world that refused to submit to his talent. A weak chin dropped from permanently pursed lips. Jem didn't hate him on first sight (he reserved that for Alexander), but he knew he would never be able to relate to anything the pampered graduate had to say.

That was obvious from his first words to Jem upon greeting him at the rehearsal room the theatrical group had booked at Goldney Hall, a residential building belonging to the University of Bristol. Being early summer, the halls were empty and Swanheart had rented a medium-sized room for their purposes at a very reasonable rate.

Jem had been full of trepidation as he got off the bus at the top of the steep road leading to the hall. He was out of his comfort zone but knew that was exactly what he needed to push himself. He'd first seen the ad in a leaflet thrust through his letterbox, the poster presumably targeting the student district in which he lived, but had also spotted it in a Bristol What's On listings magazine and decided to go for it. It had simply stated that a new, prestigious production was to be mounted by a fledgling repertory company and that actors were wanted, experience not strictly necessary. Jem had a little experience from being in school plays, but as he had always been offered the lead, he considered himself a good-enough performer to be able to give this a go. But what filled Jem with dread as he approached the grand Hall and made his stomach rock 'n' roll the way it always did in these circumstances was the fact that Jem had never been good at meeting new people.

His heart sank even more when he walked into the sunny room with its expansive view of the lush gardens the wealthy student residents regularly enjoyed on a daily basis and saw the group he would be spending the next few months with.

They were diametrically his opposite in every conceivable way. They were all about ten years his junior, fresh from, or still attending, the exclusive Bristol University. They had the guarded and resentful looks of the truly privileged when meeting those of a lower class. They exuded money and good breeding. Jem had attended a battered College of Higher Education at Northampton, which was filled with P.E. students looking for a fight, and was brought up in a small town outside Bristol, where on Friday and Saturday nights, the drinkers at the local pubs certainly found one.

Most of all, Jem felt his isolation from them in the way he spoke. As if he was branded by his background, the clumsiest of village oafs, he stumbled over his west country-tinged words that fell into silence or were sliced apart in response by refined pronunciation as meticulously cut and cold as expensive glass.

The most mannered and pompous looking of the bunch stepped forward to offer him a limp handshake. He told Jem his name was Julian

Swanheart without a glimmer of irony, and that he intended to mount a production of the earliest surviving work of literature, *The Epic of Gilgamesh*, a classic poem from ancient Mesopotamia.

He went on to elaborate how his newly assembled repertory company, Swanheart, would follow up an initial run of performances at the Bristol Redgrave Theatre with a stint at the Edinburgh fringe.

That, of course, was what had attracted Jem in the first place. He was thirty-one now, and felt that if he was ever going to follow his dream of becoming a successful actor, then now was the time. He'd been wasting his years since achieving an unremarkable second-class degree in Drama, biding his time in thankless jobs, dreaming and procrastinating, believing more with each passing day that he was not cut out for acting after all, and that only those with privilege and connections could make it.

A disastrous audition at the Bristol Old Vic Theatre School had sealed the deal. He had meticulously learned the lines to the opening monologue from Richard III, and prowling around his flat every day for weeks beforehand, he seemed to have mastered the twisted Duke of Gloucester—his hunchback grimace could have given Charles Laughton reason to cheer. But when he entered the audition room and was confronted by a stout woman with a hostile glare, his convictions had fled. Limping and lurching around in front of this stoical monument to a world he could never access, his previously masterful portrayal of festering Machiavellian bitterness had produced only poorly controlled chuckles from his observer.

"Very good," she had stopped him after three painful minutes of contorting and gurning. "And what would you do if you don't get into the Old Vic?" It was obvious the question was a test, to which he was supposed to reply that he would try again and again until he succeeded, he was that dedicated to the cause of the noble art of acting. Instead, he mumbled, "I'm working in a call center. I'll continue there, I suppose." And left, a broken man in a broken dream.

Of course, he hadn't been accepted. He'd known that from the first chuckle. That had sent him into years of despair. Rejection had never been his strong point. When he should have picked himself up again and hunted through the stage magazines for further opportunities to test himself, he preferred to slump in front of his T.V., nursing his wounds and aging away like a bad wine in a succession of temporary call-center jobs.

Seeing the ad for *Gilgamesh* had been a wake-up call. His final chance, as he viewed it. He would force himself to give it a go, to prove what his old Drama teacher had told him at school was correct, and that he did indeed have a great natural ability.

Everything that had kindled his fear of meeting and working with new people was consolidated on Swanheart's vanity production. If Julian's vainglorious personality and ambitions weren't enough, there was Alexander.

At first, Jem had almost been fooled into thinking this upbeat Scotsman of nearly his own age might be more his sort of person—he certainly seemed more weather-beaten and less detached than the rest of the cast. He hadn't been present at the first read-through, but had strutted in on the second day, cocksure and loud. His handshake was firm, and so was his gaze. He welcomed Jem in a way the others hadn't…at least for the first five minutes. Then, realizing Jem was of a different class, was circled suspiciously by the other members of the troupe, was quite clearly lacking in self-confidence, education, and esteem, and was somehow and indefinably other to Alexander's view of life and his aggrandized position within it, his attitude changed. The camaraderie vanished. Jem found himself ostracized by everyone in the play. And they still had three months to go before the first performance.

Those three months were a torment to Jem. He was pushing himself further into realms of social self-immolation with each rehearsal. It was only a matter of time before he ignited. And Alexander would provide the match.

There were also times when he lost himself. Times when he believed in himself and his talent at last. His school Drama teacher had been right then: he could act. He took the words of the play, his torturous monologues, and he soared. He had grown wings; the open hostility and indifference around him had provided the feathers, the determination to push himself like Icarus, not Gilgamesh. And he had flown. Rehearsals were torture until Swanheart said those magic words: "Let's start." And then he escaped—oh yes, he flew beyond the confines of those stately walls. Beyond the cold stares of the rest of the cast, beyond the evident resentment on Alexander's face. He flew.

But he always came crashing down. Alexander made sure of that. Never directly. The Scot never had the courage to say anything to Jem's face, no, never that; he would see the two conferring in whispers, director and the play's co-leading man—because, yes, Jem had been given the main part of Enkidu, the Wild Man, companion to Alexander's exuberant Gilgamesh.

Jem had attempted to find allies in the stoical students helping to bring this sterling production to fruition. But they avoided him, preferring the company of their own kind, their own class. Their blank gaze followed him in rehearsals as he entered the room and sat alone, always alone.

Besides Julian and Alexander, there was Lizzie, Julian's girlfriend and Queen to Gilgamesh. Auburn and fragilely pretty, she at least gave Jem the very occasional smile when their roles had the unfortunate habit of connecting. He remembered the time a bee had found its way into the Hall and bumbled against the windowpane. Its drowsy buzz was the only sound in the spacious room, as the cast had settled into silence, waiting for Julian to commence that day's rehearsal. "Summer's here," Jem said, his voice sounding excruciatingly loud and countrified to him in the utter hush that greeted the statement. Only Lizzie responded. Sitting next to him (but still at an appreciable distance), she turned her head regally and gave him the smallest of smiles, though her eyes were looking through him and beyond.

He had heard the others gossiping about her and Julian, about the rough sex games they enjoyed in the privacy of Julian's beautiful Clifton flat. Once, she'd come to rehearsals with a black eye. It didn't sound like someone was playing by the rules. Yet Lizzie refused to address the subject with her court of friends, which obviously excluded Jem. Julian had been noticeably more withdrawn that day, his normal-mannered ebullience somewhat muted.

Once, when she was wet from walking in the rain, Jem audaciously offered her his own T-shirt to keep warm, stripping off to give it to her, stricken by self-consciousness as he appeared topless in front of this hostile crew while he handed it to her. Hard eyes glittered at his nakedness. Alexander assumed control, refused the T-shirt on Lizzie's behalf, offering her his bomber jacket instead.

From then on, even Lizzie stopped smiling. Had his offer and resulting nakedness been seen as some kind of perversion?

It could only end one way.

The first performance, their opening night at the Redgrave, to a packed house of five, all parents of the troupe.

Jem knew all his lines; he knew his moves, too, even though Julian had insisted on cutting his monologues and changing the script daily throughout the preceding three months. There was nothing they could fault in his performance, he was quite sure of that. But on that opening night, as he engaged with Alexander's robust Gilgamesh and, following the script as usual, pushed the king just a little too roughly, a touch harder than he had in all the rehearsals, so that the Scot, who was a good few inches shorter than Jem and very evidently aware of it, staggered back to the lip of the stage. He didn't go over; Jem hadn't pushed him that hard. But the look on his face as he recovered, and the feverish words he whispered to the director after the curtain had dropped and a thin smattering of hollow applause from ten hands drowned out all but the anger on Alexander's face, told Jem all he needed to know about how his performance had gone down with his fellow leading man.

The play ran for four nights. The fifth and final performance was canceled due to a lack of ticket sales. After the curtain had gone down for the last time, Julian ushered Jem to one side. His callow face was as expressionless as always. He brushed at his hanging flop of hair as if attempting to act remorseful. His weak chin retreated further into his neck.

"I'm sorry. It just doesn't work between you and Alexander. There's no chemistry."

Jem stared at him. What was the director trying to say? He felt his world tumble inside himself. His world—this pretentious catastrophe of a play? Of course, it had been more than that: it was his self-worth that was tumbling. His sense of being an actor at last, of finally achieving his dream, only for his wings to burn as he spiraled, not into the sun, but into the dusty backstage gloom of a neglected provincial theatre.

"We won't be asking you to join us at the Edinburgh fringe, I'm afraid."

Jem nodded dumbly. He felt as insubstantial as a ghost, not real at all. He saw the malevolent glitter in Alexander's eyes at the stage door just before he turned away discreetly.

He walked away from Julian Swanheart's hollow apology, from the triumph in Alexander's swagger as he joined the rest of the indifferent cast huddled in the Green Room. He walked away from his one moment of blind, self-deceptive self-esteem and stumbled out into an uncertain future.

CHAPTER THIRTEEN

While they waited for D.C. Wells to fetch Whateley, Darke noticed Stone was staring at his phone with a tiny smile.

"Aneta again? She's keen."

Stone's smile disappeared, and he put the phone away sharpish. He looked like a guilty schoolboy caught masturbating.

"You could always invite her over."

He glowered at her. "I'm not inviting her over."

"Why not? She can't be that scary, surely? And you could use the company, as well as the sex."

She loved seeing him squirm. It wasn't easy to wrong-foot her boss, but this was an unexpected weakness in his armor. She was going to enjoy exploiting it.

"I don't need—"

"You just went away for a three-day break to Poland. On your own. That's quite sad. Invite her. She obviously likes you."

Wriggle on that hook, baby. The shoe was on the other foot. She was going to show him what it was like to be grilled. She was getting immense satisfaction out of this; it certainly gave her something to think about other than encroaching fatigue.

Her boss was saved from further torture by the arrival of Wells with Jem Whateley. The supporting artist didn't look happy. Not at all.

While Wells leaned casually against the wall of the production office, Whateley sat down heavily opposite Stone, who looked far more comfortable now he was back in familiar waters.

"Why have I been brought back here? Is this proper police procedure? Pretty sure you're supposed to ask me questions at my convenience if I haven't been charged with anything."

Stone smiled like a shark. "You're quite correct, Mister Whateley; you haven't been charged with anything. You're not under caution. And you're free to go home any time you like."

Whateley began to rise again.

"But I strongly advise you to remain seated and answer my questions. That is, unless you *want* me to make this official."

"In other words, you'd trump up some charge to take me in. This isn't the seventies, mate. Or the eighties. I haven't done anything." He sat back down regardless.

"I brought you here to see if you could help us with our inquiries, Mister Whateley. This is our temporary base for the time being, but we could always adjourn to the station if you *really* want." He fixed his cold blue eyes on the supporting artist. "Besides, I thought bringing you back here might help you remember something that might help us."

D.C. Wells had been under strict instructions not to tell Whateley anything regarding the murder, but Darke had the sneaking suspicion he was already well aware of what had caused the police to be crawling all over the production site. And as yet, he hadn't even asked. That was a dead giveaway that he knew more than he should.

"What am I being accused of?"

Stone leaned back expansively. "Who says you're being accused of anything?"

"Bluebottles swarming outside the base, you two vultures perched in the producer's trailer. Obviously, something unpleasant has happened, and you immediately point the finger at me."

"What do *you* think has happened, Mister Whateley?"

Whateley shrugged. He glanced at Darke and wasn't reassured by her expression.

"Okay. I don't need to pretend. I know full well what happened here."

Stone raised an eyebrow, said nothing. Waiting.

"Christine texted me, all right? She wasn't gonna keep that quiet, was she?"

"Even though everyone on the base received specific instructions not to share any information about what happened here with anyone?" Darke watched him squirm as she spoke. Now he'd dropped his crush in the shit, and he knew it.

"She's my best mate. Of course she was going to tell me."

"And is that the real reason you're acquainted with what happened here?" Stone's voice was tired. Darke could see the fatigue on his face, but neither of them was likely to be sleeping any time soon. At least, not until they'd finished with Whateley.

"Meaning?"

Stone waited. Darke knew his technique. Let them speak, let them tie themselves up in knots, or hang themselves. Why waste breath when you could often discover all you needed to know with just a pregnant pause loaded with insinuation and latent threat.

"This is ridiculous. I came of my own free will, and there's no proof against me at all!"

"What time did you leave the production base last night?" Darke lifted her biro, leaning forward over the desk next to Stone, all official and intimidating.

He rubbed a hand through his messy hair. "I dunno. Maybe eight, eight-fifteen."

"Did anybody see you leave?" Stone leaned forward, too.

Whateley shook his head. "I don't know, do I? I was in a ba— I was… upset."

"In a bad mood? Is that what you were going to say?"

"No! Like I said, I was upset."

"Upset?" Stone repeated the word, let it hang in the air. "Exactly how upset were you, Mister Whateley?"

"Not enough to kill anyone, if that's what you mean. Jesus Christ.

This is getting boring."

"Not for Guy Johns. I suspect his night was anything but boring."

"I left at eight and went straight home." Whateley fixed Stone with his most defiant glare. Stone bounced it right back.

"You didn't sign out as you were supposed to. So we have no proof that you actually left the site when you said you did."

"I didn't sign out because I was…disappointed and upset, like I said. I phoned my agency, though."

"To tell them you were leaving?"

"To tell them how I felt. They booked me for that specific job as a demon. It was a walk-on. Of course, I was pissed off when they downgraded me."

"Walk-on?" Darke made a note on her pad.

"It means specific performance upgrade. More pay, more featured."

"More kudos," Darke said.

He shrugged. "What you getting at?"

"I bet Christine Thomas was impressed with you getting that walk-on, wasn't she?"

He shook his head at her. "Cheap. Really cheap. You gonna use Christine against me, are you?"

"Just answer the question, please."

"As you pointed out earlier, I don't have to answer any questions unless you formally charge me. *Are* you going to formally charge me?" He folded his arms.

"Still thinking about it, Mister Whateley," Stone replied. "Help me make up my mind by indulging D.S. Darke." He gave a cold smile.

Whateley sighed. "Well, just to show you I haven't got anything to hide… No, I doubt Christine was overly bothered either way. I think it would take more than me dressing up as a demon to impress her."

"But I should think you felt humiliated when she found out you'd been reduced to a humble crowd extra again. Must have hurt, that." Darke had never acquired Stone's tactic of waiting; she liked to push on, burrow a point home, watch them squirm. "I mean, how can you impress someone you fancy when you're on barely minimum wage? Being picked to be special put you above everyone else, didn't it? I bet you were *furious* when you lost that job to another guy, not just upset."

"I told you: I was pissed off, yes. But not enough to kill somebody."

"No? What about if you thought Christine would be more interested in the other fella as a result?"

Whateley laughed. "What are you on about?"

"I'm just trying to put myself in your shoes, Mister Whateley. If you thought you getting the special walk-on would impress Christine, might it not have the same effect for Guy Johns?"

It was a wild shot, but worth it just to see his face.

"You're really groping in the dark, aren't you? As far as I know, she doesn't even know he exists."

"But that's just it, Mister Whateley. He *doesn't* exist. Not anymore."

He glowered at her but wisely said nothing.

Stone took over the reins. "So you say you went straight home."

"I'm not just 'saying' it. That's what happened."

"Can anyone corroborate that?"

"My pet tarantula. But he doesn't say much."

"Not very helpful. Any housemate or neighbor we can speak to?"

Whateley paused. "There's an old biddy in the flat upstairs. Always moaning about my home theater surround sound being too loud."

"Was it too loud last night?"

"She didn't complain. Maybe she was out. Or dead. She's very old."

"You've got a very strange and morbid sense of humor, Mister Whateley. Not very appropriate considering the circumstances."

He coughed, looked down at Darke's notes on the desk. "You're right. Sorry." It was the first note of sincerity since he'd been brought in. "And I'm sorry about Guy Johns, too. But I didn't even know him. Just to say hello to maybe. And whatever you think, I didn't kill him."

"We'll check with your neighbor, if that's all right. D.S. Darke will take down her details. Have you any objection to us searching your flat while we're at it?"

He shook his head in amazement. "Bloody hell. You really *do* think I did it. Is this when I'm supposed to ask for a solicitor?"

"No need for that, Mister Whateley. As I said, you haven't been charged with anything. But if we were to request to search your house, would you have any objections?"

He leveled his gaze at Stone, unflinching. "You're looking very tired again, Inspector. You really need to get more sleep. Looks like you've been up all night."

"What about you, Mister Whateley? I wonder if your neighbor would really be able to verify what time you came in. Especially if you didn't play your T.V. loud. I mean, I'm sure you don't put the surround sound on all the time, do you?"

Whateley frowned. "Okay, I'll admit I had a barney with Jimmy Dixley shortly before he was murdered, which doesn't look good, and you can join the dots between me being pissed off that Guy Johns took my job and him getting murdered too, but only if you're *really* desperate. And judging by the exhausted looks on both your faces, that's exactly what you are. So I'll be kind so we can all go home. Yes, you can search my flat as much as you like, and get the hoover out while you're at it, the place could certainly do with a clean. Just don't disturb my porn stash under the bed."

He settled back in his chair with a cheesy grin.

"Wouldn't happen to be V.H.S., would it?"

Now Whateley looked puzzled.

"Your porn stash. Would they be videos?"

"How very last century, Detective. You really need to keep up with the times. Do you mean to say you still watch your porn on V.H.S.? I bet the tapes are all worn out, aren't they?"

Darke was thinking of one particular tape, with a label saying PLEASE REWIND AFTER USE. She was thinking of the bloody thumbprint beside the lettering and found herself looking at Whateley's thumbs as he folded his hands together smugly, obviously enjoying his little dance with Stone, despite his protestations to the contrary. She wanted to grab him right now and force his thumb down onto a print pad.

"Ever had your fingerprints taken, Mister Whateley?" she said.

He turned his smirk on her. "Can't say I have. I'm pretty sure you have to be taken into custody for something for that, don't you?"

"No, sir. We just have to reasonably suspect you of an offense."

"And do you?"

"Oh yes, sir."

"Then we're at a stalemate, aren't we?"

"Sir?"

"You suspect me, yet you haven't arrested me. I wonder why? Because there isn't the slightest scrap of evidence, apart from the fact I was disappointed when Guy Johns got my job. Don't think that would hold much water with your superiors, would it? Or in court, for that matter." He stood up. "But if it would help you get some shut-eye—and let's face it, you two desperately look like you need it—I'm quite happy to let you dab my fingers all over an ink pad. "

Stone slowly got to his feet. He looked like he was struggling to hold his temper in check. Darke tensed, prepared to hastily intervene should things get too out of control. But Stone just smiled, gestured toward the door.

"You're free to leave, Mister Whateley. But I have some advice for you."

"Let me guess… Don't leave town or you'll come galloping after me with your cowboy boots and ridin' your big hoss."

Stone smiled expansively just to show he wasn't offended by Whateley's sarcasm. But Darke knew that shark smile. It was the teasing grin of a predator playing with its prey. And right now, Whateley certainly looked like a tasty morsel to her.

"I was going to tell you to be careful what jobs you pick in the future. Death seems to have a nasty habit of following you around."

Whateley paused, hand on the doorknob. He suddenly didn't look quite so cocky.

In fact, on the contrary: he actually looked more than a little scared.

Chapter Fourteen

Stone hadn't slept very well on his day off, a day off he hadn't wanted but recognized he needed. He and Darke would be of no use to the team if they were fit to drop. D.C.I. Thornton had stepped in, guiding the Murder Squad through their routine and not-so-routine paces until the S.I.O. could return to carry the reins.

As it turned out, either Thornton had been a bit slow off the gun, or there really wasn't anything helpful to go on. Stone suspected it was a combination of the two. While D.C.S. Church was morose and thunderous in turns, D.C.I. Thornton was rather shy about getting his hands dirty. And Stone could imagine his rather idle superior officer leaving most of the heavy work for twenty-four hours, no doubt bristling with impatience for Stone to get his arse back in the office.

Cooke had been busy again. The incident board had new names and new faces. Now, a photo of Guy Johns smiling in a suit, obviously from some wedding past, was attached next to Jimmy Dixley. And a photo of Christine Thomas had been fixed next to Whateley, together at last in the Murder Room, if not actually in life.

Stone tapped her picture as he briefed his team. She had obviously done modeling before becoming a supporting artist. The photo depicted her leaning against a wall in a short skirt and halter top, long legs crossed, a shit-eating grin on her fine-boned face. The picture had already earned more than a few comments from some of the more salacious officers, but Darke had soon put them in their place.

"We believe Christine is one of the last people to see him alive, so her testimony is important. We have a statement from one Jane Tighe that she saw Christine talking to him on the dining bus not long before he went missing." He had been through Jane's brief follow-up statement, which had been passed to him by the Inside Sergeant, and this was the only relevant piece of info that had stood out as pertinent and which she had not mentioned when talking to D.S. Darke. "Christine is also very friendly with our hero, Jem Whateley, so I think it's a good idea we keep both of them in our minds while we're following up leads."

"You don't think she did it, sir?" D.C. Charlie Evans was staring avidly at the blonde in the photo.

"You tell me, Stanley." Evans's protruding ears gained a pinkish tinge at the nickname. "According to Tighe, she was flirting with Johns as well. We don't know if Whateley witnessed this or not. Jane doesn't specify." He pointed a finger at Evans. "But it might be a good idea for you to follow up with her, Charlie."

Evans nodded, his ears gradually regaining their normal hue. Stone made a mental note to go easy on the lad. He didn't want Thornton to have any more ammunition against him. But even though he was outwardly gruff and bullish, and sometimes downright rude to his team, he appreciated all their efforts immensely. But he'd be damned if he would ever let them know that. That was what Darke was for.

D.C. Ming Sung had given Stone the forensics report on Whateley's Roman costume from the *Legion Britannica* production, and it had been clean as a whistle. Metaphorically speaking, obviously. Plenty of mud, but no blood. They were still waiting on tests on Guy John's clothing, hoping for some DNA samples, but the thumbprint had produced depressingly predictable results. The killer had obviously pressed John's thumb onto the tape label.

"We have a demon mask reported missing from *The Awful Dead*," Stone continued, sitting on the edge of a desk and scanning the rows of detectives. "Same pattern as the Roman job. Killer nicked a costume to dress up in—or at least we're assuming that's what the perp did when Jimmy Dixley was killed, as a Legionnaire costume was reported missing, as well as a sword. Neither have turned up despite extensive sweeps of the riverbank and some tentative diving. According to the wardrobe department on the *Dead* film, no costume went missing this time, just the mask. But then the demon costume wasn't anything that might not exist in anyone's closet at home and so easily copied: jeans, plaid shirt, the sort of retro hillbilly shit that every good hipster seems to be wearing these days." He got up, patted the photo of Martin Thorogood on the board. The #NoMeansNo campaigner was wearing a lumberjack-style red-and-black jacket. Cooke had scrawled "Hostile to violent nature of productions, present at both crime scenes" underneath.

"So, presumably, the *Awful Dead* killer wore their own clothes if they didn't belong there, or possibly a costume if the perp was an actor/extra. Either way, their gear would be covered in blood. Not something easy to hide on set unless they changed in the woods and reappeared in their own clothes. If the perp didn't belong to the production at all, the same applies. They would be splattered. Jem Whateley's costume has come back as clean as[9], which is no surprise. He left early, and wardrobe has since passed on that he handed his costume in at approximately eight-fifteen, which corroborates his statement."

He coughed. Not through nerves, just irritation. While he knew these briefs were vital, he found them tiresome. Most of his team knew what to do and didn't need him to remind them. But as Darke kept telling him, it helped unify them and focus their minds. And sometimes helpful comments and suggestions arose. So he put up with them. But never happily. Never that.

"So we have a stolen demon mask and Roman Legionnaire costume associated with the killings. What can we deduce from that?" He threw it over to them, feeling like a bullish school teacher asking his class a probing question on the use of iambic pentameter in Shakespeare.

D.S. Susan Fairchild was first to respond, which was appropriate, as she looked far more like an English teacher than Stone did. "He or she is

---

[9] Common British usage for "clean as a whistle"

playing a role."

"Care to elaborate, Sue?"

She was thinking as she spoke, as she always did. "They're responding to the themes of the production in both cases. Like they're making a statement on the contents, or..."

"Or?"

"Or joining in. Maybe they want to feel more involved, or if they're not one of the cast, to *be* involved."

"Interesting theory." Stone jotted a note on the board. *Role Player or Commentator.* "If they're making a statement, then our bearded hipster chum looks a lot more attractive." He tapped Thorogood's image again.

"Something else we should think about: the killer has been opportunistic on both occasions, waiting for the victim to be alone before attacking, which suggests someone already on site that would fit in and not arouse suspicion—like one of the extras or crew members—or someone who was in hiding. Again, we have zero C.C.T.V. footage on the *Dead* site to give us anything. So we're relying on speed cams on the roads leading to it, C.C.T.V. on the outskirts of Bristol and at any significant sites between the city and the production. I gather Ming's already busy on that."

D.C. Sung nodded unhappily. It was never an easy or fun job, sifting through hours of surveillance tape. "Nothing obvious yet, guv."

Stone nodded. Ming knew what he was doing. If any vehicles entering or leaving Bristol both before and after the murder matched with plates picked up around the time of the Roman incident, then he would have mentioned it. Of course, the killer could have used some other method of transport—bus, or bicycle even—but they would be carrying a concealed bundle of bloody clothing. Far more likely that they had either not driven back to Bristol at all, or they used back roads that avoided C.C.T.V. and speed cams, which ruled out the M32.

"What about the two videos that were left behind? We have *Caligula* and *The Evil Dead.* Both obviously reflect the relevant productions. What else do they tell us?" Again, he felt like a battered, cynical teacher, bored on a Friday afternoon, letting the class do the work. But in reality, Stone was far from bored. He had the bit between his teeth and wanted this brief over so he could get out there. He wanted screeching brakes, slamming car doors, and rapid action. He wanted *The Sweeney,* and at the moment, he was stuck with *Morse.*

"Film nut?" D.C. Wells said.

"A collector?" added Cooke.

Stone jotted both ideas on the board with his Sharpie. "Good. But where does that lead us?"

Silence. Then Susan Fairchild spoke up again. "The two productions revel in violent conduct, violent themes. So violent, in fact—especially in relation to women—that the NoMeansNo campaigners picketed both sets."

"Which brings us back to our hipster chum…" Stone sat down on the edge of the desk again. "Can we do a background on him, please, Sue? I want to know where he gets his beard oiled. Chat to his barber, his friends—if he has any—the other campaigners. Has he got a violent past?"

"So we have a possible role player, film nut, or extreme social justice warrior with a bit of a grudge. But someone who has been carefully prepping these crimes. They're certainly no impulse murders." He turned to point at the pictures of both video covers on the board behind him. "Our perp took these videos with them, intending to plant them after the kill. He or she is following a meticulously constructed plan."

"Which kind of rules out Whateley then, doesn't it, sir?" Evans's face was earnest and confused.

"Why so?"

"Because we're judging him on motive, which, in both cases, seems to be spur-of-the-moment anger or jealousy, not pre-med."

"Good point, Charlie. But not necessarily valid. He might have brought them along intending to use them anyway, and things came to a head. His history with Jimmy Dixley has been documented. And he might have been paranoid he'd lose the demon job before it happened, or he had some other motive for wanting payback against this production. We need to put pressure on him to find out. I know we've been digging into his past, but we need to widen the search, go back further, deeper. Like with Thorogood. And while we're at it, let's excavate our lovely model Christine, too."

A brief titter from the detectives, stifled by Darke's grim glare at the offenders.

"And Whateley hates the police for some reason. He's made that obvious. We need to find out why."

Cooke had been thinking. It was obvious from the frown on his face. His long legs were outstretched as usual. "Why the pencil in the ankle, guv?"

"That's my homework for tonight, Cookie: watching *The Evil Dead*. I'm guessing it might hold some clues. But certainly none on the pencil itself. I understand from D.C.I. Thornton that came up as clean of prints as we expected."

D.S. Darke made her first contribution to the briefing. She was nominally present to provide factual backup to Stone, but occasionally she thought of something he might not have considered or could not be aware of. "Shouldn't all film and T.V. productions in the area be put on hold until we've found our perp? The killer is obviously targeting them."

Stone shrugged. "The Chief Super would never allow it, Sam. He's already got Sky on his bloody back over freezing the Roman shoot. And they have a lot of clout, believe me. So that leaves us with a problem: we have to police all current and forthcoming productions with what resources we have. Which, as we all know, isn't much in today's scissor-happy political climate. But we need to speak to them, too, make sure they're increasing their own production security. That's one for you, I think, Sam. Cookie and I will be concentrating on compiling a list of upcoming attractions."

"What's that, guv? We going to the fair."

"No, Cookie. We'll be checking out what film productions might draw the attention of our killer next. This is a very bloody game they're playing, and we need to be ahead of their next move…"

CHAPTER FIFTEEN

So far, Stone had to admit he was quite impressed.

While it was obviously low budget, shot in the early 80s, and the film stock they'd used caused a rainfall of grain to cover pretty much every scene, *The Evil Dead* had undeniable power.

Forensics were still going over the VHS, so he'd had to rely on a You-Tube version on his smart T.V. It was nine o'clock in the evening, and the power of the horror movie was clawing at his tired psyche, rattling him a little. He was familiar with the main actor, Bruce Campbell, though he couldn't think why. The man was stumbling through the most horrific events with a dented charisma and battered aplomb that had Stone smiling… until he reached the tree rape.

He sat up, glued to his T.V. screen. Pressed the Rewind button on his remote, watched the scene again, paused it, looking for angles as to why the on-set killer of the rip-off "homage" *The Awful Dead* had lifted this particular vicious method of attack.

In the movie, the trees themselves had come alive, possessed by evil forces, and assaulted a woman alone in the woods. Which should have been ridiculous but was, in actual fact, pretty disturbing despite the obvious cheapness of the effects, and in its brutal depiction of a woman being forcibly entered by a creeper root, both demeaning and horrible.

Giving up on finding any analogies to his case beyond the obvious,

Stone moved on and soon found himself watching another significant jaw-dropping moment that again had him reaching for the remote to pause and replay the scene. It was undoubtedly horrible: the lady who had been raped in the woods was now possessed herself, and picked up a sharp pencil only to slam it into the bare ankle of another innocent character while making the most horrendous shrieks and cackles. The wounding was dwelt on unnecessarily, and even in this day of widespread and unrestricted blood and gore available to view in every format, and the resultant jaded attitude toward it from modern viewers, the attack was still horrifically unpleasant.

But there seemed no further conclusions to make from the two scenes other than that they were there purely for shock value. No insightful parallels, either to do with the victim or the attacker, corresponded with the crime in the woods outside Bristol, other than both attackers were "demons." He could only guess this on the part of Guy Johns's murderer, of course, going on the assumption that the killer had used the stolen demon mask to perform the execution, just as presumably they had worn the Roman costume to finish off Jimmy Dixley.

After a couple more viewings of the pencil scene, he carried on watching the rest of the film. He was nearing the climax, which literally involved all hell exploding across the screen in grainy stop-motion glory, when his phone interrupted him. It not only interrupted him, it made him jerk in his seat, so unnerved had he become by the film's relentless mood.

He switched off the film just as Ash, the Campbell character, struggled gamely to throw a human flesh-bound book onto the fire while grimacing ferociously, as if he'd had a glimpse into the future and seen where his acting career would lead him as a result of this movie.

It was the first time Aneta had actually called him rather than texted since he'd left Krakow.

"What's up, Polish lady?"

"I wanted to hear your voice again. I was beginning to forget what you sound like." And he'd forgotten how impeccable her English was, too, especially with the sexy Polish purr.

"Grumpy as usual, no doubt."

She chuckled good-naturedly. He'd had an instant connection with her in Krakow, and now he was reminded exactly why. "What are you doing with yourself, Del Boy?"

He winced. She hadn't forgotten that conversation, then. "Just watching T.V. On my own as usual."

"You want me to come join you?"

The question threw him. Her voice turned him on unquestionably, and right then, he would have loved to share a bottle of wine with her and take her to bed to chase away all memories of the unpleasant film he'd just watched. But then there would always be the difficult proposition of what she did afterward. He wasn't made for relationships. They weren't his cup of tea.

"No answer? I'm upset. Maybe you've found another lady?"

"No, no. Nothing like that. I'm just caught up with work."

"You never did tell me what you do for work."

"You never asked." That wasn't true. He was pretty sure she had asked, and he'd evaded the question. He'd been on holiday and unwilling to talk shop. Besides, telling people you're a cop often garnered decidedly mixed reactions.

"So?"

There was no harm in telling her now. And it would help avoid the thorny subject of her coming to join him. "I'm a policeman, Aneta. Detective Inspector."

She laughed, delighted by his sense of humor. "Stop teasing me."

"It's true. I'll send you a photo of my warrant card if you don't believe me."

"Wrrrr."

"Wrrr? What does that mean?"

She trilled with laughter again. "I bet you look sexy in your uniform."

"I don't wear one!"

"Wrrrrrr."

Now it was his turn to laugh. "You sound like a sexy cricket."

"I don't play sports. I told you that. I'm more of a thinker."

Was this her little joke? "Well, think about this: I'm in the middle of a case, so I should get on with it."

"It must be ten at night where you are. Why are you working late? And what case? Do tell me. Is it exciting?"

"You know I can't discuss it with you. But lovely hearing from you. I mean that."

"You, too, Del the Policeman. Speak soon."

He said goodbye and switched off his phone. The house seemed very empty now that he was alone with his thoughts again. Maybe it was the film that had unsettled him, or hearing Aneta's cheerful but brief conversation reminding him she was far away, but right now, the idea of being on his own had very little appeal.

"I'm just saying be careful."

Christine was quiet for a moment. Jem pressed the phone against his cheek as he lay in bed, wishing he was with her.

"Why don't you come and work on it with me, then, if you're so worried about it?"

He paused. Marcus at Brigstowe had phoned to offer him a job on *The Gate of Death,* a new BBC wartime series, but he'd been unable to accept. He hated turning down work.

"No can do. Marcus wanted me to do five days of continuity, but I can't do Saturday."

"Five days! Bloody hell. He only offered *me* the one day. That's so unfair. Men get all the work. Plus, you're his favorite. He's always giving you the best jobs. And why can't you do Saturday?"

"He gives me good jobs because I've proved I'm reliable. You have to build up a rep, Christine. You're still a virtual newbie."

"Prick."

"Thanks, Snaggle. You know I'd love to join you."

"You'll kick yourself when you find out what I'll be doing. It's a topless scene."

He sighed. "You're lying."

"Am not! I have to be a Jewish prisoner abused by Nazis in a brothel scene. Going to have to get my itty bitty titties out and you'll miss it…"

He went quiet at the thought of it.

"I can hear you drooling over the phone, you perv."

"Can't imagine you flashing your bits on camera. You're way too self-conscious."

"Well, as you've pointed out so many times before, I may have very small breasts, but they're perfectly formed."

"Can we stop talking about your tits, please?" He was growing hot with desire. She'd shown him them just once. They'd done a Facetime video call, and the conversation had turned a little naughty. Their relationship had suddenly turned a corner, from being mere close friends to being *flirty* friends, when she offered to show him her boobs just to prove how small they were. He had been glued to his phone screen as she slowly, and very self-consciously, began to strip off her blouse and unfasten her bra. He would never forget the sight of her slender, milky pale body, speckled with occasional brown moles like the texture of a creamy pancake. When her bra slipped free of her breasts, he'd been in heaven.

She had pirouetted demurely for the most precious ten seconds of his life before hurriedly clothing herself. "Never doing that again," she promised him. "So what did you think of my itty bitty titties?"

Now she chuckled tauntingly. "You know you want to see them again."

"Well, I can't. I won't be there."

"Your loss. Ben will be able to enjoy them instead."

"Ben?" His throat almost closed around the word. A shadow cloaked his excitement.

"He's the cameraman, darling. I saw him at the fitting, and his eyes were *all* over me. Bet he can't wait to get his lens out for the naked scene."

Jem said nothing.

"You still there, you plonker?"

"Aren't you worried about what's been happening?" he asked finally.

"Of course I am. But the agency said all productions were increasing security from now on. There will be a police presence and everything."

"Even so…"

"Don't."

"Don't what?"

"Don't try to scare me off. I'm worried enough already."

"Then don't do it."

Now it was her turn to go quiet.

Finally, "You're just jealous that Ben will see my tits and you won't."

"How the hell do you know his name anyway? Were you flirting with him at the fitting?"

"You don't own me, Jizz." Normally, he chuckled at her abusive nickname. "We got chatting, that's all. He's nice."

"Of course, he's nice. To you. Bet he doesn't know the rest of the S.A.s even exist."

She sniggered. "You still haven't said why you can't make it tomorrow."

"A Comic Con in Bristol. Shame, really. Means I lose all five days on the Nazi shoot. And it means—"

"It means you get to miss my nipples. You're such a twat. You could always drop the Con."

"I can't. I agreed to do it months ago. Can't just pull out at the last moment."

She sniggered at that. "As I said, your loss. Such a nerd."

"It's not like I'm paying to go there, is it? I'm one of the guests."

"Why the hell they'd want *you* is a real mystery. An even bigger one is why the hell people would actually pay for your autograph. Crazy." She chuckled to show she didn't mean it, *really*. Though, of course, she did. And he could understand her point; it was a mystery to him, too. He had performed as various monsters in *Doctor Who* and appeared as a Fleet Trooper in one of the new *Star Wars* films, and as a result, Film and Comic Convention organizers had started asking him to be a guest signer at their events. Like Christine had said… crazy.

"Anyway, I'm surprised you're allowed out to go to your dumb

Nerd Con. Haven't they locked you up yet?"

"That's not funny. You know I didn't do anything."

"Do I?" She paused. Maybe a little too long for his liking.

"Good night, Christine."

"Don't be like that. It's just…"

"Just what?"

"That bitch of a detective. She was insinuating things about you."

"What did you tell her?"

"I told her it couldn't have been you."

His voice softened. "Good."

"I said it wasn't in your nature."

"Good again." His voice softened even more.

"I said you weren't a maniac."

"Thanks."

"I lied, basically." She let out one of her special sardonic guffaws. "So be nice."

"I'm always nice to you. Christine?"

"Mmm?"

"Nothing. I'll see you soon. Please don't get in trouble tomorrow."

"What possible trouble could I get in? Apart from turning on all the male crew members when they see my bits?" She chuckled again. He knew she wasn't as arrogant as she was making out. It was all an act. She was very insecure, really. About a lot of things. Which was why he felt protective of her. Which was why he—

"Good night, Christine."

"Night, Psycho Killer."

He pressed disconnect and lay back in his bed. Thought of Christine, naked in front of a load of other extras and crew. In front of Ben, who seemed "nice." He stared at the ceiling for a long time before finally switching the light off.

And remained staring into the dark. It was a long time before he slept.

CHAPTER SIXTEEN

Stone looked up as Darke entered his little office in one corner of the Murder Room.

She smiled with grim satisfaction. "Bingo," she said, dropping a printed sheaf of papers on his desk.

"What's this?"

"I double-checked H.O.L.M.E.S.[10] for Whateley, but there was no fit, just like Charlie Boy said. But then I had me a bright idea…" Sam Darke already had a tinge of a West Country accent, but now she lapsed into full bumpkin mode, a habit she had when excited. It was mostly put on for her own amusement, but some of it was also because of her Somerset family background, something that Stone never failed to tease her about. But right now, he was too interested in what she had to say to wind her up. He waited for her to proceed, glancing down at the papers in front of him, then back up at her enthusiastic face.

"I rang Whateley's agency, Brigstowe. Spoke to a lovely lady there by the name of Penny. She emailed me his acting C.V. They use it to get Whateley certain featured roles that actually require a bit of acting experience every now and then. That's it on top." She indicated the first printed sheet on the small pile. "Two items of significant interest on

---

[10] Home Office Large Major Enquiry System

there, guv. If you look at it, you'll see he used to be what's called a "Scary Actor" at the York Dungeon, about five years ago in twenty-eighteen." She paused, her eyes shining with excitement.

"I phoned them just to follow up on it, see if anything of interest cropped up. and boy, did I hit the jackpot." She paused again, waiting for him to react.

"If you don't get to the point in the next five seconds, I'm gonna toss the remnants of this cold coffee all over your starched white blouse."

"Patience, guv. The first person I spoke to was a lady on the merch desk, receptionist, whatever. She'd never heard of him but suggested I speak to the manager. She put me through, and the manager told me that he hadn't actually worked with Whateley but knew all about him."

Stone leaned back. Darke was enjoying herself, maybe a bit too much. He spread his arms to prompt her.

"He's famous in the Dungeon, apparently. Got himself sacked before he finished his probation period."

"What did he do, play with the torture implements?"

"Not quite, but apparently he was too scary for the general audience. He was trying *too* hard and ignoring all the guidelines."

"What do you mean by *too* scary? It's a kind of Horror Dungeon, isn't it? Surely that's the whole idea?" Stone was familiar with the concept, having been in the sister museum, The London Dungeon, owned by the same company.

"Well, it seems he went too far with it. Maybe he was overacting, I don't know, but according to this manager, they got a record number of complaints from the public, so they let him go."

"That it? He didn't get into a fight with anyone or anything like that? Seems fairly insignificant, considering this manager who never even met him knows all about it. Surely they had lots of these so-called Scary Actors coming and going in five years…"

"Well, this particular Scary Actor made the headlines very shortly after his dismissal, guv. Seems a local rag got wind of the story of his dismissal and ran with it, sold it to the nationals. They got some mileage out of it. One of those comedy pieces. "*Is this the scariest man in Britain,*" was one of the headlines. I printed off what I could find on the net. The tabloids had a lot of fun with the idea of a scary actor who was too scary for his own good."

Stone lifted the top sheet. Under the C.V. was a black-and-white photo of a slightly younger Jem Whateley, hands together, leaning over to peer into a camera. Obviously staged by the photographer for *The Yorkshire Post*. There were more print-offs. A headline from *The Sun:* **Too Scary for Our Dungeon**.

"I think I vaguely remember all this," Stone said.

"But that's not all, guv. A week or so after this, things got *really* interesting…"

"I hope you've got good washing detergent at home, Darke, 'cause my trigger finger 'round the handle of this coffee cup is beginning to—"

He stopped short. He'd turned over a printout from another news article. A photo of a young man with a stubborn chin and a mop of dark hair. Stone read the headline just as Darke said, "Whateley's supervisor at the Dungeon, guv. He was murdered. His killer has never been found."

Jem was bored.

Despite having a quantity of fairly interesting, high-quality 8" × 10" prints arrayed neatly on the long table in front of him, he was having a slow day. The Film & Comic Con was fairly well attended, if not exactly crowded, but nobody seemed to want to look at his screenshots, let alone buy them. Of course, they were flocking to the actor at the table next to him, who was actually an ex-Doctor Who, not just an *extra* in the show.

So when his phone rang and Christine's photo flipped up on the Caller ID screen, he answered it happily.

"Hello, Saddo."

"What do you want?" He pretended to be unenthusiastic about her call, just as he always did.

"Sold any crappy pics of yourself yet, loser?"

"A few," he said defensively. "How was the nude scene?"

"All done. Only took about two hours. And youuuu missed it!"

"Great. Did the cameraman ogle your bits?"

"Oh, he did," she teased. "He loved my itty bitty titties."

"You're such a whore."

"Oh, don't be a jealous wanker all your life. Anyway, it wasn't all fun. When I wrapped early, Ben offered to take me to lunch."

He tensed, the familiar cold feeling seeping through his body. Was she really that insensitive, or just so dense she was completely unaware how hearing things like this made him feel?

"You went for lunch with him?"

"Yeah. What's wrong with that? He took me to a nice pub just down the road."

"You said it wasn't all fun…"

"Oh, Ben was *great* fun. You'd like him."

"I really wouldn't. He's surely not supposed to be fraternizing with the extras. Don't the cast and crew have an unspoken moral code about that… Don't mingle with the common scum?"

"Stop being such a prick. You sound like that silly cow, Jane."

"Was she there, too?"

"Oh yes. *All* your ladies. But she's such a bitch."

"Why? I thought you liked her."

"What gave you that idea? I was just being nice to her on *The Awful Dead* because it was the first time I'd met her. Turns out she's a jealous cow."

"What, over me?" He sounded hopeful. Hopeful that Jane had told Christine something about the two of them that might give her cause for jealousy. He knew Jane still had feelings for him.

"It's not all about you, tosser. She got riled up because Ben was favoring me in the nude scene. As if the public wants to see her baggy boobs." She snorted over the phone. Sometimes Jem really had to think hard about why he liked her so much. But he knew there was a deep loyalty and sensitivity she kept hidden as well. *Very* hidden most of the time.

"She actually phoned Brigstowe to complain. Silly bitch. Can you believe that?"

"What, because you got more camera time? Surely not."

"Well, that was the real reason, obviously. But she told Marcus at Brigstowe that Ben had been acting in an unprofessional manner toward the women in the scene. And that he was using inappropriate language in front of me."

"And did he?"

She paused. "He was nice to me. That's all I can say."

"In other words, he fancied you. Did he act inappropriately toward you? To anyone?" He frowned up at a young man in a long multi-colored scarf and floppy-brimmed hat who was examining his monster pics. He really wasn't in the mood to sell this shit anymore. The fan got the hint and moved on to the actor next door, who received him with a much more welcoming smile.

"Not that I saw. He has quite a flirtatious nature, shall we say."

"He shouldn't be flirting with you when you're half naked. He's in a position of power, an important member of the crew! He should have been more professional!"

"It wasn't like that. He was just cracking jokes about the ladies. Nothing detrimental."

"Jesus, Christine. Those women would have been feeling self-conscious enough without that jerk making pervy references to their bodies."

"Only to me! I didn't think anyone else had heard it. Bet that bitch Jane was listening because she wanted the attention, really."

"So what happened? What did Marcus do about it?"

"There's not a lot he can do, is there? I bet he thought Jane was making it all up to get attention from them, to sound woke, or some such bollocks. Can't believe the silly cow told them he was flirting with me."

"And then you proved Jane wrong by going for lunch with him?" His voice was terse and cold.

"You *are* in a bad mood, aren't you? What's the matter? Everyone realized you're an extra and not a superstar? Bet *nobody's* bought your pics."

He sighed. "I'm sorry. I'm not having a go at you."

"Yes, you are."

"All right, I am!" he snapped again. "You shouldn't have gone for lunch with him. That will make him behave even more badly on set. He obviously thinks he can shag any female S.A. in sight."

"He's not—"

"Don't even fucking go there with the 'he's not like that.' He so obviously fucking is!" He hadn't realized how much he'd raised his voice until he saw a mother hurrying her two children away from his table, the boy and girl of maybe nine or ten giving him disappointed looks.

"I'll cut you off if you shout at me."

He tried to calm himself, but everything seemed to be slipping away from him. And besides acting, Christine pretty much *was* everything to him.

"Did he… Did he try anything with you?"

She was quiet for a moment, during which his imagination conjured up all sorts of scenarios.

"He didn't shag me against the bar in front of the lunchtime drinkers, if that's what you mean. Oh, and it wasn't just Jane who tried to ruin what might have been a really lovely morning."

They were back on safer ground. "Go on," he said, forcing himself to sound more cheerful.

"One of those desperate NoMeansNo twats had a go at me as I was driving out the gate. Can you fucking believe he actually stepped out in front of my car and waved me down to have a pop at me??" Her voice was high-pitched with indignation.

"Really? Were they protesting about the naked scene? They seem to be on every set these days. Maybe moral standards *are* slipping more."

"Fuck me. You'll be voting Tory next. Yes, he must have guessed I was in the brothel scene, although how he knew that, I have no idea."

"It's not much of a stretch. There was an interview with the writer in *The Daily Mail Online* the other day, and he was talking about it, trying to defend the scene from accusations of exploitation and degradation of women."

"He obviously didn't do a very good job, judging from this nut job's behavior. Proper freak. Hipster wanker. Big, pretentious-shaped beard; oversized, black studenty glasses; lumberjack gear. You know how much I hate those morons."

"Of course, he wasn't smooth and smiley, like *Ben* obviously is."

"Don't start that again. But as Ben was following me in his *Beemer*..." She let the significance of that sink in. "...to meet me for lunch, he saw it all and got out to sort the freak out."

"What a hero." Another family was converging on him. He'd had enough of Christine for one morning anyway, so he prepared to get rid of her and start trying to make some money.

"He was, actually. Ben saw him off. Gave him a right good flea in his ear. Probably get himself into trouble with the producer over it if that weasel complains. But the bearded freak was well scary. Talk about over-enthusiastic. And he's a *bloke*! Which makes what he's doing even more suspect. If it were a woman, I'd sympathize much more with what they were trying to say. But this jerk was obviously just out to look socially aware. My bet? He was trying to get into the knickers of one of the women he was picketing with."

"Very astute observation, no doubt. Anyway, I'm glad you got released early. Doesn't sound like a good one to be involved with after all, if the campaigners are at its throat. Maybe say no if Brigstowe offers it to you again."

"You've changed your tune. You were slagging those woke wankers off when they protested against *Legion Britannica* and *The Awful Dead*. But, of course, you were *in* those productions, weren't you? Don't be a hypocrite, Jeremy. I know you like a bit of exploitation and degradation every bit as much as the next man."

He *hated* people using his full name, something she was very aware of.

He smiled up at a teenage girl who was cosplaying Jodie Whittaker, the recent Doctor Who. Her parents displayed the usual mixture of embarrassment and excitement that marked them out as fans, too. The teenager was far cooler in her approach. She was giving Jem a very stern and reproachful "get off the phone" look.

"Look, I have to go, Blondie. Catch you soon."

"Bye, loser. I'll let you know how my next date with Ben goes."

He tried to smile at the teenager as he put his phone down, but as was often the case, speaking to Christine had made that very difficult.

"I remember the case. Maybe *that's* what I was thinking about and not the headlines regarding Whateley's dismissal. Quite a fuss over it, if I recall correctly." Stone was still staring at the article in *The Yorkshire Post*. "The Dungeon was closed for a long time afterward. Bad publicity, having *real* horror happening in a pretend horror setting. People generally prefer their scares to be fake. Was Whateley interviewed in connection with the murder?"

"The file's there near the bottom, guv. I got onto Yorkshire C.I.D. as soon as I read the article and they emailed me the files straightaway."

Stone didn't rummage through the sheaf to find it just yet; he wanted to hear Darke out fully first.

"And?"

"They interviewed all of Dave Fenton's work colleagues. He was a fairly popular supervisor apparently, no obvious grudges. Whateley was still living in York, and his interview's on file. Nothing suspicious. Had an alibi for the time Fenton was murdered. Having a meal with his girlfriend, apparently. But what really grabbed me by the throat were the details of the murder scene."

Stone could wait no longer. He shuffled through the notes with mounting excitement. When he found what Darke was referring to, he read the scene of crime report swiftly. Then he looked up at Darke.

"We've got him."

She nodded enthusiastically. "Everything matches. A grisly death in a fabricated horror setting. ..." Fenton's body had been strung up on the flayed Viking exhibit, his eyes removed messily, with what Yorkshire detectives had assumed to be one of the torture implements that had gone missing from the museum at the time: an authentic medieval eye gouger.

Darke was about to continue, but Stone beat her to it, reading aloud from the report in front of him. "And a V.H.S. videocassette positioned next to the corpse..." He scanned the S.O.C. addendum. "*Mark of the Devil.* Yes, I remember there was one of those scare-mongering articles in one of the tabloids; a minister tried to drum up electoral publicity for himself by having a go at Video Nasties again in the wake of the murder, when all the details were eventually leaked to the press. Very familiar. As you said, Sergeant: bingo."

"But his alibi?"

"We'll destroy it. There's bound to be a hole in it. Chase up the girl-friend who made the statement."

"But that's not all, guv."

"There's more?"

"Christmas has come in October. There's a lot more. There was more than the York Dungeon on our friend Jem's C.V. Apparently, he also acted in a play in twenty-thirteen called *The Epic of Gilgamesh.* Like with the York Dungeon, I used my friend Google to find out all about the play and its performances. And guess what I found?"

"Do tell. Another murder?"

"Not quite. A disappearance. One of the actors vanished soon after the play had finished its run at the Bristol Redgrave Theatre. A young man named Alexander Fergus. His parents reported him missing, and the whole troupe of actors was interviewed as a matter of course, including Jem Whateley. But he was never found."

"So, no sensational murder this time, no V.H.S. marker?"

She shook her head.

"You say he was never found?"

"No, sir. Occasionally, a new Chief will come in and open the case again, but no new evidence has justified reopening it formally."

"Who was the S.I.O.?"

"It's in the file, guv. You might get a surprise."

"Well, it wasn't me, that's for sure. I was on the Gloucester force back then."

"And I was a fresh-faced D.C. in Devon and Cornwall."

"Keeping me in suspense, Sergeant? I've still got some coffee left in this cup."

"It's all there if you look."

"I'm getting a headache. Who conducted the interview with Whateley?"

"D.C.I. Thornton, sir."

She waited for him to react. But he said nothing, eyes down on the files in front of him again.

"So?"

"So what?"

"Do we pick him up?"

Stone nodded, almost absent-mindedly. His brain was fizzing. He could imagine exactly how Thornton had run the case ten years before. No wonder Fergus had never been found. The Chief was well known—amongst his subordinates at least—for cutting corners, avoiding the hard slog that was required from a S.I.O. in such cases. Thornton was lazy, edgy, and resentful, and Stone pictured him filing the case peremptorily under "Missing Persons." He wouldn't have chased it down as thoroughly as he should have. Stone was certain of that. His boss had only been promoted on the back of being married to the Chief Constable's daughter. And if the Chief Constable should get to hear the rumors dogging the office about Thornton having a young mistress, it obviously wouldn't go down too well. But they were rumors, just like the mutterings about Thornton being slack and idle were opinions. Stone would certainly not act on them.

What he would do was go and talk to the man.

And then he'd pick up Jem Whateley, and this time, hopefully, charge him.

CHAPTER SEVENTEEN

"Didn't Yorkshire get in touch about Whateley, sir? Especially when he moved back to Bristol. That should have flagged his connection with the historic Alexander Fergus case."

Thornton looked evasive. He was a balding, stoop-shouldered stick of a man in his early fifties. Far too old to be messing around with one of the uniformed constables—if the stories were true, that is. Stone believed them.

"There may have been a conversation. I would have to look back at the files."

"I've saved you the bother." Stone dumped the paperwork on the desk in front of his boss. Thornton eyed it distastefully, flicked through it tentatively as if he might catch something from it. "Nothing pertinent or concrete," he summed up, pushing the files away. "This Whateley character had an alibi in the York case and nothing whatsoever to suggest he was involved in the Bristol disappearance five years before. I do hope you've got something more substantial on him now." He frowned up at Stone, his dark, furry eyebrows knitting with irritation. "Don't go doing something you'll regret."

"Regret, sir?" *Like taking positive action toward solving a case, you mean?*

"If you're intent on taking this man in, make sure you have enough for the C.P.S."

Stone hesitated, and Thornton pounced. "Yes, there are similarities between the historic cases and the ones we're working on today. But let's not be rash. Are they mere coincidence? Whateley had an alibi in York. The case made the papers, obviously—all the details were widespread, including the V.H.S. being left at the crime scene. We could be looking at a copycat."

Stone had considered that, of course. But Whateley was at the heart of all the cases, both historic and present day. "I'm convinced he's our man, sir. We can hold him for twenty-four hours at least while we find something definite to stick on him. Maybe some evidence in his flat. Like a V.H.S. collection of horror movies or something."

"If he *is* your man, I'm sure he's more careful than that. But search away." Thornton's gaze wandered to the window of his office, apparently more interested in the bright October sunshine playing on the rooftops outside than he was in his subordinate officer's intentions of solving the case.

"You could always speak to the lady who supplied his alibi in York again. See if she has anything new to say."

"Bit hard, sir."

Thornton faced him again slowly, bored. Maybe he was thinking of that pretty constable. "Why's that?"

"She's dead, sir. Died a few years ago of cancer."

"Well, we can't blame him for that, I suppose." He smiled at his own unfunny joke. "Bring him in for questioning by all means. But before you even think of charging him, make sure you can find something a bit more watertight than the circumstantial evidence you've got on him at the moment."

More paperwork for both of us. That's what you're thinking, isn't it? The D.C.I. never changed. His success rate was always a good percentage, but only because he refused to ever take a risk and formally charge suspects without having a damn good chance of them reaching a courtroom. The fact that he'd given in so relatively easily on Whateley gave Stone an added impetus. The lazy D.C.I was normally averse to even bringing suspects in for questioning, fearing his detectives might freak out and actually arrest someone, heaven forbid. He must think Stone was on to something after all, even though he would never admit it. And he would never admit it because it would make him look like he'd been deficient ten years before when he spoke to Whateley in relation to Alexander Fergus's disappearance, if Stone was proved correct.

He left the office, managing not to slam the door. Darke was waiting for him outside, ready and eager as always.

He felt the old thrill of the hunt course through him. "Let's go," he said.

Jack Regan was back in the room. Soon there would be squealing brakes and doors slamming. Stone grinned like a shark as they set off down the corridor, collecting Cooke along the way.

CHAPTER EIGHTEEN

Jem Whateley lived on a once-genteel street in Hotwells, Clifton's less-prosperous neighbor. When they received no answer from repeatedly ringing the bell, Darke flipped through her notebook 'til she found his number. She shook her head at Stone after several attempts to reach him on his mobile proved fruitless.

"Could he be working?" Darke asked.

Stone was pensive. "It's Saturday, but I suppose so. I guess being an extra isn't a nine-to-five job. Try the agency."

After a few moments, Darke shook her head again. "Agency bookers are clearly nine-to-fivers. The automated reply gives an emergency number, though." She tried it, and after a brief chat, she thanked the person on the other end. "Spoke to Penny, the lady who sent me the files. She's looking after out-of-hours office calls."

"And?"

"She ran a quick check, and Jem Whateley isn't on any jobs with them today."

"So where is our man? Out shopping, at the flicks?"

"Penny suggested we try Christine Thomas. It's well known in the office that they're thick as thieves, apparently."

"Good shout. Got her number?" Stone was very aware that an elderly lady was peering at him from an upstairs window. He smiled and waved, then moved to the door again and pressed the top bell. A few seconds later, a creaky and hesitant voice responded. "Yes? May I help you?"

"Police, Madam. Could we have a quick word?"

"If it's about that dreadful man in the flat below, I already spoke to a policeman. Colored fellow, but he was very nice."

Stone winced at her blinkered phrasing. The older you got, the less you learned, it seemed.

"I just wondered if you knew where we could find Mister Whateley?"

"I don't know, young man. And I don't care. At least I don't have to put up with his beastly music and blaring television today."

Stone was just about to ask her to let him in when Darke nudged his shoulder. "Heads up, we've got a full house again." She switched her phone off and placed it in her jacket pocket.

"Did your parents drag you to bingo on a Friday night when you were a kid, by any chance?"

"Spoke to the delightful Miss Thomas. She told me where to find Jemmy boy."

"And are you going to tell me?"

"You're going to love this, guv…"

The panel was going well. Even though Jem hadn't made much money selling signed photographs of himself in monster costumes, he was enjoying being on a stage, sitting next to the ebullient former *Doctor Who* actor and being asked questions by an earnest middle-aged man in a way-too-small *Star Trek* sweater.

It was at times like these when he felt he'd actually achieved something. He was being treated like a star, even though he knew he wasn't one. But he could live with that. Okay, so he would have much preferred to achieve this very low-level celebrity status through solid acting work and not by stumbling around in a sweaty monster suit, but at least right here, right now, he was being recognized, appreciated, even if come next week he would be back to being ignored and disrespected as an extra again by both cast and crew on some filming job.

From his raised position sitting on the stage, he scanned the large sports hall where the Con was being held. Trader tables laden with action figures, toys, and replica props from a pantheon of science fiction franchises filled the space. Cosplayers strutted and swanned around the aisles and in front of the stage, seeking attention. There were curly-wigged Tom Bakers with voluminous scarves; Mr. Spocks with plastic pointed ears; Princess Leias in white robes and sweaty-looking Chewbaccas; Belles and Beasts, Robocops and Wonder Women. None of them ever bought Jem's signed autographs, and he had built up a healthy disdain for their posturing. The former Doctor to his left, however, seemed to delight in their craving for the spotlight, assuaging their egos with bland compliments. But then he was being paid a solid fee to appear, and one of his tasks was to judge the tedious Cosplay competition at the end of the day.

There was only a relatively small audience filling the three rows of plastic chairs arranged in front of the stage, and there were many gaps—the former Doctor had been on the road attending Cons a lot over the last few years and his value to Con attendees was diminishing somewhat. And besides, it was well over thirty years since he'd been in the program. But the size of the crowd didn't bother Jem. He was grateful to have an audience at all.

"So, how does it feel to be a Cyberman?" Paul, the interviewer in the *Star Trek* sweater, asked him.

Jem took the microphone from him to give his reply. "Sweaty most of the time. Put it this way: you don't want to be around at the end of the day when I take my helmet off." He waited for laughter, but nothing. He elaborated, "Full of sweat, you see. Tip it upside down and it's like pouring water out of a kettle." A few disgusted noises.

"Care to tell us about any interesting locations you've both worked in?"

The actor who had once been Doctor Who was a natural anecdote-teller. He regaled the diminutive audience with colorful tales of yore for five minutes, dropping in the names of well-known guest actors with whom he had enjoyed filming, mostly in quarries and airfields in decades past. Then Paul handed the mic to Jem.

"Disused nuclear power stations at four a.m. mostly. Grimy warehouses and smelly tunnels. Oh, and the Clifton Suspension Bridge in a Dalek. That was fun." The glazed expressions that greeted his words were starting to deflate his enthusiasm. A few were getting up to leave, obviously bored. "But I'm not always behind a mask," he said, almost plaintively. "I've played Nazi officers and terrorists, too, so you can see my face in some episodes."

But Paul had noticed the lack of response he was getting and was already reaching for the microphone. Jem held it away from his grasping fingers, desperate to elaborate further on his skills beyond the monster suit. "I've done proper acting, too. I was the leading man in a play, and I've… I've had lines of dialogue in lots of shows. I'm not just a Cyberman, you know."

Paul managed to retrieve the mic. "But that's what you're famous for, Jem. You should be proud."

"But I've done other things…" His voice trailed off. Paul was addressing the audience, asking if they had any more questions for the two guests on stage.

They did, but they were all for the Doctor. Jem was beginning to feel like an imposter sitting next to him. He was beginning to wish he'd listened to Christine. She'd told him the attendees wouldn't be interested in a nobody like him.

Paul was threading his way through the audience rows, handing the mic to those with questions for the celebrities. Now he returned to the stage, asked the crowd if they had one last question. A hand shot up toward the back of the audience, where a knot of bored cosplayers and a few traders and casual drifters had gathered, mainly because there wasn't anything else to watch or do.

"The gentleman in the trench coat at the back," Paul said, climbing down off the stage again to make his way toward the raised arm. Jem had lost interest, was checking out the clock on the far wall. 3:30. After this he would beat a despondent retreat, get the hell out of this dump.

"I've got a question for Jem," a voice boomed into the microphone.

Jem twisted around, trying to locate the source of the voice. He could see Paul standing next to a figure, microphone outstretched, but the man's face was hidden behind the large head of a Stormtrooper.

"Care to tell us about *The Epic of Gilgamesh*, Mister Whateley? I'm sure we'd all like to know what it was like being an actor on that production." Jem twisted in his seat, trying to get a better look, but the Stormtrooper was joined by a *Game of Thrones* giant, and the speaker was completely blocked. He could just about see some long blonde hair and part of a face clearly belonging to a woman standing next to him, and they looked vaguely familiar, but the invisible man had more to ask:

"What about The York Dungeon, Jem? How was that? Bet that was fun, eh?"

A knot of coldness tangled inside Jem. He began to suspect who was speaking even before the man asked his next question and then began pushing forward through the crowd, past the Stormtrooper, and into sight at last, followed by the woman he now recognized and another man, almost as tall as the *Game of Thrones* giant. He was still clutching the microphone as he advanced on the stage.

"I bet it gets very competitive being an actor, doesn't it? Or even an extra? Because that's what you are really, isn't it, Jem? An extra playing at being an actor." The man stopped right in front of the stage, staring up at Jem with a knowing sneer. "And when other extras get better parts than you, I bet it doesn't feel good, does it? I bet it makes you mad. In fact, I bet it makes you so mad you feel like you could just kill…"

Paul was struggling through the milling cosplayers, vainly trying to reach the microphone now. But Detective Inspector Stone hadn't quite finished; he evaded the grasping hand, turning to the interviewer with a stern look. "Hold on there, Captain Kirk!" D.S. Darke was standing like a statue of doom behind him, expressionless. "Yes, I've got a question, all right, if you don't mind steering the Enterprise to another galaxy for a minute or two longer." He faced the stage again. "In fact, I've got several questions. But maybe you'd much prefer I didn't ask them right here, Jem the Cyberman. How's about you follow me and my team here in our own space cruiser back to the Planet Mee Mah, Mee Mah—or as us Earthlings know it a bit more prosaically, Avon and Somerset HQ—and you can have a Gargle Blaster, or even a cup of tea, while you answer them all at your leisure."

The cold knot tightened. "Am I under arrest?" He was very aware that the audience was deathly still now. He had their full attention at last.

Stone stretched his arms expansively, and Paul eyed the outflung microphone but decided right now would not be the best time to retrieve it, considering the profession of the man in possession of it. Stone drew the mic back in to answer Jem.

"How about I put it in more Comic Con-friendly terms: I'm asking for the pleasure of your glittering company down at the Space Station. I will be interviewing you under caution, so be a good monster and lurch down from that stage. D.C. Cooke, care to give the Cyberman a hand?"

Jem rose from his chair as D.C. Cooke read out the charge. He was very aware that the *Doctor Who* actor was gaping at him, too, just like everybody else. He'd achieved his dream in a very twisted way: he was on stage, and all eyes were on him.

For the first time that day, he was definitely the most interesting person at the Con.

CHAPTER NINETEEN

While Jem Whateley was escorted to an interview room by D.C. Cooke and briefed on his rights, Stone ambled over to the coffee machine at the far end of the corridor.

"That was quite some stunt," Darke told him. "You know he could probably sue for defamation of character?"

"Bollocks. He's guilty. All I did was pull him in for questioning."

"You did a lot more than just arrest him, guv, and you know it. You *destroyed* him in front of that crowd."

"It's not like he has to worry about his reputation as a famous actor, is it?" Stone popped two coins in, pressed the Latte button.

"If we're wrong about this—"

"We're not wrong, Sammy. I saw it in his eyes on that stage. He knows we've got him." He turned to her as the machine sprinkled and sprayed into the cup. He winked at her. "Cheer up, for fuck's sake. He's a wrong 'un. Too much of a coincidence that he didn't have anything to do with four separate incidents, all involving him."

"If he gets a good solicitor…"

"There will be something in his flat that will convict him, I'm sure of it."

"Then why did he consent for us to search it?" Darke crossed her arms worriedly.

Stone collected his latte and smiled. "Stop brooding. We'll find something. And there's a good chance Forensics or C.C.T.V. will pin some shit on him. If we find any D.N.A. traces on those tree creepers, which I'm sure we will, we'll stuff him for Christmas, like the turkey he is."

Darke shook her head slowly. "I still think you could have gone about it a bit differently. All that piss-taking. The Con attendees could make a complaint, too. This could all backfire if we're not careful. You weren't exactly subtle." She allowed a small smile. "You were enjoying yourself too much."

"Subtle, my arse." He took a sip, beamed at her. "Anyway, you were the one shouting 'Bingo' earlier. What's made you change your tune? The Chief got your ghost? He's scarier than any Halloween spook, I admit, the crabby, creepy, old skirt lifter."

She nudged him out of the way, ordered a cappuccino for herself. "I'd love to see his face if he heard you referring to him like that." She chuckled despite her qualms.

"Oh, I say that to his face every time he asks for a report. Doesn't blink an eyelid, the bastard. Too busy thinking about that sexy young constable he's given extra duties to." He took another sip. "Shall we crack on? I can't wait to hear what stories our traveling thespian has to tell us about York and beyond."

"You're in a good mood. And that always worries me." Darke waited for her cappuccino to fill. "Let's just play this by the book, eh, guv? We don't want him squealing harassment. Especially if we *can't* pin anything on him."

"You sure *you* haven't been sleeping with Touch 'em Up Thornton, too? You're beginning to sound like him."

"Cheeky git. I'd rather sleep with *you*, and that's a disgusting enough thought." She winked at him and added, "…Sir."

"Thanks. Don't think Sophie would approve. I've got something you don't need, remember, Sergeant?"

"It's certainly not morals, if that's what you mean."

"Now who's being cheeky."

Stone led the way down the corridor toward the interview room. D.S. Fairchild met them on the way, and she had some papers in her hand.

"Just found this, sir. Bit more history on Mister Whateley you might find interesting."

Stone glanced at it, and his smile widened. He thanked Fairchild and turned to Darke.

"I hope you've sharpened your critiquing skills, Sergeant." The shark grin came out to play. "Because we've got a performance to judge."

Jem Whateley had been briefed by the duty solicitor, and D.C. Cooke had outlined the potential charges against him, and he wasn't in the best of moods.

"You're trying to pin York on me!" he burst out when Stone and Darke entered the interview room. "*Again!*" His brief[11] urged him to remain calm and wait for Stone to press record and announce himself, Darke, Whateley, his brief, and the reasons for his arrest.

"Do you understand exactly why we have taken you into custody, Mister Whateley?" Stone began. Whateley sat back with a more-than-grieved expression, while his brief gave him a meaningful glance.

"I understand you obviously haven't a clue what you're doing if you're trying to pin Dave Fenton's death on me again after all these years."

"We understand you were dismissed from your position at The Dungeon. Care to elaborate on that?" Darke's voice was smooth and honey-sweet, but her eyes were a cold blue.

"Dave got me the sack, but then you probably know that already." He glanced defensively at his brief, shrugged. "It's no secret; it's bound to be in your files. He was a cunt. Excuse my language, but he was."

"Did you not get on?"

"I wasn't bothered about the bloke either way. But he had it in for me from day one."

"Why was that?"

---

[11] UK informal: a lawyer who will speak for someone in a court of law

"He was jealous." He kept his eyes fixed on the D.S.

"Like you said Jimmy Dixley was jealous?"

Whateley threw his head back and looked up at the ceiling, sighing dramatically. Then he returned her gaze as steadily as before. "It happens. You must be really desperate if you're dredging up the York Dungeon business again after all this time."

"Unsolved murder case that you were connected to. And now we have two more that you're connected to. Not such a desperate stretch, I would have thought." Darke watched his reaction for a few seconds, but he was giving her nothing. A slow smile tugged at Jem's lips. "So why was Dave Fenton jealous of you?"

"I was put on a two-week probationary period by the manager as a Scary Actor. I was wowing the crowds. Big time. They loved it. I was scaring the shit out of them. Dave hated me for that because he was no longer getting such a big reaction from the public. They all wanted to see me instead."

"He was a Scary Actor, too?" Darke consulted her file. "I thought he was the Supervisor."

"He was. But he was required to work the crowds, too."

"Is that the only reason he was jealous?"

The small grin grew wider. "Nope. He liked to think he was the big cheese with the women as well. When I appeared on the scene, I took away his glamor."

"Which women would that be?"

"Other girls who worked at the dungeon. And the groupies."

"Groupies? You saw yourself as a bit of a rock star, then?"

Jem laughed, but his eyes had taken on a distant light. Taken back down memory lane to a time when he obviously thought he was something. Darke waited patiently.

"Yeah, groupies. Funny, thinking back on it. They loved coming to The Dungeon, used to hang around with us in the evenings down the pub."

"So Dave Fenton grew so jealous of you taking the groupies that he managed to get you fired?"

"I only had one girl. But Steve, the assistant Supervisor, was telling everyone at The Dungeon the next day after I pulled her, and I could see Dave's face. He *hated* it. Next day I got dismissed. He was in charge of my probationary period. It was easy for him. Made out I'd been scaring the kids too much, that sort of thing."

"Wasn't that what you were supposed to do?"

Jem's smile faded. The memories of his actual dismissal were obviously not as pleasant as those of the groupies. "The Dungeon received a letter, apparently, complaining I scared some seven-year-old kid witless. Fenton used that against me. The manager explained my job was to entertain the public in an amusing way, with lots of jokes and stuff. Nothing too creepy. Steve, he came in to watch me in the Guy Fawkes chamber one day to assess my progress. He told me afterward he had genuine chills down his spine."

"So Fenton might just have had a point."

Jem shrugged. "The majority of the public loved it." He turned to his brief. "Are you going to get them to explain why they're dragging all this up again when it was put to bed five years ago?!"

The solicitor advised Whateley to continue to answer the questions as the past case had modern parallels.

"But I had a set-in-stone alibi. That's why the Yorkshire police dropped it." He leaned forward, addressing Darke like she was a child. "It's. All. In. The. Files."

"Yes, it is, Mister Whateley," she replied. She glanced down at the papers. "Gillie Peters? Was she the groupie you mentioned?"

Whateley sighed. "She became my girlfriend."

"And you were with her on the night of February eleventh, when Dave Fenton was murdered."

"All night. I'm glad you can read."

His solicitor glowered at him. "I'm sorry, but this is extremely frustrating. You interrupt me in the middle of a Comic-Con panel, making me look like a villain in front of a crowd of people who will *never* forget it, just to make allegations that are nearly as old as his attitude." He gestured at the 'til-now silent Stone, who didn't respond.

"It says here that you spent the night together at your flat in York." Darke tapped the file. "Shame we can't question her again, really, isn't it? You never know, she might have decided to change her statement..."

"Are you trying to pin her cancer on me as well?"

Darke glanced at the file, ignoring his insensitive facetiousness. "You split up a month after the incident, I see. Why was that?"

"I moved back to Bristol. She worked and lived in York. Long-distance relationships, et cetera, et cetera."

"If she was a groupie at The Dungeon, she was obviously quite infatuated with you? You being the big new thing on the scene."

He sighed again. "Predictable. I know what you're insinuating, and it's bollocks."

"What am I insinuating, Mister Whateley?"

He glanced at his solicitor, who chose that moment to intervene. "I think it would be better if you didn't answer that one."

"No, no. It's fine." Whateley's chin stuck out again as he made the decision. "She didn't give me an alibi because she was obsessed with me, if that's what you're getting at."

"Luckily for you, we'll never be able to answer that, will we? Unless we spoke to her family and friends. I wonder if they might be able to provide a different slant on your relationship."

Another shrug.

Stone cleared his throat. "Okay, Mister Whateley. Let's talk about Alexander Fergus, shall we?"

"Wondered when you were going to join in. Another blast from the past. We really *are* wasting taxpayers' money today, aren't we, while the real murderer goes free to kill again."

Stone ignored that. "Care to tell us about your relationship with Mister Fergus?"

"Another cunt. Excuse my language again."

"There seem to be a lot in your past, don't there?"

Shrug. "The acting profession tends to attract 'em, I'm afraid."

His brief leaned forward, conferred in a low voice with Whateley. Jem shook his head. "For the benefit of the tape, my solicitor has just recommended I don't elaborate on my relationship with Alexander Fergus, as his disappearance was not a murder inquiry and therefore should not be connected to this case. Sorry, mate," he said, addressing his brief. "But I see no reason not to volunteer the info. The guy was a creep and a narcissist. Massive ego. Again, I was asked about his disappearance years ago by you lot in Bristol. Can't remember having the honor of speaking to Sergeant Seventies here, though." He bared his teeth at Stone. A thought appeared to strike him. "So, wait, you're saying Fergus was murdered, too? I thought he'd just realized what an arsehole he was and fucked off to start up again elsewhere. Oh, and of course you've decided with an insight that would make Officer Dibble proud that I offed him as well? Beautiful."

"You don't like the police much, do you, Mister Whateley?"

"You make it easy. Hang on; we seem to be on a loop here."

"So it's safe to assume you and Mister Fergus didn't get along?"

"You can assume what you like. He was an absolute wanker, like I said. Sorry, he was a very unpleasant and distasteful person. That better?"

"What was the nature of your disagreement?"

Whateley paused, glanced at his brief. The solicitor was about to speak when Jem beat him to it. "He got me sacked from the play we were working on." He shrugged at his brief again. "It'll be in the file, I bet. And the other members of the theater troupe can verify it easily, if they haven't already done so."

The solicitor didn't look happy. "Can I remind you, you're under caution, Mister Whateley. Do I need to repeat what that entails?"

"I'm fully aware of what it entails. But I have absolutely nothing to hide. He wanted me out of the play, so he got the director to remove me before they went to the Edinburgh Fringe with it."

"Just like Dave Fenton got you sacked from the York Dungeon?" Stone frowned. "Bit of a pattern here, Jem? Wouldn't you say?"

"Patterns happen. Patterns aren't evidence. Look, I'll tell you why I don't like the police. Because of what they tried to pin on me in York, despite the fact I had an alibi. Because of the way they treated me, like I was an evil, murdering scumbag. Just like the way you've been treating me, Detective Inspector Stone." He took a breath, leaned forward, eye-balled Stone. "But here's the news, Officer Dibble: I didn't do it. None of it. I didn't do it then, and I didn't do it now. Someone killed Fenton in a horrible way, yes, and someone killed Dixley and Johns in equally horrible ways—I've read the papers and heard the rumors on set. As for good ol' Alexander… I haven't a Scooby what happened to that prick, and I don't care. And yes, I can see why you're coming for me. But, hell, even though it'll be November fifth in a couple of weeks, I'm telling you clearly and emphatically, you've got the wrong guy."

Stone looked round at Darke. "That's all right then; we can all go home."

"Okay," Jem got up.

"Sit down, Mister Whateley. We're not quite done yet. I've got something else for you." He withdrew another file from the others on the table. "You grew up in Wolton On Edge, I believe, twenty miles out of Bristol?"

"Well done, Detective. You'll crack this case yet."

"Thank you, Mister Whateley. I try my best." Shark smile. "And my officers have certainly been trying their best, too, as you'll see. Because they've unearthed, only within the last hour, something that adds to the pretty pattern that's emerging."

The solicitor intervened again. "Is this some new evidence against my client? In that case, I should have been thoroughly briefed beforehand."

"Relax. It's not what you'd call evidence—just another segment in the bizarre mosaic of Mister Whateley's life. A bit like that colorful Roman floor they unearthed a few years back, piece by piece. That was in the same neck of the woods as your old hunting grounds, I believe."

"Nevertheless, I should be given time to look at the information and discuss it with my client."

"If that's what Mister Whateley wants…" Stone held out his hands, all benevolence.

Whateley thought hard. You could read it in his face. Then, "I want this done, so I can go home and get on with my life. Spit it out, Detective Try Hard."

"Quite inventive with the nicknames, aren't we? I bet you had a few for your old Drama teacher, didn't you?"

Whateley froze. "What?"

"Missus Carruthers. Don't tell me you've forgotten her. The play she produced and directed is on your acting C.V. Right at the bottom. Apparently, she taught Drama at your school back in the year two thousand. You were in the sixth form, I believe. "

His gaze hardened. "What about it?"

"Another death. You really have some track record, don't you?"

"Leave her out of this." Whateley no longer looked so cocky.

"Why would we do that, Mister Whateley? Was she somebody else you 'disagreed' with?"

He took a deep breath, and his brief asked if he wanted to take a break while they discussed this new information. Jem's face slowly relaxed, and he shook his head.

"Like I said, I've nothing to hide. And no, I didn't disagree with Missus Carruthers. She was a brilliant teacher. She showed me how to act. She started me on my journey."

Stone sat back, waiting for him to continue. When nothing else seemed to be forthcoming, he spread his hands. "That it?"

"What d'you want to hear? She was my favorite teacher."

"And she died, Mister Whateley. In unfortunate circumstances. Just like all the others."

"You're full of crap, and you're the only one in this room who doesn't know it. Yes, she died. I know that. I went to her bloody funeral." He stabbed a finger down on the desk. "It was an accident. That was the coroner's verdict. It was in the local papers. A terrible accident."

"She burned to death, Mister Whateley. In her own Drama Hall."

He shook his head, laughed bitterly. "Jesus wept. Is this all you've got on me? You're really stooping low when you bring up the one person who inspired me the most as a kid, who prompted me to get up on stage in the first place. And you want to sully that memory with your shitty, dirty little insinuations? I'm ashamed of you, Inspector. I knew you were desperate, but this…" He looked down at the desk, his face clenched.

Then suddenly he looked up again, right into Stone's eyes. "She smoked. Way too much. The coroner said she must have fallen asleep going over a script one evening after school had finished and dropped her fag. That's it." He turned to the solicitor. "I'm done talking to these people."

The duty solicitor nodded, looked at Stone. Stone grimaced. "I've got just one more question for you, Mister Whateley. I believe I may have mentioned it before, but do you have a particular interest in old horror films? Particularly ones on V.H.S.?"

Whateley put his head in his hands. Rubbed his eyes. Then looked straight at Stone. "And like I said to you before, I might have had one or two years ago, and I used to rent a few from the old rental library in Wolton, just like everybody used to do in those days before it closed for good. But I've long since moved on, Detective. Upgraded, like most everybody else." He glanced at Stone's retro short spiky haircut. "*Almost* everybody else."

"What about horror films?"

"I'm more of a Sci-Fi fan myself."

Stone nodded, considering. "That's interesting. And it fits with you prancing around in *Doctor Who* monster costumes, I guess." He nodded again. "So you wouldn't be able to tell me much about films like *The Evil Dead* or... what was it called?" He consulted the file emailed from Yorkshire C.I.D. "*Mark of the Devil?* That sounds like a nasty one. Ring any bells?"

"Never seen it. Sounds lame to me."

"But I'm sure you're aware it was positioned next to the body of Dave Fenton in the York Dungeon. Surely the Yorkshire detectives mentioned that?"

"Guess so. It was five years ago."

"Funny that you wouldn't be more familiar with it. It made all the papers. Quite a story. Man strung up on a torture display, his eyes dug out with a medieval eye gouger. Ever see one of those?"

Whateley closed his eyes. "There were lots of torture implements at The Dungeon. Lots of them genuine articles. There was bound to be a gouger among them."

"But you can't specifically remember it? Just like you can't specifically remember the V.H.S. video? Bit odd, that."

"Why? I was shocked at the time, and even though I didn't like the jerk, I wasn't gloating, believe it or not. I'm not a dark tourist, or dark voyeur, or whatever the hell you call it. I didn't immediately rent out *Mark of the Devil* when I read the newspaper article. And like I said, there were *lots* of horrible things in The Dungeon. But I didn't use any of them on Fenton."

His eyes darkened, and again that far-away look stole over him. *Down memory lane again*, Darke thought. Stone stood up, tucked his pen in his inside jacket pocket, a surefire sign they were having a break.

Darke switched off the tape machine. "Interview halted at seventeen-fifteen. Officers Stone and Darke leaving the room."

Stone nodded to Whateley. "We'll speak later, bud. Go relax in your five-star room, ask for a cuppa from the nice duty sergeant. Wouldn't want you claiming police brutality, would we?"

But Whateley didn't reply, even to his solicitor's instructions. Darke could see he was still somewhere else. From the look on his face, this particular Memory Lane wasn't one he wanted to share.

CHAPTER TWENTY

February 2018

It was ten past five. Another twenty minutes and The Dungeon would be closing. And even though Jem enjoyed his job (which was basically scaring the pants off people for a living), he was always a little glad when the big oak doors were finally shut on the seemingly endless stream of tourists. It was tiring work, and quite often his voice, having endured being contorted into a menacing croak all day, would be worn out and husky by the end of it.

He propped Dick Turpin's feet up on the ledge fixed to the gallows pole, ready for the dummy to spring forward and swing on its rope when Jem pushed the little red button, and waited until he could hear the excited chatter of people approaching.

They were in the next room now, listening to the hologram of Dick in his prison cell, regaling them with tales of his wicked highwaymen adventures. Now Dave Fenton was doing his little routine next door, cracking the exact same jokes he used every time about modern-day highwaymen nicking motorway traffic cones, and as usual, there was no reaction from the crowd. No surprise there: the jokes weren't even remotely amusing, and simply ruined all the atmosphere the Turpin hologram had so wonderfully created.

Then it was Jem's turn.

He was waiting for his cue behind the door leading from the cell to the hanging square. Dave cracked his final feeble joke, and there was the cue: "If you'd all like to make your way toward that exit, you'll be able to witness the final end of Britain's most notorious Highwayman."

Jem froze, timing it just right. Then, as he heard the tourists' footsteps shuffling toward the door, he began to slowly push it inward. The door creaked wonderfully, and he could sense the crowd in the other room freezing, not knowing what to expect. He could sense Dave waiting, too, and hating Jem for the reaction he was getting before he'd even emerged into view. He'd told Jem repeatedly that he was supposed to burst into the room, crack a few jokes in a silly *Monty Python* voice and boisterously usher the crowd into Tyburn Square.

Jem was having none of that.

The door creaked again, inching open. Jem, bent over to simulate a broken neck, his head at a twisted angle, shuffled into the cell where the group of tourists was waiting.

They were transfixed.

He said nothing for a moment, returning their stare, breathing heavily and croakily. Hell, he was outdoing himself today; he was even creeping himself out.

He loved this. He had them rooted. And he knew he looked great: he had the best costume in The Dungeon, and he knew exactly how to milk it to unnerve the punters to the hilt. He was wearing a low-crowned undertaker's hat, a long frock coat, and black mittens. His face was painted white, long streaks of black ran from his eyes to his lips. Around his neck was a length of gallows rope. Tied to it was a dead rat (rubber, of course, but realistic for all that).

He stretched out a hand, his head cocked back on one shoulder like Frankenstein's hunchbacked assistant, Ygor, and gave his challenge. "Who wants to see 'im 'ang, then?" His voice was a punk Freddy Krueger mixed with crow-rasp cockney. He gave a shuddery laugh, looking straight at Dave as he did so. He had been warned once already to tone down his act, the supervisor claiming they shouldn't try and freak out the public too much because the props were scary enough as it was.

Again, Jem was having none of that.

He shuffled backward, drawing the tourists on with a beckoning hand, giving Dave one last smirk as he did so. The supervisor watched him, frowning. He was wearing a barrister's wig and a jovial red gown and would have looked far more in place at a courthouse than at a museum of horror.

Jem closed the door after the last of the crowd had entered and thumbed the prop mechanism hidden on the wall. One of the tourists shrieked as the old lady model leaned out from a window above the make-shift courtyard and emptied a bucket of "sewage" over the crowd. It was only water, but it had the desired effect. The narrator's deep tones on the soundtrack were holding the group enrapt now, building the atmosphere up nicely for the execution itself, and Jem had nothing to do but lurk around and snigger occasionally, slowly edging his way around the crowd toward the scaffold.

He'd already hanged Dick five times that afternoon, but this would be the last one of the day, so he was going to make sure it was special. He cuffed the dummy's realistically sculpted head and mocked the rogue until the crowd tittered expectantly. He surveyed the audience regally from his vantage point on the scaffold. They were all staring up at him. One young girl was looking distinctly nervous. Jem would target her in a minute.

"God save the King!" he roared in a drunken, throaty voice and pressed the button. The dummy sprang forward from its perch, swinging nicely on the rope—sometimes the mechanism didn't work and Jem would have to give the highwayman a helpful push.

"Go for it, Dick, my son," he chortled as the crowd stepped back a pace or two, responding wonderfully to the dramatics. Jem gurgled and choked, aping Dick's noises on the soundtrack, and then astonished the entire group of tourists by taking a mighty leap from the scaffold, landing just in front of them with a psychotic grin.

He winked at the teenage girl. "You wanna feel the caress of my noose?" he rasped, holding out the rope around his neck. The pretty brunette squawked and burrowed into the little crowd to hide. Jem rounded on the others. "Who's next for an 'angin' then?"

Nobody volunteered. They were all spilling toward the narrow exit tunnel, the young girl and her plumper female friend shrieking deliciously at the back of the queue as Jem swaggered after them, breathing hard like an asthmatic maniac.

Then they were gone, and Jem was alone. He straightened up, stretching his back to get rid of the cramp the awkward posture had given him. The tourists were milling about in the shop around the corner at The Dungeon exit now, and at last there was silence. He coughed, his throat sore and dry, done for the day.

Dave was waiting for him in the main torture room. A big wooden wheel hung on one wall, the fiberglass body of a man stretched across it, wrists and ankles tied to the spokes. Below it, a window displayed another dummy staked out with a cage on its stomach, a mechanical rat inside gnawing away at the dummy's fiberglass innards. Dave was standing in front of a flayed Viking, his head just below the victim's peeled-back ribs.

"Need to see you in the manager's office after you've changed."

The creep had taken off his wig, and his dark hair stuck up messily on his head. Jem straightened to his full five-foot-eleven, and though they were both about the same age, Dave looked older, face puffed with his own pomposity. He walked off, leaving Jem to take in his words. The bastard had heard about Gillie then. He wished Steve could keep his bloody trap shut, just for once. But it wasn't his fault she fancied Jem more than she did Dave. He guessed the supervisor was going to whine at him about scaring the tourists too much again as an excuse to vent. He could deal with that.

Time to get this shit off his face and go home.

The Dungeon was empty of guests, the big main doors locked now, but the props still whirred and clunked around him as he thumped along the wooden boards in his boots, heading for the rear of The Dungeon, where the staff room was located. The manager would always be the last one out, and it was her responsibility to switch off all the electrics. As a result, the exhibits were still active, albeit performing only to themselves in the empty rooms. To themselves, and Jem. The others would all be in the staff room scraping greasepaint off their faces. He didn't mind being on his own amongst The Dungeon's exhibits. In fact, this was his favorite time of day.

It always felt like The Dungeon belonged to him alone as he stalked through the creepy corridors, entering the sixteenth-century Doctor's Surgery with its container of leeches on one shelf, then out past the Plague Pit, pausing to appreciate the gruesomeness of the corpses piled in a cart next to it. On he went, through the "excavated cellar," triggering the ghosts of Roman Legionaries as he did so, the centurion's trumpet echoing eerily, followed by the jangle of armor and tramping sandals. On past Little Ease, the four-by-four-foot barred cage with its cramped occupant squeezed into a living hell; around the corner, pausing again to admire the realism of the drowning prisoner chained in a stone well as water rose above his lips. Gurgles and chokes on the soundtrack. The moans of the tortured, the clank and rattle of wooden props, the *clump*, *clump* of his own boots—this was Jem's world.

A man on a rack moaned as his body was stretched, but he didn't look at Jem as the actor strode past.

Anybody else would have been scared stiff. Jem reveled in it all.

He chatted amiably enough to the other actors as they all took off their make-up and changed into their casual clothes, but they seemed more subdued than usual. Even Steve, his best friend in The Dungeon, seemed to be having difficulties meeting his gaze. Jem scowled when he saw Dave in the mirror entering the staff room; he turned, tossing the piece of sponge he'd been using to clean his face into a bin. Plucking his coat from the rack, he left the staff room and followed the supervisor to the manager's office.

Sheila Watts was forty-ish, portly, with a blank mask of a face. Jem couldn't ever remember seeing her smile in the two weeks he'd been there. She looked even more uncomfortable than usual. Fenton sat beside her at the desk, opposite Jem. He looked even smugger than usual.

"I get it," Jem said. "Tone it down, Jem." He gave them a big smile. Sheila looked at Dave to break the news. He coughed dramatically.

"I'm sorry, Jem. Not as simple as that this time." He grimaced slightly as though what he was about to say would hurt him more than it would Jem, but not *really*.

Jem waited, an old, familiar coldness creeping up inside his body.

"It's the letters," Sheila said as if that was self-explanatory. "I'm afraid to say your probationary period has not been successful. We will pay you a week's wage in lieu, and, of course, your P-forty-five will be sent out tomorrow. But we'd like to thank you for the work that you've done for us." She looked to Dave again for support. He nodded brightly, as if she'd just delivered some good news.

Jem stood up. He wanted to say something incisive and dignified, but there was nothing.

Feigning concern for Jem's future career, Dave offered: "I hear Mc-Donald's pays almost as much per hour as we do, and they've always got vacancies."

Jem found some words at last, or at least two. "Fuck you." That was all he had. And it wasn't much. He bowed with open mockery. Smiling broadly, yet his thoughts were black and dangerous.

He left them, Sheila with her blank face and Dave with his triumphant smirk. The staff exit lay at the other end of the empty shop with its rubber severed limbs and bouncy spiders. He grabbed a severed finger from the display by the till, a last gesture of defiance, and the exit door clanked firmly shut behind him.

CHAPTER TWENTY-ONE

He couldn't wait to get inside that tight, blonde pussy.

At least, he imagined it would be tight, but that was purely from judging how slender she was. He couldn't envisage someone that slim having a Bagpuss.

The text she'd sent him almost made his hands shake as he aligned the final shot. But Ben Trenchard was a professional, if nothing else, and he wouldn't let pussy distract him from crafting a perfect pan across the set of the Nazi Death Camp.

Wrap was called, and everybody scrambled to get the hell out of Auschwitz. Everybody except Ben. He hung back, dawdling with his equipment.

"What's up, Ben?" asked James Radley, one of the grips. "Thought you'd be in a rush to get back to the missus." He winked cheekily. He knew Ben was having problems with his girlfriend.

"She can go fuck herself," Ben responded, taking out his phone. "G'night, James. See you tomorrow, mate."

James picked up on the cameraman's mood and left him to it. Ben went to the honey wagon in the production unit car park, dawdled some more, looked at the text again. He'd got Christine's number off her before they'd finished lunch. Of course he had. But this wasn't it. And he certainly hadn't given her his. He didn't want her phoning him at home, not with Jackie the way she was at the moment. She already suspected he was up to something. She always did. To her credit, he had to admit she was pretty much always right, too.

He fired a text back:

> Can't remember giving you my number—not that I mind of course! And this isn't the number you gave me.

While he waited for her to reply, he read her original text again, the one she'd sent a quarter of an hour before the production wrapped for the day.

> Hi Ben. I want to see you again!! Hope you don't think I'm being too presumptuous, and I'm guessing you wouldn't want people to see you out with a humble SA—I know how much you value your secrecy. So how about I meet you in an hour at the SS Camp set? That would be a real turn on! Christine xx

He didn't have to wait long for her reply.

> It wasn't hard to get it. Lots of people know you on set. Don't worry, I was discreet and didn't tell anyone I wanted to meet you again. Just said I wanted camera advice for my own photography company I'm trying to set up. Oh, and this is my sister's number. My phone died on me.

Who the hell could she have got his number off? He didn't like that. One major possibility was that silly, old slag, Jane. He'd seen her chatting to Christine just before he took her for lunch. Jealous cow. Two shags and a risqué blowie in the supporting artists' green room tent after wrapping on a shoot a few months before, which had admittedly been fun (Ben loved risks, they made him hard) and was about all she'd been worth, and then Ben had moved on. But he could imagine the poison she'd poured into Christine's ear. But it obviously hadn't worked, had it?

He wondered what had happened to that other twat he'd seen her hanging around with on other productions. Another extra who thought he was an actor. So many of those around. But Ben had assumed they were together as they seemed so close. Daft fucker had delusions of grandeur all right, both as an extra and as a lover; definitely a case of benched in the friend zone. Ben chuckled to himself. He'd watched the sad arse trying to shuffle into frame on many productions, overacting in the background as if he thought the camera was on him, instead of the guy just being a walking prop for the principal actors to stand in front of. Ridiculous. No wonder Christine had subbed him. He'd have to ask her about him, though. It would make him even harder to think he was fucking the girl the silly sod fancied.

He hung around the base camp, waiting for the rest of the crew to piss off. Last to leave, Jacob Scorby, the producer. He clocked Ben and ambled over for a chat, puzzled why the cameraman was still there. Ben brushed him off with an excuse about wanting to look over the set one last time as it got dark, prepping a shot for the next day. Jacob applauded his professionalism and dedication, and off he fucked, thank the Lord.

It was 5:30 now, and dusk was settling on Auschwitz as he sauntered toward the mock-up of the Birkenau Death Camp. He passed the security guy sitting in his car at the end of the track that led to the set, exchanged a nod and a smile, and passed on.

He paused at the railway tracks the set designer had laid leading up to the camp and looked up at the austere and disturbing-looking set, made even more sinister by the fall of night. The huge gatehouse was a silhouette against the evening sky, the doors open, framing darkness. The iconic gatehouse was a true symbol of evil, a screaming mouth into hell. The Gate of Death, the prisoners had called it. He had been filming it from different angles all day. He stepped onto the rails, strode slowly toward the opening. Birds seethed mournfully as they circled their nests in the trees at the far end of the camp set. The wicked barbed wire fences and turrets were black against the fading light.

He stepped into the archway.

Okay, he was here. So where was Christine?

He became aware of a figure approaching through the dusk. He strained his eyes to see, but it was becoming too dark.

His phone vibrated in his pocket. He pulled it out. **Guten Tag.**

He smiled at the slowly approaching figure silhouetted against the slightly paler sky. He could make out she was wearing a German officer's hat (at least, that's what it looked like from this distance) and a long SS officer's coat.

"You playing dress up?" he called, not too loudly to attract the attention of the security man at the end of the drive, although the man was too far away to hear anything really, and he was in his car. Still, Ben didn't want to take any risks.

His phone vibrated again in his hand.

I know you like women in costume so I borrowed this

She was texting as she walked, the sexy slut. By the time he'd read it, a huge grin on his face, she had approached to within ten feet.

"You know me too well," he said. He peered at the shadow beneath the cocked hat, but her features were indistinguishable. The coat made her figure larger.

The vibration came again.

Turn around Sexy. I'm going to pretend to arrest you and march you up into the Gatehouse. Oh and please unzip. I want you ready for action!!

He laughed, delighted. "Oh, come on. Not getting my pecker out here! Not yet!!" But he was thinking of the sentry room the set designer had created above the gateway. There was a bed, basic and simple, but that was what she obviously had in mind. He turned around, and though his hand wandered down to his zip, he didn't act on her suggestion. He could feel his growing arousal, though, and that nearly persuaded him to do so.

He could hear her boots marching through the grass toward him. She'd really made an effort for him! Jane must have told him how he liked to play dress-up sex games, the minx. Oh, this was *too* good!

He could feel her breath on the back of his neck. And now he was fully aroused.

His phone vibrated.

AUFWIEDERSEHEN ARSCHLOCK

He blinked at the text, confused. What did that mean?

Then he felt something cold, metallic, and horribly sharp slip around his throat from behind, draw tight against his neck as strong hands applied pressure.

Barbed wire!

He could feel the vicious spikes dig and rend at his throat, the wire constricting his breathing. He choked, twisted, tried to throw the assailant off him, but the pressure intensified, the nasty snags biting deeper. He flailed madly, bucked backward, hoping to catch the attacker off balance, but the steel coil tightened its grip around his throat like a barbed wire python. His hands tore at it, trying to pry it loose, but the hooks only lacerated his fingers.

The night became darker as his vision began to fail. He collapsed to his knees, facing the large, forbidding shadow of the turret house. The archway screamed.

The Gate of Death.

"Pleaseee…" he croaked. But his voice went unheard, even by his killer.

The birds circled mournfully above their nests at the far end of the camp, only settling down as darkness completed its fall.

Silence over Birkenau.

CHAPTER TWENTY-TWO

There was no music this time on the way to the unit base.

Stone really wasn't in the mood. The thrill of the hunt had turned on him. He was the hunted one now, and he didn't like it. Not one bit.

The papers would be full of his failure within hours. Inspector Clueless Fails to solve Movie Murders, or something equally garish.

Wells parked up at the base, and Stone and Darke followed him glumly down the track toward the Birkenau set.

It was now after one in the morning. The production security man had forgotten about Ben Trenchard for a few hours, then remembered that he hadn't seen him leave again. When he'd spotted Ben's car still parked at the base, he went straight to the Death Camp set to check if he was there, then phoned the police immediately, shaken to hell by what he found. The call had come through at around 11:30, and Stone had wasted no time getting to the base.

The security man was waiting for him by his car, looking thoroughly miserable, accompanied by a uniformed officer. Stone ignored him for now, walking toward the gateway, illuminated now by the production arc lamps that Stone had ordered to be switched on.

He walked under the archway, Darke and Wells at his side. The irony of the constructed set not passing him by at all. This was the second time in a month he'd walked through the Gate of Death.

Another uniform was on duty at the S.O.C. Forensic bugs photographed the corpse, took notes. No white tent this time. The barbed wire sentry fence prevented that, and the closed-off nature of the guarded set protected the scene. Stone approached with an acid stomach and an acid expression. The chief forensics officer, Harry Grimes, pulled his mask down to speak, but Stone ushered him to wait. He approached the body.

"Fuck's sake," said Wells.

Stone said nothing.

Ben Trenchard was naked to the waist, crucified upside down on the barbed wire fence, his wrists and ankles knotted with wire. He wore a crown of barbed wire thorns of sorts, albeit one that had slipped down around his throat.

Stone continued to say nothing.

Hughgroves, the pathologist, was bending over the body, straightened as he saw Stone.

Stone waited for him to speak, fury building slowly, inexorably inside him.

"Probably about six or seven hours ago. I would say that makes it around six-thirty, seven this evening. Cause of death, as you can see."

Stone didn't trust himself to speak. Not yet. Darke came to his rescue. "Any other injuries?"

Hughgroves's right eye spasmed. "It would seem the barbed wire round his throat was the only assault. His larynx was crushed and lacerated. Difficult to say until I've examined him properly at the mortuary, but preliminary inspection suggests he was attacked from behind."

"Would it take someone with considerable strength to do that to him?" Darke stared at the inverted corpse with apparent dispassion. Stone was once again reminded of how efficient she was, just when he needed her to be.

"The victim's not a particularly big man; in fact, quite short, five-seven, at a guess. And a slim build. So it would not have taken an especially powerful man to overcome him, particularly if they struck from behind." Stone heard Hughgroves's response, registered it, filed it for later. Right now, he had to control his rising anger. He turned away, glanced back at the ominous Gatehouse. Play with fire, and you get…crucified and hung upside down half naked on a sentry fence. It sounded like a joke. A very dark, macabre, and cruel joke. And maybe that's what it was. The Roman slain with his own sword, the demon raped and choked to death by a tree root, and now the cameraman on a production duplicating Nazi atrocities experiencing an only too real one himself

"So it wouldn't necessarily have been a man?"

Stone turned back to hear Hughgroves's response.

"Not necessarily, no. A relatively robust woman could have managed it."

Darke turned to Grimes, the chief forensics officer. "Apparently, he was strangled with barbed wire. But wouldn't that have resulted in the killer's hands being lacerated, too? Possibility of not just the victim's blood being found in the grass?"

Grimes indicated a patch of grass with a square of police tape around it just in front of and to the side of the Gateway, which they had missed as they strode toward the killer's showpiece display hanging on the fence.

"Blood spatter found there, so we're guessing that's where our man was killed. We're checking it, obviously, but judging from the previous S.O.C.s, this perp isn't going to make it that easy. My guess? The killer wore reinforced gloves to handle the wire, maybe extra padding."

Darke nodded glumly.

"Where is it?" Stone broke his silence at last, glaring at Grimes.

"What?" Grimes frowned at him, his weak face attempting a gruff expression. He didn't like Stone. Not many people did. That wasn't his problem.

"The tape."

Grimes lifted his eyebrows in an ironic expression, gestured for the Detective Inspector to come closer to the corpse. "You're going to love this." He crouched, peering behind the crucified corpse. Stone bent to follow his gaze, already convinced that he wouldn't. The top of a fat VHS box poked from the waist of Trenchard's jeans, the plastic wedged tightly between his belt and the skin of Trenchard's back.

"Pull it out," he ordered, straightening up and putting on a pair of gloves handed to him by one of the C.S.I.s.

Grimes did as he was instructed. The arc lamp shone on the grotesque artwork. The title *SS Experiment Camp* screamed above a topless woman strung upside down on a barbed wire fence. Stone took it, opened the box. A grubby tape sat snugly inside its plastic pouch, a bloody thumbprint on the label.

"Take it away," he said gruffly.

Darke gave him a look. He ignored it. He was just fine, thank you. "What was he doing here on his own?" he said to her.

The uniformed cop spoke up, obviously excited to be part of it all. "The security guy said the victim told him he was coming in here to recce the set, sir."

Stone glared at the young constable. The cop visibly paled, if that was possible, considering the color of his complexion already. Then Stone nodded. "Silly fucker." Not sure if the D.I. was referring to him, the cop looked away hurriedly. But Stone was turning to Wells. "Talk to the security bloke. Ask him if he heard anything and why he waited so long to check on Trenchard. I bet he was in the land of fucking nod, all parked up like a warm bug in his cozy car."

He looked at Darke, and he could hear the anger in his own voice, but there was nothing he could do about it. "Why was the stupid bastard out here in the dark on his own? Everyone else had packed up for the day. Surely he was sick of seeing this set? Doesn't add up."

Darke had obviously thought of something. She put a hand on Grimes's shoulder. The C.S.I. chief turned, his expression softening when he saw it was Darke who had touched him. "Did you find his phone?"

Grimes blinked. "Not on his body, no."

"Then where is it? He was the D.O.P. on a film set. He wouldn't go anywhere without his phone."

"Check the area," Stone told Grimes. "I'm guessing the perp took it, for whatever reason. But let's search anyway. This fucker likes playing games; maybe he's hidden it somewhere. I'll get some more bobbies up to help you." The chief was about to turn away when Stone stopped him. "How did the murderer get in? Assuming he didn't tiptoe past Rip Van in his cozy car, that is?"

"Follow me." Grimes set off across the short grass and mud covering the entire prison camp, heading for the far end. Stone and Darke followed. The camp was not to historical scale, as Stone knew from his own visit to the museum, so it didn't take them long to reach the furthest fence, studded by a sentry tower at each corner. Grimes shone his torch on the wire. A gap had been cut in the middle.

"Cutters?

Grimes nodded.

"The fucker came prepared again." He glanced at Darke. "Too much of a coincidence our camera pal came here at the same time as his killer, especially when filming was done for the day. Let's find out why. You could be right, Sam: maybe his phone can tell us." His anger was beginning to recede as his detective instincts kicked in. He had a job to do.

"If we can't find the actual phone, we can speak to his mobile provider, check who was the last person to contact him."

Darke nodded. She was already on her phone as Stone peered at the gap in the fence again. Beyond it were thick woods. A local scenic area five miles from Taunton. The killer could easily have parked up in a picnic area, taken his time cutting through the wire as dusk fell. But how had he lured the cameraman to his death?

As they marched back toward the corpse, Darke voiced what had been eating away at Stone since he'd first received the call.

"What about Jem Whateley, guv?"

Stone didn't answer.

"Looks like we got the wrong man."

Again Stone refrained from answering her. But Darke wasn't going to let that stop her. He knew she'd kept her thoughts to herself during the drive from Bristol, but now that they'd examined the S.O.C., she could no longer hold back.

"He was tucked up in custody when this happened. We got it wrong, guv."

And he knew that she was only being polite with the "we." There may be no "I" in "team," but there was certainly an "F" in "Fucked up."

And he'd done that all by himself.

PART TWO

FREEZE FRAME

CHAPTER ONE

Another producer, another production office trailer.

Stone was sick of the sight of both. He let Darke do most of the talking, content to sit back and stare blearily at the corpulent young exec.

He'd managed to snatch three hours of sleep before heading back to the production base near Taunton. At least Cooke had done the driving. He'd left the huge detective to talk to various crew members to find out if anyone knew of anybody Ben Trenchard could have been meeting after wrap, in the dark. Stone had already asked Scorby.

"He told me he wanted to recce the set one last time." Scorby shrugged. He was trying to carry off an *enfant terrible* Tarantino air, but his lazy eye and drooping jowls worked against the image.

"Why would he do that in the dark?"

Scorby blinked at the D.S., spread his hands in an exaggerated *je ne sais pas* manner that irritated Stone.

"Surely he wouldn't be able to see much," Darke prompted.

"I think he wanted to catch the dusk light, make some plans. He wasn't just a cameraman; he was our D.O.P., too."

"D.O.P.?"

"Director of photography," the producer explained loftily. "And a damn good one, too."

"Can you think of any other reason he might have wanted to go in there after the production had closed for the night?"

Scorby shook his head. But a slightly shifty look had momentarily appeared in his one good eye.

"If you know something, we need to hear it."

He frowned, regarding Darke as if summing up her talents for a role. "Sometimes he strayed."

"What does that mean?"

"He…he had a bit of a wandering eye, I suppose you could say."

He wasn't the only one. But Stone was too tired and depressed to appreciate the irony of the producer's statement. He'd had to release Jem Whateley first thing this morning, and that had worsened his mood.

"You're saying he made a habit of…assignations on set after hours?" Darke glanced at Stone. This could be what they needed.

Stone stirred himself. "Any idea who he might have been meeting?"

Scorby shook his head vigorously, his expression revealing he thought he'd said too much. "He was very discreet. Always."

"So…" Darke locked eyes with the producer. "Was he married?"

"No, no." One eye went off on a different orbit as if alarmed at the prospect. "But he had a steady girlfriend. Lovely lady. Jackie."

"And was Jackie aware of his…transgressions?" Darke uttered the word like it tasted dirty.

Another *je ne sais quoi.* Stone forced himself not to lose his temper. "But *you* were."

Scorby sighed. "He had a taste for the female S.A.s. Unfortunate. But there we are."

"Any in particular?" Darke picked up a pen, pulled out her notepad.

"I don't remember their names," he said. "I just heard rumors about it. I never *saw* anything."

Darke put her pen down again, disappointed. "Can you think of anybody who might know?"

Don't shrug. Don't you fucking dare.

Scorby shrugged, looked a little complacent. Glanced at his watch.

"I'm *so* sorry we're keeping you from your movie, Mister Scorby." Stone's voice was laden with sarcasm. "But we seem to have a problem, don't we?"

"Which is?"

"You don't seem to be giving us any information. Which means we won't be able to let you carry on with your little masterpiece until you do."

Scorby lost his smugness, dropped the whole casual Tarantino thing. He looked like a chubby puppy that had been kicked.

"But we have a very tight schedule…" he pleaded.

Stone ignored that. He'd found Scorby's obvious weakness. "And you have a D.O.P. who's D.O.A. Had you forgotten that?"

Scorby added sulky to his whipped look. "Of course not. But we can get around that. There are others I can speak to…" He trailed off, realizing what a prick he sounded.

"You seem to be missing the point, Mister Scorby. You won't be needing *any* cameramen for quite a while."

"That's ridiculous." His face reddened. "I realize these are very tragic circumstances, but even so, we have a movie to deliver on time and on budget. Any more delays would be unthinkable at this point."

Stone restrained himself from chuckling ironically. "Your schedule and your budget are so irrelevant right now that I'm almost amused you're mentioning them. *Almost.* But Mister Scorby, I'm also tired, and when I'm tired, I get a little irascible, so please do forgive me if I don't give a mole's anus about your cheap little Nasty Nazi flick."

Scorby gaped. Darke interceded rapidly. "The sooner we get leads we can work on that will help us find whoever did this to Mister Trenchard, the sooner we can green-light your production again."

Scorby nodded at her gratefully.

"Is there anything you can tell us that might help? I'm referring to anybody who might have a grudge against Mister Trenchard, or the production itself."

"The production *itself?*" Scorby looked horrified at the thought.

"This isn't the first film to be targeted, Mister Scorby. In fact, this is the third production to become the scene of a murder inquiry in the space of a month, as I'm sure you're aware. It's no secret that someone unknown is targeting movie sets. You must have seen the news, read the papers. We put out a request for all productions in the South West to increase their security measures. Did you comply with that?"

It was as if Scorby's head had been so full of schedules and budgets that he hadn't even entertained the notion that his film was now severely implicated in an ongoing murder case. But the light was beginning to dawn. Slowly but surely.

"So you think whoever did this wasn't just after Ben but…"

Stone enjoyed connecting the dots for the producer. "You're *all* at risk. It could have been any of you."

"But… Why?"

Stone enjoyed parodying the producer's shrug, too. "That's what we're here to find out. I'm not saying this wasn't personal against Trenchard, but the fact that other people have been murdered on different sets leads us to the conclusion the perpetrator wants his very own special wrap party, and the list of those invited is getting longer all the time."

Scorby paled. In the immortal words of Ant and Dec in the Australian jungle, *It could be you, Scorby.* Stone smiled thinly.

"So, now you've had a reality check… Any suggestions as to who might have it in for your film and the other productions involved?"

Scorby put his head in his hands, whether in contemplation, despair, or both. Stone waited patiently. For a few seconds, anyway. Then he got up and paced around the caravan. More mug shots on walls. More actors he didn't recognize.

Darke crossed one leg over the other, watching the sweaty producer intently. "Any actors you fired, ex-crew members who might carry a grudge for whatever reason, that sort of thing?"

Scorby took his hands away, and one eye focused on the D.S. "There *is* someone you could talk to…"

Stone turned back to look at the corpulent producer slouched in his swivel chair. He hadn't shown any signs of grief or compassion toward his dead D.O.P.

Darke picked up her pen again.

Scorby hesitated. "Of course, it could be nothing…"

"We'll decide." Darke opened her notebook. "Please go on."

"We…" He cleared his throat. "…we had to let our original script-writer go. He wasn't happy about that. Not at all."

"So it was an acrimonious severance of the ways?"

Scorby nodded. Darke scribbled a note.

"He threatened us with legal action. It was all very unpleasant."

"Name?"

"Jack South. He, uh… His original script was far too exploitative. You see, we are trying to tell a sensitive, sympathetic story here. Jack didn't get that. His screenplay was loaded with sex and gore."

Stone grunted. Scorby glanced up at him.

"So you cut out all the sex and gore?"

Scorby looked a bit uncomfortable. "Not *all* of it, or we wouldn't have been able to tell a serious story in the way it actually happened. Obviously."

"Obviously. So, was there a scene in the film where someone gets stripped and hung on a barbed wire fence?"

"Of course not!" Scorby added outrage to his repertoire. He puffed himself up a bit, struggling to remember he was Tarantino-esque. "South's script had lots of things like that in it, though, which we cut out. Our present screenplay bears very little resemblance to South's."

"And I can imagine he didn't like that much," Stone said.

"He got paid. I don't know what his problem was."

"To be fired from a production must be pretty upsetting, even so," Darke said.

Shrug. "He got paid," South repeated, as if that covered a whole pantheon of sins.

"And did he go quietly into the night?"

Scorby blinked at Stone, tried manfully to bring his other eye to bear on him, too. "I don't understand."

"Did he make any threats when you told him his script was shit and that he had to vacate the premises forthwith?"

"It wasn't like that! He wasn't expelled from school, Inspector."

"I'll repeat my question: did he go quietly?"

Scorby looked away. "Not exactly."

"Then tell us exactly."

"He… He said he would dirty our name—*my* name—in the industry. But he was full of shit. And besides, ours wasn't the first production to let him go."

Stone sat down at the table opposite Scorby again. "And which productions might they be?"

Scorby looked at his messy desk as if that would provide help. "I think he'd written a treatment for *The Awful Dead,* amongst others. Could be wrong, but…"

"That *is* interesting." Stone glanced over at Darke, who scribbled in her pad. "Where can we find this maverick?"

Scorby picked up his mobile, scrolled until he got a number, then read it out for Darke.

"Address?" It took him longer to find that. He had to burrow amongst all the paperwork on his desk before giving in. "My secretary will be able to provide that," he said eventually. Looking relieved, he glanced at Stone hopefully. "Is that it?"

"Not yet." Stone smiled grimly. "Tell us a bit more about this Jack South. Was he a particularly violent man, would you say?"

Shrug. Stone kept his smile. "He was a shit scriptwriter, that's all I know."

"You can tell me more than that, I'm sure."

"I didn't have much to do with him. Mostly contacted him by email and phone. Only met him a couple of times."

"And you didn't form an opinion of him?"

"Yes, I did: the guy was an asshole." Scorby looked pleased with that character summary.

"I need more than that. I meet a lot of arseholes in this job." Stone paused to let the significance of that sink in.

"He argued about every script change, every detail. He was short-tempered and precious. A dick, in other words. But like you said, there are a lot of 'em about."

"Especially in your industry, it seems."

Scorby let that fly. "We done?"

"Still no."

Scorby sighed. "What more do you want? I have financiers to call, distributors to appease. Stopping production on this film is not just a pause; it's a serious exclamation mark in my career." He looked pleased with that turn of phrase, too. Stone had a feeling he'd used it many times.

Stone leaned back, making himself comfortable in the plastic chair.

"Did you like Ben Trenchard?"

"What's that supposed to mean?"

"It's a very simple question, Mister Scorby."

"I don't know why you're asking it. It's hardly relevant."

"On the contrary. It's extremely relevant. You've spent the last half hour moaning about costs and delays. And do you know what you've left out?"

Scorby let loose one of his patented expansive shrugs. Stone got up from his chair, leaned over the desk, pushing his face right into Scorby's.

"You forgot to say you're sorry. You left out the bit about how terrible you feel about Trenchard losing his life. You omitted concern, Mister Scorby." He straightened up, nodded to Darke. "Don't worry; we'll let ourselves out." He paused at the door. "Oh, and Mister Scorby?" He smiled grimly. "Good luck with your financiers."

CHAPTER TWO

Cooke ducked his head as he entered Stone's office.

"Finish whatever you're doing and stretch your legs over to Martin Thorogood's house."

"That prick? You reckon he's our man?"

"I don't know, Cookie. Just grill him. He's got a major hard-on for one of the women protestors, and he'll do anything to impress her. I particularly want to know where he was between five and midnight, the evening of Trenchard's murder. And speak to a few of the other campaigners as well, especially Tina Bell. Get corroboration from them, if you can. Otherwise, Thorogood's girlfriend, wife, boyfriend, transexual non-binary lover—whoever the fuck can tell you where he was."

Cookie grinned at his boss. He turned to leave.

"Oh, and Cookie?"

The tall D.C. waited expectantly.

"Know anything about Video Nasties?"

Cookie looked blank for a second, which wasn't a huge change from his normal expression. "*Driller Killer, I Spit on Your Grave...* that sort of thing?"

Stone nodded. "*SS Experiment Camp, The Evil Dead.* They're both listed as former Video Nasties. Looks like our perp is playing a game with us that involves them. Find out everything you can on Video Nasties so I can brief the team. And most importantly, cross-reference any upcoming productions that could possibly be linked to any Nasties. Apparently, there's an official list of them, if my memory serves me correctly. Find it and go to work. And get Ming to help you."

After he'd gone, Stone sat gazing at the wall for a short while in deep contemplation, then got up, left his small office, and strode across the Inquiry Room to collect Darke.

The Merc glided to a halt on double yellow lines outside Brigstowe Agency. Stone switched off the engine and the music, much to Darke's relief. She could tell his mood had lifted a bit since the previous evening; she'd had to endure half an hour of The Damned's cartoonish anarchy blaring from the car's speakers, which kind of confirmed it. The hunt was on. Stone was back in the game.

"If you love this music so much, why don't you consider getting a Mohawk?" Darke deadpanned as she climbed out.

Stone slammed the driver's door. "And that wouldn't look at all stupid, would it?"

"Noooo."

He wanted to ignore her cockiness but was unable to resist. "My older brother was a punk. And it's not about a haircut or a leather jacket with studs on it, Darke; it's an attitude, a way of viewing the world and cutting through the bullshit. Which is what makes me a bad cop: I don't toe the line."

"You're a great cop."

He turned to her, surprised, as if suspecting she was still being flippant.

"Not to the Super and his cronies, I'm not. I'm an embarrassment, a fart in a lift. The foul smell nobody wants in their nostrils."

"I've almost gotten used to it." She winked, and he sighed in exasperation.

A biting wind swept across from the Avon gorge half a mile to their left. They could see the magnificent Clifton Suspension Bridge from where they stood. A few pedestrians braved the gusts as they crossed the walkways. It was a dull, cold November day, and Darke shuddered inside her jacket.

Stone prodded the bell of Number 39. A tall Georgian Townhouse, now converted into flats, Brigstowe Agency was situated on the ground floor.

Darke was eyeing Stone's long, brown overcoat. "Is that new?"

"Yeah."

"Where did you get it?"

"AllSaints. D'you like it?"

"I'd like it on a guy in his twenties. When do *you* get time to shop in AllSaints?"

The door opened, and a woman in her early thirties with an oval face and prominent curved nose appeared. Her long, dark hair was instantly clutched by the wind. She stepped back into the building, and Stone followed, warrant card held aloft.

"Detective Inspector Stone, Detective Sergeant Darke," he said automatically.

The woman peered at them blankly.

"Perhaps I could speak to the proprietor?"

"I'm afraid he's away." She made no move to let them in, her whole demeanor guarded, bordering on irritable.

"Are you one of the bookers?"

She blinked at them a few times before replying, her hair frolicking around her face. "I am, yes."

"Then maybe we could speak to you."

"I'm afraid you've come at our busiest time. The afternoons are when we place all our bookings." Still, she made no move to let them pass.

"Is that the police?" a male voice from inside called.

The woman turned her head as a man appeared in the doorway behind her, a headset around his neck. He beamed at them openly, his eyes lively and interested, contrasting with the blandness of the rest of his boyish features. "Let them in, Penny. They're probably here to discuss these appalling crimes. Is that right, Detectives?" He glanced at each of them in turn.

Penny frowned and finally stood aside, as did the man, who stretched out an arm for them to enter.

Stone and Darke followed them down a bare hallway and through a door to the left, finding themselves in a waiting room filled with plastic chairs stacked in piles. Photos of supporting artists in various colorful costumes adorned the walls.

"This is where we register everyone each year," the man told them chirpily. "But come through to our actual office." He led them down another short corridor beyond the reception area and through another door on the left. Penny immediately retreated to her desk, her hand reaching impulsively toward her own headset abandoned amongst the workload on her desk. Stone could see red lights bleeping on the headset receivers next to their respective P.C.s.

"I'm afraid you're going to have to ignore any calls for the time being," D.S. Darke said forcefully. Penny grimaced at her.

"Of course," said the man. "Can we get you anything to drink? Tea, coffee?"

Stone and Darke declined, looking around the office. There were two more desks, one at the head of the room.

The man saw Stone look at the latter and ushered him toward it. "This is Jason's desk. He's the proprietor of Brigstowe. Please take a seat." He pointed Darke toward the other empty desk.

"And where is Jason at the moment?" asked Stone, settling himself behind the desk. Unlike the others in the room, it was tidy.

"He's away, I'm afraid. In Cornwall for a week's holiday."

"This him?" Stone picked up a framed photo of a middle-aged man with dark hair. He had pale makeup on his face and dark kohl around his eyes. He was wearing filthy white robes and clutching a dagger.

"Oh yes," supplied the man cheerily. "That's his Banquo's Ghost. He's very fond of that photo."

"Bit creepy looking," was all Stone could muster.

The man sniggered. "I think that's the point." As if suddenly remembering his manners, he approached Stone with his hand out. "I'm sorry. I didn't introduce myself. I'm Marcus. And this is Penny." He waved a hand toward Penny, who forced a smile. Crossing to take Darke's hand, Marcus beamed at her. "I didn't realize Detective work appealed to such attractive people. You could be on our books. I could get you *lots* of work." He smiled expansively. Darke didn't twitch so much as a lip, staring at him disparagingly. Undeterred, Marcus skipped over to his own desk, perched on one side. Stone gave her a subtle grin.

"So, how can I be of assistance?"

"I'll need to speak to your boss. Could you give his number to D.S. Darke?"

Penny spoke up. "I don't think he'll appreciate being contacted while he's on holiday."

"I don't care if he's on a one-way trip to the moon. I want his number."

Penny scowled but pulled a small sticker pad toward her and wrote down the number. Darke collected it, added it to her phone list.

"Is he aware of what's been happening over the last few weeks? Not really a good time for him to go on holiday, is it?"

Penny stared at him as if he were being particularly offensive. "Of course he is. We *all* are. But he hasn't been on holiday for years. He needed the break. It was his one chance to be with his son."

"He's been taking the whole affair very badly, I'm afraid," Marcus said. "He takes it all so personally."

Stone stared at him. "Why would that be?"

"Because it's mainly our S.A.s who are on set when these awful things have happened. And one in particular who I believe has had rather a rough time of it."

Stone grunted. "If you're referring to Jeremy Whateley, he has been answering questions, yes. But I think you already know we let him go this morning."

"About time, too!" Marcus looked annoyed for a second, then the blandness returned. "He's a lovely chap. Wouldn't hurt a fly."

"Seem to remember they said the same about Tony Perkins in one of his roles."

Marcus pursed his lips, rolled his eyes to one side. The reference had sped over his head, apparently.

"We've recommended Jem have a few weeks off filming," Penny said.

"And how did he respond to that?"

"Not well. But he respected our position."

"Which is?"

She looked annoyed. "The fact that one of our S.A.s has been arrested and questioned by police in connection with a murder inquiry—"

"Three murder inquiries," Stone added.

Penny sighed. "Doesn't look good for our image, does it? Productions might be deterred from booking through us."

"Are you the only agency Jem works for?" Darke had her notebook out again.

Penny shrugged. "Probably not. He's a professional supporting artist, so he'll need to be with more agencies to be able to survive, but you'd need to ask him that question."

"What's his relationship like with the rest of your supporting artists?" Stone asked her.

"Why are you still interested in him? You just said you released him."

Marcus intervened hastily. "As far as we know, very good."

"It wasn't very good with Jimmy Dixley, was it? And by all accounts, he was angry and jealous when Guy Johns nicked his job. Any connection to Ben Trenchard?"

Marcus paused, looked uncertain. Penny stepped in. "A complaint was made about him." Marcus shot her a look, but she ignored it. "Jane Tighe phoned us to say he was pestering the female S.A.s again. Apparently, he's well known for it."

Stone glanced at Darke, who was busy scribbling in her pad.

"Any particular S.A. he was targeting?"

Penny didn't hesitate, ignoring Marcus's warning glare again. "Christine Thomas."

Stone raised his eyebrows. "You're a mine of interesting information."

"I'm just trying to speed this process up, Inspector," Penny said, giving Marcus a sharp look in return. "We have an incredible work-load we need to be dealing with."

Stone ignored that. "What was the exact nature of Miss Tighe's complaint?"

Penny held his gaze steadily. "She said he was flirting openly with Miss Thomas, to the embarrassment of other S.A.s. She said it was incredibly unprofessional of him, and it left a bad atmosphere on set."

"And did Miss Thomas welcome the attention?"

Again no hesitation from Penny. "Apparently so. But that's beside the point."

"Why's that?"

"Our S.A.s are not employed to fraternize with crew members. It's one of the most stipulated regulations in our handbook. Which is why Jane felt compelled to make an official complaint."

"And did you act on her complaint?"

"Not much we can do without upsetting the production. But I did send out a general email to all our S.A.s reminding them not to fraternize with cast and crew."

"Are you aware that Miss Thomas and Mister Whateley are very good friends?" Darke asked, looking up from her pad.

Marcus looked down at his desk. From being the gushing, overly helpful one, he'd now swapped roles with Penny to become the reticent party in the room. But it was clear Penny's desire to get them out as soon as possible prompted her sudden urge to cooperate.

"Of course. He introduced her to our agency. Their friendship was hardly a secret."

Marcus said sadly, "I'm afraid Jem obviously has it quite bad for Christine."

"And would Mister Whateley have been aware of the attentions Ben Trenchard was showing Miss Thomas?"

Penny shrugged. "You'd have to ask him that."

"Oh, we will." Stone frowned at her. He remembered Sam Darke had told him a lady called Penny at the agency was very helpful and lovely and sent her Jem's C.V. Her lovely qualities were definitely absent today.

But then, of course, they often were when people had to deal with Stone rather than Sam Darke. Their problem, not his.

"Anyone else complain about Ben Trenchard? Any signs of hostility toward him from other S.A.s besides Jane Tighe? You must have your ears to the ground concerning S.A. gossip on set."

"Jane wasn't *hostile* toward him. She was concerned about his behavior toward female S.A.s, and quite rightly so." She drew in a breath, composed herself. "And we don't encourage gossip, no matter what you like to think, Inspector. But there have been occasional complaints over the years. I'd have to check the records. Nothing extreme springs to mind, though. Marcus?"

Marcus shook his head. "Can't think of anything. I've been on set myself and noticed his behavior toward the female S.A.s, however."

Stone frowned. "What were you doing on set?"

"Jason very much encourages a hands-on approach within Brigstowe. Isn't that right, Penny? He likes us to attend film shoots fairly regularly to help the A.D.s sign people in and out, that sort of thing. And, of course, we do the occasional S.A. role ourselves." He seemed to brighten up again now that he was talking in more general terms.

Penny added. "It gives us a chance to observe our S.A.s in action."

"Spy on them, you mean?"

"No!" Marcus was adamant. "We're there to support them. In fact, I was supposed to be on the *Legion Britannica* shoot, but they didn't have a spare costume in my size. Just as well! So awful."

"And I was supposed to be on set next week for the Auschwitz drama," Penny added forlornly. "Doesn't look like that'll be happening now."

"Jason really likes to get inside his S.A.s' heads," Marcus said. "To understand how we can support them better. It's not spying."

Penny tapped a pen on her desk pointedly. "Anything else we can help you with. As I've pointed out, we are—"

"Incredibly busy. Yes, I can see the flashing lights. But we're not done yet."

Penny sighed, fiddled anxiously with her headset.

"We're going to need a list of all your S.A.s. Send it to the same email address D.S. Darke gave you. Have you got any people on your books with criminal records?"

"All S.A.s have to submit a D.B.S. certificate in order to receive work nowadays, Inspector." Penny briskly shook her hair off her shoulders. Stone smiled thinly at her body language. He wasn't going to be hurried.

"But that only covers a certain period, doesn't it? Have you got anyone on your books who has displayed unpleasant, antisocial, or violent tendencies, would you say?"

"If they displayed such tendencies, they would be removed from our books promptly." She looked to Marcus for support. He nodded.

"Penny's right. We don't tolerate bad behavior."

"Unless it's an important crew member."

Marcus looked offended. "But that's completely out of our control."

"What about Jem Whateley and Jimmy Dixley's public on-set argument? You didn't suspend Jem afterward, did you?"

"We discussed it, actually," Penny said.

"But we came to the decision that Jem was a valued member of our little S.A. community," Marcus interjected. "No history of problems from him. And a very good performer. We're always offering him special roles, featured work. Jobs that are more advanced than merely being an extra in a crowd." His eyes took on a gleam. "It's what makes our jobs interesting, when we see our S.A.s stretch themselves and achieve success, no matter how minor it may seem to others. Acting is acting, whether you only get one or two lines reacting to a principal cast member or you're the star of the show." He smiled, and his bland face glowed with enthusiasm.

"I bet that can put some noses out of joint," Stone said.

"What do you mean, Inspector?"

"If our pal Whateley is getting all the plum roles. I can imagine that pisses off some of your other supporting artists."

Marcus maintained his smile. "We like to think our S.A.s are proud of each other's commitments rather than resenting them."

"And besides," Penny added. "Marcus said he *offers* Jem plenty of upgraded acting roles. That doesn't necessarily mean he gets them. It's up to the productions."

"And does he? Get them, I mean."

Now it was Marcus's turn to fiddle with his headset. He lifted them from around his neck and placed them over his ears as if hinting that the interview was over and they had calls to make and receive. Penny allowed herself a little smile, her eyes full of wry humor as she answered Stone.

"Of course not. At least not in the majority of cases. This is a very competitive business, Inspector. Each actor or S.A. is up against hundreds, thousands of others for each job."

"Cutthroat."

"Excuse me?"

"You missed out 'cutthroat.' Isn't that what they say about the acting industry?" He got up from his chair, glanced at Darke, who also rose. Penny looked relieved. Marcus gave them a final bland smile as Stone thanked them for their time and let themselves out.

Back on the blustery street, Stone buttoned up his coat. A traffic warden had plastered a yellow penalty charge on the windscreen. Stone peeled it off and stuffed it in his pocket.

"You need to stop collecting those," Darke said. "There are more enjoyable hobbies."

Stone ignored her. "Phone this Jason guy. I don't care if he's having the time of his life on a freezing-cold beach in Cornwall in the middle of November. Tell him to get back here A.S.A.P."

He climbed behind the wheel of the Merc. Sat thinking for a while, his hand on the ignition key.

"Can't help thinking I'm missing something," he said while Darke got in beside him and looked up Jason's number.

"It's like the penny's landed inside the slot machine but not been pushed over the edge yet." He grunted in frustration. "Only it's not a penny; it's a fucking pound." He switched on the engine, and the raucous blare of "Smash it Up" filled the car.

CHAPTER THREE

"Thought they'd thrown away the key on you."

Christine let him into her flat with a cheeky smile. She was wearing a floral T-shirt and brown slacks and looked surprised to see him.

Jem went straight to the lounge as if searching for any male visitors, and satisfied they were alone, he settled himself on the small settee. He glanced around at her familiar furnishings, Klimt's *The Kiss* print still hanging above the fireplace, the bookcase filled with astrology and self-help books, a copy of John Fowles's *The Magus*, which she was re-reading for at least the fourth or fifth time, on the coffee table. He pulled a face when she eased herself into an armchair next to the fireplace.

"Aren't you going to sit next to me?"

"I don't want to get murdered, do I?" Another show of teeth.

"Thanks, Snaggle." Her smile closed down immediately. He felt a bit guilty. He picked up some magazines on the seat next to him. "Come on, sit next to the jailbird."

Christine remained where she was. "I'm amazed to see you out and about. Didn't they even give you an electronic tag?"

"You don't seem too upset about your lover."

Her face dropped. "You're such an insensitive prick."

He shrugged. "He was a sex pest. You *do* know that, don't you? It's common knowledge amongst S.A.s."

"He was charming to *me*. Polite, engaging, fun to be with. Every-thing that you're not, in fact."

He snorted.

"Are you trying to tell me he got what he deserved?" Her eyes were cold, hostile.

"Of course not." He looked away. "Sorry. I guess you're upset."

"Prick."

"You only went on one date, didn't you?"

"It should be me interrogating *you*. Can't believe they let you out."

"So you keep saying. Would you rather they hadn't?"

She didn't answer, looked out the window of the second-floor flat.

"Christine?"

"What do you want me to say?"

"That you believe I didn't do it for a start!"

"They let you out, didn't they?"

He got up, walked to the window.

"Don't act all hurt. What the hell was I supposed to think? They arrested you!"

He spun round to face her, and she flinched a little at the look in his eyes.

"How long have we known each other?"

She stared at the carpet.

"*How long?*"

She played with her hair, gave him a shy look.

"We went to school together. Grew up together. Moved to Bristol, if not together, then near enough at the same time. And you could hon-estly believe—"

"I didn't *know* you at school. You were five years older. I only got to know you later."

"What are you saying??"

"Stop being a drama queen. So what. You didn't do it. So who did? This is all getting too close."

"It's been too close since Dixley bought the farm."

"Another of your enemies."

"Fuck me. You're unbelievable."

"*I'm* unbelievable? *You're* the one who nearly got charged with murder."

He let that go. She got up, went to the kitchen, came back with a bottle of wine and two glasses. "Sorry." She handed him a glass.

He looked at her. "Me, too. I can't believe you were on the same set as him, that's all. The same *day*. I couldn't handle it if—"

"Are you *crying?* O.M.G., you *sweetheart!*" She threw her arms around him and hugged him compulsively. He squeezed her back, kissed her hair.

She released him. "Don't get any ideas, Buster." But she was grinning her old, loopy grin.

He sat down on the sofa again, and this time, she joined him. They sipped at their wine in silence for a few minutes. Finally, Jem put his glass on the small table.

"Are you giving it up?" he asked her.

"What?"

"Don't be dense—S.A. work."

She thought about it. "I don't know. I must admit I'm pretty traumatized about what happened to Ben. Can't think about it at the moment. I'm definitely having a break. Unless some really good job comes along. Hopefully, they'll catch the lunatic who did this soon because I can't afford not to work. What about you?"

"Brigstowe has politely *requested* I take a few weeks off. But they can fuck themselves. Like you, I need to pay the bills. There are offers coming in from other agencies, so we'll see."

Christine fidgeted on her cushion. "Just be careful."

"Stop that; you don't want me to think you actually like me."

"I *do* care about you, you prick." She gave him the finger when his smile broke out. "But don't get too excited. I'm not about to sleep with you."

"You'll give in eventually."

She laughed. It was good to hear. She looked fantastic. He drew in a breath, judging everything he said. "You know how much I care about you."

She took a sip, changed the subject. "Ben, Jimmy, and Guy. Three dead now: Two of them S.A.s like us. That's terrifying." She searched his face, her blue eyes darkening. "Who do *you* think did it?"

He took a deep gulp, finished his glass, held it out for a refill. "I haven't a fucking clue, Christine. And more worryingly, I don't think the police do either." He smiled grimly and took another gulp of wine.

CHAPTER FOUR

It was with some trepidation, but also a fair bit of excitement, that Derek Stone entered the bar.

She was already there, in a cozy corner at the back. Why she'd chosen The Hatchet was beyond him. Besides being the oldest pub in Bristol, it was also a hangout for bikers, punks, Goths, and hairy bastards of all kinds. Was she baiting him? There could be a fair few in here who might have had a run-in with him throughout his glorious career in this city.

He paused as he reached her table, looking down at her with a cautious smile. She tilted her head to look up at him, her dark eyes full of mischief and uncertainty, a curiously attractive mix. He had to admit, she looked good. Her long, dark hair tumbled over the fake fur collar of her coat. One epically long leg was folded over the other. She pouted as she scrutinized him.

"You could look more pleased to see me." Her words were almost lost beneath the heavy metal on the sound system.

He spread his hands. "I'm pleased to see you, Aneta."

"Sorry?"

He raised his voice. "I said I *am* pleased to see you!"

"You could *sound* more pleased to see me."

He laughed despite his consternation. He'd forgotten she had the power to make him do that. He hadn't met many women who could actually make him laugh, although Darke had her moments.

"You should have given me more notice."

"I wanted to surprise you. See if you had a wife and child."

He shook his head. He wasn't sure what she wanted, what she was doing here in the U.K. He would have to make it plain that he had no room in his life for relationships.

"You look scared."

"It's the music."

"Bullshit. You're scared of me. Don't worry, Detective Inspector; I'm only here for beer and sex."

He twitched instinctively when she used his title, glancing around to see if anyone was listening. Luckily, it was early evening and the pub was only a third full.

"Oh, I'm sorry. Don't you want everybody in here to know you are a policeman?"

"I'd get you a drink, but I see you already have one."

"Get me another. Vodka and coke."

He gave her another cautious smile and set off for the bar.

His thoughts bounced chaotically around his head while he waited for the drinks. What the hell was he going to do with her? What was she really after—a holiday, a romance? He'd only met her the once in Krakow. He didn't have time for this. He really didn't. Not with a full-blown triple murder investigation hanging over him. The Chief had lain into him before he clocked off for the day. The mantra was the same: get this case done. Not to save further lives, but to save his reputation, so the credit-stealing bastard could hold his head up at the golf course with the Chief constable again. Stone should have been clocking up the overtime, searching for the killer, not socializing with a pretty Polish woman in a biker bar.

He felt overdressed, obviously. While the brown Heron coat might look trendy (on a twenty-year-old), he was still wearing his rumpled suit under it, though he'd ripped the tie—which, with each passing day, was feeling more and more like a hangman's noose—from his neck as he entered the pub.

To his right, a huge metalhead was glugging from a bottle of New-castle Brown. Stone eyed him warily. The guy ran his gaze over Stone's clothes and lost interest, returning to his conversation with a scantily clad rock chick next to him.

Across the far side of the bar, a punk with a bright green Mohawk was watching him closely. He felt like pulling out his *Machine Gun Etiquette* CD and waving it at him, but that would have been beyond pathetic. He doubted this lot was into his music anyway; his tastes were locked in the seventies.

He grabbed the pint of Butcombe and Aneta's vodka and made his way back to the table.

Aneta had taken off her coat, revealing a tight black sweater and short skirt, and he glanced shiftily at her figure. She caught him looking.

"Naughty policeman," she chided him.

"Stop saying that," he hissed, settling down on a stool opposite her.

She laughed. "Wrrrrr."

"And don't make that sound. You know what it does to me."

"You're off duty now, Detective Inspector."

He glanced over his shoulder. A couple of bikers with shaved heads and impressive beards were passing their table. They glanced at him guardedly.

She was laughing again, a very infectious chuckle. He found himself smiling naturally for the first time in weeks.

"It *is* good to see you, Aneta."

"Really? You didn't look so sure a minute ago."

"It's just…" He hesitated. There was no way he could tell her about the job. Just no way. "I'm really busy at work at the moment."

"I guess you are. Have you caught the Video Nasty Killer yet?"

He jerked, spilling some beer. "What?"

"Oh, come on. It's in all the papers. That's what they are calling the murderer."

Stone was well aware of the fuss in the newspapers, especially the tabloids. He'd tried his best to ignore it. "I— I'm not…"

"Please don't say to me you are not involved with this case." She sipped her vodka, kept her eyes locked on his, the mischief still rampant in their depths, though the uncertainty had faded. She had judged his reaction, his body language, and knew that, for the most part, he was definitely pleased to see her. "Because I know that would be a lie."

He shrugged. "I can't talk about it, Aneta."

"So you *are* involved. Of course you are. A detective inspector in the Avon and Somerset C.I.D. would naturally be at the center of such a major case. How exciting!"

"What are you doing here, Aneta?"

She pouted again. "Change the subject, I see. I told you, I'm here—"

"For beer and sex. I got that. How long are you thinking of staying?"

"Don't worry, Derek the Detective: I won't keep you from your killer for long."

He took a gulp of beer. "Did you fly in this afternoon?"

"It's only two and a half hours from Krakow. It is nothing. I should come see you more often." She laughed at his expression. "I am here for two nights only. I wanted to see Bristol—and maybe see you."

"Where are you staying?"

"With you. If your wife doesn't mind."

He began to bluster, then realized from her cheeky smile that she was winding him up again. "You're welcome to stay, of course. But only for the weekend. Then I have to concentrate on nothing but the case."

"I have a hotel already booked, my gallant policeman. But surely you should be working the weekend as well to catch this killer." The music chose that moment to stop, and her last few words were loud in the sudden quiet. The bikers who had settled at the next table were watching them with open curiosity.

"Shall we go somewhere a little more discreet?" he suggested.

"Like your house? Ah, I knew you couldn't resist your little Polish lady for long, Detective Derek."

"For fuck's sake. That's not what I meant, and stop with the names. "

"It *is* what you meant. I can read it in your eyes. Okay. If you want to ravish me at your house, I am willing." She was talking deliberately loudly to antagonize him. It was part of her mischievous personality, and he had to admit it was frustratingly endearing.

He led her out to his Merc, parked a few roads down from the ancient pub.

He opened the door for her, slid in next to her, and reached for the key.

"You look tired," she said, fastening her seat belt. "Haven't you been sleeping?"

He fired up the engine. The Damned's *The Black Album* was in the CD slot, Dave Vanian wailing about Doctor Jekyll and Mr. Hyde.

"Oh, you like punk rock music, yet you hate that pub."

He pulled away from the curb, unsure how to answer.

"Maybe you should have a Mohican haircut." She giggled.

"Where are you staying?" he asked, ignoring her jibes.

"With you, tonight, you lucky, lucky, Mister Punk Policeman."

He poured her a glass of merlot as she settled in his living room, eyeing the rock magazines, the large smart TV, and the general ephemera that constituted a single man's domain.

She chuckled at his framed *Great Rock 'N' Roll Swindle* movie poster. "Do you wish you had been a rock star instead of a policeman?"

He sat on the sofa next to her, took a sip of his wine before answering. He was very conscious that only a few inches separated their bodies. "I'm not in the slightest bit musical. So no."

"I can see you in a band," she carried on, a twinkle in her eye.

Despite his qualms, his fear of relationships and mess, and the enormous pressure he was under to solve the case, he found he was relaxing, enjoying her company far more than he had expected.

"Playing a triangle? Because that's about all I could master."

"I don't know what a triangle is," she said, looking confused. She stared at him thoughtfully. "You don't look like a guitar player. And definitely not a drummer. Have you got a good singing voice?"

He laughed. "If you think a bear guzzling gasoline has a good singing voice, then yes."

She chuckled warmly. "Bass player. Definitely. You are long and skinny, like your hero." She pointed at the cartoonish, oversized image of Sid Vicious on the movie poster, looming over Big Ben. Abruptly, without the slightest change of tone, she added. "How are you going to catch this killer?"

He took another gulp of wine, set the glass down. "I told you, I can't talk about it."

"The killer is leaving clues for you," she continued, ignoring him. "The papers say that Video Nasties are left at the scene of the crime. Is that true?"

"What did I just say to you?"

"I'll take that as yes. In Poland, we are not familiar with your Video Nasties. Horror films are not so popular. But I like them. And I have looked up about these Nasty films."

"Are you listening to a word I'm saying?"

"Only in Britain did this happen. A peculiarly British phenomenon. Very interesting. But I am sure you know all about it."

He thought of Cookie, hoped he was doing his homework, and suddenly felt ashamed that he hadn't undertaken the job of researching the Nasty Phenomenon, as Aneta had referred to it, himself.

He sighed, not wanting to discuss it and at the same time wanting *very* much to discuss it.

"It's in the papers, Derek. Relax. I am only talking about what is already known to the public. The papers are asking what Video Nasty the killer will choose next to implement his M.O."

He glanced at her sharply. Were the tabloids—and it had to be the trashier papers—really playing these games? He should have been on top of it. Their scurrilous resources just might drag something out of the shadows that could be useful. He made a mental note to get Ming on the job of scouring the papers the next day.

"It's a message."

"What is?" His voice was sharp as a gunshot. Her change of conversation had unsettled him. He no longer felt relaxed. He was tense, wire-taut again. He gulped at his wine.

"What the killer is giving you." Her eyes were no longer playful but earnest. "It's a clear message. Maybe you are chasing down certain people you suspect, but I can see from your body language you are not finding what you want. Maybe you are too close to see. Look wider, look at the broader picture, too, at what this killer is telling you; the films themselves maybe point toward something."

He thought of his persecution of Jem Whateley, of how it had led him down a blind alley. Had his focus been too narrow? Part of him still believed Jem was in some way implicated in the crimes, but he couldn't understand how. Too much of a coincidence otherwise, surely? That all three murders involved people he was either jealous of or had been fighting with. All the police instincts he'd honed over the years were insisting he'd been right to chase Whateley. But what Aneta was saying was uncannily on the money. How could she have picked up so much just from reading the papers? He looked at her sharply.

As if reading his mind *again*, she smiled waspishly. "And now you are wondering why I am so interested in your weird British murder crimes? Are you going to shout at me for talking business?" She winked playfully.

"I want to know how you jump to the conclusion that I've been chasing certain people. Please don't tell me the papers are following my every move?"

"Of course they are. Like you, they have their informants. What do you call it, sneaky noses?"

"Snouts." He almost smiled, but he was unsettled by her words. Of course, the papers would be hounding him, using their own sources to dig deep. And they already knew Whateley had been arrested and then released. He'd expected that, though he hadn't bothered following their reports. For a moment he had worried they were onto the other suspects he had in his sights. He sighed. Of course not. How could they? She'd obviously been busy reading while on the plane, at the airport, that's all.

She sipped her own wine, the movement slow, seductive. Her voice was seductive, too, the accent lulling him. He felt the wine and Aneta's presence slowly working on him. He thought of what they might be doing very soon in his bedroom (after he'd tidied away the dirty underwear and socks that would inevitably be curled up on the carpet). He felt a warm glow start to creep up his body.

And then she ruined it again.

"For a sleazy crime, you need to find a sleazy man."

He put his glass down, exasperated. "For the last time, can we stop talking about this? I'm actually glad to see you, Aneta. I really am. But you have to stop worrying at my case like a sexy, little Polish terrier." He leaned back on the sofa. Silence for a moment while she sipped her wine, unconcerned by his outburst. Then, giving in, "What do you mean by 'a sleazy man'?"

She put her own glass on the table, leaned toward him a little. "Well, obviously the person who did this is depraved, whether they are man or woman. They are killing people in most violent and sadistic fashion, copied from very violent and unpleasant films. Do you agree so far?"

He nodded.

"But what do you know about these films that the killer is using as macabre set dressings at each crime? Like grisly metaphors. Like grave markers." She was becoming more excited as she continued, and Stone was catching some of it now. She was putting thoughts into his head that should already have been there.

"Metaphors? What d'you mean by that?"

"Like I said, the killer is sending you an ironic message. You have to analyze what that message is and why the killer is sending it to you."

"You think the videos are the key?"

"Of course. They are essential components of the killer's modus operandi. You know this. But what do they tell you? This is where you must concentrate. Maybe the answer to that will lead you to this monster."

He thought again of Cookie, sweating over his video viewing. Stone was already chasing the nasty angle, obviously, but Aneta was looking at things from a fresh angle. He had assumed the video nasties were just a cruel joke, a mocking gesture. What if they meant more?

"You mentioned a 'sleazy man'…"

"Besides you, you mean?" Her eyes momentarily regained their naughty twinkle before seriousness chased it away. "You obviously don't know much about these films. Probably because they are not starring Sid Vicious, or…whoever that is." She pointed at another framed movie poster, *Apocalypse Now*.

"You kidding me? You don't know Martin Sheen?"

She ignored that, caught up in her own excitement. "To know about sleazy films, you need to speak to someone who understands them."

He scratched his nose. "And who do you suggest, Aneta Conan Doyle?

"I am not here to do all your work for you, Derek. First, you must pay me." She winked again.

And this time, he could resist no longer. He leaned forward and pulled her to him.

Sid Vicious leered down at them as they kissed while Johnny Rot-ten vomited into the Thames.

CHAPTER FIVE

Cookie took the stand. Apparently, his skill set had no end as he showed off his professionally prepared slide show. Stone and Darke were sitting at the front as D.C. Cooke started the slides with a brief introduction, reading aloud from the words on the screen.

"The Video Nasty phenomenon originally came about due to public and political outcry in the early eighties when a large number of unclassified films released by fledgling and maverick video distribution companies released uncensored material following a loophole in the law. Only films shown at the cinema were legally bound to be assessed and censored first by the British Board of Film Classification. The law didn't take into account the invention of video cassette recorders, which began being manufactured in the late seventies but became an item in pretty much every household by the early to mid-eighties." He paused to make sure they were all listening.

"Very good, Professor Cooke," Stone said. "Your research is definitely showing."

"Something is," D.C. Wells quipped. "His fly is undone."

Cookie checked his trousers before straightening again with a mortified expression. "Do you want to hear this or not?"

"Let the big lad speak," Darke chided them. "It's not often he's so eloquent."

"He's nicked it all off the internet," Ming pointed out. "I helped him."

"If I may continue," Cookie said in his best Boycie. General laughter. It was good to see the squad relaxing, if only for a short while, after the constant pressure they were under to bring this case to a conclusion. For this reason more than anything, he was prepared to let Cookie do a Led Zep and ramble on.

"As a result of the floodgates being opened on a torrent of films claimed to be unsuitable for viewing in the home, the Video Recordings Act was set up in nineteen-eighty-four, which stated that commercial video recordings for sale or rent must carry a B.B.F.C. classification. A list was then compiled by the Director of Public Prosecutions of seventy-two films that were believed to violate the Obscene Publications Act of nineteen-fifty-nine. These were films deemed most likely to 'deprave and corrupt.' The list was modified as prosecutions were dropped or failed, resulting in a definitive list of thirty-nine titles that were actually prosecuted. This became the hardcore thirty-nine." He stopped for breath.

"Shall we cut through the bullshit a little?" Stone interrupted. "Are any of the videos left at the murder scenes on this list?"

"Yes and no," replied Cooke. "Looking back to the York Dave Fenton inquiry, the video found next to his corpse, *Mark of the Devil*, was on a section three sub-list, which consisted of films still liable to be seized by police under a 'less-obscene' charge. These were films that attracted their own fair share of notoriety. *The Evil Dead*, which was one of the major objects of the Nasty witch hunts, was actually never prosecuted but remained a hot potato until a censored version was released a few years later. This, of course, is the baby that ended up next to Guy Johns's exposed and desecrated anus in Lords Wood."

"Can we show a bit more respect for the deceased?" Darke was not as enamored of Cooke's rough talk as some of the male detectives filling the room.

"Sorry, Sarge. Where was I? Cookie glanced back at the screen.

"Finishing off, we hope," Stone said.

"He's normally very quick at that; his missus told me." Wells again.

Cooke ignored him. "The important thing to remember is that our perp seems to be picking films from these lists. *SS Experiment Camp* was a major league Nasty, definitely one of the most prosecuted on the top list of banned thirty-nine. But apparently, mostly because of the cover. Which I'll show you in due course."

"What about *Caligula*?" asked Stone.

"Things get complicated there. It was dubbed 'the most controversial film of the eighties,' and was objected to by the B.B.F.C., Customs and Excise, and various lawyers due to the copious amounts of sex and violence, and, in fact, never made any of the lists because it didn't get a video release until nineteen-ninety, and that was heavily cut."

"Impressive stuff, Cookie." Stone meant it. Cooke hadn't read the last bit from any screen. He'd obviously been diligent with his homework.

Cooke then proceeded to take them through an A to Z of the infamous 39 Video Nasties. He'd copied photographs of all the covers and accompanied each lurid shot by reading out the film in question's even more lurid tagline, throwing in a gritty little précis every now and then to keep his audience awake.

"*Axe*. 'At Last… Total Terror!'" He glanced back at the artwork gracing the screen. A huge axe occupied the foreground, buried in a shadowy skull. Satisfied they'd taken that in, he activated the PowerPoint to the next shot.

"*Absurd*. 'Brutal!… Shocking!… Violent!… Savage! Not for the Squeamish.' Apparently, this one's called *Horrible* in France. Bit of a statement of the obvious there."

"Both titles are grabbing me," Ming remarked from just behind Stone. "Is it all about your sex life?"

Guffaws all around. Stung, Cookie moved on to the next cover. "*Anthropophagus the Beast*. Interestingly a clip from this one made the six o'clock news in the early nineties, following another clamp down on video nasties. Crazy, giant bastard on a Greek Island who eats his own intestines, apparently."

"Definitely all about Cookie on his summer hols then," Ming couldn't resist adding.

"All right, calm down," Stone said over the resulting mirth. "Let the giant bastard enjoy his holiday slides."

"Do you want me to continue or not?" Cookie asked with a wounded expression.

"As long as it doesn't take all day." Stone stretched his feet out and crossed his arms.

"*The Beast in Heat*." Cooke turned to view the image on the screen, which depicted a buxom woman being pursued by a hairy, apelike brute. A massive swastika floated in the background. "This one's interesting. Not the film itself, which is, apparently, utter garbage, but its collectability status. One of the hardest-to-find Nasties on the list, with prices ranging up to a grand on eBay and through private sellers. Safe to say our perp won't be dropping this one at the scene of the crime."

"And people pay that sort of amount?" Stone straightened in his chair. A grand for an old VHS was silly money indeed, especially for what was, by Cookie's own account, a terrible film.

"Apparently so. I've done a bit of research. As soon as it appears for sale, it's snatched up. The prices are increasing. It's rare because the distributor didn't release many copies."

"Any other expensive ones?"

"*The Devil Hunter*. Another piece of cinematic feces by all accounts. But rare as a nun's orgy."

"Is that on the list, too?" quipped Wells.

"It would certainly be on mine if it existed," Cookie said with a straight face.

"All right, less locker room, more Murder Squad, please." Darke put the office back in order.

"*Blood Bath*. 'They came seeking pleasure, they found death.'" The cover displayed a bloody machete being wielded and an octopus tentacle looped around a corpse's throat.

"Sounds like the massage parlor on City Road," Wells chortled. "Some of the women in there could give you a coronary."

Darke glared at him. Cookie flicked on to the next slide.

"*Blood Feast*. 'Nothing so appalling in the annals of Horror.'" Nubile woman being bisected with a chopper.

"How many did you say are on this list?" Stone asked as the slide show flicked to the next cover.

"Thirty-nine, boss."

"We're not sitting through another thirty of these. Cut to the chase. What have you learned about the Nasties that might be relevant to the case?"

Cookie shrugged.

"You've just been having a good time, haven't you?" Darke shook her head.

Cookie was thinking. You could tell from his vacant expression. "I think what's relevant is that any one of these films could be used for reference by the perp." He looked pleased with that.

"Except for *Devil Hunter* and *Bitch in Heat*," Ming slipped in. "Because they're too expensive to leave around."

"Unless our perp has lots of money," Stone said. "And judging from the films he's left behind so far, even if he hasn't got money, he's certainly a collector. How much are *SS Camp* and *Evil Dead* to buy on V.H.S.?"

"Give me a minute." Cookie whipped out his phone and searched. Then whistled. "*SS Camp* is going for two hundred and forty pounds. *Evil Dead* original release one hundred pounds."

"Not cheap, then. So that doesn't rule out the other two. Main thing I asked you to do, besides pleasuring yourself to naked S.S. babes and octopus sex, was to cross reference possible connections to upcoming productions. Did you manage to do that between all the sweat and tissues?"

Cookie looked hurt again. "Yer. Ming and me had a look. If you'd let me get as far as *I Spit on Your Grave*, you'd have seen what I was building toward."

"Give us the cut version."

"There is a British remake in pre-production right now, to be filmed in Bristol, Somerset, and South Wales."

"Of *I Spit?*"

"Yer." Cooke had long since gotten accustomed to his peers mocking his peculiar version of yes and stubbornly continued to use it all the time, as if it was part of his post-modern ironic repertoire. Or maybe it was just his Gloucestershire farm upbringing rearing its rustic head.

"Then we need to be all over it. Let's chat with the producer, director, screenwriter… Hell, let's talk to the honey wagon cleaners that are booked for it. We want to know everything about this flick before it even sets up cameras. Good work, Cookie. Any others either shooting or being planned with links to Nasties?"

"I've made a list, guv. Nothing too obvious. But then some of them could just have minor elements in them this nutter might pin a Nasty to. I'll go through it with you later. But *I Spit* is the big one. It's a red flag to this mad bull."

Stone had to agree it seemed a very likely candidate. "Excellent work, Cookie."

The big D.C. grimaced, which was his version of a smile, and began striding away from the PowerPoint.

"Just before you quit the limelight, how did it go with our NoMeans-No pal?"

Cookie paused. Sneered. "He's got 'wrong un' written all over him. But as per[12], he used the ladies as a shield. Told me to ask them where he was, meaning he was clinging to 'em like dried snot throughout the day. Annoying bastard, if you don't mind me saying."

Stone nodded. "Can they corroborate his whereabouts during the time Trenchard was killed?"

"They'd all pissed off home by then, according to Thorogood. Tina Bell said the same. She couldn't confirm where Thorogood went after that, though. She said he asked her for a drink, but she declined, which doesn't surprise me. Guy's a slime."

"Because he protests against inequality for women and the distasteful way they're treated in the film industry?" Darke's face was stern. "Is *that* what you mean, Detective Constable?"

Cookie had spoiled his trousers on what had otherwise been a day of unusually high achievement for the big lug. Stone grinned, moved them on rapidly, climbing to his feet to take center stage.

---

[12] Common British usage for "as per usual"

"What Cookie's superlative presentation skills have steered us toward is a better understanding of the mentality of our perpetrator and the M.O. being utilized. We can see the killer knows their Nasties, which suggests a horror fiend or a deviant collector. Maybe someone who has access to these rare and extortionately priced videos through other means. I want to know if any S.A.s, crew members, or actors on the three affected productions have any known affiliations with film markets, film fairs, conventions, or old video rental libraries. This nut job is clearly influenced by these films. I'd go so far as to say he or she has an unhealthy obsession with them. We've already discussed the idea of the killer being some kind of role-player. What about a thwarted actor? Or is the perp making some kind of ironic statement with these Nasties? Critic with a grudge? Targeting certain people in the industry or just showing off?"

"What d'you mean by showing off, guv?" Wells asked.

"Leaving Video Nasties behind at crime scenes like a graffiti artist tagging walls. We have here a serial killer Banksy, chucking V.H.S. boxes around instead of spray paint. Showing off. Leaving a message." A memory of Aneta naked in bed flashed into his mind. He got rid of it quickly. "The killer thinks they're clever and artistic, in a very twisted way. That's definitely what I'm picking up from this fucker. A sick puppy with a creative bent. But where's the perp getting these films? Find out." He scanned the rows of faces in front of him. "Get onto film collectors and sellers advertising on the internet, find out if they've flogged any Video Nasties lately. Check out film convention organizers, eBay sellers who specialize in horror films, ask if they've supplied to regular buyers. Horror movie mags—I'm sure there are a few available on the newsstands. Speak to the editors, read the classified ads, see if anyone is after Nasties."

D.S. Fairchild's phone rang, interrupting him. He waited for her to answer before continuing.

"We let Whateley go, but we'd already searched his premises. Nothing to get excited about. We've got absolutely sod all back from forensics on all three murder scenes. Blood at Auschwitz was all Trenchard's, as expected. But we have a unique angle on the *SS Experiment Camp* and *Evil Dead* copycat killings in that, in each case, the gender of the victim has been reversed. The cover of *SS* shows a naked female, but our perp strung Ben Trenchard on barbed wire; likewise, in the Sam Raimi flick, the tree roots rape a woman, not a man. Was this deliberate? Is this a crazy S.J.W. twist?"

He paused to let that sink in. "This fruitcake is thorough. But is he Thorogood? I want that greasy spoon watched. Does he secretly love horror films? Does he pester Tina Bell? What's his favorite porn mag? Does he *really* believe this S.J.W. stuff, or is he using it for his own sticky ends? Charlie, I think you're the man for that. Get in his face. Stalk him like he clearly stalks his female friends. And what about the other women campaigners? We don't know enough about them. Get on it. I'll let D.S. Darke allocate that one."

He wracked his brain for other loose ends he could send his trusty D.C.s to tie up. "Guy Johns's demon costume came back with prints all over it, but nothing we can spotlight. Blood traces were all Guy's. Just like with *The Evil Dead* and *Caligula* tapes, there were no prints on the *SS Experiment Camp* V.H.S. either—apart from Ben's bloody one. Looks like our Nasty Nazi racially cleansed the lot. How about C.C.T.V. coverage of roads into Bristol on the nights concerned, Ming?"

D.C. Sung pulled a face. "Still viewing footage of cameras around and outside Taunton. Nothing significant yet, guv. Blanks from the other two nights. All vehicles entering Bristol at that time accounted for, with no suspicious motives. Of course, the killer might not have been returning to Bristol."

"And yet Bristol has been the center of the map as far as these killings are concerned." Stone pointed at a map on the incident board, with three pins indicating the murder scenes. "And the perp could have used back roads into the city with no cameras, as we discussed. Keep up the viewing, though, Ming: it's good for your posture." He let out a long breath, strolled along the row of desks and expectant D.C.s.

"We talked about how opportunistic the previous murders were, whether the perp was biding his time to strike in hiding or walking about as a member of the production. But this new murder suggests something else. Was he meeting someone? Was the perp invited onto the set especially? Still no sign of Trenchard's phone, but I will be speaking to someone I gather our Ben would very much have liked to have met as soon as I wrap this up. Sue?"

D.S. Fairchild was waving at him from her desk, having finished her conversation.

"Just heard back from Ben Trenchard's mobile supplier. The last recorded call to his phone came from a mobile reported stolen two weeks previously."

"Why doesn't that surprise me? Thanks, Sue." He glanced back at Cooke's PowerPoint screen, still showing the last video cover he'd clicked on. It was titled *The Burning.* "The Most frightening of all maniac films," ran the tagline. As he stared at the hideous image of a man consumed by flames, he was again struck with the feeling he was missing something. And just like the day before on leaving the Brigstowe Agency, he knew it was no good trying to corner that feeling. That way, it would only recede even further down a misty tunnel of insubstantial memory. No, he would just have to wait until it ambushed him unawares, like a maniac leaping from a bush with an axe.

What had the tagline screamed? "At last…Total Terror."

He knew full well from all the frantic calls productions in the South West were making to Avon and Somerset for more protection that the killer had certainly achieved that.

And, contemplating another Nasty Cookie had so diligently shown them, this reliance on tagging the S.O.C.s with horrible videos was patently and morbidly *Absurd.*

But that didn't help Stone in any way or form.

He looked up to see D.C.I. Thornton beckoning to him from the back of the Inquiry Room, clearly hunting down updates. Here was someone else who wanted a *Blood Feast.*

And all the plasma would be Stone's.

CHAPTER SIX

"What do you want?"

Christine Thomas's voice on the intercom was aggravated. Well, that was a shame. After being growled at for an hour by Thornton about how he needed to "close down this case" within the next few days or The Super and the Chief Constable were going to use Stone's balls for Christmas tree decorations, he wasn't in the mood for pretty, spoiled little girls.

Her flat was in Clifton. Of course it was. Stately townhouse, a nice, quiet road. How could she afford that on a supporting artist's wages? Had to be Mummy and Daddy.

"It's Detective Inspector Stone, Miss Thomas."

"I know. I peered out of the window. What do you want now?"

"We need to speak to you. Let us in please."

"It's not very convenient."

Tough. He could feel his temper rising. Darke gave him a warning look.

"Here or at the station, Miss Thomas. Your choice."

The front door clicked open.

Stone followed Darke up the immaculately maintained stairwell to the first floor, waited while the D.S. rapped on the door of Christine's flat.

She answered after keeping them waiting as long as she could. She looked petulant and sulky. She led them inside and stood impatiently in the middle of the lounge without offering them seats. Stone didn't mind; he chose the sofa, as did Darke. Christine remained standing. She clearly wanted to hurry this along.

"Please sit, Miss Thomas," Darke said, a note of irritation in her voice, too.

"I don't see the point of you being here. What have I got to do with all this?"

"I believe you were familiar with Ben Trenchard," Darke said while Stone picked up *The Magus* from the coffee table, flicked through it, dropped it again.

"I knew him a bit, yes. He was the cameraman on the film I've just been working on. But I'm sure you know that. And, of course, I was sorry to hear about what happened." She shuddered. Putting it on? Stone watched her body language closely. There was something she was hiding.

"I hear he was… How shall we put this…interested in you."

Christine stared at him, lips pressed tightly together. *Is that what you didn't want us to know?* She hadn't exactly been discreet, by all accounts, about going for lunch with him, a tasty snippet of info the security man at the gate had readily provided. A "blonde, pretty woman in her thirties, supporting artist."

"I think he liked me, yes. But he was friendly with a lot of women on set."

"But you went out for a drink with him?"

She looked away, her face twisting, looking worried. Suddenly she looked Stone straight in the eye. "Did this happen because of me?"

"What d'you mean by that?"

"Was he killed because he took me for lunch?" She looked terrified. *An act?*

"Now, why would you say that? Do you know someone who might be jealous of you?"

She looked away again.

Darke took out her notepad, always a sign she was interested. "Would that person be Jem Whateley?"

She gave a little shrug. She looked uncomfortable.

"But we both know that was impossible, don't we?" Stone said. "Jem was locked up in a cell dreaming of you when Trenchard was killed."

She nodded but still looked unhappy.

"Does he have anyone who might possibly act on his behalf? While he was banged-up, I mean?"

"You mean a hitman?" She sneered. "This isn't Miami!"

"No, it isn't, but it's not looking like the chilled-out green city it used to be anymore, either. Answer the question."

"I don't know."

"But according to our records, you know him very well. Come from the same town, don't you? Grew up together."

"Not exactly." Looking defensive now. Trying to distance herself from him? "He was five years older. We didn't hang out until a lot later. After school."

The cover of *The Burning* on Cooke's slide show suddenly slipped into sharp focus in his mind, triggered by her words, and the nagging feeling that had tormented him just before entering Thornton's office that he was missing something was at least partially satisfied. He knew there were other relevant but infuriatingly elusive connections still floating around waiting to be made in the morass that was his brain, but he'd snag them eventually, too. Just as he always did, *usually* just in time for it to be useful on a case. He might be forgetful, his frazzled memory a well-worn tool, scratched and dented, but it tended to get the job done in the end.

"Would that be the same school in which a Drama teacher burned to death?"

She looked startled. "Do you want to pin that on me as well?"

He stared back without answering.

She finally sat down in the armchair. "I was not much more than a child when that happened. It was horrible. The Drama Hall was partially burned down. They abandoned it and built a new one closer to the school. The old one you had to cross the playing fields to get to. Pretty isolated. We used to keep away from it after that. We thought it was haunted."

"Haunted?" Darke took an interest, leaning forward.

"By old Missus Carruthers. The Drama teacher. But we never saw anything. Think it's still there, half burned down. I don't know why they didn't demolish it. Probably a financial thing, too much cost involved, as usual. So they'd rather leave it there, fenced off like a creepy memorial." She shuddered again, yet this time it looked more heartfelt, like the nasty event from her past had more meaning than the present-day murder. "Horrible."

"And did the stories about it being haunted also involve rumors about how she died?" Darke was clearly fascinated. But then, morbid things always did have a draw for her. She might have the brightest blue eyes and the sunniest of smiles, but some of her interests were as dark as her name. Which certainly helped, with some of the grisly details they were involved with in their line of work. Stone returned his gaze to Christine.

"She always had a fag in her hand. Chain smoker. I can remember her quite clearly, sitting in her little office in the Drama Hall or outside the door, puffing away at a cigarette. The Drama Hall was very old. It might not even have belonged to the school and was just used by them, so maybe it was down to a rights issue why the ruin was never rebuilt. I don't know." She looked at Stone with an odd smile. "She dropped her cigarette, didn't she? That's what the papers said. She fell asleep reading her precious scripts—she was mounting a new play—and dropped off and burned."

"Does that amuse you?"

She snarled. "Oh, fuck off. I'm trying to be helpful here. Of course it doesn't. I was fond of old Missus Ruthers, as we called her. I'm remembering painful things and trying to keep a brave face. Or am I under suspicion for burning an old woman to death, too?"

"Nobody said you were under suspicion for anything, Miss Thomas," Darke said quickly.

"You clearly think I'm involved in something." She looked away, angry… *Scared? Or acting again?* Stone was beginning to enjoy himself, relaxing as his professional police hound instincts clicked and whirred like cogs in their usual fashion. They might need oiling, just like his memory, but they still operated pretty well. This young woman fascinated him. She was paranoid, scared, combative, secretive (guilty?), and feisty all at once. He could spend all day asking her questions and watching her twitch. But they didn't have all day. He had to pull this in.

"So, how was lunch with Mister Trenchard?" he asked, returning her thoughts to the present.

She shrugged, looked at the carpet. "Very pleasant. He was nice." A flicker of sadness on her face? Regret?

"Did you arrange to meet again?"

She looked up, and the fight was back in her eyes. "Yes, Inspector, in the S.S. Death Camp at midnight."

"Did I say Trenchard was killed at midnight?"

She scowled. Shook her head.

"Where were you that evening, Miss Thomas?" Darke had her eyes fixed on Christine like a ferret about to take down a mouse. He would have to tease her about that later. She wouldn't warm to the comparison.

"You should know."

"Should I?"

"You mean your duty sergeant hasn't told you? I was at Avon and Somerset police station, asking to see my friend." The wicked smile was back.

"You were visiting Mister Whateley? What time would this have been?"

"I can't remember exactly. Seven-ish. Why don't you check?"

"That's that then," Stone said brightly and patted his knees as if about to rise. "But there's one more thing I need to ask you."

"Go for it, Columbo."

Darke gave him a wry smirk. He smiled expansively at Christine.

"You don't seem to be taking the murder of your date very seriously."

Her eyes narrowed. "I already explained that. I'm dealing with it in my way. And he *wasn't* my date. We had a very quick lunch. I hardly knew him."

"Did you like him?"

She put her head in her hands, rubbed her face. "Yes. He was charming. And good looking. And I'm fucking sorry he's dead, and I'm very worried that the crazy fuck who's been murdering people on film sets is going to come after me as well. Happy now?" She looked up at him, her eyes deep and spooked. Acting, or legit? Stone's nose was letting him down for once because he couldn't decide.

"Why would you think they're after you?"

She got up, moved to the window, stared out at the November rain that had just started. "I don't know. It just feels…personal? And way too close for comfort."

"Then my suggestion to you, Miss Thomas, is to stay away from film productions. At least until we find the perpetrator."

"Very kind of you to think of my safety," she said coldly. "But it won't pay my bills, will it?"

He stood up, prepared to leave her with one last question—*another* last question. Darke rose, too, notebook still in hand for any possible revelation.

"Can you think of anyone—besides Jem Whateley, that is—who might have an issue with Trenchard? For whatever reason? Maybe someone was angry or jealous of him? Did he mention anything over lunch?"

"He didn't mention his girlfriend, that's for sure. I didn't know he had one until I read the paper." She remained with her back to them, staring gloomily out at the rain.

"There are probably lots of women who fancied him. On set, I mean. Female members of the crew, maybe. Definitely S.A.s."

"I can imagine," Stone said. "For a cameraman to go out with an S.A. must be a big deal—for the supporting artist, at least. I can imagine you ruffled some feathers."

She shrugged. "There's always competitiveness and jealousy on set, for a whole load of reasons."

"Can you think of any particular female S.A. who might have been more than usually jealous?"

She turned round. "There's always bitching on set, too. I'm not going to be one of them. And I'm not going to do your job for you either. I have to look after myself now." She looked a little scared again.

"Would Jane Tighe be one of those female S.A.s?"

She sighed. "Who knows?" She smiled wryly. "You'd have to ask her. But I'm sure she wasn't the only one. Like I said, plenty of bitching on set. And Ben was a good catch."

"Pity you didn't land him, then." Stone smiled back to show her he wasn't being mean, *really*. "Take care, Miss Thomas." He followed Darke to the door, pulled it closed after him.

"She's spooked," said Darke as they made their way down the stairs.

"Wouldn't you be?"

Darke opened the front door, grimaced at the rain. "Could be an act. She *is* an actress."

"She's an extra. Big difference."

"You like her, don't you?"

"Darke? Get in the car."

He glanced up just before he closed the car door.

Christine's face was still at the window.

CHAPTER SEVEN

It wasn't very far to Gibbet Lane. The address Stone was looking for was just three miles outside the South Eastern limits of Bristol.

"You seem perkier than usual," Darke said as the Merc left the last suburb behind and entered the lush countryside. "Why does that make me suspicious?"

"You've got a copper's mind." Rolling Somerset hills opened up all around them, and the sun had emerged to brighten the landscape. "You just don't know when to switch off."

"You keep smiling to yourself as well."

"Let it go, Sergeant." There was no way he was going to tell her about Aneta. Just no way. He suddenly realized she would be gone the next day and was shocked at how sad that made him. One more evening with her, and then he was determined to forget her, concentrate on the case. "Did you brief Wells on Jane Tighe?"

"Smooth convo gear change. He knows what he's doing; he'll go gently."

"Don't want her spooked."

"Is that why you sent Wells instead of interviewing her yourself?"

"She's a gossip. Potentially, a malicious one. And also a potentially useful witness to Ben Trenchard's behavior and those involved with him. If we go in heavy-handed, she'll freak and clam up."

"Great name," Darke said as Stone turned right onto the sinister-sounding Gibbet Lane.

"Thought you'd like it. Probably used to hang highwaymen here." Half a mile down the narrow, winding road, Stone pulled up outside the gates of a low-lying, Los Angeles-style ranch house, all stucco walls and myriad extensions. They could see a splendid chandelier inside one of the windows.

"Bit bling for a writer," Darke said as Stone killed the engine.

"Must be doing all right for himself. According to Scorby, he's the 'go to' script writer in the South West. Also, according to Scorby, he's a hack."

"Doing all right for a hack."

They left the car on the verge outside the gate, and Stone walked up to the entry box, pressed the button.

A woman's voice greeted them, sounding wary. Probably thought they were trying to sell her something.

"Could I speak to Jack South, please. Detective Inspector Stone and D.S. Darke." He waved his warrant card at the security camera fixed above the front porch. The gates clicked and whirred inward. The door opened before they got halfway across the gravel drive, and a woman wearing riding galoshes waited for them. She had long, dark, curly hair and a very healthy complexion. She smiled tautly at them.

"I'm afraid you've missed him. Can I help with anything?"

Stone crunched to a halt. "Do you know where we can find him?"

She paused. A worried look erased the smile. "Is there something wrong?"

"No," Darke said emotionlessly. "We just need to follow up on some inquiries with Mister South. Could you tell us where he's gone?"

She frowned, not sure whether to tell them or not, until Darke's open smile finally won her over. "Okay. Well, he's not gone far. He's taken Jolly for a walk." She smiled again at their confusion. "Our retriever. He usually strolls down to Stanton Drew stones every morning. There's a footpath around the back of the house, if you want to go that way. Cross a couple of fields, follow the stream, and you're there." She

glanced at their polished shoes. "But you might find it less messy to drive."
She smiled that controlled smile again. "I do hope Jack isn't in any trouble."

"Just routine," Darke said as they turned back toward the car.

They followed the sat nav to Stanton Drew, passing a quaint cottage erected in the middle of a crossroads that looked like a giant mushroom. Darke gazed at it through the windscreen as it drew closer. "Fancy living in there? Would suit you. Bit odd."

Stone ignored her childish conversation and took a tree-lined lane that meandered up toward the village of Stanton Drew. They followed the brown sign indicating the Stanton Stones and were soon pulling up beside a farm building and a small row of cottages. A stile opened onto a field glistening with dew in the thin November sunlight.

They left the car and climbed over the stile. They could see the ancient stones leaning at the far end of the field. Not a large circle, but impressive nonetheless. The two detectives scanned the stones, searching for the figure of a man with a dog.

"There he is," Darke said, pointing toward the last stone on the right. A man was reclining on the flat rock, a Golden Retriever sitting at his feet.

Stone eyed the moist grass and occasional cow pats with trepidation.

"Just make sure you don't get cow shit on your Heron," Darke said with a cruel smile.

"I'm not gonna lie down on the grass, Darke. We're not having a bloody picnic." He paused, looked at her hopefully. "Unless you've brought a pork pie and some crisps?"

"I've got a bottle of Malbec in my bra as well, guv."

"Wondered why you looked so lumpy."

"You're *definitely* in a better mood today. Met someone nice, have we?"

Stone scowled. The detectives canned the chat as they drew closer. The man noticed them and sat up, the dog eyeing them curiously.

Jack South was in his late thirties, with short, dark hair, an oiled goatee, and a wide smile, wearing jeans and a well-worn leather jacket. He looked urbane and content.

"Down, boy," Darke warned Stone between her teeth when she spotted the goatee.

"Jack South? D.I. Stone and D.S. Darke. Your partner told us we'd find you here. Could we have a word?"

"You can have several," he said with a disarming smile. "I'm not in a rush." He shuffled his bottom to the edge of the flat stone, which rose about three feet above the ground, dangled his legs over. "Darke and Stone? Can I steal your names for a script I'm working on? I couldn't improve on those. What's this about?"

Stone ignored the writer's flippancy. "We'd like to discuss your involvement in certain productions. Particularly the one called..." He trailed off, realizing he didn't have a clue what the Auschwitz-based film was actually titled. He turned to Darke.

Jack South came to his rescue. "*The Gate of Death.*"

Stone nodded. Of course it was.

"I'm sorry to disappoint you, Inspector, and to bring you all this way for nothing, but I can't really help you with much." He leaned down and stroked the head of the retriever that was still watching Stone with big, brown eyes.

"We understand you wrote the screenplay," Stone fastened another button on his Heron coat.

"Nice coat," South said with another winning smile. "AllSaints?"

"Could you answer the question, please?" Darke cut in, her stomach unable to deal with Stone's preening. "This is a very serious matter."

"Sorry, Sergeant," South said, rolling his eyes at Stone, who narrowed his own warningly to show he was above flattery and conspiratorial laddishness.

"I wrote the original draft, yes," South continued. "But the producer, in his wisdom, decided his ideas were rather loftier than mine, apparently, and demanded a rewrite. When I told him that would involve neutering the projects and making it as exciting and appealing to the public as an episode of *Country File*, he got all bitter and twisted and had me replaced."

"And how did that make you feel?" Darke asked.

"Obviously upset. But not enough to kill the D.O.P." He dropped his jaw in mock amazement. "Tell me that's not why you're here? Has Scorby been making accusations? I'm a bloody screenwriter, not a psychopath."

"Nobody's been making accusations." Stone eyed a crow that was perched on a nearby monument, watching them. He'd never liked crows. Evil things. "We're just talking to everybody involved in the production in question. We were also told you provided a screenplay for another film recently?"

"Which would that be? I'm very prolific." Another boyish smile. It didn't work on Darke.

"You seem to be doing very well on it," she said tersely. "Nice house you have there."

The smile tucked itself away. "That mostly belongs to my wife. She came into an inheritance. But my screenplays have earned me a good living; I can't deny it. Even the ones that get dropped by sanctimonious idiots who think they're the next bad boy of cinema. They still paid me for it, so as long as I get the gold, they can be as self-righteous and hypocritical as they like."

"Hypocritical?" Stone dragged his attention away from the crow, which was pecking at his nerves.

"Of course, he's a bloody hypocrite. He claimed my script was too exploitative. And then I hear they've got a gratuitous whorehouse scene with lots of naked women. Could you please explain to me how that is *not* exploitation?" His eyes were hard and cold, the charm offensive forgotten.

"I can see that makes you angry, Mister South," Stone said.

"It makes me bloody furious. But not enough to kill anyone. And especially not a cameraman. Why would I?" He laughed at the ridiculousness of the suggestion. "Trenchard had nothing to do with me. I don't think I ever met him on one of the very few times I called in to the production to talk with Scorby. Cameramen don't hang around with producers or scriptwriters. They're usually busy filming."

"We're not saying you *did* kill him," Darke said. "You seem determined to make that supposition all by yourself."

"We asked you about another film you worked on," Stone interrupted. South and Darke were obviously not clicking. And she'd warned *him* about behaving himself just because South had a goatee! "*The Awful Dead.* How did that work out? Not very well, from what I hear."

South looked confused. "I didn't work on that."

Stone watched him carefully. "Our source tells me you did. And apparently, it was another situation where your script was rejected."

"Would this be Scorby?" South laughed mirthlessly. "He's so full of shit! He probably just wanted to stir it, drop me in it with you guys because he knew that *Dead* crap had a similar unfortunate incident."

"Why would he do that?" Darke stepped closer to him. The retriever whined.

"Because I called him a twat to his face, because I insulted his whole pathetic production and threatened to bad mouth him to all my scriptwriter buddies. Which he richly deserved."

"And did you? Bad mouth him, I mean?"

He glared at her. "No. I was just angry. But I'm not vindictive. I just wanted him to sweat because he was such a prick."

"Because he didn't like your script?"

"Because he was a *prick*."

"For a screenplay writer, your vocabulary seems a little limited," Darke said. And then, as South's face darkened, she carried on, "So, you didn't have a script rejected or rewritten on *The Awful Dead*?"

"No!! And even if I had, which I've just categorically explained to you never happened, I wouldn't be so insecure and psychopathic as to kill somebody for it. Especially an innocent extra or a bloody cameraman! I'm a writer. Do you know how much time they spend on sets? We're the great Unwanted on productions. They mess with our words and twist the final product to their own blinkered design, and they sure as buggery don't want us on set to get in the way."

He shuffled off the stone, dropping to his feet to confront Darke, all six-five of him. She returned his angry glare undaunted.

"Calm down, Mister South," Stone said, eyeing a cow wandering toward them dubiously. He'd never liked cows either. He'd been chased by a herd once as a child. Terrified him. "Nobody's saying you did anything. But you do seem very worked up about Mister Scorby."

South turned to him, and the anger began to drain away. He sighed. "You're right. I *am* worked up. If Scorby's been spreading shit about me to you, he's probably done it to other people in the industry—potential employers, producers, directors. But I would never even contemplate writing a script for such a low-brow, derivative piece of shit like *The Awful Dead*, and I resent him fabricating such lies just to deflect the heat from him onto me. Purely motivated by ill will and grudges, that guy."

Stone was still watching the cow from the corner of his eye. Darke glanced at him, wondering if he had any further contributions to make.

"Look, detectives, I can see you've got a job to do, and I sympathize with it. What happened on those two productions was appalling. Hideous. Heinous and evil. Is that enough adjectives for you, Sergeant?" He gave her his patent smile again. "Wouldn't want *another* critic of my words now, would I?" He dropped the smile again when it bounced cleanly off the D.S.

"So you have no idea who might have had a grudge against either production, or anybody involved with them?" Stone asked as the cow moved slowly past the reclining stone.

"Sorry. Can't help." He fished his dog lead out of his jacket pocket. "Come on, Jolly." The dog leaped to its feet, all wag and tongue.

"Not done yet, Mister South," Stone said. Why were people always in a hurry to get away from him? He thought about Aneta again. One more day, and he was wasting it here in this field of stones and cows and crows. At least *she* didn't seem to want to escape him.

"What more could you possibly want from me? I've told you all I know."

"You mentioned Scorby might prejudice you with other producers. And you yourself threatened to bad mouth him amongst your script-writing circle. You must have your fingers in a few pies locally."

South was bending down to attach the lead to the dog's collar. He straightened. "Meaning?"

"Meaning you're a very well-established writer in the South West. You said it yourself. So you must have your ear to the ground."

He nodded, pleased that the line of questioning had swapped an accusatory tone for a more flattering one. "You want to know if I've heard something? I just told you I can't think of anyone involved in those productions—"

"What about other productions?"

"What?" South frowned at Stone.

"Future films, upcoming movies or TV shows. We have a killer who's targeting them, Mister South. So if you can give us any information at all about people involved in the industry who might possibly be in danger, or can think of anyone who bears a grudge or a grievance, no matter how small and insignificant you might think it is, who might be connected to projects we don't know about yet, I'd really appreciate your input. I guess what I'm asking you, Mister South, is whether you know of any wrong 'uns out there. You know the industry well. You know the people. Is there *anyone*—and I don't care if it's a producer, director, writer, clapper board holder, or on-set caterer—who has a particular edge, shall we say? Someone who might raise just the slightest of alarms in your mind."

South thought for a moment. Darke and Stone waited. They could both see his expression change, the brief flit of an idea behind his eyes.

"Is it really for me to cast doubt on others? The way Scorby did with me? Hardly seems fair."

"This is a murder case, Mister South. There's nothing fair about it. Tell us what you know."

"It's probably nothing."

"We could fill a dozen police cells with 'probably nothings,' Mister South."

He grinned. "Can I use that line in one of my scripts?"

Stone's expression told him all he needed to know on that score. He got serious again. "There is a director who I've heard certain things about. And, um, I *have* worked with him as well. In fact, he has a production coming up soon. I provided the script."

Darke had her notebook in her hand as if by magic. "What's it called, and what's the director's name?"

"It's a crime drama. Nothing major. He's probably changed the title by now, as he never liked the one I gave it, which was *Walking Shadow*. You know, from the Macbeth quote?"

"Too literary for him?" Darke said.

"On the contrary, this guy thinks of himself as a bit of an intellectual.

But he didn't like me providing the intellect, so he probably changed the title for one of his own. He didn't think much of my script either, and we had a few creative differences shall we say, so I walked."

"Creative differences?"

South hesitated. He looked guarded now. "Can you promise this goes no further?"

"Unless what you tell us has any direct relation to a current crime, then we will keep your confidences to ourselves, yes," Darke told him.

He nodded, still unsure. "I've seen and heard some kinky things in my time. Caught a couple here amongst the stones once when I was out walking Jolly. The girl was giving the guy a blowie right here in the open in broad daylight. They barely stopped when they saw me. Reckon they enjoyed me being there. And Josh, who owns the farm next to the stones, told me he caught another couple in his shed over there by your car. They were rutting like bunnies at the back of the shed, behind the combine, completely naked. He sent 'em off with a flea in their ears. Must be the stones. Appealing to their wild pagan natures, or something."

"Is there a point to this, Mister South?" Darke was getting impatient.

South scratched the back of his head. "The director's name is Julian Cranleigh. The NoMeansNo campaigners will be all over his new film. I understand they're picketing pretty much every production involving women and violence in the region, though, so that's not much of a surprise. And for once, it's not because of the script or the themes. It's because of the director."

Julian Cranleigh. Again that nagging nudge to Stone's brain that he needed to connect some dots. But right now, nothing. "Go on."

"He's got a reputation. A very low-key one, and I've only heard rumors, nothing concrete." He glanced at Darke. "It seems he has a very unhealthy relationship with his wife. He gets a kick out of beating her when they're having sex. And apparently, she likes it." Darke held his gaze until he dropped his own. He looked at Stone instead, who glared impassively back.

"And what makes you think that?" Stone remained expressionless.

"Like I said: rumors. From other writers and actors who've worked with them. You see, she's an actress, too. She works on all his productions." He started to say something, paused, then said it anyway. "Okay, she told me."

"His wife?"

He nodded.

"She's as fucked up as him. No wonder the NoMeansNo campaigners protested about Cranleigh's last film when it came out on D.V.D. They boycotted various H.M.V. stores, apparently. He's a twisted fuck."

"You sound bitter."

He smiled wryly. "You were about to add 'again,' Sergeant. I'm obliged to you for not doing so. No, I'm not bitter on this occasion. I'm guilty."

"Why would that be, Mister South?

"He chucked me off the *Walking Shadow* production. Got a new scriptwriter to take over. Good luck to them is all I can say."

Bit of a pattern there, eh? Stone was about to say but restrained himself. He put his hands in the pockets of his new coat. "So what exactly are you guilty of, Jack?"

He gave Stone a sheepish grin. "This is where the confidential bit comes in. Please don't repeat any of this to Emily. It would certainly end my marriage."

"We'll do our best."

"I'm only telling you this because I want to contribute in any way I can to help you with this case. Movies are my lifeblood. I hate what's happening and want this sick puppy caught. I'm not saying it's anything to do with Cranleigh; all I can tell you is he's pretty sick, too." He breathed in, staring at the dead tree just beyond the stone circle. More crows were arriving, croaking mournfully. Stone heard them clearly as he waited.

"I've always had a weakness for beautiful women." He glanced at Darke, then quickly away when he saw her hard, cold stare. "He, uh. caught me."

"Caught you?" Stone prompted, although he'd already guessed.

Jack grimaced, but Stone could see he was also preening. "I made a big mistake."

"What did you do, Mister South?" Stone asked.

"She seduced me, Detective Inspector. And I gave in, like the Silly-Billy I am. No wonder he decided to replace me. He doesn't like other people playing with his toys, you see." He studied the crows with a distant smile. "And he caught me playing with his most prized toy of all." He pursed his lips ruefully, but Stone wasn't fooled. He wanted to share this with them. Not only was he enjoying the memory, but it added to the rakish air he tried so hard to cultivate. Just like the goatee. "I plucked forbidden fruit, Inspector Stone. I slept with his wife."

Darke grunted, signaled to Stone that it was time to leave.

"Well, then, it seems to me you should be more careful, Mister South."

South cocked an eyebrow eloquently.

"If he's as twisted as you say he is, you might want to look over your shoulder a bit more. Happy writing."

He left South with a decidedly unsettled look on his face and strode off between the cow pats in pursuit of Darke.

CHAPTER EIGHT

He didn't know what to say now the time had come.

They embraced one last time. She leaned in for a kiss; he went for passionate, but she kept it short.

"Goodbye, Detective Derek." Her eyes were twinkling but also sad. Confusion filled him. He didn't want her to leave. And yet, he wanted her to leave.

He couldn't do this. Not just the relationship thing, that had *never* been him, but more importantly, being distracted by Aneta's undeniably pleasant and exciting company just wasn't what he needed right now. Thornton wanted his scalp as it was. Maybe afterward…

She studied his face for a reaction, seemed about to say something, then changed her mind and instead said, "And remember: your killer is very creative. You should be looking for someone who is imaginative, manic, and incredibly vicious. Someone with a violent past."

He nodded. He didn't want to talk about it, but he had nothing else to say to her. People pushed past them, eager to get the security checks over with. She looked at the airport conveyor belts, clutched the handle of her suitcase with finality.

"I know we will never see each other again, Derek, but it's been fun."

"Don't say that. We will."

She shook her head, certain. "No. We won't. I will never hear from you again. And that's for the best, I think. You live here, and I in Poland. Take care. And good luck finding this beast." She leaned in, one last kiss on his cheek, then turned her back on him. He waited until she was through the security checks, wondering if she would look around, but she didn't.

He made his way down the escalator to the Departure Hall, conflicted, alone again.

As it should be.

"Julian Cranleigh, guv?" Darke stood in the doorway of his office. "Found him?"

"Ohhh, yes. And you'll be very interested to hear it."

She sat down, the glint in her eyes fading as she looked at his face. "You all right?"

"What have you got, Sergeant?" He wasn't in the mood for her probes today. Had he ever been? He kept his secrets, his lies, all to himself. Best way. He was D.I. Stone, gruff and bullish; what you see is what you get. There were no hidden depths. D.I.s didn't need them. *He* didn't need them.

She shrugged his mood away. "I ran a search on Cranleigh, and guess what I found on his C.V.?"

He glared at her.

"He's been a director for years, had a couple of minor T.V. successes and one small cinema hit, but he started out in theater…"

He gave her a "just fucking get on with it" expression. Undeterred, she did so. "Remember our friend Jem was in a play ten years ago? Well, guess who directed it? Under the name Julian Swanheart?"

"*The Epic of Gilgamesh?* So that's where I knew his name from. And Thornton will probably have spoken to him back then, too, when Alexander Fergus went missing. Swanheart? What kind of wanky name is that?"

Darke grinned, glad to see some of her boss's edge back. "He's currently working on the project South mentioned, starts filming next week in Bristol and then London. And he didn't change the title. Still called *Walk-*

ing Shadow. Shall we go speak to him?"

Stone thought about it for a second. "Not yet. Not entirely sure what he's got to do with any of this, if anything at all, despite South's character assassination, but you can run over Thornton's archive interview with him, see if it offers us a clue. Could all be just coincidence. But still interesting. Good work, Darke; we'll chase Swanheart tomorrow. But I want to follow up on a lead Wells has given me first." He tapped a piece of paper in front of him with a scribbled name and address.

"He contacted a couple of editors of horror magazines to see if any of them could point us in a useful direction, and one of them runs a mag called *Horrorscope*, published in Bath. He came up with someone who might give us some valuable insight into the whole Nasties thing."

Darke peered at the scribbled address. "Bridgewater?"

"What's wrong with that?"

"Nothing. Just in the middle of nowt, as my Dad used to say." She picked up the piece of paper. "The Video Coffin? What the hell is that?"

"This guy Gaz Jenson used to run a stall at Saint Nick's Market in Bris, according to the *Horrorscope* editor. Wells pushed him a bit, and the geezer spilled some interesting stuff on Jenson. While he sold legal, certificated vids and then D.V.D.s when that format came along on his stall, he also used to flog illegal and highly collectible V.H.S. nasties from a lock-up to certain 'special' customers. Had quite a few of those apparently, this editor reckoned. He moved down to Bridgewater about six or seven years ago; no idea why. But according to Wells's source, this Gaz guy is a walking, talking A to Z of Video Nasties."

"Thought we had Cooke for that."

"Be interesting to see a list of his 'special clients.'"

Darke nodded. "That's cheered you up anyway. You looked like your face had slapped your arse when I walked in."

"What has? And remember, I'm your bloody boss, arse-slapped face or not."

She did her best cockney. "The possibility of some action, guv! Brisk drive dahn to Bridgewatah, talk to a snout. Get some tasty info on some villains."

Stone sighed. "Get out. And be ready in ten."

Darke stopped at Wells's desk. "Good work on the Bridgewater lead."

He nodded. He hated compliments. He was about to continue with his work searching records, but Darke hadn't finished with him.

"Any idea what's up with him?"

"Who?" Wells's brown eyes narrowed at the D.S.

"The boss. He seems…out of sorts today."

Wells shrugged. "He's always out of sorts. Thought you knew that by now, Sarge."

"Yeah," she bit her lip, pensive. "Even so."

"Thornton's been mounting him on a daily basis, Sarge. Probably needs a funnel to take a dump now. Probably that."

"Gross. And I don't think it's that. Thornton's *always* giving him a hard time. When he can be bothered to leave his office, that is. This is something else. And it's not just this case. I'm used to him being moody when he's in the middle of a murder inquiry, even one as bad as this. This is different and weird. He's up and down like a yo-yo lately."

"Women." Wells gave up on his work, leaned back in his swivel chair.

"Hmm?" *Was he being a sexist prick?* Not usually Wells's style.

"Women trouble, boss."

"Oh. You think?"

Wells nodded. "Can read him a mile off. Yesterday he was all manic, excited, like a bloody kid at the Christmas tree. Today he's like a neglected puppy. Gotta be a woman."

"Well, thanks for that insight, Mister Relationship Guru. Any woman in particular?"

Wells shrugged. "He's not daft enough to tell me, is he?"

"I thought you guys always did the locker room thing?"

"What?" Wells's voice rose in indignation. "You think I'd share a gym locker room with *him*? Outta your mind. Besides, can't really picture the guv'nor in a gym, can you?"

"I meant metaphorically, Wells. Never mind. Carry on frowning at your screen."

He raised an eyebrow at her, but she was already moving on. She glanced at Cooke, slumped with his long legs protruding beyond his desk. *Nah.* Stone was thick with the giant D.C., but not thick enough to confide anything like this to the blabbermouth. Besides, she didn't want Cooke thinking he knew something she didn't. She collected her coat, glanced at the weather outside, and left her umbrella on her desk.

She'd get it out of him on the way down to Bridgewater.

CHAPTER NINE

She got nothing out of him apart from a string of swear words and sexual advice.

"Touchy," she said as the Merc swept past the giant wicker man with his arms outstretched as if pleading with the cars streaming along this stretch of the M5 to slow down. She remembered the figure used to be far more imposing, surrounded only by fields; now a brand-new housing estate had sprung up to either side of its wicker clutch, cornflake-box new builds gathering behind the sculpture as if preparing to attack.

Stone turned off at the junction and followed the sat nav through Bridgewater.

"It's that Polish girl, isn't it?" Darke persisted. "Why don't you tell me."

Stone ignored her, turning up the Ghoultown CD. That was certainly one way of shutting her up. Spaghetti western guitars and trumpets mixed with tequila-soaked vocals. At least it sounded more modern than his usual tastes, if not at all easier on the ears. She gave up, let him brood.

The Video Coffin looked just like a normal terraced corner house, apart from the garish but badly peeling sign above the door and the lurid posters in the windows. Darke was unimpressed with the titles and artwork they revealed. *Bloodsucking Freaks* and *Entrails of a Virgin* didn't promise chilled tea-time viewing.

Stone didn't waste any time pushing through the door.

The shop was filled with movie-based paraphernalia, character figures, T-shirts, mugs, posters, books, soundtrack CDs, shelves of DVDS and Blu-rays, but only a few retro VHS Cassettes, which, while certainly horror, didn't seem to Darke's admittedly untrained eye to be quite the sort of collectible items they were interested in.

A door at the back opened, and a man emerged to greet them. Late forties, slender build, dyed black hair in a rockabilly style, tattoos of skulls and vampires and other weird shit, wearing a *Texas Chainsaw Massacre Part 2* T-shirt.

He gazed at them suspiciously, clearly smelling filth. It didn't just take their suits to give that impression, Darke had long ago realized that. It was their faces, their eyes. She'd resigned herself to the fact that she'd never be mistaken for a children's author or a florist.

"Help you?" he said, meaning the opposite.

Stone did the honors with his warrant card and the introductions. The man grunted.

"Gaz Jenson?"

The Video Coffin proprietor nodded unhappily. "I ain't got nothin' illegal in stock, if that's what you're after."

"That's a shame, Mister Jenson," Stone said smiling, "Because that is *exactly* what we're after."

Jenson crossed his arms. "Got a search warrant?"

"So you *do* have illegal items?"

"Never said that, did I?"

"Relax, Mister Jenson. We're not here to confiscate your wares, although we *are* very interested in them."

The wariness gave way to confusion. Stone elaborated. "You've probably heard about the recent murders in the area?"

Jenson frowned. "What's that gotta do with me?"

"Like I said, we're not here to penalize, but to ask for your help."

He glanced at Darke mistrustfully. "I ain't got nothing—for you to penalize anyways."

"I dare say that's true, Mister Jenson," Darke said, picking up a tattered VHS from a nearby shelf and examining it. "*Dawn of the Mummy*," she read the title aloud. The cover depicted a bandaged fiend emerging from a sand dune. "Tasty stuff."

"You can *see* it's true," he insisted. "Got a big red B.B.F.C. sticker on it. That means it's certificated."

"Yes, I can see a sticker; you're right," she said slowly. "But anyone can put that on there. I think to be truly certificated the B.B.F.C. logo would need to be printed."

Stone looked at her curiously, Jenson with a new hostility. She shrugged. "I remember my Dad renting some films when I was a kid, and some of the more dodgy ones had fabricated stickers like this. Even back then I had a suspicious nature." She put the video back and looked at Jenson.

He shrugged. "Everything I got like that you can get on the internet these days anyway. Even the really nasty ones you can buy in H.M.V. now, so don't give me that bollocks." He tilted his head back, defiant mode engaged.

"Doubtless, that's true," Stone said, "but we don't give a shit. Do I have to explain again that we're not here to give you a hard time, Mister Jenson… Gaz, old son, let's be friends." Stone smiled mockingly, baring his teeth. Jenson looked even more dubious.

Darke stepped up to the counter. "Let's cut to the chase. We just need a little chat about Video Nasties, and a little bird tells us you're The Man."

Jenson stared at her, then Stone, still confused. Then, a light dawning in his eyes, "Wanna know about the nasties, huh? You think I can help you catch your killer, dontcha?"

Stone kept his smile. "You're getting there, Gaz."

"I sell Horror shit. How is that gonna help you? You think me giving you a Mark Kermode on the cinematic qualities of *Driller Killer* and *I Spit on Your Grave* is gonna lead you to your man?" Now he was relaxed enough to smirk. Stone smirked right back.

"You're the expert in the whole area, according to our source. But it's not reviews I'm after, Baz. It's your customers I'm interested in."

Another cynical gleam of understanding, followed by a series of expressions ranging from cautious to calculating. "What's in it for me?"

"You mean, apart from helping Avon and Somerset stop this blood-sucking freak, to reference one of your own classics?" Stone picked up a mug from the counter. Pretended to drop it. "Oops. Butterfingers."

Jenson laughed. "Are you for real?"

Stone replaced the mug and dropped his smile instead. He leaned over the counter, fixing Jenson with a hard "I will mess with your life" glare. Darke had seen it plenty of times before. It verged on the cartoonish, but there was also a definite edge, too. It unsettled villains and fellow cops alike; it wrong-footed them, leaving them unsure whether he was a lunatic or a comedian. It often left her unsure, too, and she knew him better than any other person alive.

Jenson unfolded his arms, the calculating look vanishing. He glanced nervously at Darke. She watched him impassively.

"What's this, bad cop and even soddin' worse cop?" He tried to laugh again, but the mirth got lost along the way. Then, "You ain't got no cause to come in here like this. It's bloody harassment. I ain't done nuthin' wrong."

"You're obstructing the police. Last time I checked, *that* was wrong." Stone let the statement sink in. "And you're murdering grammar. That's offensive, too."

"But I haven't obstru—" He stopped speaking as Stone's face softened into a sly smile. "Ahhh, you bastard. You're pullin' my dick, aintcha?" He smirked again, almost appreciatively.

"Wouldn't dream of going anywhere near it, Gaz," Stone winked. "Now, could we get down to business and see your 'client list'?" He loaded the last two words with all the sarcasm Darke thought they deserved, but it was lost on Gaz.

"I ain't got one as such, and before you start getting all Flyin' Squad on my arse again, that's not me being obstructive. People just come in and browse, or they phone me if they're lookin' for somethin'." He shrugged. "Client lists are for hairdressers." He looked pleased with his little joke.

Darke was sifting through the few VHS boxes on the shelf. "These aren't Nasties, are they? Where d'you keep them?" She turned to face Jenson again.

His face had that annoying calculating look again. Darke decided to go easy on him. "As we said before, we're not going to confiscate them. We just want to defer to your expert knowledge."

Again, the sarcasm flew completely over Jenson's head. He nodded, making his mind up. Stone waited, eyeing him dangerously.

"If I show you them, do I get a special mention in the papers or on the news? Like official expert advisor to the cops and shit like that?"

"Be better than putting an ad out that, wouldn't it?" Stone was mocking him, but Jenson didn't pick up on it. He nodded eagerly, or as eagerly as a tattooed guy with a psychobilly cut and a *Texas Chainsaw* Tee could manage.

He crossed to the shop door, locked it, then, after asking them to follow him, led the way out behind the counter and into a grubby hallway. He took them right to the back of the house and out a door, across a small yard to a surprisingly large shed with a flat, corrugated iron roof.

Jenson produced a key and opened two padlocks before ushering them inside, flicking a light switch as he did so. A bare bulb in the ceiling and a single window encrusted with grime and cobwebs barely illuminated the dusty, cramped interior that was completely filled with VHS boxes. Some were on shelves, others on a workbench, but most were piled on a rug on the floor. There must have been hundreds, maybe even thousands.

"Welcome to Video Nasty Heaven," he quipped proudly.

"Or Hell," Darke said, gingerly picking up one of the cassettes in its fat plastic box from the top of the nearest pile. She wiped away a thin layer of dust on the cover to reveal the title, *Night of the Demon,* and the bold, red type that stated: **Warning—this film contains scenes of extreme and explicit violence**.

"That's one of the best," Jenson said approvingly. "Guy gets off a motorbike to take a piss, gets his dick ripped off by a crazy Bigfoot."

"It happens, I guess," Darke said, dropping the video on the pile again.

Stone was on his haunches sifting through another pile. He held up a cobweb-strewn *I Spit on Your Grave* like he'd won the lucky dip. "Well, look at what I found. I've heard of this one."

"Sure you have," Jenson said. "Leader of the pack, that one. King of the Nasties."

Stone shook the cobweb off his hand. "Then maybe you should keep it in better conditions."

"I try me best, but it's bloody hard work, cleaning…" Jenson complained. "…and Nasties just seem to attract dust and spiders."

Darke stared around at the collection of antique videos covering the floor space, some battered, their plastic boxes tattered, some almost pristine, apart from the ever-present dust.

"It's like a mecca for horror fans," she said. Jenson beamed proudly, like she was praising his children. "Got to be worth some money, all these."

"Yep. Gold mine. That's why I'm very careful. Got this wired up to the security system, though I only arm it at night." He pointed at a red light winking in the ceiling. "Anybody tries to steal my babies, I'm gonna know about it."

"Touching," Stone said. He picked up another film from a cardboard box near the workbench. "Hang on… Isn't this one a real rarity?" He held up a VHS with a brute chasing a scantily clad woman Darke recognized from Cooke's slide show.

"Hell yeah," Jenson boasted. Despite his earlier misgivings, he was enjoying himself now, showing off his prized but decidedly perverted wares. "Fetch up to—"

"A grand," Stone finished for him. "Yeah, I've heard. Not managed to sell it then?"

"I've sold two other copies over the years. Rare as crow's teeth. But I've been collecting for decades. My passion, y'see, horror. And Video Nasties were always the forbidden fruit, the bad boys of the genre." His eyes glowed with enthusiasm. "I've probably got the finest collection in the U.K. Lots of other collectors buy from me as they know I've usually got the goods. Or the bads, if you like." He winked.

"Other collectors?" Stone was examining *The Last House on the Left*. He dropped it back on its pile. "Any names or numbers?"

"I remember what they bought more than who bought it. That ain't much help, is it? But there have been some characters in the past. I remember one nut telling me he drove all around the country visiting video rental shops a few years back, lookin' for Nasties. Told me he even went all the way up to Scotland, and all he found was a copy of *The Slayer*. Minor Nasty," he explained.

"Can you recall anything about this nut? Age, looks, that sort of thing?"

Jenson shook his head. "Nah. Too long ago now. Probably gettin' on for ten years. Just remember him tellin' me that."

"Was he from the Somerset area?"

"Sorry, man. My mind's had a lot to cope with over the years. It's watchin' all these videos. Rots yer brain." He cackled.

Stone had moved on to the workbench, stepping carefully around heaps of VHS boxes, all with their grotesque and hideous cover art. "This looks familiar." He picked up another film, showed the cover to Darke. She nodded when she saw the naked woman crucified on barbed wire.

"Have you sold one of these lately?" Stone held it up like an exhibit at an auction.

"Not for a while. Quite common that one."

"What about this one?" Darke had pounced on another familiar title.

Jenson nodded. "People still buy this rough 'n' ready old V.H.S., even though you can bloody get it uncut on four K Ultra fuckin' H.D. nowadays." He took it off Darke, admiring the cover. "*The Evil Dead*. Still one of my faves. Never gets old."

"Wonder if it's anyone else's fave. Who's bought it off you recently?"

He shrugged. "Dunno. Like I said, it's popular. Can't remember exactly who I sold it to or how long ago. Faces tend to blur in my memory."

"That's unfortunate," Stone said. "How about *Mark of the Devil*? Sold that one recently?"

Jenson paused as if remembering something. Then a leer appeared on his face. "Haven't had that one for a long time. Maybe only ever had the one copy. Don't see it around much."

"But you remember selling it?"

The leering look remained. "Now, some faces you just *don't* forget. Or figures."

"A lady bought it?" Darke asked, wading through the drifts of Nasties toward him.

"Real beauty," he winked at Stone.

"How long ago was this?" Darke felt her own excitement build.

Jenson wracked his addled brains. "Dunno. Maybe four, five years ago. Can't be more exact than that. But I reckon a good five. Never seen her before, and never seen her since. Only come in the once, more's the pity. Fit as fu— Er, I mean, beautiful, she was. Don't get many customers like that, I can tell you. Normally sleazy blokes."

"Any distinctive features?" Darke asked. "And I don't mean how big her breasts were," she added as another sleazy grin appeared on Jenson's face.

"Blonde and skinny," he replied, winking at Darke. "Just how I like 'em."

She gave him a lizard stare. "But her name would be beyond you?"

He shrugged. "Too many years have chugged over the hill. But she might not even have given me her name at all. Collectors like to keep their privacy. Especially in the bad old days when possessing all this stuff would get you an unwanted holiday at Her Majesty's worst establishments." He grinned happily. "Luckily, them days are long gone."

Darke was scarcely listening. She had her phone out, was scrolling through names on Facebook. "But you remember her face?" She held up her phone for Jenson. "Was this her?"

Jenson peered at the profile pic of the good-looking blonde woman in her mid-thirties. His trademark leer returned. "Could be. Yeah, I reckon it is. So *that's* her name…"

Darke closed the image before he got any ideas, looked triumphantly at Stone.

Stone handed the copy of *Snuff* he'd nearly trod on to Jenson. "Good work, you sleazy bastard," he said and waded after Darke through a sea of Nasties toward the door.

CHAPTER TEN

Hi Christine. I would like to suggest you for an exclusive role in a new British zombie movie! The director has hand picked you from our books and really thinks you have the ideal look for this role, which will be on an acting contract rather than being an SA job. They are on a tight budget as it is an independent film but are offering £350 per day for a week in January. They would like you to attend an audition TODAY at 3 p.m. I do hope you can make it, as we think you would be perfect for it. Please text back YES or NO with the code Zombie! Penny XX

Christine read the text and then re-read it, her excitement mounting. It had come through on a different number than the last few Brigstowe texts she'd received, but that was quite a common thing. They were always changing their phones and adding new numbers. She thought about her trip to the salon she'd booked for that afternoon and the drink with Jem she'd arranged for afterward. Both could be postponed easily. Three hundred and fifty pounds a day was too good to pass up, and besides, Penny said it was a proper acting role! Her excitement mounting, she didn't waste any time texting back: ZOMBIE YES

She didn't have to wait long for a reply.

Excellent! The director has some pretty precise instructions for the audition so please read the following carefully. The audition itself is quite an unusual one and you will be required to react spontaneously to every event that unfolds, which basically involves you running from a zombie and pleading for your life! The actual shooting days will require your character to have a lot of dialogue with one of the principal cast members so I hope you are okay with that, but today will simply be a screen test to see how well you respond to the scenario. The director will actually be made up as the zombie! This particular director favors a very hands-on approach to make it easier to choose exactly who is best for the role from personal interaction. There will also be a hidden camera present to judge your reactions. The director has run this scenario before with other actors but feels you have the best look. Please don't contact the office regarding this as today is our busiest booking day and we are snowed under! Further instructions will be attached to a post when you arrive at the following address. The director's number is 07565532433 which should only be used in an emergency. Good luck!
Penny xx

Christine didn't recognize the address, but when she added it to the maps on her phone, it proved to be only a thirty-minute drive, just outside Bristol, a spit of land between the Avon & Somerset canal and the River Severn.

What to wear, what to wear! The address looked like a towpath, which could be muddy. She decided on jeans and a thick beige sweater, topped off with a trendy cape just to add an extra dash of style.

She still had five hours to wait. She thought about ringing Jem to talk about it but remembered he was on an S.A. job in Stroud. She texted him instead. She decided to make a coffee while she waited for a reply but had only just added half a teaspoon of brown sugar to her mug before he replied.

Where is it? Can you still make drinks at 5?

She sent him the address and told him she could, but only if he was buying.

Another five minutes, then:

I did a shoot there once. Another low-budget zombie film for Brigstowe three years ago. Very atmospheric location. They had us extras dressed as zombies emerging from the River Severn, attacking the cast who were hiding in the ruined boats. We were bloody freezing in that water for hours! Typical way to treat S.A.s. This director sounds a bit of a character, audition-ing you dressed as a zombie! I'd add a Lol, but we both hate that. Good luck! See you later xxx

Christine wasn't overly bothered about silly bastards dressed as zombies freezing in the muddy waters of the Severn; she was too excited about the audition, which promised to be an adventure in itself.

She washed her hair and applied her makeup, looking forward to boasting to Jem later about the £350 per day. She felt a little guilty about it, as she knew how much he wanted to bag some meaty acting roles, but there was nothing she could do about that, was there? There might be a job for him as a zombie on the film again. He might even get lucky and reprise his fun time wading out of the Severn. She chuckled at that, made another coffee, and got ready to leave.

The sat nav took her down a small lane off the A38. She could see the old Severn Bridge on the horizon, striding out of the afternoon haze. A sun hung low behind the steel structure, splintering light through the arches and gilding the enormous cables.

Her Mini Cooper navigated tight bends and potholes with aplomb, and soon she was crossing a small, black-and-white timber bridge on the canal, and the voice on the sat nav told her she'd reached her destination.

She parked on the shoulder at the side of the road. Only one other vehicle was parked there, a Suzuki Jimney, but she didn't pay it much attention. Nerves were knotting her stomach now; she had only done two auditions before for acting roles Brigstowe had set up for her, and she hadn't gotten either of them. But she was determined to bag this one. She'd practiced a screaming face, gurning[13] a terrified expression in the mirror, which had only made her giggle, but she wouldn't let that deter her. She could do this.

She followed the towpath toward a small electrical substation, which had been mentioned in the address, and found the post beside it. And there, pinned to the post, was the envelope with her name scrawled on it, just as Penny had promised.

She glanced up and down the towpath. Nobody in sight. Such a lonely spot. She felt a touch of unease, thinking of the murders that had plagued productions lately. Her excitement and ambition dominated, however, and she pulled the envelope off its nail, tore it open feverishly.

A single typed sheet of paper. She read the instructions, and the unease trickled away. This was *sooo* cool. The note told her to follow the footpath to the right of the electrical substation and enter the field next to the river, where she would find ruined barges. She was to wait beside the most rotted one, in which a phone would be hidden and set to record, so she must favor the rear end of the boat so as best to capture her reactions for later assessment. The director would approach her made up as a zombie, and she was to then run and hide inside the boat. Her performance skills would be assessed, so she was encouraged to give it as much energy as she could; however, to deter any interruptions from possible passersby, she was requested to mute her screams.

How much bloody fun was this? She couldn't wait to tell Jem.

She folded the note, shoved it inside her pocket, glanced at the eerie substation with its generators and dynamos. A low hum emerged from it. To the right, just as the note had described, a footpath led through a screen of trees and entered a field, the muddy greenery of which she

---

[13] To make a grotesque face

could just glimpse through the close branches.

She looked down at her knee-length boots in dismay. They were her best. The mud would undoubtedly ruin them. Couldn't be helped. And besides, she could afford new ones if she got this job. She cleared her throat nervously, ready to let loose muted screams.

Muted screams? That was going to be difficult. She'd have to mime them.

She stepped gingerly along the path, careful to avoid the worst patches of mud, and pushed between the groping branches into the field, besides which a broad stretch of the River Severn glistened in the last of the afternoon sunlight

She saw the barges straight away. And suddenly remembered she had been here before, long ago as a child with her parents. And now she remembered what she had called these old barges, her mother laughing her approval. Ghost boats. It was certainly an apt name. The barges had once plied their trade up and down the Severn, but they had long been requisitioned for another purpose entirely. They had been beached in the mud to protect the riverbanks several decades ago and were now decaying wood and steel corpses, a graveyard of hulks.

Christine eyed them warily. They were undoubtedly an eerie sight, wooden ribs black against the lowering orange sun, steering handles smothered by thick mud.

She searched for the most ruined one, and scanning the muddy banks, she spotted a piece of cardboard attached to a particularly dilapidated barge, with the one word inscribed on it in felt pen: AUDITION.

She searched the field for the director but could see no one. River birds ululated, lamenting the imminent dusk. There was still plenty of light left for her to give the performance of a lifetime, though.

She started toward the barge, her boots soon slavered in mud. Still no sign of anyone else. Forebodings reared up again, the eerie isolation of the setting unnerving her. What the hell kind of director would bring her here to audition? Okay, so it was certainly atmospheric enough for a horror film, but even so, did they really have to go to such lengths just for an audition? A horrible thought burrowed inside her mind. What if it was all a trap? Had the Video Nasty Killer, as the tabloids delighted in calling the murderer, lured her here?

She tried to calm herself. Of course not. The killer only struck on movie sets, and there was no cast or crew here, apart from Christine and an eccentric director… She gazed around at the riverbank with its creepy ghost boats, the shimmering water, the trees hiding her from the towpath. She hoped a rambler would show up on the path someone out enjoying the evening splendor, but nobody appeared.

Stop being a pussy! The director wanted it atmospheric. And Penny had arranged it all. Everything was kosher.

She carried on toward the barge. It was sunk into the bank, tilted at an angle, so that one bulwark reared up against the sky, splintered wooden planks poking up like fingers, metal struts rusted and caked with dried mud. The tide must reach this far then. She eyed the river nervously, but its gentle lapping remained a good hundred yards away.

She decided to walk around the hulk, and as she passed the decaying prow, she saw the zombie.

It was standing perfectly still in front of another hulk and had been hidden from her sight by the bulwark of the one next to her. As promised, the director's features were covered in makeup, the details of which she couldn't discern from this distance, apart from the dead-white foundation and what she assumed was a grimy wig. The zombie's clothes were filthy rags covered in dried stage blood.

So when was she supposed to start acting? She froze next to the rusted prow of the audition hulk, watching the figure for any potential cue.

As if it had been waiting for her to hit her mark, the figure began to lurch forward through the long grass, stumbling over tussocks toward her.

That'll be it, then!

She put on her most horrified face, began to edge around the front of the barge, hand to her mouth to stifle a scream. The figure tottered closer, arms outstretched, and she saw gnarled "zombie" gloves, the latex ripped and plastered with fake blood.

She inched sideways around the lower flank of the tilted hulk, away from the approaching director. This bulwark was almost completely rotted, the ribs filthy and slimy with mud. She glanced behind her, hoping she was in view of the phone camera because she couldn't see anything inside the wreck. Further along, there was a gap in the wooden bulwark, allowing access to the interior. She guessed that was where she should make for, as the note had specified she hide inside the barge.

The zombie was closing in now, and she could make out more details. The gruesome face makeup had been expertly applied, blacking on the teeth, making them look gapped and dirty, blood smeared around the eyes… Which looked oddly familiar.

Maybe she'd worked with this director before. She contorted her face into a silent scream of pure terror and crept sideways along the bulwark, all the while hoping she wouldn't slip up in the drifts of mud that encroached on the hulk.

She made the gap, stumbled backward through it as carefully as she could. The deck of the hulk consisted of a soup of mud and marsh grass. Her boots sunk up to the ankles. She ducked toward the rear of the barge, keeping the terror plastered across her features, hoping the phone—wherever it was—was capturing a perfect close-up.

She cowered against the rearing opposite bulwark, waiting for the zombie to appear in the gap. A long, thick splinter of wood stuck out from the bulwark, jabbing at her back, so she moved aside, still trying to look terrified. She made sure she kept away from it, pressed against the dirty wood next to it. The splinter was almost a foot long, jagged, and nasty. They could have bloody removed all hazards first, surely? Health and bloody safety!

The zombie appeared in the gap, snarling, face contorted. It lurched through the opening, filthy work boots grasped by the hungry mud slowing its entry.

Christine pulled her face into a mask of fear, opened her mouth, miming her best scream yet. If only she could let out a real one!

There was definitely something familiar about those eyes, and the face, disguised as it was under layers of grisly makeup. The zombie staggered toward her across the mud-claimed deck of the barge, now only three yards away.

She flattened herself further against the dirty bulwark—she hoped she would get expenses for her ruined cape—and opened her eyes as wide as they would go, emoting pure terror, baby!

And realized why the zombie was familiar.

Her wide-open mouth froze in confusion. Was this a joke? This certainly wasn't whom she expected to see.

The zombie's right claw shot out, seized her by the back of her head, gloved fist bunching around her beautiful blonde hair.

What the fuck!! That bloody hurt! She was about to break the act, tell the zombie that it was taking the audition just a little too seriously, when the hand pulled her head viciously sideways, twisting her entire body around until her face was inches away from the splinter.

And then she understood.

There was no hidden phone, no camera.

There had never been any audition.

How could she be so fucking stupid?!! Because she was dumb. Born fucking dumb. A blonde through and through. That's what they said, what they ALWAYS said.

She struggled against the zombie's grip, but it was too strong, moving her face nearer to the jutting shard. Panic forced a gabble of words from her: "Okay, you've scared me! Brilliant makeup! Your plan worked. You got me to act terrified, and here it is! You'll never get better!! You can stop this now!" And then, at last, when she knew reasoning was never going to help her, she screamed a proper scream, one that tore at her vocal cords and drifted across the empty riverbanks and the ghost boats beached in the mud. "You can stop this now!!

The zombie's hand propelled her head forward, the thirteen-inch splinter shearing through her right eye and into her brain.

The audition was over.

CHAPTER ELEVEN

Jem waited patiently in the Cafe Nero at the top of Park Street, trying Christine's phone intermittently. When she still hadn't shown up for their rendezvous by 5:35, and all he could reach was her voice mail, he decided to call Brigstowe. A vague alarm bell was ringing; even though it was highly likely Christine had just been delayed, he hoped Brigstowe could update him on his friend's whereabouts. *But surely she would have texted. She'd never left him waiting like this before.*

Penny answered, sounding flustered. He was hoping to get Marcus, as he knew the agency was just about to close for the evening; the male booker was a lot friendlier and more supportive of Jem in his various S.A. and acting assignments, and Penny could be tetchy.

"I can't divulge info about other S.A.'s assignments, Jem." He could tell she was impatient to get off the phone and go home.

"But I already know what job she was on, Penny," he insisted. "She told me you booked an audition for her today on a zombie job. But she's forty minutes late and not answering any of her calls, and what with this maniac on the loose on film productions…" He left that unfinished, but Penny was quiet for a moment.

"Hang on a sec, let me just check with Jason," she said finally. He was on hold, Coldplay gnawing at his anxiety even more until she returned. "Jason didn't send Christine on any jobs, Jem, and neither did I.

You must have your wires crossed."

The gnawing increased. "What about Marcus?"

"Not in today; he's only a part-timer, remember? We haven't heard of any zombie production. What seems to be the problem here? Maybe she's pranking you."

Now panic was setting in. He cut the connection, his fingers shaking as he searched for Stone's number.

The D.I. answered after the fourth ring.

He tried to quell the fear, but his voice trembled as he told Stone about the text Christine had received. Stone was maddeningly obtuse and asked him to repeat and clarify details until Jem had to refrain from screaming as he related the nature of the text and the isolated spot Christine had been summoned to. "It's been used as a film set before," he croaked, images of zombies rising from the river filling his mind, all of them reaching for Christine.

"We've been trying to get in touch with Miss Thomas, too," the detective replied stoically. "She's not at her flat." That was enough for Jem. He hung up while Stone was still in the middle of urging him to remain where he was and they would check on her. Fuck that.

He ran down the street toward the meter where he had parked his '76 Beetle, bashing people out of the way, scrabbling the keys out of his jacket pocket, then fumbling them in the door lock, dropping them, forcing himself not to panic. Rush-hour traffic locked him in, had him screaming at the jam, clawing at his face impotently until each traffic light deigned to turn amber. Not waiting for green. He jumped a red at the St. James Barton Roundabout, his speedo flicking to forty as he barreled past the rearing sculpture of a bear painted with a black-and-white zig-zag effect. The Migraine Bear, Christine had called it. He tried to shut her out of his mind, all the happy, funny things they had done together— at least until he found her safe and well.

Caught on another red behind a queue of cars as he neared the beginning of the M32, he dialed her number again, reached voicemail, and slammed both fists on the steering wheel, hitting his horn by accident. The heavy-set driver of the car in front leaned out of the driver's side window to yell obscenities, but now the light was turning and Jem gestured furiously for the man to drive. The guy took his time deliberately, and Jem was about to jump out of the Beetle and shriek into the man's florid face when he finally inched forward. Jem sped past him on the inside lane, causing another car just behind to blare its horn at him, but Jem was oblivious, gunning the old Beetle to fifty, then sixty in the 40-mile zone, pressing redial with his free hand as he did so.

It was 6:15 on his dashboard clock as he swept down the country lane toward the river, and darkness pressed in on him, his beams picking out moths and hedges, and beyond, the slightly paler expanse of the river, lights twinkling across the water from the furthest banks.

He remembered exactly where to go, and at last, he reached the rickety canal bridge, was halfway across before his headlights picked out the Mini Cooper parked on the shoulder on the other side.

A sob broke out when he saw it. He'd prayed he'd been wrong, that his growing suspicions were unfounded, but here was proof that he wasn't. She would never have left her car here in the dark for so long, would have responded to his frantic repeated calls and texts. He slammed the Beetle to a stop next to the Mini, practically falling out of the door, tumbling against the passenger door of Christine's car, peering inside desperately even as he heard another vehicle approaching the bridge from the direction of Bristol and headlights caught him in the act. He didn't wait for the new arrival to reach him but set off, haring[14] down the towpath.

He heard Stone calling his name, but he didn't stop to answer, slowing down only when he reached the electrical substation, panting as he turned to veer down the muddy path, slipping and sliding through the mud, whisked by branches, and out into the field.

Pale starlight and the twinkling of houses from across the river allowed only the vaguest impressions of the marshy bank. The darker silhouettes of rotting hulks loomed out of the night. Jem stopped, breathing heavily, fumbling for his phone, turning on the flashlight app. The small finger of light was meager but guided his steps across the tussocks toward the barges.

---

[14] Running

He could hear Stone following him, still calling his name. Jem swung once to acknowledge him, the phone's light beam just reaching the detective as he pushed through the bushes into the field.

"Whateley! Stop!"

Jem shook his head helplessly, turned back toward the boats. The beam of light swung over the nearest hulk, moved on, picking out more tussocks and glistening patches of mud. Jem stumbled, fell headlong into the grass, almost dropping his phone. Was on his feet again as Stone puffed up behind him.

He passed the first barge, flashlight swinging to capture the next one, its rearing bulwark stark black against the only slightly paler sky.

AUDITION. The beam displayed the notice attached to the decaying planks.

He tottered toward the prow of the barge, beam swinging across the expanse of slime and grass ahead and then back to the boat, picking out the rusted metal girder in the prow, moving around to the port bulwark sunk lower in the mud.

The torch beam picked out the shine of the VHS box nestled in the mud beside a gap in the planks, and Jem heard Stone swear as he stumbled around the barge in time to see it, too.

Jem stopped, transfixed, the light playing over the garish illustration of a rotting hand erupting from grave earth while a swollen red sun hung in the background. Lurid yellow letters spelled out *Zombie Flesh Eaters*, and Jem's beam shook as it moved on, found the pale, pale hand protruding from the gap in the jagged planks just behind the box.

Waves lapped gently in the starlight, and a train rattled along on the other side of the river.

"Whateley," called Stone softly, "Don't..."

But Jem was on his knees in the mud, holding that cold hand in his; his phone dropped, falling against a tussock, the flashlight spotlighting the wrecked face that lay just inside the barge.

And stuck upright in the mud next to Christine's head, a rotting glove covered with makeup and blood, frozen in a grotesque wave.

PART THREE

PLEASE REWIND TAPE AFTER USE

<h1 style="text-align:center">CHAPTER ONE</h1>

"I didn't expect anything else," Stone said when Wells passed on the news from the C.S.I. team that Christine's phone had not been located at the S.O.C.

"Get onto Tech, see if they can track it and any calls to it besides Whateley's. Though the bastard's probably dumped it by now. I doubt the same phone the perp contacted Trenchard with was used to text Christine anyway. Probably another stolen mobile. But go through the motions anyway."

Wells nodded.

Stone turned to the rest of the Murder Squad. There would be no fooling around today, no jokes, no innuendo. Every man and woman in the room knew exactly how high the stakes were now. Four murders in and they were still fumbling in the dark. Thornton was apoplectic with rage. Stone could feel the daggers, and his back was bleeding.

But he didn't care about Thornton, or the Super, or the Chief Constable for that matter. His own career was supremely unimportant right now. This was personal. The killer was dancing round them, taunting, flaunting.

And he had liked Christine Thomas.

He'd liked her spirit, her sassiness, even her scorn. Admittedly, he hadn't liked her as much as Jem Whateley…

"The killer's getting bolder, taking more risks." He surveyed the team. Darke sat to one side, sullen, quiet; Cooke, blank-faced as ever, was sitting upright for once at his desk; Wells frowning. Ming cowed; Sue Fairchild fragile, stunned; Charlie looking strained, no longer as eager as a rookie, tainted somehow by the killer's poison. They all were.

"Christine Thomas was killed near a public towpath, out in the open. A walker could have stumbled upon them, heard her screams. And yes, it was the middle of nowhere, but there are canal-side cottages further down the towpath. We need to speak to the residents of those cottages as a matter of urgency. Who might they have seen? And somebody could easily have been walking a dog at the time the murder happened. Does this mean the perp is losing control, or do they just not care anymore? Does that mean we can expect them to slip up? We need to be ready." He took a deep breath, feeling sick from fatigue and stress. "And the M.O. is changing: this time the killer didn't use a current film set, though Whateley says the murder scene was once used for a zombie movie. And this time a glove was left, along with boot prints."

Charlie spoke up. "Any luck with those, sir?"

"The prints? Nothing yet. Likewise, the glove. Was that dropped by accident or left deliberately? I'm going for the latter. This bastard is enjoying themselves. Each crime scene is being constructed, *designed*. Like a movie set." He let that sink in. "The glove rising from the mud, the provocative tree root, the corpse on the barbed wire, the V.H.S. boxes. Set decoration. All this indicates the strong possibility the perp is working within the film industry. Could be a technician, a crew member, rather than an actor, but I want all options covered."

He scanned each of their faces again, waiting for questions. Nothing. Like him, their tanks were nearly empty.

"We have one lead. I think it's important. Christine Thomas bought a V.H.S. copy of *Mark of the Devil* from a trader in Bridgewater five or so years ago. The same video that was tied to the York supervisor murder. Was it the exact same copy of the film? We don't know, but the coincidences in this case are stacking too highly otherwise. Does that mean she was involved in the crimes? Not necessarily. Does it mean she knew the identity of the killer? I think the answer is yes, which could be a factor in her death." He turned to Cooke. "I want a list of all her known associates of the last ten years, particularly anybody involved in the T.V. and Film industry." Cooke nodded, made a note on a pad in front of him. "Find out if she knew any film collectors. Speak to her friends, family. Let's hear all about her past relationships. Talk to exes. I want this fucker. And I can smell the sick bastard. We're close, even though it doesn't feel like it right now. Maybe the killer felt threatened, backed into a corner, so they got rid of Christine Thomas, who might have led us to them."

Sue Fairchild cleared her throat. It was a habit of hers, prior to speaking. She was always so preciseand emphatic in her speech, and she didn't want something as petty as phlegm impeding her words. "I ran checks on former video rental shops in the Bristol area and possible links to film production personnel." She waited; they all waited. "I came up with nothing, I'm afraid. No extras or crew members on the lists of productions affected have documented past links to rental libraries."

"It's not necessarily something that would be documented, Sue, but thanks." Stone hadn't meant it harshly, but weariness made his words sound clipped.

"I realize that, sir." The stick in her back tautened, and her voice was decidedly more prissy. "But video libraries should have had customer lists. And if anybody used to work in a video library it could have shown up on C.V.s. I also ran checks on addresses to see if anybody of interest used to live above or next to a library. I was quite thorough."

"I'm sure you were, and you're right; it was worth a try. Thanks, Sue…" A memory raised its head suddenly, causing him to falter. "Wait a minute." He snapped his thumb and forefinger. "Whateley mentioned a video library in his hometown when we last questioned him. Said he used to rent titles from it. Get it checked out, Sue. Speak to Whateley again, find out everything he knows about that rental library."

She nodded, her expression prim.

Stone turned to the rest of his team. "So we have a definite link between York and Whateley, and a potential one to Christine with *Mark of the Devil.* We also have a connection to *The Epic of Gilgamesh* between Whateley and a director acquaintance of the scriptwriter Jack South—Julian Cranleigh, or Swanheart as he used to call himself. As I said before: too many coincidences, and I hate the 'C' word. Cranleigh is directing a new movie called *Walking Shadow*, which, according to D.S. Darke, starts shooting this week. We also have another production commencing in two days, and this one promises to be the most provocative. It's an *I Spit on Your Grave* remake. The ultimate Video Nasty. So I want us to have a permanent set presence on that one. It's a red rag to our killer. Has to be. But this time, he's not going to get the chance to play copycat. We'll be ready for him. I'll pressure Thornton to get enough uniforms so that every possible inch of that set is covered. I'll have a bobby squeezing out soap for visitors to the honey wagon if I need to, ladling out sprouts and fries in the catering truck. Every D.C. in the squad will be blending in, brushing up on their film-making knowledge. We're going to be all over it like a halo of plain-clothes flies."

Charlie was obviously bothered by something; that was evident from the way he was fidgeting in his seat.

"Charlie, either you have lice in your Y fronts or you've got a valuable contribution to make."

"Yes, sir." Charlie's jug ears reddened, but he continued regardless. "Why hasn't this *I Spit* remake been canceled? Surely with the murders focusing on films in the area, it's a crazy idea to carry on?"

"Good point. The answer, as always, is money, Charles. Greedy financiers see the negative publicity as hype and raising awareness of their nasty little film. Believe me, we could get it shut down, and I've already spoken to the Chief about this, but he agrees with me, that this could be the trap we need to catch our killer. Although if you ask me, anybody still prepared to work on it is either very greedy, very brave, very desperate, or very stupid. Possibly a combination of all of those. But it's in our interest that it *does* get the green light. The killer will surely be unable to resist. And this time we *will* be ready."

He finished on an upbeat note deliberately. Their loss of morale had not gone unnoticed. What he didn't tell them was that the reasons for D.C.I. Thornton agreeing with him about permitting the *I Spit* movie to go into production were probably not prompted by the same motivations as Stone. Stalled productions cost money, not just for the producers but for the local area, which would benefit from the added employment and investment opportunities. And film producers had influence and high connections—especially the one attached to this movie, it would seem: Thornton was more motivated by wanting to avoid a pernicious frown from the Chief Constable on the golf course than the actual prospect of Stone potentially snaring the killer. The *I Spit on Your Grave* remake was go-go-go.

And Stone would be there for it. Every clack of a clapper board would be observed by one of his team; every extra taking a piss in the honey wagon, every costume change, every comb lifted in the hair-and-makeup truck, every meal devoured in the dining bus, all would be undertaken under watchful eyes.

Finally, Stone turned to Darke.

"And I haven't forgotten Cranleigh. Let's pay him a visit. Like I said, I'm not very fond of the 'C' word, and Swanheart sounds a right one."

Darke smiled thinly. It was obvious she knew he was trying to raise some swagger for her sake, for the team's. But there was only so far you could get on diminished swagger, only so far you could walk the walk before the limp became only too painfully evident.

CHAPTER TWO

All those wonderful titles. A cornucopia of illicit gore. It was a VHS wonderland of plastic boxes offering the most gorgeously disturbing artwork you could imagine. Often, retreating from the present, it was therapeutic to languish in the hall of memories, each one of which came with its own special, lurid tagline, and even more-lurid cover art.

Simply glorious. Halcyon, sadistic salad days.

Late at night, tiptoeing silently down the stairs from the flat above so as not to wake the parents, leaving the light off so as not to attract attention from the street, then dancing up the aisles of videos, face out on their shelves, a grim gauntlet, but a delicious pleasure! Running fingers over the plastic covers, summoning the contents forth with the merest touch. Wallowing in the unspeakable, unable to see most of the titles because of the obvious age restriction enforced by conservative parents but letting the mind unleash their secrets instead, a TV screen of the imagination flickering as the films played there, uncut, unfettered, undesirable! The joy, the joy!

The joy remained, undimmed by time; on the contrary, sharpened by the bittersweet passage of the years.

Of course, there had been those occasional and oh-so-pleasurable stolen moments when both parents were away for the evening. It was never difficult to persuade (usually involving a bribe) the teenage punk who worked evenings at the video library to surrender a title for illicit viewing when the watchful guardianship of Daddy was taken out of the picture. If anything, the clerk had taken a sick pleasure in playing his part in corrupting the child. He had found it downright funny and had even tutored the child regarding which titles to pick. "*I Spit on your Grave?* That'll tickle your bone. Or *Driller Killer?* That's the stuff. The blood flows in rivers. It says it on the pack. Just don't tell your fuckin' old man."

Depraved and corrupt. Isn't that what the Obscene Publications Act was so keen on warning the nation in regard to the Nasties?

But define that. What did it actually mean? Surely cassette tapes with grainy definition and rips and dirt obscuring the picture (no matter how vile and distasteful the contents) couldn't be blamed for what the child had become? And what exactly *had* the child become?

What indeed…

Not corrupt.

Not depraved.

A seeker of truth in art, unfettered, unchained. An enabler. A creator, if you like.

So, if the child had become Frankenstein, who was the monster?

Could the child be both?

A video library of the soul, a holy source from which flowed rivers of blood.

And then the movies died.

The day the *truly* corrupt and depraved destroyed the dreams *and* the nightmares.

And they came in uniforms of blue.

"Fuck off. Just *fuck off.* How the hell would I remember who owned it? Why aren't you doing something fucking useful, like finding out who actually killed Christine. Tell that useless sod Stone to get his arse out of his cozy office and catch the bastard!"

The phone went dead in Sue Fairchild's hand. She pulled a face, replaced the receiver, called to Stone who was conferring with Ming over the lack of results gleaned from CCTV footage.

"Any luck, Sue?"

"No. And he was most unpleasant. He said he didn't know who used to own the video library."

"Think he was telling the truth?"

"No reason to believe otherwise. He sounded quite adamant."

Stone nodded. "Check with estate agencies in the town. Find out when it was sold, who by, and to whom. Let's wrap this up."

She frowned, gave him a tight little smile, and nodded slowly, making him aware with her expression that she was really the Inside Sergeant and she should be dealing with witness statements and members of the public calling *her* with info, not chasing leads outside her assigned duties. But she would do it because she had enough time and she was a dedicated professional officer. Just as long as he understood all that.

Penny's face dropped when she answered the door and saw Jem. She tried to cover it immediately with a sweetly insincere smile, but Jem didn't care. He swept past her into the office, waving away her expressions of sympathy regarding Christine.

"I need to see Jason."

Penny nodded, granting him a little leeway considering the circumstances. She preceded him down the short corridor to Jason's private office where the proprietor spent most of his time rather than occupying his desk in the call center with the bookers, knocked once, and opened the door for him.

Jason sat behind his desk in the small, plain office, an uncertain smile on his lined face. He was edging into his mid-fifties, eyes a little pouchy, hair a little dyed, chin as uncertain as his eyes.

He offered Jem a seat as Penny withdrew.

Jem stared at the picture of Jason's family on the desk, a blandly pretty wife, a gawky teenage son.

"I was so sorry to hear about Christine," the boss of Brigstowe said. "I know how close you two were."

Jem nodded, moved the conversation along to where he needed it to go. "I have to work more than ever now, Jason. Give me anything you've got; I don't care what it is, even being a patient on *Casualty*."

Jason attempted a strained smile. "You hate being a patient on *Casualty*."

"It doesn't matter. Anything. I need to be out of the house, I need to be—"

"You need to rest, Jem. *That's* what you need. You've been through a traumatic experience."

"No!" Jem rose from his chair, his volatility not selling his cause and realizing it, but he was past all rational behavior now. "Just give me *something…*"

Jason looked away. "Go home, Jem. We'll be in touch if we find suitable work."

He would do nothing of the kind, and Jem knew it. They thought he was a liability, would fly off the handle on set, lose his cool, spoil their precious reputation.

"You owe me, and you know it. Christine died because somebody impersonated Penny. They used Brigstowe to kill her. You *owe* me."

Jason knew Jem's intentions full well. He could read them in his bloodshot eyes, that was evident enough. "Let the police catch whoever did this, Jem. Please just go home and try to get some sleep. You look drained."

"I look 'drained.' Is that all you've got for me? Is that really the best you can do?"

He turned and stormed out of the office, slamming the door behind him, leaving Jason grimacing.

Instead of walking down the corridor to the reception area and the exit, he hesitated outside the door opposite Jason's that led to the mini call center where Penny, Marcus, and the occasional temp worked, fielding calls from S.A.s hungry for work and booking jobs with productions. He didn't bother knocking.

Penny and Marcus were both in the middle of calls, headsets on. They looked up as he entered, and he waited impatiently for them to finish their conversations.

Penny finished first, removing her headset carefully and smiling sadly at him. Her pinched face looked even more sour from the attempt at sympathy.

"Did Jason send you in?"

"Yes," Jem lied. "He said to prioritize me for any work."

Penny looked unsure. Did she know he was lying? Presumably, they'd all had some conversation regarding him and what protocol to follow. He didn't care. They would give him work. They owed him.

"I don't think we've got much on at the moment."

"Check. You'll have something."

Marcus had finished his call now and dropped his headset on the table with a sigh. "Hey, Jem. Good to see you." His smile was as bland as his face. Forgettable looks, forgettable personality. Insipid as a daytime TV presenter.

"I need work. Anything. Priority. What have you got?" He glanced from one to the other.

Penny was scrolling desultorily through items on her PC now, but Marcus looked more thoughtful.

"Might have something for you. Just came in."

Penny gave him a warning look, but Marcus ignored it. He'd always been the more-supportive member of Brigstowe. He had got Jem the best jobs every time.

"Stand in on a new indie production. Not much money, but it's above standard S.A. rate."

"Got anything on *I Spit on Your Grave*?"

Penny looked confused. Marcus frowned.

"A remake of the old Nasty film. It's starting this week."

"Not one of ours, I'm afraid," Marcus said. "We're not supplying for it."

"I need to get on it. Can't you give them a ring?"

Marcus shook his head. "We don't have a contract with the production. Sorry, mate. I would if I could."

Jem stared at the booker intently. "Do you have any other horror films at the moment? That is, if those bloody NoMeansNo campaigners haven't frightened them all off."

Penny stiffened. "I happen to agree with their cause. Too many films ignore women's rights these days. We're not a commodity for abuse and disrespect." Her voice had lost any trace of sympathy now.

Marcus chuckled. "Now look what you've done. You've set her off."

Jem didn't care. He didn't smile, didn't bow to her principled pressure. "If they stop me finding this fucker, then I'll be going after them as well." He breathed in, gazed at the rows of supporting artist photos lining the walls as if searching for his prey amongst their black-and-white faces. "If I'm going to find the killer, it'll be on that set. I'm sure of that. And I'll tell you something else." He swung his gaze back to the two bookers. "I'll recognize this bastard as soon as I look into their eyes."

Marcus raised his hands. "Mate, I feel your pain. No horror films as such on our books right now, but this stand-in role is a good one. It's a thriller, and you would be required to provide a performance as well as stand in for one of the main actors."

Jem nodded. "I'll take it."

Marcus smiled conspiratorially. "Just don't tell Jason. He'll kill me."

"He bloody will," Penny confirmed.

Marcus shrugged. "You owe me one." He winked at Jem.

"Thanks. I appreciate it, Marcus. You understand why I'm so desperate to work right now."

Marcus nodded. "It's called *Walking Shadow*. Starts tomorrow. You're not claustrophobic, are you?"

"No, why?"

"Because you'll be wearing a stocking over your head."

Jem frowned. "Am I a bank robber?"

Marcus paused, as if wondering how to put his next words. He glanced at Penny nervously, then smiled up at Jem. "No, mate." His smile wavered.

"You're going to be the killer."

CHAPTER THREE

Jem was carrying a plastic cup of tea to the dining bus when he almost walked right into Julian Swanheart.

The years fled down a long tunnel, rebounded to greet them. Their eyes locked, Swanheart's confused at first, then a vague light of recognition dawning; Jem identifying him in that immediate shock of meeting. His tea slopped over the brim of the cup, scalding his hand, and he jerked his eyes away as Swanheart strode on, pretending he didn't know him.

Shaking tea off his fingers, Jem stared after the director's retreating back. *Fucker.*

The shame and hurt of his severance from the fledgling theater company ten years before resurfaced. Memories of failure were never far from Jem's thoughts; memories of bitter resentments even closer. Just like he could never forget people who had wronged him in his pursuit of an acting career, forgiveness was out of the question, too.

Swanheart had looked a lot older, obviously, but that floppy, sub-Hugh Grant hairstyle remained, albeit sprinkled with a touch of frost; the weak eyes had looked more defensive, embittered by egregious fortunes. The chin was sliding into pouch, his belly, too, bound in by a suede jacket and purple slacks.

Jem remained staring after the theater director who had sacked him from *The Epic of Gilgamesh* ten years before, and his anger, barely subdued since Christine's death, simmered dangerously. That he was the director on *Walking Shadow*, too, Jem had no doubt at all. A brief search on IMDb on his phone soon confirmed it. So, while Jem's career had led him to being one of the industry's bottom feeders, the most despised of all performers, an *extra*, Swinehart had achieved all his ambitions, and here he was at the helm of a medium-budgeted British movie. Bastard.

Called to set an hour later, he tried on his stocking mask for the first time. The set was actually a location on the sprawling Downs, a huge area of natural beauty situated near Clifton, a large portion of which production security had closed off from the public for the evening's shoot. Jane Tighe watched him from the sidelines, her role today that most abhorred and detested by supporting artists (and everyone else in the cast and crew): the dreaded 'passerby.'

Jem received his instructions from the Third Assistant Director. He was to lurk behind a tree until the actress walked past, then jump out. She was going to scream, and Jem, masked and clad head to foot in a black jump suit, was to strangle her. He would then leave her corpse half concealed in the bushes and flee as a handful of late-night revelers strolled past, one of these being Jane.

Jem nodded when the A.D. had finished, waiting impatiently for the main actress to arrive for him to get it done. He was already regretting accepting the job; he felt like he was wasting his time here. Every instinct was urging him to leave, to somehow inveigle himself onto the set of the *I Spit* remake instead, which was filming at Leigh Woods on the outskirts of Bristol over the next few days.

He had contacted several agencies, but only one had the contract, and they had nothing for him. He had determined that, after this night shoot was over, he would head straight to Leigh Woods regardless, hang around in the vain hope of spotting his new nemesis. That the murderer would be attracted to the infamous franchise like a homicidal moth to a flame, Jem had very little doubt.

And, as he had told Penny and Marcus, he felt sure he would know the killer as soon as he saw them.

When Julian arrived on the set to take his position behind the monitor at the far end of the cordoned-off area of grassland, he was either very careful not to look at Jem or had already completely forgotten about him.

His frustrations rising, Jem waited. It was another ten minutes before the actress had finished having her hair and makeup done and finally arrived on set. It took Jem a little longer to recognize her than it had with Swanheart. She looked frumpier, and her hair was no longer the glowing auburn that had stolen his attention so much on *Gilgamesh*; now it was a more-prosaic, dull blonde, and like Julian, she had gained a few unflattering pounds, though her regal beauty was still largely intact.

He was wearing the stocking over his head so there was no chance of her recognizing him. Even if he hadn't been, he was sure he would have been long-relegated to oblivion in her memories, even though he was convinced Julian had known him.

His resentments simmered. So they were still together. In what capacity he was not entirely sure, but at least they were still working in union. Jem wondered if Julian was still indulging in his rough sex games. God, where had *that* recollection come from? It had been many years since he'd even thought about this couple.

He remembered her bruises, the proud demeanor regardless, her seeming insouciance as she brushed aside the concern from other *Gilgamesh* cast members. Of course, she had never implicated Julian in her injuries, but she hadn't needed to; they had all known.

The Third A.D. introduced Jem to her, and of course, he remembered her name now—Lizzie. But while it was impossible for her to see his features, she didn't react at all to *his* name. Why should she? It was all so long ago. She smiled politely, her eyes dull, empty.

The First A.D. called, "Rehearsing... and *action!*" Jem tried to concentrate on his role, but this new twist had thrown him even more. His leap out of the bushes was lackluster, and having to put his hands around that long, still-lovely neck had been just too weird for him to carry out with the necessary aggression. He felt Swanheart's eyes on him from behind the monitor.

"Cut!" The First sounded angry. "Reset!" He marched over to Jem, his tired features strained with impatience. "Can you put more *oomph* into it this time, Jed?"

"It's Jem."

"Jem, yeah. Give it more bollocks, mate." He turned, trotted off to the side, waited for the sound and camera operators to announce their readiness, the clapperboard was clacked, withdrawn, and the First yelled: "For a take this time, lots of hush. And… Action!"

Jem put more bollocks into it. All the fury and grief that had been escalating found an outlet. He flew out of the bush, his hands clawing at Lizzie's neck, his body landing on top of hers as they sprawled on the grass. She gave a shriek far more realistic than the yelp of the rehearsal. And Jem squeezed.

And as he squeezed, he was sure her eyes could see beneath his stocking mask, could see *him*. She started to choke, gagged, her eyes filling with fear. Genuine? He realized with a shock far worse than a plunge into an icy mountain tarn that he was actually crushing her throat with his hands.

He rolled off her, stood up, aghast. She got to her knees, coughing, helped to her feet by the First. Jem froze, horrified by what he'd just done. But the First was looking happy as he received the director's signal on his earpiece. "Got that. Moving on."

Jem peeled the mask from his face. Lizzie glared at him sullenly, a weird light in her eyes. She caressed her throat as if checking for bruises.

"I— I'm so sorry," Jem stammered, rooted like an inadequate schoolboy.

"What for?" she said, her mouth twisting into an ugly smile. "You just got a bit carried away, that's all."

"Did I— Did I hurt you?" Self-disgust flushed through him.

She laughed coldly, glanced across at Julian. The director was staring at them with a curiously immobile face. "Wouldn't be the first time a man's got carried away with me." Her eyes were cruelly playful.

Jem hung around while they set up for the next scene, just in case they needed him again. Jane sidled up to him.

She was wearing a short leather jacket and trendily ripped jeans too young for her. Her lined face looked anxious.

"You all right?" she asked him.

"No."

"Of course, you're not. I'm so sorry about Christine."

"Are you? Now you've got less competition in the blonde S.A. stakes." Contrition hit him as soon as the words were out. "I'm sorry. I didn't mean that."

"Yes, you fucking did." Hurt made her look older. "But I'll let you off, considering what you've been through."

"You don't have to."

"I know I don't. But the way you attacked that actress proves you're not ready to be on set yet. You should have some time off."

"No."

"Really. You should. I care about you, and I can see you're not ready for this."

He tried to smile for her but couldn't. It was getting colder as the evening wore on, despite the bright arc lamps set up around the area of the Downs in which they were standing. Other extras waited patiently while the crew moved cameras, set up lighting, and checked the monitors.

A switch was suddenly thrown in his head. "I've never been ready for *this*." The rage was back; it had never gone away, and now it needed an outlet. "D'you think this is the kind of career I had in mind all those years ago? Standing in the shadows while *real* actors strut their wares in front of me, detesting me because I deign to share a set with them? Do you think I fucking wanted *this*?" His voice was rising, and Jane was glancing around nervously.

"They think we're beyond contempt, and they're fucking right. We *are*. We come into this industry without proper training and expect to be treated like actors. Well, we're fucking *not*. It's taken me all this time to realize it. We're a fucking joke. Breathing furniture, walking props. Nothing. Believe me, they can't feel as much contempt for us as I do for myself. And we *let* them treat us like this! Taking crumbs from the table and accepting it, being grateful for it. You know the way we get treated, and you deserve better, Jane. We all do."

There was nothing stopping him now, not Jane, not the First, certainly not weak-chinned Julian, even if he had deigned to look Jem's way.

"Those NoMeansNo campaigners… They should be protesting about the way *we* get treated, not moaning about tits and arse and simulated rape, for fuck's sake. Left to stand in the rain and subzero temperatures wearing a T-shirt in the middle of winter, or forced to stand for hours in thirty-seven-degree heat in Roman armor while the cast and crew are popping open ice-cold cans of Coke and not giving *any* to the pitiful S.A.s. Or made to queue for fucking hours for slop while crew members and actors push in front of you. *Actors…* fucking spoiled wankers. Every one of them. When we're told to stop talking on set, these cunts are singing and braying loudly. We're the shit on their shoes, Jane. Shit. *Shit.*"

He collapsed onto a park bench behind them, the tide of grief and fury ebbing, for the moment at least. Jane was staring at him in shock and embarrassment. The First A.D. shrugged, walked away to speak to the director. The actress Jem had strangled glanced at Jane, her eyes cold, and there it was—contemptuous. She, too, walked away.

Jane sat down beside Jem. She put a hand on his knee. He was trembling, face as white as the moon emerging from the clouds above.

"I'll get you a cup of tea," she soothed.

He was shaking his head. "You think I've gone too far, don't you?"

She chuckled drily. "I think you'll probably never work for this production again, yes."

"I meant everything I said." He was staring across the patch of grass toward the monitor. Julian was chatting to Lizzie now. Their eyes swung toward him, but it was his turn to look through them.

"Except for that bollocks about the campaigners. I can't seriously compare the degradations of a humble S.A. to the depravity thousands of women have undergone at the hands of filthy perverts masquerading as producers."

"Goooood," Jane said with another chuckle. "I'm so glad you said that. Pity that actress didn't hear you recant."

"Although that dickhead who's always hanging around with the female protestors needs a bloody slap. He was twatting about outside the car-park entrance when I drove in, but he couldn't get past security. You know he had a go at Christine when she went for lunch with Ben

Trenchard? Maybe I should vent on him instead of these silly fuckers." He put his head in his hands.

"Interesting," Jane suddenly said.

He didn't react, rubbing his eyes, still slumped forward on the bench.

"It's that copper who interviewed us when Guy Johns got killed. What's he doing here?"

Jem's head snapped up. There had been a police presence when he arrived at the production base, two uniformed cops, which he understood was going to be standard procedure until the Video Nasty Killer, as the papers continued to dub the murderer, was caught. But he hadn't expected Stone.

He and the blonde D.S. were talking to the First, who was pointing out Julian.

Stone then made his way through busy crew members and milling extras to the monitor where Swanheart was still sitting.

Jem watched intensely as Stone spoke briefly to the director, who reluctantly got up from his chair, passed some instructions to the First, and then followed the two detectives as they strode purposefully away from the set. Stone turned his head once in his direction, but Jem wasn't sure if he had seen him or not.

"Stone's onto something," Jem said to himself. "He must be."

"We'll find out in good time, I'm sure," said Jane.

Jem continued to stare after the three figures as they threaded their way through the throng toward the director's isolated trailer, which was situated at the far side of the unit base car park.

He squeezed the rolled-up stocking in his hands as if practicing for a retake with Lizzie's slender throat in his grip. Jane gave up trying to speak to him, and soon the Third A.D. was signaling to her to come and rehearse her passerby scene.

She turned back once; his gaze remained riveted on the distant trailer, his hands still crushing the stocking in his lap.

CHAPTER FOUR

"So, how can I help you, Inspector?"

Julian Cranleigh signaled for Darke and Stone to sit on the sofa inside his trailer. While still relatively cramped, it was the biggest 3-Way on the site. Cranleigh perched on the edge of a small desk so he could look down on the detectives from a greater height. The motive for the positioning was not lost on Stone.

"You're obviously aware of the murders taking place on various film sets in the region?"

"Of course. Tragic. Utterly heinous." Cranleigh's face remained fairly impassive, though he tried to load his voice with the required sympathy. He brushed at the Hugh Grant flop of hair and studied them with distant blue eyes. "But what, pray tell, does it have to do with me? Are you concerned something similar might happen on my set? We already have stringent security measures in place, and a couple of your wonderful chaps patrolling the area, too."

"I'm glad to hear you feel secure. And I really *don't* want to rattle you unnecessarily…" He glanced at Darke, who just about managed to keep from grinning. Of course, he wanted to unnerve this pompous prick. "But every production in the area needs to be absolutely on their toes."

Cranleigh nodded ingratiatingly.

"But there are a couple of other matters we want to talk to you about. We've been led to believe you yourself have had issues with the NoMeansNo campaign."

"Good God, they never let it lie, do they?" He smirked at Stone for laddish support, got none, and cleared his throat. "They've been victimizing me, Inspector. You should be talking to them, not me, though thankfully there's only one of the lunatics picketing our production today. A *man*. Clearly a virtue signaler. Obviously likes to portray himself as the Good Guy to get some… Anyway, in answer to your question, yes, they *have* dogged my career. Made bloody pests of themselves."

"And why is that, Mister Cranleigh?"

He looked evasive, fidgeted on the desk, his body language not so pompous. "You'd have to ask them that."

"But I'm not, am I? I'm asking you."

Cranleigh was beginning to realize that he couldn't bamboozle this policeman with his superior intellect and public-school charm. It left him looking like a rather foolish boy. He fidgeted with a thread on his beige jacket. "It's a personal matter, that's all. Nothing really to do with my films or plays."

"Would it have something to do with your wife?"

He looked up at Darke sharply. He tried a dismissive smile and a grunt, but Darke was watching him ferociously.

"I can assure you there is nothing untoward in our relationship. And I fail to understand what this has to do with your investigation."

"We need to cover every angle, Mister Cranleigh. And your name has been put forward as one of interest." Stone studied the director's petulant features, looking for chinks. "Would you describe your relationship as healthy?"

"Of course. Don't believe everything you read in the papers, Inspector."

"We've heard otherwise from different sources."

Cranleigh's face adopted a calculating look for a second, then he sighed. "You've been talking to that worm, South, haven't you? Of course he's going to vilify me. He slept with my wife, so I sacked him. He'll say anything to blacken my name."

"What would your wife have to say on the matter, do you think?" Darke tilted her head to one side as if asking a child an innocent question. "We'll be speaking to her as well."

"Look, I appreciate you have jobs to do, but I have a film to direct. Is this absolutely necessary?"

"What about your sex life, Mister Cranleigh? Do you visit S. and M. clubs, fetish bars, that sort of thing?" Stone this time, voice casual, eyes unwavering.

"That is absolutely, categorically none of your business." Cranleigh rose from the desk, spluttering with outrage.

"Sit down, Mister Cranleigh. Unless you'd rather continue this conversation down at the station?"

"This is outrageous. I've only too willingly agreed to help you, even though I am extremely pressed for time, but I did *not* agree to suffer your filthy accusations. If this line of questioning continues, I shall be forced to contact my solicitor."

Stone gave him his shark smile. "That won't be necessary, Mister Cranleigh. We're just trying to discover whether you are acquainted with any potentially violent characters who might help us with our enquiries."

Cranleigh calmed a little, and this time he opted to sit in the plastic chair next to the desk, bringing him down to the same eye line as the detectives. "I'm not acquainted with violent people, Inspector. Sorry to disappoint you." He stuck his weak chin out in an effort to regain his dignity.

"What about *The Epic of Gilgamesh*?"

Julian looked momentarily startled. "What about it?"

"You directed it under the name Julian Swanheart, I believe."

"Yes. What possible relevance does that have to your inquiries?"

"You may remember one of your leading actors from that production. A Mister Alexander Fergus?"

Cranleigh tried to look solemn. "Yes, a perfectly dreadful time. I gather he was never found? I spoke to the police at the time."

"Any theories?"

Cranleigh paused as if racking his brains. "None whatsoever. He just vanished shortly before we were due to take our play to the Edinburgh fringe. Very popular chap. Can't think what happened. I felt dreadfully sorry for his parents."

"Was he as popular as you remember him being, though?"

Cranleigh frowned.

"There was one member of your cast who didn't get on with him, wasn't there?"

Cranleigh shook his head. "I'm not following you."

"But somebody is apparently following *you*."

Now Cranleigh was getting there. His face was suddenly host to a variety of expressions: suspicion, reflection, a touch of fear even. "You mean that extra? The one standing in for our killer?" His voice had attained a nervous edge. "You think he might be involved in the murders?"

Stone leaned forward. "Do *you* have any cause for believing he might be?"

Cranleigh hesitated. "It was common knowledge he and Alexander didn't get on… You think he might have murdered him?"

"Did you ever see them behaving violently with each other?"

"Nooo… It was more their body language. They hated each other." Cranleigh's face was pale. "Should he even be allowed onto my film set if you believe him to be a suspect? I shall have to notify the agency that we don't require him after today."

Stone ignored that. "What about any other members of your *Epic* production." He tried to keep the sarcasm out of his voice but wasn't sure he did a great job. "Do you recall anything about them? Are you still in contact with your former cast?"

"Good God, man. That was ten years ago. I've moved on from those days."

Stone looked around the immaculate, hi-tech trailer interior. "I can see that. But I still want you to answer my question."

"Apart from my wife, no." A flicker passed across his face, barely detectable. But Darke saw it.

"You don't look entirely convinced on that score, Mister Cranleigh," she pushed. "Are you absolutely positive you haven't been in touch with any previous cast members from *The Epic of Gilgamesh*?"

Again, that uncertain look.

"You need to answer the question," Stone said more forcefully. "If there *is* somebody else who can help with our investigation and you don't tell us, it could be seen as obstruction."

He nodded ingratiatingly. "There is someone…" His tongue passed across his lower lip nervously. "But you have to promise confidentiality."

"We can't promise anything, Mister Cranleigh. What do you need to tell us?"

"At least…" A pleading look came into his eyes. "If I tell you, does my wife have to be informed?"

"Answer the question, Mister Cranleigh." Darke's gaze was unflinching.

He hesitated, mouth open. It was almost as if he wanted to tell them. A boast? He came to a decision and a wily smile replaced the uncertainty. "As long as it goes no further," he said, as if completely ignoring their previous response.

He leaned back against the wall of the trailer and sighed theatrically. "I have only kept in contact with one person from those days. Apart from Lizzie, of course. The rest have faded into deserving obscurity—until that extra popped up today, I hadn't seen him either."

"But wasn't he an actor in your play?" Darke asked.

"It didn't get him very far, did it? No, he has attained his level, bless him."

Stone did his best to disguise the distaste in his voice. "You were telling us about this other person…"

"Yes. Alice. Lovely girl. Still is actually." Again, that detestably complicit smile that Stone didn't return.

"Do you have her details?"

Julian hesitated again, then held his hands up in mock surrender. "Okay. I'll give you her address and number. Just remember our little promise." He gave them a ghastly smile and fetched a pen from his inside jacket pocket, hurriedly scribbling on a Post It note before handing it to Stone.

"And has Missus Cranleigh kept up this relationship with Alice?" Darke asked, clearly already guessing the answer.

"God, no. And it would be curtains for us if she ever found out, so please, I am relying on your discretion. And again, I fail to see how Alice can help you with your current inquiries."

"We'll be the judge of that. So there's nobody else from the *Gilgamesh* days you can think of still on the acting scene?"

"Don't be absurd. They were all rank amateurs. So no, apart from Lizzie, of course. And that…extra. But I don't call hanging around in the background sniffing for crumbs acting, do you?"

He was still sneering as they left the 3-Way.

Lizzie's trailer wasn't quite as spacious or comfortable as her husband's, and the sofa on which Stone and Darke were squashed together was significantly smaller.

Lizzie poured herself a glass of water from the tiny bathroom and then stood with her back to the small, glazed window. Night pressed against the pane, though the light bulb was bright enough for the detectives to see the wary look on her face.

"We really should be more careful whom we allow the agencies to send us," she said scornfully. "You know he actually strangled me during that last take?"

Stone nodded, searching her long neck for marks and finding none.

"So, it was a surprise to see him on set?"

"Of course. I haven't seen him for ten years."

"Anybody else who you might have come into contact with from those days?"

"No. I think our lives have all moved in different directions."

Darke glanced at Stone. "So, you haven't run into Alice Garfield in recent times?"

She looked surprised. "Alice? Absolutely not. Where did you get her name from? Is she implicated in this?" A thought struck her. Her face darkened.

"Is something the matter, Missus Cranleigh?"

"What? No. Of course not. Can I help you with anything further?"

"Alexander Fergus," Stone said. "Any ideas what might have happened to him?"

She shook her head. "I'm afraid not. We were all shocked when the police told us he had been reported missing. Such a lively character."

"Would you say any members of the *Gilgamesh* cast had any personal problems with him?"

"What? No. Of course not. He was a gregarious chap. Everybody liked him."

"Except Jem Whateley. They didn't like each other, did they?"

"Maybe you should ask him that. And I really don't think one of your suspects should be playing the role of a killer on our production, do you?"

"We have no reason to believe Mister Whateley is a danger to anyone, Missus Cranleigh. But are you absolutely sure there was nobody else who might have had a grudge against Alexander?"

"No, no. I went through all this years ago with you people. Why are you dredging up the past? Let it be."

Stone got up from the cramped sofa. Darke rose, too, straightening her slightly rumpled suit. "But that's the problem, Missus Cranleigh," Stone said, staring into her hazel eyes and giving her the grimmest of smiles. "The past won't let us."

CHAPTER FIVE

Alice Garfield was in her mid-thirties, brunette, with flashing green eyes. Her eyes flashed even brighter when she opened the door and D.S. Darke raised her warrant card.

"Goodness me, how on Earth may I help you, Sergeant?" She peered closely at the ID, her frown the only sign of lines on her finely boned face.

"I need to speak to you about a matter concerning our current investigation into a number of recent murders, Miz Garfield." She let that sink in, going for gold straight away, no messing around. Alice blinked in shock, then leaned forward to peer up and down the terraced Totterdown street.

"You'd better come in before the neighbors think *I'm* involved." She paused as she let Darke into the short, bright hallway. "Goodness me," she added, quickly closing the door behind them. "You're not here to tell me you think I *am,* are you?"

Darke smiled. There was something invigorating about the woman's breathless enthusiasm, not to mention her dazzling eyes, her sophisticated speech. She could certainly see why Cranleigh had been tempted. And more than once, by his own account.

Alice led Darke into a small, cozy living room, bright white walls, floral suite, a print of Van Gogh's *Wheatfield with Crows* on the wall above the settee, to which she promptly ushered Darke. The D.S. was glad to have been given the option of making this call; Stone had gone onto the set of the *I Spit on Your Grave* remake, which was also in the middle of an evening shoot. Darke hadn't fancied that. Not at all. Alice Garfield was a much pleasanter prospect.

Declining a cup of tea, Darke explained exactly why she was here, seeking information on any previous cast members of Julian Cranleigh's old play.

"Gosh, that was a while ago. And my memory's never been great, I'm afraid." She flashed another dazzlingly white smile. Yes, Darke could see exactly why Cranleigh had been moved to infidelity. What she couldn't understand was what a pleasant, attractive, and obviously intelligent woman like Alice saw in a creep like Cranleigh.

"I was only twenty-five at the time. Gosh. So long ago. It gets away from you, doesn't it?" She settled at last in the armchair next to the door. "I'm sorry, but I don't think I'm going to be much help to you."

Darke hated to wipe the lovely smile off Alice's face, but there was no way around it.

"I understand you're still acquainted with Julian Cranleigh?"

That did it. The eyes flashed with a different light. The smile evaporated. A wariness crept over her face. "I—I know Julian, yes. We remained…friends…after the play finished."

"I understand you're rather more than that, Miz Garfield."

She stared at Darke intently, wondering quite what to say.

"We have it from Cranleigh himself, Miz Garfield. His wife is unaware, as far as we're concerned."

Alice looked down at her hands in her lap. She clasped them before looking up again. "I suppose you must think I'm a terrible woman." She held Darke's gaze. "Believe me; I'm not proud of myself."

"I'm not here to judge."

"No. I can do that all by myself." Her gaze wandered to the print on the wall as if seeking solace from the flaming swirl of color.

"Did he promise you good parts in his productions?"

Alice looked Darke squarely in the eye again. "I don't even have that as an excuse, I'm afraid. I stopped acting shortly after *Gilgamesh*. After poor Alexander..." She kneaded her hands together. "It all seemed so tragic. I—I found a different path in life."

"May I ask what as?"

"Of course. I'm a playgroup supervisor. I look after children." She found a smile again.

Darke nodded. She could see the trim, energetic woman bouncing around a playgroup with children.

"No, the attraction to Julian was not motivated by ambition." She cracked a weak smile. "I loved him. Especially back then, when he was full of passion and endeavor." The smile faded. "I'm afraid we were seeing each other back then, too. " She lowered her gaze. "Behind poor Lizzie's back. I know what you must think of me."

"And now? Has the affair really continued for ten years?"

She shook her head sadly. "I think I clung to him after that dreadful business with Alexander. And he couldn't bear to break up with Lizzie."

"Did he—" Darke paused, measuring her words. "Did he ever beat you?"

"You know about that, too?" Another smile, this one ironic. "No. He never hurt me." Her eyes were wide as she returned Darke's gaze. "It was Lizzie, he always told me. She enjoyed the games. The rougher, the better." She looked down at her hands again. "If he had ever tried those games with me—" She broke off. "No... He *did* try with me. I remember now. Just after *Gilgamesh*. He wanted me to hit him. I said no. He never asked again. And I know *exactly* what you're thinking..."

Darke gave her an innocent look.

"You're wondering why I continued to have an affair with him, aren't you? After that, after Alexander, for ten bloody years..." Her gaze lost focus. Then she glanced at the print above Darke's head again. "I wish I had an answer for you, Sergeant. I really do. Maybe it was because he made me feel more special than any other man before or since."

"Because he didn't beat you?"

"No! It was more than that. He was imaginative. Clever. Warm. But don't think I was stupid enough to believe he would ever leave Lizzie. They were too similar. I realized that soon enough. They were born for each other."

"Then…"

"All I can say in my defense is that it has only ever been a very *intermittent* relationship. One of mutual suitability. Friends with occasional benefits." Another weary smile. "There have been many men since I met Julian. But none seemed to stick like he did. Even if I only ever saw him every few months. And as for Lizzie…"

Darke waited. The cuckoo clock on the wall announced seven o'clock. Alice waited, too, for the wooden bird to cease its plaintive call.

"Though I do feel dreadfully guilty about the whole business, please don't think otherwise… I nevertheless often suspected she knew all about our very intermittent affair."

Darke cleared her throat.

"But did you really come here just to ask me about my sordid dealings with Julian? Are you seriously suggesting Julian is involved with these ghastly murders?" Her eyes retained their sparkle, but now they were skeptical, too. "Yes, he's an insufferably pompous man. But he's got a very warm heart, and he's loyal to his old friends. And I really don't see him being implicated in something as sleazy and inelegant as these Video Horrible Murders, or whatever the media is calling them."

Darke nodded. "Former *Gilgamesh* cast members?" she reminded Alice.

Alice gasped theatrically. "Of course, that's what you were asking me, and I've chewed your ear off reminiscing about Julian. You must let me cast my mind back…" She put her hands to her head as if that would help her.

"Do you know," she said eventually. "I really can't think of anyone else apart from Julian and Lizzie. And dear, old Alexander, of course."

"No?" Darke prompted. "What about Jem Whateley, who played one of the main roles with Alexander?"

Her eyes widened even more. "Gosh! Jem!! He was the Wild Man, Enkidu! Of course, how could I have forgotten Jem?"

"Have you seen him since the play finished?"

She thought about that. "No," she said finally. "Pretty sure I haven't. But…" Her eyes were roving the room, not exploring the features of the lounge but events from a decade past.

"There *was* someone else. I just can't quite recall… When you mentioned Jem, it triggered some very distant recollection. Someone who was close to Jem, maybe? Certainly not Alexander. Oh gosh! My memory is so frustrating." She banged her head gently with her fists.

"Close to Jem? A girlfriend, maybe?"

"I…" She shook her head slowly. "I just can't remember. Just something very vague about someone following him. Maybe a bit *too* interested in Jem, if you get my drift. But I can't for the life of me remember whether this person was male or female, let alone conjure up a name!! I'm so sorry. And it probably isn't relevant anyway."

Darke frowned. *Was this something?* She didn't want to make assumptions, and her next few questions would have to be very gentle and careful so as not to cause Alice's overworked and, by all accounts, unreliable memory to go into meltdown.

"Following him? Could you explain what you mean by that? Stalking him, you mean?"

"No, no, I don't think it was anything like that. Oh! It's just not coming into focus. Just a flicker of a memory of thinking someone had a crush on him, maybe. Was that it? Oh, I don't know. Not a crush. Perhaps something a bit different. An obsession sounds too severe. Was it a man, was it a woman?" She shook her head again and made a frustrated noise with her lips. "I think someone else noticed it, mentioned it in passing to me. But I have no idea who said it or who it was about. But I don't even think Jem was aware of it." She smiled apologetically at Darke. "Not a very good witness, am I?"

"You've been very helpful," Darke said, trying not to show her disappointment. "But if you *do* remember anything…"

Darke rose to her feet. Alice half rose, too, still deep in thought. "No, nothing sparking the old synapses, I'm afraid."

Darke smiled, charmed by her gentle eccentricities. She was like an old lady from the 1930s trapped in the body of an attractive young woman. It was a very appealing mixture.

Darke had made it to the door of the living room when Alice's voice made her stop.

"Wait!"

Darke turned, one eyebrow lifting enquiringly.

"My feeble brain may not remember, but I have something much more reliable that will hopefully give us the answer."

Darke raised both eyebrows this time.

"I got my father to film the play with his camcorder. I've still got the tape somewhere. I'm pretty sure I'll remember the mystery person when I see them on stage!"

And now Darke's smile was every bit as wide as Alice's.

CHAPTER SIX

"Where are you, Tina?" Martin tried to keep the longing out of his voice but failed. "It's seven o'clock now, and nobody apart from me has turned up."

"I'm sorry, Martin." The voice on his iPhone didn't really sound it, though. "I won't be coming today, or any other day for a while. And neither will the others."

"But why? You know what Jack South told us: there is a scene of protracted violence against women in this film. By a man wearing a stocking mask, for God's sake. It's filthy, degrading, an utter exploitation of women, and it has our cause written all over it. And it's directed by a man with a proven track record of wife beating. So why aren't you here with me?" His voice had taken on a whiny note that he also fought to control.

Beyond the patch of rough ground where he was parked on the edge of the Downs, he could just see a security man in a hi-vis manning the entrance to the unit base. Martin had been waving banners at anyone who drove in or out all afternoon and evening. He'd rung Tina three times already, and this was the first time she'd answered the phone. Clearly, she'd been avoiding him.

"Jack has an ax to grind, Martin. He only gives us these script leaks to strike back at producers or directors who've bad-mouthed or sacked him. We're not going to be his pawns anymore. He's a bitter man, and his screenplays are just as chock full of depravity and crimes against women as the productions we've been picketing. We've just been unwittingly aiding him in *his* cause, not ours."

"What gives you that idea?" He squeezed the phone, feeling his last link with Tina breaking. "Jack believes in us."

"No, he doesn't! We should have looked at *his* work before blindly accepting his condemnation of other people's scripts. Janet sent me a D.V.D. of a film based on one of Jack's screenplays. *Slasher School*. It's vile, Martin. I couldn't stomach more than twenty minutes of it—absolutely abominable atrocities committed to the female form. We're done with Jack's leaks. And we're done picketing films. For a while, at least." Her voice was determined, angry. She sighed, tried to soften it a bit. "I've been summoning the strength to tell you all day. I know how fanat—*committed*—you are to this campaign, and I was reluctant to cause any bad feelings between us, but I think it's best if we don't see each other for a while. I hope you understand."

This was too much: one horrible revelation after another. He collapsed onto a nearby park bench. "But… I *am* committed. I thought you were, too. Just because Jack has written some bad stuff doesn't alter the fact he's been tipping us off to other disgraceful films that certainly need protesting against. Maybe he's reformed and seen the error of his ways."

"I don't think so, Martin." She sighed again, obviously wishing she could end the conversation. "He was just settling scores and using us to do it. Like silly sheep, *baa*-ing when we're told to. Well, no more. He even contributed a script to *Walking Shadow*, which was apparently nastier than the one they're going with. But there are other reasons why we've decided to call it quits."

"To get away from me? Is that one of them? What have I done to you, Tina? You know how fond I am of you, and how dedicated to the cause I am."

Another, longer sigh. Silence for a moment. He pictured her pixie-like face frowning with exasperation, and his heart died. Far from being seen as a heroic campaigner for women's rights in her eyes, he had become a nuisance. A pest.

"We think you're just a little *too* dedicated, Martin. You weren't doing us any favors. I'm so sorry to be blunt. But more importantly, we decided to stop because of these awful murders."

"But… But surely that's all the more reason to continue. The killer is copying the depraved acts in films like this. So we need to stop them from being made."

"That's one way of looking at it. Another is that we're showing the killer where to strike. Our protest could be seen as providing a hit list for the murderer. We're marking out his territory for him! Or her!!"

Martin felt his world slipping out of his grasp. "Tina…" he whispered plaintively. But she either didn't hear or chose to ignore the begging in his voice.

"Besides, we've achieved our goals. To a certain point, at least. Women have always been scapegoats for male entertainment and their sense of personal failure, fantasy figures for men to play out their patriarchal urges against. To unload their sexual frustrations and whims. But that is beginning to change. And we've played our part. We've raised awareness, even if only to a small degree. But it all counts, Martin. And you've played your part, too. And we thank you. But now it's time, for us at least, to step back."

He had so much he wanted, *needed* to say, but the words weren't there. He stared at his placard lying in the grass.

STOP DEGRADATION OF WOMEN IN FILMS!

Were *those* his words in paint on wood? He didn't think so anymore. Nothing made sense now.

"Goodbye, Martin."

The phone went dead. She was gone.

As the utter numbness of that realization struck him, he heard a distant crash of glass.

He turned, knowing what the cause of the sound was even though his car was hidden behind a copse of trees at the edge of the rough area.

Only distant light from a park lamp beyond a clot of bushes and from the production base and the city below the sweep of the Downs illuminated the area, and poorly at that. The knot of trees where his car was parked was thick with shadow.

His heart was too heavy to be unduly moved by this new twist. Some horrible opportunist had obviously spotted his laptop he'd been foolish enough to leave on the front seat.

He made his way toward the Renault, but not *too* fast—he'd been hurt enough for one evening. He didn't particularly relish encountering a desperate junkie in the lonely dark.

He crept nearer the trees. He could see the dull gleam of the Renault's bonnet through the conifers around it. His was the only car there this late in the evening. Should he phone the police? But the thief would be long gone before he even reached his car. No point. He held his breath as he crept closer, edged around the branches of the nearest tree.

As he'd suspected, his car had been broken into, the passenger window shattered. He could see from this distance that his laptop was gone. Just like the cowardly thief.

He felt like crying. This, on top of Tina abandoning him—it was too much. Too much. He walked around the front of the Renault to the driver's door and unlocked it. Shards of thick glass lay on both seats, some hanging from the passenger window like webbing. He brushed the fragments away from the driver's seat and sat down, inserting the key in the ignition. A great sob traveled up from deep inside him.

He looked at his pitiful face in the rearview mirror, pale and pathetic. A shadow behind his reflection moved in the mirror. A dark head, features mashed together by a stocking mask. The head moved forward as the body lunged at him from the back seat.

And a screwdriver plunged fiercely into the back of his neck, slammed home with awful force.

From the back seat, the figure in the stocking mask leaned hard on the handle of the screwdriver, riding out Martin's death struggles, inching the specially sharpened blade of the tool further into the neck until the bit popped out from the campaigner's throat. Blood chugged in a steady flow down Martin's jacket and shirt, pooled in his lap, painted the dashboard, speckled the rearview mirror. Relatively few drops spattered the figure in the back seat.

The figure left the screwdriver in its fleshy socket, pushed up the passenger seat, and opened the door. Climbing out, the killer dropped a rucksack onto the grass, withdrew some wet wipes from inside it, mopped unhurriedly at the blood on the jumpsuit sleeves before tossing them into the back of the car. Finally, the figure pulled a VHS box from the rucksack where it nestled beside a couple of others, and leaning back inside the car, tossed it carefully onto Martin's lap. The cover glinted dully in a reflection from the distant park light. The killer read the title out loud, relishing the words. "*The Bogey Man.*"

Job done, and only one more to perform.

The killer closed the passenger door, pulled off the stocking mask, and dropped it through the shattered window to land on top of the glass on the passenger seat. No need to worry about forensics anymore. Time to wrap all this up.

The killer strode away from the Renault, heading across the dark expanse of the Downs, away from the entrance of the production site, looking for a less-conspicuous access point.

The rucksack on the figure's shoulder was a bit lighter now. Though the soft clunk of VHS boxes thumping together as the killer moved signified more titles were about to be unearthed.

> *"Catch, catch a horror taxi,*
> *I fell in love with a video nasty…"*

The killer hummed the song gently, voice low. It was the killer's tribute anthem, whispered every time the deed was done. It was perfectly appropriate, this *Damned* tune from the 80s, and though it was the only song by the band the killer knew, it was the consummate soundtrack to these acts.

"Catch, catch a horror train,
Freeze frame gonna drive you insane."

The killer particularly liked that last line. *Didn't drive me insane, though, Mummy dearest.*

The killer was as mentally sound as they come.

Almost time for the curtain call.

"Shadows fall and all is gloom
You're not so safe
In the safety of your room."

Cue guitar solo. A chuckle in the dark. Just so damned good…

Every murder should have its soundtrack.

CHAPTER SEVEN

When she opened the door to leave Julian's trailer, she certainly hadn't expected to see Jem Whateley waiting outside. She tried to control the shock, not let it show on her features. Her heart revved inside her chest.

How long had he been there? It was past eight o'clock now, lunchtime on the night shoot, and every other member of the cast and crew was busy eating in the two dining buses at the other end of the site.

Jem gestured at the "Do Not Disturb" notice attached to the door. "I need to speak to him for five minutes."

She stared at him. What did he want? What could he possibly know about all this?

"Have you been here a long time? I don't think he likes people hanging around outside his three-way."

He shook his head. "Just finished my dinner and thought I'd have a word with him. I saw the police interview him. If he knows something, I want to hear it. I'm not asking though."

Insolent fucker. Know your station, boy.

"He's not here," she said curtly. "Probably gone back to the set to tweak a few things while it's quiet."

He continued to stare at her. Did he remember her from ten years before? They had both visibly aged. He looked hardened, resolute. There was a simmering anger in his eyes. It was obvious he no longer cared whom he upset.

She came to a decision. He had made it easy for her. "You want the killer caught, don't you?"

He didn't answer, eyes traveling right through her.

"The Video Nasty Killer." It sounded ludicrous. The words hung between them.

"Meet me in five minutes in the car park. I'll be in a cream Rover."

He tilted his head to one side questioningly.

"I can't talk right now. But I might be onto something I can only tell you."

"Why not the police?"

"Do you want to know or not? I can't tell them. You have to trust me on that. But this involves all of us now—all of us from *The Epic of Gilgamesh*. We thought we'd escaped its shadow, the shadow of Alexander's disappearance. But we never did."

He stared at her for a few more moments, then let her pass.

We thought we'd escaped its shadow. She walked off toward the car park, her own words repeating in her brain. *But we never did.*

We never did.

Alice Garfield had spent some time searching for the illusive video tape. After nearly half an hour had been wasted while she pawed through boxes, drawers, and cupboards, Darke was convinced she was never going to find it, but then she finally reappeared in the living room clutching a Super VHS tape—a much smaller variant of the standard VHS.

"Now I have to find the camcorder to play it in," she said ruefully.

Frustration gnawed at Darke.

"And the special lead to attach it to the T.V. Oh, dear. Would you like a cup of tea while you're waiting?"

There was only one car with headlights on and engine running in the unit car park. All the other vehicles were empty and dark. *Walking Shadow* would be filming for another few hours yet, the estimated wrap time being midnight, but Jem no longer cared if he was needed on set now that lunch was over. If Lizzie had something important to tell him, he wasn't going to miss it. Did she know the identity of the killer? And where had Julian "gone" to, exactly? Did she mean he'd returned to the set or left the production for the night?

He couldn't see her in the darkened interior of the car, but the vehicle with the lights on was certainly a cream-colored Rover. As he approached, he could just about make out her darkened silhouette in the dim light from the dashboard. She wound down the window.

"Get in the passenger seat," she told him brusquely. Her face looked strained and anxious in the dark.

He did as instructed, opening the door and sliding in beside her. As he closed the door again, a cold, metal object pressed against the back of his neck.

"Don't move, don't speak, or I will discharge this nail gun and a five-inch tack will be embedded in your brain."

His body iced over with shock. The voice was a creepy croak, distorted, so he couldn't tell if it belonged to a male or female. The metal object in his neck pressed tighter. Next to him, Lizzie looked desolate. "I'm sorry," she moaned. "I was told if I didn't lure you in here, my husband would be killed." Her lip trembled.

"Look in the rearview mirror," the grotesque rasp instructed Jem.

Now following the instructions of a different director, Jem again did as he was told. His body stiffened even more when he saw the reflection of a dark figure in the back seat, wearing a black, woolen ski balaclava. He could just about discern a shadowed glint behind the white-rimmed eye holes. A shiny nail gun was held in the stranger's right hand, its barrel pressed against Jem's neck. He recognized it as similar to one he'd seen in a local branch of B&Q a few years back. Pneumatically powered, compressed air would slam a nail forward with sufficient power to puncture his skull with ease at this close distance.

"Drive," the intruder croaked at Lizzie. She obeyed instantly, turning the car toward the entrance of the unit base car park, where a bored-looking security guard was chatting to a uniformed cop.

"Don't stop or I fire."

Lizzie gunned the engine, the Rover bouncing only slightly over the smooth grass of the car park. As the Rover neared the entrance, Jem tensed, expecting a sharp agony at the base of his skull at any second. The policeman and security man turned to face them as they drew level.

"Wave to the nice men," the horrible croak told Lizzie.

She took one hand off the steering wheel, gave the men a quick wave. Jem gave her a sidelong glance without moving his head. Her face was immobile now, frozen.

"Smile," the croak warned her.

Again, she obeyed. The two men smiled back, waved briefly, and the Rover was through the entrance and turning onto the road.

"Drive 'til I tell you to stop."

Jem concentrated on trying to detect some hint as to the identity, or even gender, of the whisperer, but it was so strangled and unnatural that it was impossible.

With the cold metal against his nape, Jem carefully rolled his eyes toward Lizzie again. Her face was white in the dash lights, staring expressionlessly ahead. He switched his eyes to the mirror again as the Rover hummed along the road that cut through the dark expanse of the Downs.

"Did you kill Christine?" he asked, his voice sounding more defiant than he felt.

"I said, don't speak."

After another five minutes of silence, as they were nearing a car park viewpoint on the cliffs above the Avon gorge, the whispery croak came again. "Pull in here."

Lizzie did as she was instructed. The car park was empty. Far across the plunging gulf, Jem could see the opposite cliffs of the gorge, and to the left, the illuminated splendor of the Suspension Bridge.

"Switch off the engine."

When she had done so, Jem heard a rustle from behind, and then the intruder pushed something forward for him to see, a black leather glove clutching a hip flask.

"Take it," the voice ordered. The nozzle of the nail gun poked him again. "Carefully. Make no sudden moves or your brain will grow a nail." A hiss followed. A stifled laugh?

Jem took the flask with his right hand. He heard liquid slosh inside.

"Good." The nail gun's cold kiss against Jem's nape was a little more insistent.

"Now drink it."

Jem understood the words, but his brain refused to act on them. He continued to hold the flask in his lap, his eyes fixed on the shadow in the balaclava and dark jumpsuit in the mirror.

"It's very simple," the voice croaked, and suddenly the nail gun shifted, was pointing against the back of Lizzie's slender neck.

"I know you are a gallant, noble man. You will not refuse me and let your co-star die."

Jem gathered himself to yank at the door handle, throw himself into the car park. As if reading his mind, the hoarse croak warned: "Open that door and she dies. Do you want that on your conscience?"

Slowly, Jem relaxed his body. His thoughts were a whirl. What had the stranger meant by "co-star?" Was it just an ironic turn of phrase, or did it hold more significance? Again, as if reading his thoughts, the croak emerged from the balaclava.

"The stage is set. The lights are low. The audience is waiting for the players to arrive." A pause, then, "That's you two."

Lizzie released a sob.

"Stop that!" the horrible voice growled.

Jem flicked his eyes to the side, saw Lizzie's body trembling. He could have jerked open the door right then and either run for help or attempt to struggle with the figure in the back seat. But he knew he would never be able to forgive himself for Lizzie's death if his gambit failed.

Another hiss from the back. "Do you like my ski mask? I bet you don't know which film it's from?"

Jem darted a look in the rear view. Again, a distant twinkle in dark eyes, lost in shadow. The mouth hole was too small to show any lips and partly covered the mouth, so the voice was further muffled by wool.

"*Toolbox Murders*, of course. How do you like my Cameron Mitchell impression?" As if to encourage a positive response, the nail gun prodded the back of Lizzie's head.

"But I'm afraid I have to switch now and play a character from another film." The gruff whisper caught and hitched with excitement. "I'll let you guess the title, though it isn't really important in the scheme of things. I'll give you a clue: it isn't a Video Nasty. Yes, sadly I'm shifting from my usual MO just for you, Jem."

Hearing his name croaked by the intruder was an icy waterfall in his heart. Who was this monster? And why were they so familiar with him? More importantly, and certainly more terrifyingly, what did they want with him?

"If you don't mind, I will keep the ski mask on for the time being. At least until we're ready for the show to begin."

Jem let his eyes rove the shadowy car park, hoping somebody would appear. Trying to stall for time, Jem asked, "What show?"

The croak intensified with sudden anger. "I said *no talking*!"

The nail gun pushed more urgently against Lizzie's neck. She let out a stifled moan of terror.

"Let me give you a choice," the gruff whisper continued. "In the flask you hold is a harmless drug that will put you to sleep for a few hours should you drink it. Just long enough for us to reach our destination. If you choose not to drink it, not only does our wonderful actress here die an excruciating death, but you will *never* discover why I killed poor Christine."

Jem's body went rigid. Slow-building rage began to push away the fear.

"Of course, you could refuse to drink and let Lizzie die, and maybe you could overpower me afterward, unless I manage to fire a nail into, say, your eye socket as we struggle. But I would be very reluctant to do that, the reasons for which will become all too apparent later. I really don't want you dead."

Jem didn't realize how tightly his fists were clenched until that moment. He opened them slowly, tried to control his breathing, the dark rage that was clouding everything. He needed to think carefully.

But the figure in the ski mask was impatient. "We must move quickly now. Drink the drink and you shall save the actress and discover the facts about your Christine. Fail to drink and Lizzie dies, and even should you manage to overcome me, I shall *never* reveal my secrets about Miss Thomas, to you or to the police. And if you run, you will never know who I am or why I have done all this for you. This I guarantee."

For you. Jem racked his brains for any significance in those words, but they were meaningless to him. Was this some insane game? Why would this maniac want to do anything for *him*? He wanted more than anything to know who lurked behind that black balaclava. But could he risk drinking an unknown drug to find out? Christine's pale, beautiful face filled his thoughts. His heart clenched like his fists had done.

Jem's gaze dropped from the horrible ski mask to the darkness beyond the windscreen.

"Time presses. You must decide *now.* Save the actress and know everything, or watch her die and risk a lifetime of not knowing."

Not knowing.

He didn't care about his own death anymore. And hadn't since Christine was murdered. His life had no meaning now. If he let this chance go of discovering why she had died and by whose hands...

Not knowing... Yes, that would be far worse than dying.

He looked down at the flask in his lap.

Sue Fairchild put the phone down and leaned back in her chair.

The estate agent had kept his word and returned her call, even though it had taken him some time to do so. He impressed on her wearily that he had closed his office nearly two hours before and this was overtime.

He had warned her when she first asked him to trace the owners of the video rental shop in the small Cotswold town of Wolton that it might take some time to find out as he would have to sift through several files and wade back through many years to locate the details she wanted, and he was a very busy man with various property deals that needed his urgent attention before he went home for the night, etc., etc.

Sue had listened patiently and then told him he would be assisting the police in a confidential and highly important case and that any co-operation he gave would be greatly appreciated. She had suspected that that wouldn't be enough to stop him chasing down his "urgent" property deals first, and the fact it had taken him so long only confirmed that conviction. But, late as he was, the estate agent had finally come through.

She looked down at the name she had written on her pad and tried to quell the excitement rising inside her. Wouldn't do to jump the gun. She had always prided herself on her coolly meticulous efficiency.

Then she opened up the witness statement files on her PC. Of course, not all of the statements were from actual witnesses; many of them were just records of the interviews conducted by Stone and other D.C.s with relevant people connected to the case. She scrolled through until she found the match she already knew was there to be made.

Then, remaining as calm as ever, she reached for the phone again, and dialed Stone's number.

It had taken another ten minutes or so of tinkering, but Alice had finally connected the TV to her camcorder and pressed play.

Darke had sat through nearly forty minutes of pretty amateurish acting, the slightly grainy tape showing an almost empty theater and even emptier gestures on the part of most of the wooden thespians involved.

She had already recognized a young Jem Whateley, looking ridiculous in a loin cloth as the wild man Enkidu, although he had obviously looked after his body more back then. It was harder to judge his acting, though, as the script was so portentous and archaic even Anthony Hopkins would have struggled with it, and there were far more melodramatic gestures than emotive close-ups.

Alice had kept up a commentary throughout, pointing out various actors, but in reply to Darke's questions, had remained uncertain as to whom exactly she was looking for.

Another character had just walked into the background, obviously playing a very minor, non-speaking role. Darke frowned at the grainy image. Then sat bolt upright, her blood tingling.

"Wait!" She pointed at the pale figure on the screen. "Pause it!"

Alice fumbled with the remote and the image froze, the actor at the back of the stage quivering, features blurring as the picture jerked to a halt.

"Rewind!"

Alice did so, then pressed Play again. The character walked onto the stage, face turned toward the audience, toward the camera.

So much younger, of course, and the quality of the recording was not great… But Darke recognized the pale figure immediately.

She scrabbled for her phone.

Stone was in the production office of the *I Spit on Your Grave* remake, grilling the producer and co-producer of the film, when his phone began to trill.

The first call was from the Murder Squad office, either Sue or Ming. But even as he moved his thumb toward the answer icon, another call merged with the first. Sam Darke. Stone had always viewed mobile phones as a necessary evil, and this confusion of incoming callers momentarily baffled him as he tried to work out which one to respond to first.

The two film producers watched him scornfully as he fumbled.

Stone finally managed to press one of the two merging icons and Sue Fairchild's calm and collected tone told him exactly what she had discovered.

He stared at the two faces in front of him as he listened, his pulse quickening.

He was on his feet before she had finished, almost forgetting in his excitement that Darke was still trying to get through.

But all he could think of now was the echo of a voice telling him something he should have remembered a long time before:

"I was supposed to be on the Legion Britannica shoot myself, Inspector, but they didn't have a spare costume in my size…"

And then, as if to taunt him further, the words of the *Legion Britannica* costume supervisor he'd interviewed days before that:

"One size fits all, Inspector."

One size fits all.

CHAPTER EIGHT

"I would have spotted it earlier when I ran a cross-check on film personnel and video rental libraries," Sue explained defensively on the phone as Stone raced to the address she gave him, Cookie wasting no time firing up the blues and twos[15], the light flashing across suburban streets as the Merc sped toward its destination.

"But Brigstowe was never listed on the call sheets the producers supplied us with, as they don't have a direct presence on set. And Wolton isn't in the Bristol area, which is where we were concentrating. But as soon as I heard the name Carruthers from the Estate Agent, I remembered. The Drama teacher mother who burned to death in an old school building, and according to the Estate Agent, a father whose video library business was closed after he received excessive fines for renting out prohibited Video Nasties. It all fit."

"Good work, Sue. We're on our way now. D.S. Darke and D.C. Wells en route to the agency premises in case the perp's holed up there."

After wasting ten minutes ringing the doorbell at the Kingswood residence, a Victorian terraced property. Stone knocked on the door of the house on the right, Cooke took the left.

A spindly woman emerged with a cigarette and a grumpy attitude.

"I dunno where 'e's to. Strange un', that boy. Never quite could put

---

[15] British police term for the lights and siren on the patrol car.

me finger on it, but…whass he done then?"

Stone returned to the car and had Sue on the phone in seconds. "Try Jason Gold's number—the Brigstowe Boss. Find out if he has any idea where our bright-eyed boy could be. And find his car reg, get onto Control. If he's on the road, I want him found."

He collected Cooke, who had received a similar negative result from the neighbor he spoke to, and the Merc peeled away. While Cooke drove, Stone rang Darke, who was just pulling up at the Brigstowe address in Clifton.

"Door's open, boss. Not liking the look of this."

"Don't enter. Repeat, don't enter," he told her. "Be there in ten." He turned to the massive D.C. in the driving seat. "Put that fucking giant hoof down, Cooke."

Darke and Wells were still waiting outside the Brigstowe premises when they arrived. They looked solemn, strained.

"Do we call for armed back-up, guv?" Darke asked as soon as Stone jumped out.

"Fuck that. I get the feeling the bastard's long gone anyway." He moved toward the door that hung ajar, a light from the hallway spilling out onto the pavement.

They could hear nothing from inside. Stone led the way, followed by Darke, then Wells. Cooke brought up the rear.

The reception area was empty, apart from a VHS box propped against a water urn. Stone eyed it apprehensively. *Night of the Demon.* He'd seen a copy of that one at the shop in Bridgewater.

He gestured to the others to stay put while he advanced down the short corridor to the bookers' call center. The door was closed. Gently, he turned the knob, then threw the door back, staying flat against the wall. Ever so carefully, he eased his head around the door jamb.

Empty.

He turned his attention to the door opposite—Jason's office. Stone repeated the procedure.

This time when he peered slowly around the door jamb, the sight awaiting him caused even a veteran like Stone to freeze over with shock. An involuntary grunt tore from his mouth. He advanced carefully into the room.

Jason was lying on the carpet. His intestines had been dug out, flung wildly around the room, which looked like a psychotic artist had sprayed scarlet paint around the walls, furniture, and curtains. A length of small intestine was draped across the framed family photo. Jason's mouth was locked open in shock, eyes caked with his own gore.

The room stank of exposed innards and hot blood.

He withdrew from the room, peered down the corridor to where his colleagues waited. "Wells, call it in. Forensics, pathologist, the lot. Darke and Cooke, check the rest of the building, see if there's anyone else here."

They soon found her. Darke's voice was a little shrill as she called from the direction of the reception area. Stone followed her voice, found her in a small room that obviously served as a kitchen.

Penny Hargreaves was bent in a frozen position over a cooker in one corner, her head forced on top of one of the hot plates, which was now turned off. That it had once been very hot indeed was evident from the reek of burned flesh and the gristly, charcoaled mess that remained of one side of Penny's face.

"Fuck me," the usually stoic Cooke muttered.

Stone stared at the corpse for a moment. Cooke backed out of the kitchen, holding his nose. Darke remained. "He's completely lost it," she said.

Stone said nothing.

"Gone fucking hog wild," was Cooke's muffled verdict from behind a handkerchief.

Wells's call came from the reception area. "Boss? We've got a match on the suspect's vehicle. One of the uniforms called it in from the set of *Walking Shadow*. Suzuki Jimney. It's in the car park."

Stone was running before Wells finished. "We got the *wrong production*!"

Darke followed him out to the Merc at a brisk trot. "All the evidence pointed to *I Spit on Your Grave,* boss. We couldn't be everywhere at once."

Stone was in the driver's seat this time, barely waiting for Cooke to squeeze his massive frame into the car before he sent the vehicle lurching away from the curb.

"A.P.W. already out on Marcus Carruthers, guv," Wells greeted him as Stone leaped out of his Merc at the unit base car park. Wells and Darke followed the D.I. as he led the way across the grass. A uniformed constable and a security man had waved them in and now waited for them to approach. A young A.D. hovered nervously behind them.

"Any sighting of Marcus Carruthers on this production?" he asked the constable.

The uniform glanced at the A.D. "This chap says he was sighted once around seven-fifteen, sir."

Stone turned to the A.D., callow, scared, barely out of his teens.

"What was he doing here?"

"He… He was the booker from Brigstowe Agency. They sometimes… sometimes had a presence on set, signing S.A.s in and out, sometimes they… Now and again they worked as S.A.s, too."

"And was Marcus booked as an S.A. today?"

The A.D. shook his head, looking miserable. "No. I happened to see him walking through the unit base at the time I mentioned to the constable. I didn't think much of it, because…as I said, bookers were often on set."

"The perfect disguise, guv," Darke said. "We were so busy looking at extras, actors, and directors, we overlooked the invisible presence on every set. Easy for him to get around unquestioned, and therefore have access to every facility on site, too. Costumes, armory."

Stone didn't trust himself to speak. His thick, woolen Heron coat suddenly felt too hot. He needed air, but he was already outside breathing it. Forcing himself to get a grip, he focused on the callow young A.D.

"Anybody reported missing on set?"

The A.D.'s radio was crackling, an urgent voice asking for him.

"Ignore that," Stone said.

The A.D. looked even more unhappy. "The First's requesting my presence on set, Inspector," he pleaded miserably.

"Then let's not keep him waiting. I want to see Julian Cranleigh as well."

"That's why the First is so upset," the A.D. whined, trotting to keep up with Stone's rapid strides toward the cluster of trailers and 3-Ways. "The director's gone missing. Nobody's seen him since lunchtime. No answer when we knock on the door of his trailer. The First's standing in for him, handling scenes. He's not happy. Our lead actress, Lizzie Cranleigh, and a stand-in's gone missing, too."

Stone glanced at him but didn't stop, heading for the 3-Way in which they'd interviewed Cranleigh hours earlier. "What's the name of the stand in?" But he had already guessed the answer before the A.D. gave it.

A large **Do Not Disturb** notice was affixed to the door of the director's plush 3-Way. Stone paused. "Has anyone been inside?"

The A.D. shook his head. "The First nearly did, after knocking several times. But Julian's always been adamant that he doesn't want anybody to enter when that sign is up. He's got a bit of a temper, sir. It became a bit of a..." He hesitated, aware that Stone looked as unhappy as his immediate superior, the First A.D., sounded.

"Bit of a what, son?"

"A joke, sir. We knew that every time he put that notice up, he was... getting it on...with his wife."

"Make a habit of that, did he?"

"Normally only at lunchtimes, sir. The First didn't want to cause a scene by walking in on him..."

Stone sighed, reached out, and yanked at the handle.

Inside, the 3-Way was dark. Stone scrabbled for the switch, and the room was instantly bathed in harsh light. The main room was empty and seemed undisturbed. Stone glanced at the door to the small bathroom, which was closed.

Stone pushed it open. It wedged against something inside. When he saw the trickle of blood running under the half-open door from whatever was stopping it moving further, he turned back to Darke. But she had followed him up the steps and had already clocked it. She was calling the station for another team of forensics before he even opened his mouth.

Pulling on his forensic gloves, he edged around the door.

Julian Cranleigh was slumped naked in the open shower cubicle, an outflung foot resting against the inside of the door. Blood had pooled an inch deep around the body in the shower tray, the drain clogged. A closer look revealed the reason for the blockage: Cranleigh's penis had been severed and was curled next to his naked buttocks, partially preventing his life fluids from seeping away.

Scarlet handprints splayed against the half-open glass door. Cranleigh's throat had been hacked open for good measure. A DVD floated in the backed-up tide of red. Stone fished it out, shook off the blood. Darke was impassive behind him in the half-open doorway. She saw the title, too. *I Spit on Your Grave.*

"He's laughing at us," Darke said, her voice sounding strange.

Stone didn't trust his own either. He turned the DVD over, examined it carefully, the 18 certificate inside the red circle embossed with the BBFC letters.

"Change of M.O.," he said, and yes, his words sounded as strangled as Darke's.

"Boss?"

"It's a legally certificated D.V.D., for fuck's sake. Why the change from V.H.S.?"

Darke thought about it. They could hear Cooke talking to the young A.D. outside. "Making some sort of ironic comment?"

Stone didn't reply. He placed the DVD carefully on the wash basin, turned back to the body in the cramped cubicle.

"Why was he taking a shower mid-way through the shoot?" He glanced round at Darke.

Darke thought about it, her eyes averted from the naked, gory body in the cubicle.

"Very convenient for the killer," she said. "I've seen the film, guv. Thought it might come in useful, having a knowledge of the major nasties. Fiercely intelligent pro female slant to it, believe it or not. Main rapist gets castrated by his female victim in the bath. But… How could Carruthers have known he'd catch him in the shower?"

Stone didn't have an answer. He became aware that Cooke was calling him from outside. Darke edged backward to let himself out of the cramped bathroom.

Cooke was leaning inside the 3-Way.

"Just had a uniform radio in from the other side of the Downs, guv. Another body found. Parked in his car with a screwdriver through his head and a video in his lap."

Would it ever end?

He stepped down from the 3-Way. The A.D. was staring at him with a face whiter than a pillowcase.

"Don't go in there, son," he said kindly. He turned to the constable who had followed them from the car park. "Make sure nobody except forensics enters."

The uniform nodded.

He turned to the security man, a burly middle-aged grafter in a hi-vis. "Any vehicles left the site since lunchtime?"

The man's face crumpled in thought. "Yeah," he said. "Missus Cranleigh. Around about eight, eight-fifteen."

"Was she alone in the car?"

He looked uneasy, as if he was about to be accused of not doing his job properly.

"I think someone else was in the passenger seat. But it was dark. Couldn't see properly."

"Anyone else? Maybe in the back seat?"

He shrugged. "They went past pretty quick. Might've been. All too shadowy. Sorry, like."

"What car was she driving?"

He brightened a little at that. "A cream-colored Rover. She drove Mister Cranleigh here in it this afternoon. Don't think he could drive."

"Reg?"

He knew that, too, and his expression was a lot happier when Stone walked away, already on his phone calling it in.

CHAPTER NINE

"Welcome back," a familiar voice greeted Jem as he rose from the depths of unconsciousness. "I must apologize for being so melodramatic on the way here. I should really leave that to you thespians."

His vision was fighting for focus, his thoughts even more so. A blur next to him, somebody seated, subdued lighting, the hum of a generator.

His head ached abominably. He blinked at the figure facing him in the rickety wooden chair to his right and his vision finally swam clear.

He was staring into the hollow eye sockets of a filthy skull. Threads of hair still clung to it in places, the teeth locked around skeins of cobweb. A dead worm was lodged half in the cavity where the nose had once been.

A groan tore from his throat. A skeleton was propped in the chair beside him. A rotting T-shirt and jeans still clung to the emaciated frame.

"And do say hello to your old friend, Alexander. What a lovely reunion!" The voice again, the voice he recognized. But none of this made sense. Was he still drugged? He had taken the drink (had he a choice, really?) and soon the velvet gloves of oblivion had folded over him. And now? "Shame I had to gag the lovely Lizzie, but she did scream so. And besides, it's *you* who will be doing the acting tonight."

He shook his head to clear it, aware for the first time that his arms were suspended above him. He cranked his neck to look up, saw the rope fastening his wrists to a blackened beam four feet above. His shoulders ached from the tension.

He twisted his head, searching for the origin of the voice, saw Lizzie similarly tied to his left, a gag secured around her mouth. She was staring at him with teary, fear-widened eyes.

Finally, his gaze found the speaker.

He was dressed from neck to toe in what had previously been called an asbestos suit, the bulky coverall nowadays made of aluminized materials. An ugly flamethrower was cradled in his arms, a petrol tank slung over his back. A bulky hood with a wide visor was draped on a stool beside him.

"Yes, a truly heart-warming reunion of a talented cast. There's Alexander next to you. Did you know I buried him under the burned planks of this very stage shortly after killing him? Nice of him to join us above ground again. Such a shame Julian couldn't join us, too, but we actually have a much better director on hand to give sage advice. Say hello to mother, Jem." The figure gestured into the shadows to its left with the barrel of the flamethrower. Jem strained to see what was there, just in front of one of the old-fashioned stage lamps fixed to a charred post. Another skeleton, propped up on another rickety wooden chair, its bones as blackened and charred as the post behind it.

"My mother directed you in your first triumph, Jem," Marcus continued, his bland face shining with exultation, Saturday night TV presenter looks, except for his eyes, which were joyous, more animated than Jem had ever seen them. "Surely you remember your tremendous portrayal of the Wolf Boy—your first ever performance—in *Dark of the Moon,* staged right here in this Drama Hall."

He gestured with the flamethrower at the blackened beams and half-burned wooden walls surrounding them, the shreds of curtain that had survived the inferno more than twenty years before. With a shock, Jem realized the booker was telling the truth: he was indeed standing on the stage where he had first experienced the pure adrenaline rush that only performing before a live audience can provide. Except now it was black with soot, the "wings" were half disintegrated, windows long gone, and he could see gaps in the roof where the conflagration had torn its way through. The old Drama Hall had always been a fire hazard waiting to happen, but health and safety legalities had not been so stringent in those days. The death of his old Drama teacher, Mrs. Carruthers, had changed all that. *Mrs. Carruthers.*

He stared at the man in the fire-proof suit. Of course. Same surname. But how had he not remembered him from school? A glimpse of a quiet, slightly younger boy lurked in the wings of memory, but it was insubstantial, forgotten.

As if reading his thoughts, Marcus smiled. "Is it all making sense at last, Jem? I see you remember all this. But do you remember *me*?" His smile was a grimace. "Not the confidant, ebullient Brigstowe booker you've become familiar with, but the painfully shy and inward youth who watched your first performance from the sidelines. Always from the sidelines. Because Mother would never let me play with the big boys."

Was he joking? Was all this some elaborate prank? But the sheen on Marcus's bland face was that of madness, not good humor. Bland, bland, so bland he was practically invisible, unless you were staring right at him. Mr. Forgettable.

"She told me I couldn't act. She told me I was wooden. 'Wood, wood! I'm surrounded by wood,' she used to cry. Do you remember? Of course, you don't. Because she never said it when you were around. You were her stage darling. Her protégé. Oh yes, she predicted such wonderful things for you. She envisioned such triumphs. The future was bright for you. But for me?" He tapped himself with the flame thrower. "Not so much.

"I was the eternal set dresser in my mother's eyes. Destined only to lurk in the shadows, in the wings, while those with the real talent strutted and fretted their hour upon the stage. Of course, you don't remember me. But I *never* forgot you."

Jem was still trying to take it all in. He tried to speak but his throat was clogged. He coughed. Beside him, Lizzie hung limply, eyes fixed on their persecutor.

"How *could* I forget you, with Mother's glowing testimonials roasting my ears on a daily basis. Anybody would have thought *you* were her son.

She was so proud of you. Even though you only did two productions here at school before leaving for your bright future. But as it turns out, Mother's future was brighter than yours, wasn't it? She went up like a torch. Such a shame she took a lot of this gorgeous old Drama Hall with her." He gestured around him with one gloved hand.

"Have you been back to see it in recent years? You should have. It's been left to rot—a bit like Alexander. Barbed wire and corrugated iron fencing protecting it from the curious. The school couldn't do anything to restore it as it was on private land that didn't belong to the council. And the owner never bothered. So many years later, I bought it. And here we are. Do you like what I've done with it?"

Another gesture with the hand not holding the flamethrower. By now Jem was becoming accustomed to the dim lighting, and he could make out the scattering of VHS boxes littering the stage, and beyond them the flicker of small TV screens, maybe five or six of them positioned in the shadows along the back wall. Old school VCRs lurked beside them, one for each TV. His numbed mind tried to make sense of the still pictures displayed on the screens, different images of freeze-frame atrocity on each of them. One showed a machete buried in a bloody face, another a buzz saw bisecting a head, the others depicting equal depravity. A gallery of gore.

"A selection of gory greatest hits from the Nasty parade," Marcus quipped as he noticed Jem staring blankly at the TV screens. "I've paused them at particular moments of interest as you can see. These crazy films act as my muse; maybe they'll do the same for you. Because believe me when I say it, this is all for *you*." A dramatic pause, a mock bow, made more grotesque by the fire suit. Everything about Marcus was jarringly different: the naked mania on his face finally allowed out to play, the overly theatrical verboseness, the hammy mannerisms. The bland mask of conformity he'd worn for so long had slipped completely away.

"I stage managed every detail to get you here so you could shine at last, in the epic performance of your lifetime. You just weren't getting the breaks, were you, Jem? Well, here's your chance: your own special platform. Prove Mother right. Let me see your star blazing out… " He paused, pursed his lips thoughtfully.

"Because up 'til now, your future just hasn't been as spectacular as any of us believed it would be. Even *I* began to doubt: was Mother wrong to be so supportive of you, I wondered, as your career continued to stall? Because, darling thespian, of *course*, I followed it. I followed *you*. *The Epic of Gilgamesh* should have been your chance to shine. I was already on board as the set designer when you walked in; it was me who pushed the leaflets asking for actors through your letter box. I knew you would be unable to resist. But you can't remember me from that production either, can you? The invisible stagehand, with a very minor background role. Don't worry; you weren't alone. I'm pretty sure Lizzie didn't recognize me either, did you, darling?" He waved the flamethrower nozzle at the hanging actress. A stifled cry came from behind the gag. Marcus ignored it.

"I followed you and Christine to Bristol, you see. All the better to study your glittering career. That was not so glittering—but through no fault of your own, I'm sure. You tried. Your audition at the Bristol Old Vic, for one. How could that have failed? Obviously, I didn't see it, but I knew you had gone for it. How did I know? And here's where it might become a little difficult between us…"

Jem tried to speak again, and failed again, the waves of dizziness ebbing and flowing. None of this made sense.

"Your beloved Christine is how."

Jem's head, which had been slumping with fatigue, jerked up again.

"We had a little thing, you see. I'm so sorry to tell you this now, but I did promise to reveal everything if you accepted the drink. Please don't let it come between us. Not now, on the night of your greatest triumph." He smiled as if Jem understood perfectly what he was talking about.

"Five or more years ago, it was, dear boy. Just a brief fling. Nothing special—though she did go shopping for me in Bridgewater when I was renting a flat in York for a couple of weeks. She found me the exact V.H.S. I wanted, too, and sent it to me. What was I doing in York, you ask? Can't you guess? I followed you there, too, obviously. I was so excited to hear you had become one of the Scary Actors at the Dungeon. I just *had* to come and watch you perform. I came every day for a week. And *still* you didn't recognize me in the crowd of tourists lapping up your performance. And my dedication was rewarded: you were *glorious.* Everything my mother had said about you was starting to come true."

A beatific smile, which soon curdled. "Until that supervisor ended it all. I overheard him threatening you one day when I had wandered off from the rest of the crowd to look for you, just maybe to see if you *did* recognize me. Of course, he had to go. So two or three days after he sacked you I hid behind an exhibit after the museum closed and waited for him. I'm telling you parts of your history, Jem. The least you could do is *listen.*"

Marcus's voice had risen sharply and petulantly as Jem's head slumped, the effects of the drug still pulling him toward sleep. He struggled to raise it, to focus on what was being said, though the tide of insanity was mostly washing over him.

"But I was talking about Christine, wasn't I?" He patted the flame-thrower. "She was never good enough for you, Jem. She was way too dumb. I only went out with her to stop her from dragging you down. I told her not to tell you because by then I had started work at Brigstowe—purely because I knew you were one of its S.A.s—and I didn't want my relationship with her to cause problems between us. But to illustrate how dumb she was: even after the press had printed all the details of Dave Fenton's murder at the York Dungeon, and the discovery of *The Mark of the Devil* tape nestled beside his corpse, she still couldn't conceive I could possibly be involved."

He shook his head in mock disbelief. He looked like an oversized action figure with his smooth, regular features and ridiculous fire suit. "She asked me, of course. But I told her it was just a coincidence and that *Mark* was a popular collector's item. I told her to keep it quiet, though, because the police might be less inclined to believe me than she was."

He showed his gleaming teeth in a weird snarl. "She asked me *again,* all these years later, after I killed Dixley and Johns. She was easy to convince though, all over again. She just didn't have it in her to believe I could be implicated, bless her. Dumb, dumb, dumb."

"But one thing she had in her favor: she could *see* me." He tapped the breast of his fireproof suit with his free hand. "And *you* couldn't. You always looked right through me without even being aware of who I was. Even at Brigstowe, I was just a voice on the phone, a booker without a face. A nobody to you. But that just made me want to impress you even more, to be personally responsible for elevating you to the rightful position of eminence Mother always believed you should attain."

His voice took on a reasonable edge, as though he was discussing a booking. "Lizzie will be the witness. And Alexander, of course, though he can't comment any longer, sadly." A pause, a thoughtful expression, then: "And most importantly, Mother. She'll be watching your delivery *very* carefully."

But Jem's mind was clearing now. He had shut out this latest dribble of insanity because something Marcus had mentioned earlier, something far more vital, was shearing through the swamp of his mind. A name. And a face, swimming into sharp focus along with that name.

"Christine…" His voice just a croak, but Marcus heard it.

"Oh, forget her. You really need to, especially if you want to impress me tonight the way you always did my mother. Christine was just a distraction you didn't need. Your unrequited desire for her was holding you back. You needed to concentrate on your acting goals, not some dumb blonde."

He started ranting about other names, other apparent obstacles, negative elements, and threats to Jem's alleged career—or to his ability to concentrate on the prize and progress without being held back by his own jealousy or desire. Names that barely registered, let alone the motivations for killing them: Alexander, Fenton, Jimmy Dixley, Guy Johns, Ben Trenchard, Martin Thorogood. All sound and fury, signifying nothing.

All except the one name.

Christine.

"In a way you could say I set-designed your life, Jem." He held out his free hand demonstratively, a flourish. "Just like I set-designed mother's plays."

He approached Jem, shuffling awkwardly along the stage in his fire-proof suit, flamethrower lowered in the cradle of his right arm.

"It had to be the right video for each job, you see. I'm nothing if not meticulous in my craft. I always strove for perfection in my Murder Art. Every execution was to facilitate your arrival as the actor you and I know you can be. Everything detrimental to that had to be cleared. Whether that was someone taking your job or your girl. Even that silly man waving placards was an obstacle in your path. You told me yourself he and his campaign could frighten off productions. You see how thoughtful and creative I've been?"

He allowed himself a self-congratulatory smirk. "Incidentally, do you like my costume? A fire-approach suit, I believe it's called. I always had a knack for obtaining costumes. And I've worn some good ones, haven't I? Romans and zombies, and everything in between." He shifted the flame-thrower slightly, the barrel glinting under the stage lights. "I was going to use that drill to illustrate my point tonight," he indicated a power drill plugged into a socket attached to the generator just behind him. "But there wasn't a relevant *costume* to go with it. Not like with this choice. Have you seen *Don't Go in the House*? Of course, you haven't. Very suitable, actually. First time around I didn't have all the gear, but now I really do. Full circle."

His smile looked unhealthy, all wrong. "Any questions before we begin?

Why the Video Nasties, maybe? Surely you want to ask that one? No? A commentary on the vicious dog-eat-dog nature of the acting business and the decline of moral standards in the industry… or just because I liked them? As that unspeakable moron on the reality show likes to say: '*You* decide….'"

He turned his attention toward Lizzie, who was struggling against her bonds and making game efforts to speak through her gag. "Hush, Lizzie. I've already said you're not here to act, just to inspire Jem. Don't make me burn you before I'm ready."

He swung toward Jem again. "Anything else before we make a start? Shall I remind you how I helped mold your career at Brigstowe? The more I studied your progress as an extra, the more I became convinced I could help you. Didn't you appreciate me putting you forward for all the best roles? Of course, you didn't always get them, but I gave you the opportunity. Yes, it became an obsession: I suppose you *could* call it that. Mother was driving me on to help you. I felt that all along. This was all done in her memory." He smiled again, and it was *almost* a normal smile this time. "I'm half envious of you, half infatuated—I admit it! Shall we begin? Enough of my ham, though I must admit I'm rather enjoying this little performance of my own. I can see the appeal. But I've talked long enough. Certainly far, far more than that quiet, introverted young man who watched you from the wings on *The Epic of Gilgamesh.*"

"She wasn't…" Jem's words were a clogged whisper.

"What's that?" Marcus stepped closer.

"She…wasn't…dumb." He lifted his head, glared at the booker with the most violent hatred he'd ever felt in his life.

"Oh, don't be so silly," Marcus scolded him. "We have far more important things to concern ourselves with now."

"I'm going to… kill you."

"*Kill* me? No, darling, you're going to *perform* for me."

He turned back to the stool behind him and, allowing the flame-thrower to dangle on its strap, picked up the hooded visor with both hands before facing Jem again. "What I want is very simple. To commemorate our historic reunion, here where it all began, I'm going to ask you to act. That's what you were born for, wasn't it? All you need to do is recite some lines from *Dark of the Moon.* I'm sure you can remember them. The prize for a stirring recital is that darling Lizzie here gets to keep her beautiful face. If you disappoint me… Let's just say, she'll start to lose her looks far more quickly than she anticipated."

The haze was beginning to close on Jem again. He blinked it away, tried to concentrate on Marcus's insane words.

"Wh…what?" he managed to gasp as Lizzie pulled frantically at her bonds, muffled screams emanating from behind the gag.

"You heard me. Show me proper acting or Lizzie burns. And remember, Alexander's watching, too, your old friend and co-star…and

Mother, who gave you your first role, so make it good, make it *real*."

"No." He shook his head to clear it, unsure precisely what he was refusing, but unwilling to contribute to this lunacy.

"No?" Marcus shuffled closer. "Did you just say no? Wrong answer, I'm afraid." Abruptly he pulled the hood over his head. Jem could see his manic eyes behind the transparent slit of the fireproof visor. Then clasping the flamethrower with both hands, he raised the muzzle…

And pressed the trigger.

Chapter Ten

A long tongue of flame stretched from the nozzle, played over Alexander's dirty skull, caressing it, igniting the bone.

The flesh on Jem's face singed from the proximity. Lizzie's thrashings intensified.

Just as suddenly, Marcus cut the flame, removed the hood, dropped it beside him. "Does that inspire you to reach emotions you've never reached before?" He swung the nozzle toward Lizzie. "Next time it will be her beautiful face the flame cradles so lovingly." He lowered the muzzle, watched Alexander's skull continue to burn. His rotting T-shirt caught, then his jeans. Marcus made no move to douse the flames. Instead, he shuffled toward the rear of the stage, picked up a remote from the burned remains of a table. He pointed it at one of the VCRs arrayed against the back wall.

"Maybe a soundtrack will help you emote." He thumbed the remote and a tinny soundtrack of electronic warbles and whines erupted from the TV screen as the image sprang to life. A shriek rose above the "music," followed by more screams, more cheap and nasty soundtracks unleashed as Marcus aimed the remote at each VCR in turn. Soon, all six screens were in action, the horrible music digging into Jem's mind.

Marcus dropped the remote, shuffled back to Jem and Lizzie. The muzzle lifted.

"Now let's try again, shall we? I'll make it easy: you obviously can't remember your *Dark of the Moon* lines. I'm being unreasonable, aren't I? It was more than twenty years ago, I suppose, even though *I* remember them clearly… Marvin Hudgeons." He adopted a ridiculous American southern drawl. "I loved your dance, Jem. Remember that? You were supposed to dance in time with the villagers, but you changed it up, created your own unique jig. Now *that's* acting." He dropped the accent. "See, I can't do it like you. But, as my mother was so fond of telling me, I'm not an actor."

Jem was more interested in something else he'd noticed. Just before the cacophony of Video Nasty soundtracks had kicked in, he had heard a definite creak from the beam supporting his and Lizzie's weight. He glanced up at it. The beam was half burned through, and the violence of Lizzie's struggles was causing it to crack, even if only slightly. He looked quickly at Marcus again before the madman could notice.

"Got another idea. You might go for this one. I'm being sporting, you see." The flames from Alexander's corpse were dying down a little, but the light danced eerily on Marcus's blandly crazy face.

"How about we get you to do an encore of your Richard the third? You know: the one you did for your audition piece at the Bristol Old Vic. I'm sure Lizzie and I would love to hear that." He gestured at Lizzie with the barrel. "Same rules apply. If I'm not convinced by your portrayal, if I don't think you're putting your *heart and soul* into it, Lizzie fries. For real this time." He bent, picked up the hood, placed it on his head, placed a finger on the flamethrower's trigger.

Lizzie's eyes were imploring Jem, her body thrashing manically. Did he hear another crack of wood over the squeal and piping of cheap, synthesized music? He had to play for time.

"Okay!" It came out as a rasp. He cleared his throat, tried again. "*Okay*. I'll do it. I'll fucking *do it*!"

Marcus's eyes flashed with triumph behind the visor. And even though his voice was muffled, Jem could just hear the jubilant shout: "*Now* you see me…"

And Jem let rip. He knew this had to be the performance of a lifetime. If not just for Lizzie's sake, then his own, too. This was his moment, his biggest audition yet, and the role he would win? Their lives.

So, he began. He summoned up the half-forgotten words, let them trip from his tongue while he dangled from the rope and the Video Nasties wheezed and screeched in the background.

"Now is the winter of our discontent,

Made glorious summer by this sun of York..."

He coughed away smoke from the dying flames next to him, carried on bravely.

And the words came. They flowed. He was back in that audition room in the Old Vic, the woman with the cold face watching him, chuckling at his antics as he shuffled around the room, Quasimodo without a bell rope.

"And all the clouds that lou'rd upon our house

In the deep bosom of the ocean buried..."

The muzzle wavered, lowered.

"Grim-visaged war hath smooth'd his wrinkled front...

I that am curtail'd of this fair proportion,

Cheated of feature by dissembling nature..."

He knew his own features were animated, twisting with his passion, capturing the villain in all his tics and Machiavellian glory. The half-ruined Drama Hall was forgotten, Marcus, too. Even Christine, in this climax of his thwarted art.

"Deformed, unfinish'd, sent before my time

Into this breathing world, scarce half made up,

And that so lamely and unfashionable

That dogs bark at me as I halt by them..."

How he could remember the lines he had no idea, but they continued to tumble from his lips just as they had eight, nine years before, conjured from a secret place, carrying with them all his hopes, all his dreams, all his aspirations.

The muzzle drooped even more. Marcus was scrabbling at the visor, ripping it from his head. He stared at Jem in astonishment.

Which rapidly turned to dismay.

"What... What's this?" His mouth gaped, but not in awe. Not in awe, at all. "Is this the best you can *do*??" His expression was appalled.

"Wood. Wooden…" He shuffled forwards, unbelievingly. "Is this what Mother was so ecstatic about? This hammy blandness? This *nothing-ness*???" Like a critic without a pen, words literally failed him for a handful of awful seconds. But his face said it all. His lifelong mission to elevate and celebrate the one person his mother praised above all living things was all for…

"*Nothing*. You're nothing…" He finally found the word he wanted, repeated it as if struggling to comprehend how he could have been so monumentally misled.

"I give you the platform you've been waiting for all your life to emote *real* passions, and you give me…*this*?"

Jem was too stunned to speak. Even Lizzie had stopped wriggling, her eyes turned on the booker.

"Mother was wrong. You *never* had a bright future. You speak like an extra, you look like an extra. You *are* a *fucking extra*!"

He was raising the barrel of the flamethrower again.

And then everything happened.

The half-burned-through beam gave way at last under their combined weight, the rope fastened to it sliding free, dumping Jem to the floorboards, soon after followed by Lizzie, whose gag finally slipped free in the process, her scream, bottled for so long, reaching a peak that rose above the tinny soundtrack wails.

Jem rolled, was on his feet in seconds, charging at Marcus even as the booker's finger began to close on the flamethrower trigger. Jem smashed into him like a Rugby forward, sending Marcus spinning to one side and back, the flamethrower dropping from his grip, swinging on its strap.

Jem carried on his charge, heading for the object he'd noticed earlier, the only weapon he could lay his hands on.

The power drill.

He snatched it up, depressing the trigger to make sure the plug was connected, and Marcus was lurching round in his cumbersome suit to face him, flamethrower snatched up again. Then stopping, facing Jem, perfectly still. Jem paused, too, locked in the terror of the moment.

"This was never just about me, was it?" Jem whispered, revving the drill. "It was more about me finally seeing *you*. Well, hear this, you fucker. *I still can't see you.*"

Marcus lowered the flamethrower nozzle. Looked at Jem with a stunned light in his eyes.

"The blood flows in rivers," the booker said.

Jem launched forward, jammed the bit against Marcus's smooth forehead, pressed the trigger, the whine of the drill mingling with Marcus's scream, with Lizzie's scream, with the screams of Marcus's beloved videos.

And Jem was screaming, too.

Slo Mo.

Men were running into the Drama Hall. Lizzie saw them burst in, two of them with assault rifles, Detective Inspector Stone behind them, his D.S. alongside him.

But it was all in slow mo. Their jerky movements caught in quicksand as her eyes tracked them across the room. All totally unreal. Part of the endless nightmare she'd found herself in since around eight that evening.

She felt she was no longer a part of the action. Had she ever been? It was a drama between two actors and she was relegated to background.

She crouched on the wooden planks of the stage, the half-burned stage, and watched the slo-mo events unfold.

"Armed police!"

"Put the drill down!"

Jem, crouching over the bucking body of Marcus, blood spraying the extra's face as he leaned in on the whining tool, applying all his weight.

"Drop the drill!"

Jem retracting the whirring, bloody drill bit from its socket in Marcus's forehead, spinning around. Staggering forward, eyes wide and lost, the tool continuing to whine madly.

Lizzie yanked herself free of the nightmare, finding her voice in a moment of icy clarity:

"Shoot! He's going to kill *me* next! *Shoot*!!"

"No!"

Even as Stone's shout echoed across the room, the shooter was already acting on a split-second decision as per his training and pulling the trigger of his Heckler & Koch G36. Would he regret that call? Would it torture him in the nights to come? The bullet sped to Jem's brain regardless of regret or instant decisions with endless repercussions.

Jem dropped beside Marcus's body.

In the stunned silence that followed, Lizzie was the first to move.

She got to her feet, picked up something she had landed on when she fell, glanced at the shiny, lurid, plastic cover without emotion.

Nightmares in a Damaged Brain, the title screamed.

She tossed it onto Jem's lifeless body and walked toward the police.

EJECT TAPE

Stone hadn't said a word to her since Lizzie got in the back of the Merc.

It had been the blonde D.S. who explained to her how they found them. Stone had apparently remembered Christine Thomas telling the detectives about the burned-down Drama Hall where Marcus had set fire to his own mother when not much more than a child. They had reached the abandoned building, set far back from the school, in less than forty minutes.

They had asked her questions after a medic had been called to check her over. Had she really felt threatened by Jem at the end? Of course, she replied. He had gone hog wild; she had no doubt he would turn on her next.

She had cried and looked traumatized when they told her Julian was dead.

It had been so hard not to laugh at Darke's forced expressions of sympathy. Of course, she knew her husband was dead.

It had been she who killed him.

She'd bought the DVD from the Bristol branch of HMV the day before. The idea to kill him had been festering in her mind for years, and the Video Nasty Killer was a gift. It was certainly plausible the maniac would target Julian, too. Especially with Julian's notorious reputation; his projects had been boycotted before by women's rights groups, and she could let the cops find a motive there, if they wanted. When the police mentioned that bitch Alice's name, she knew he'd been seeing her again. He had been fucking her for years (that much was obvious) and she had always turned a blind eye to it, stupidly believing he had stopped. But she had finally realized there was only one really good way to stop him.

Years of abuse, a decade of beatings as part of his pathetic sex games, and Lizzie pretending she liked it so as not to lose him. But now he had made it. She could afford to cut her ties with her share of the money he'd earned as a rising *enfant terrible* of the cinema. The British Coppola, that's how he liked to think of himself. What a sleazy, little twat.

She had waited for lunchtime, then put the notice up on the door, knowing full well nobody would dare interrupt the infamously irascible director.

He had looked at her with his hang-dog expression when she entered. She knew exactly what predictable buttons to press, started undressing even as she closed the door. He could never say no. And he'd never let *her* say it, either. All those times when she'd tried to insist she didn't want it, the rough play, the rape. Because no should mean no, isn't that what they said? Julian never understood that. To him, no was a green light for his perversions.

It was so easy to lead him into the shower, to strip naked for him, while his weak protestations that they didn't have time soon trailed away when she took him in hand.

She knew what he liked.

But he hadn't liked *that*.

When she had finished, she removed the gag from his mouth that was part of their ritual, rinsed the shaving blade and her body clean in the shower, standing astride his corpse, so calm, so collected. Then she had stepped away from him, drying herself nimbly.

Free.

At last.

Carrying the bloody gag, towel, and blade, she looked back once before shutting the bathroom door.

He looked so sad, slumped in the shower cubicle, blood continuing to pump from his throat and the stump she had left of his cheating manhood. She got dressed again, without any regrets, certainly without tears.

Of course, there was a risk she would be seen leaving, but she would just have to run it. She had reached a point where she no longer really cared. She was free of his squalid tortures, and worse, his infidelities. She could face anything after a decade of that.

As it happened, two people *did* see her.

The first caught her in the middle of getting dressed, pushing open the door of the trailer without a by your leave.

She remained incredibly calm as she looked at the figure framed against the darkness outside. He said nothing, the ski mask he had finished putting on as he entered hiding his features. She saw his eyes through the holes, looking at the DVD in her hand, and his head tilted ironically. She knew what he was thinking: upgrade. Did he approve? Then he saw the bloody gag she was just about to hide in her bag, the blade lying on top of it.

"I beat you to it," she said with a stoicism born of abuse. "You can go now."

"I see you," he whispered in his theatrical croak.

"But I didn't see *you*," she replied.

He had nodded. And told her what to do if she wanted to remain innocent of her crime. She had agreed. And why not? Whateley meant nothing to her. She had lured him to her Rover as promised in exchange for the killer's silence.

Imagine her shock when, ten minutes after the killer left, she stepped out of the 3-Way and saw Jem waiting.

But everything had gone so smoothly in the end.

Poor Jem.

He had to go, the loser. She couldn't have him placing her at the scene of Julian's murder, could she?

Maybe she would even have felt guilty…if he hadn't been such a weasely prick.

She'd heard him ranting to his friend earlier, the poor, misunderstood fucking worm of an extra. All the suffering women have endured through-out their careers and you compare that to your *terrible* experience of being overlooked and lost in a crowd of 400 losers. Tough life, mate. Try having some fat, balding, grease-ball producer trying to get into your knickers every time you walk on set, then we'll talk, you pathetic wanker.

#NoMeansNo. He actually fucking said NoMeansNo. Prattling about starting his own campaign for overlooked and unappreciated supporting artists.

Let the fucker take a bullet for his fellow extras.

If there was any justice, he would end up a fucking martyr.

She glanced out of the window at the night as the Merc sped toward Bristol.

Whateley was as deluded as the nut job he killed. Now they would both get a paragraph or two in the rags; hell, maybe some twisted fucker would even make a movie out of it.

There's your fame, you cunt. The extra who plays you might get twelve words and a walk on.

Did she feel sorry for Jem the loser, for Julian the sadistic, cheating, woman-beating coward, for the demented Marcus and his mother fixation?

Did she bollocks.

She was careful not to let Stone and Darke see the smile as she stared out of the window.

It was beaming inside her though.

Did she feel sorry?

Hadn't she screamed at them to stop? The drill, the fists, the flame-thrower. She'd given them all plenty of warning.

Because NoMeansfuckingNo, motherfuckers.

She saw Stone's eyes on her in the rear view.

And it was so very, *very* hard to stop herself from grinning.

Acknowledgments

Big thanks to Christopher Pearson for his invaluable technical advice and assistance with police matters and terminology. Any errors and flights of procedural fancy that may occur are naturally down to me!

ABOUT THE AUTHOR

Mickey Lewis is the author of nine novels. Under the name Leo Darke he has written *Mr. Nasty*, *Pandemonium*, *Lucifer Sam*, and the soon-to-be-released *Sawney Bone*. He also contributed two original novels to the *Doctor Who* range for BBC Books, *Rags* and *Combat Rock*, along with trying his hand at a couple of twisted, surreal children's fantasy novels, *Gorebone* and *Mad Demon Fox and the Halloween School*.

Away from writing, Mickey Lewis has been a mainstay monster on *Doctor Who*, appearing as a Cyberman, Dalek, and Sea Devil amongst other villainous creatures. He's also popped up in the *Star Wars* universe in three recent movies. He lives and lurks in Somerset, plotting wicked tales by the sea.

Rock Out with

"Leo Darke has created a heavy metal nightmare made of hard-driving prose, a dark sense of humor, and a jovial nod to 1980s horror fiction. There's sex, gore, and suspense to spare, and it all unfolds to a heavy metal beat. An enjoyable read."

—Ray Garton, author of *Crucifax* and *Ravenous*

The Day the Music Died

When a private jet carrying internationally acclaimed rock band Cat O' Nine Tails vanishes over the Indian Ocean, the shockwaves were felt around the world. There was no wreckage, no bodies, no black box recordings to provide clues as to what happened to the musicians.
They were simply gone.

Rock 'n' Roll Will Never Die

Just as the world is recovering from the loss of Cat O' Nine Tails comes news that the jet carrying the band has mysteriously re-appeared in the same air space from which it had vanished six months ago. Was it a publicity stunt? The band is unable—or unwilling—to answer that question. They were "lost. But now we're back..." with the promise of a new album with a killer new sound coming soon. There's something definitely not right with the band, but the nation is too firmly in the grip of Cat O' Nine Fever to notice. And as the formerly affable, much-loved Cat O' Nine Tails gears up for a new stadium show, it falls to Cat's original front man, sacked years before, and the members of a virtually unknown punk band, Lucifer Sam, to uncover the real threat behind the massive publicity drive.